Galaxy
The Prettiest Star

Galaxy
The Prettiest Star

Written by
Jadzia Axelrod

Illustrated by
Jess Taylor

with Cris Peter

Lettered by
Ariana Maher

Sara Miller Editor
Steve Cook Design Director – Books
Amie Brockway-Metcalf Publication Design
Tiffany Huang Publication Production

Marie Javins Editor-in-Chief, DC Comics

Anne DePies Senior VP – General Manager
Jim Lee Publisher & Chief Creative Officer
Don Falletti VP – Manufacturing Operations & Workflow Management
Lawrence Ganem VP – Talent Services
Alison Gill Senior VP – Manufacturing & Operations
Jeffrey Kaufman VP – Editorial Strategy & Programming
Nick J. Napolitano VP – Manufacturing Administration & Design
Nancy Spears VP – Revenue

The "Progress" pride flag in the DC logo
designed by Daniel Quasar

GALAXY: THE PRETTIEST STAR

DC Comics, 2900 West Alameda Ave.,
Burbank, CA 91505
Printed by Worzalla, Stevens Point,
WI, USA. 4/8/22.
First Printing.
ISBN: 978-1-4012-9853-1

MIX
Paper from
responsible sources
FSC® C002589

Library of Congress Cataloging-in-Publication Data

Names: Axelrod, Jadzia, writer. | Taylor, Jess (Illustrator), illustrator.
| Peter, Cris, illustrator. | Maher, Ariana, letterer.
Title: Galaxy : the prettiest star / written by Jadzia Axelrod ;
illustrated by Jess Taylor with Cris Peter ; lettered by Ariana Maher.
Description: Burbank, CA : DC Comics, [2022] | Audience: Ages 13-17 |
Audience: Grades 10-12 | Summary: Taylor Barzelay seems to have the
perfect life with good looks and good grades, but they are actually an
alien princess from the planet Cyandii, and after six long years of
accepting the duty to remain in hiding as a boy on Earth, it all changes
when they meet confident Metropolis city girl Katherine.
Identifiers: LCCN 2022001580 (print) | LCCN 2022001581 (ebook) | ISBN
9781401298531 (trade paperback) | ISBN 9781779508751 (ebook)
Subjects: CYAC: Graphic novels. | Extraterrestrial beings--Fiction. |
Gender identity--Fiction. | Self-acceptance--Fiction. |
Princesses--Fiction. | Love--Fiction. | LCGFT: Genderqueer comics. |
Romance comics. | Graphic novels.
Classification: LCC PZ7.7.A96 Gal 2022 (print) | LCC PZ7.7.A96 (ebook) |
DDC 741.5/973--dc23/eng/20220131
LC record available at https://lccn.loc.gov/2022001580

For the girl who
needed this book
ages ago, and
couldn't find it.

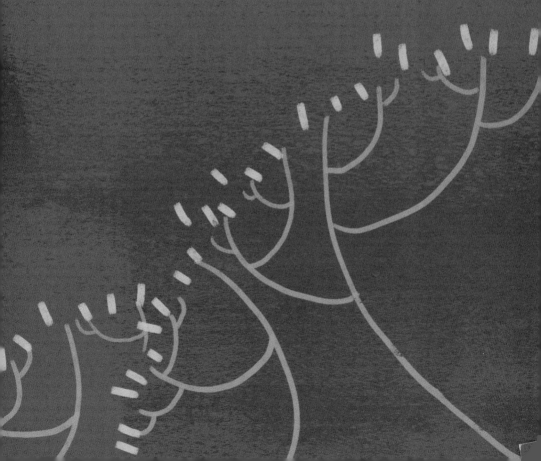

chapter 1
Aladdin Sane

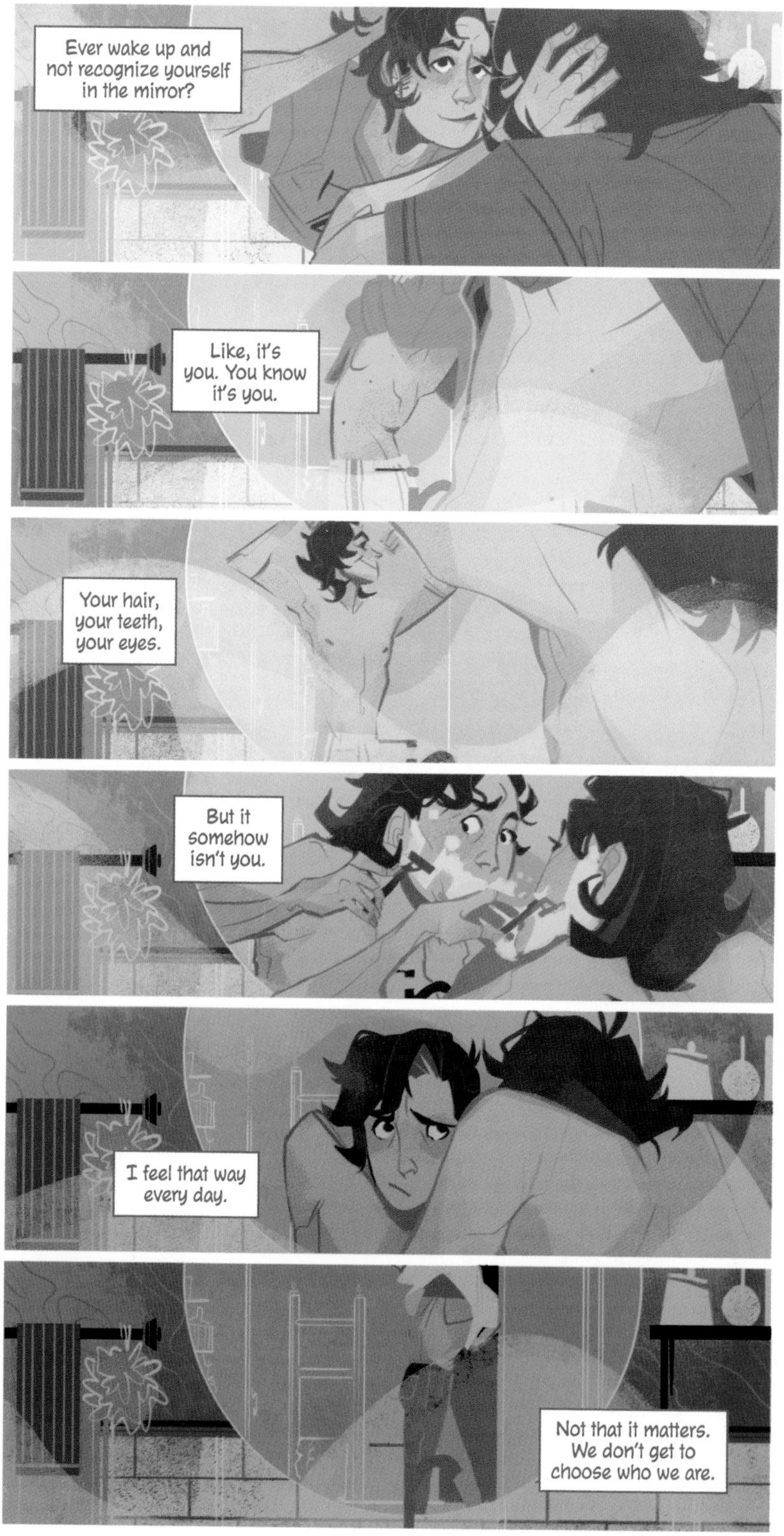
Ever wake up and not recognize yourself in the mirror?
Like, it's you. You know it's you.
Your hair, your teeth, your eyes.
But it somehow isn't you.
I feel that way every day.
Not that it matters. We don't get to choose who we are.

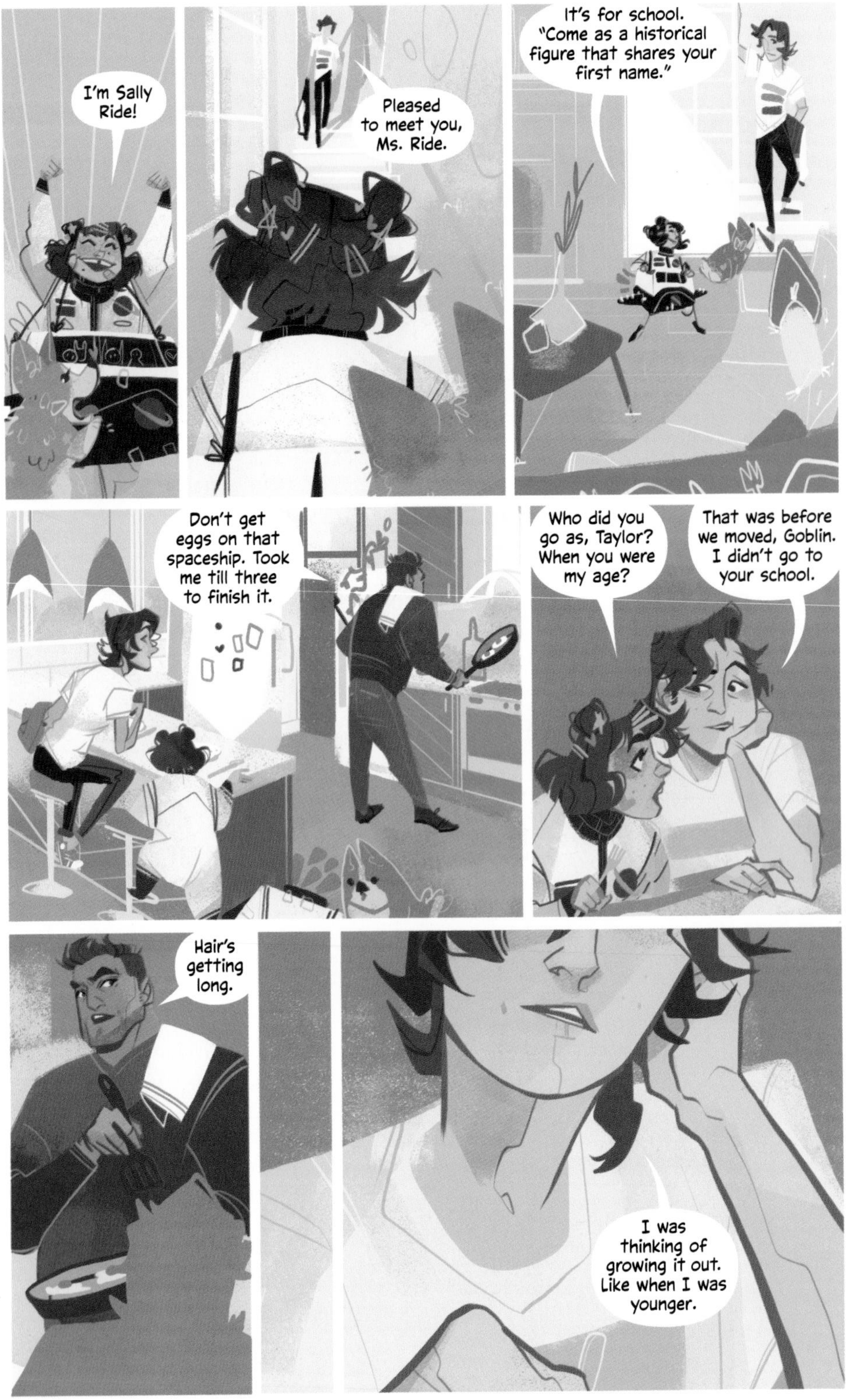
I'm Sally Ride!
Pleased to meet you, Ms. Ride.
It's for school. "Come as a historical figure that shares your first name."
Don't get eggs on that spaceship. Took me till three to finish it.
Who did you go as, Taylor? When you were my age?
That was before we moved, Goblin. I didn't go to your school.
Hair's getting long.
I was thinking of growing it out. Like when I was younger.

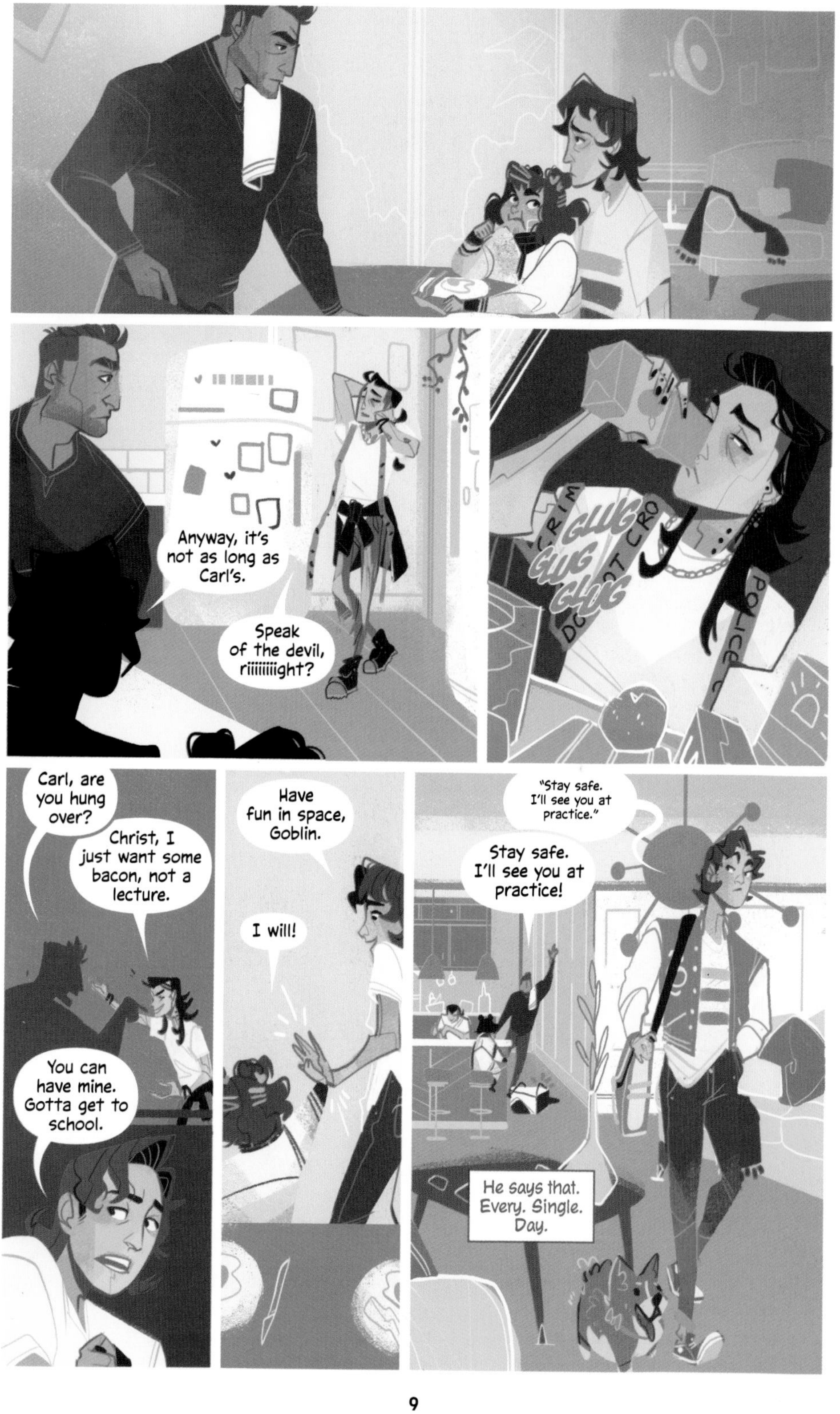
Anyway, it's not as long as Carl's.
Speak of the devil, riiiiiiight?
GLUG GLUG GLUG
CRIM DO NOT CRO
POLICE
Carl, are you hung over?
Christ, I just want some bacon, not a lecture.
You can have mine. Gotta get to school.
Have fun in space, Goblin.
I will!
"Stay safe. I'll see you at practice."
Stay safe. I'll see you at practice!
He says that. Every. Single. Day.

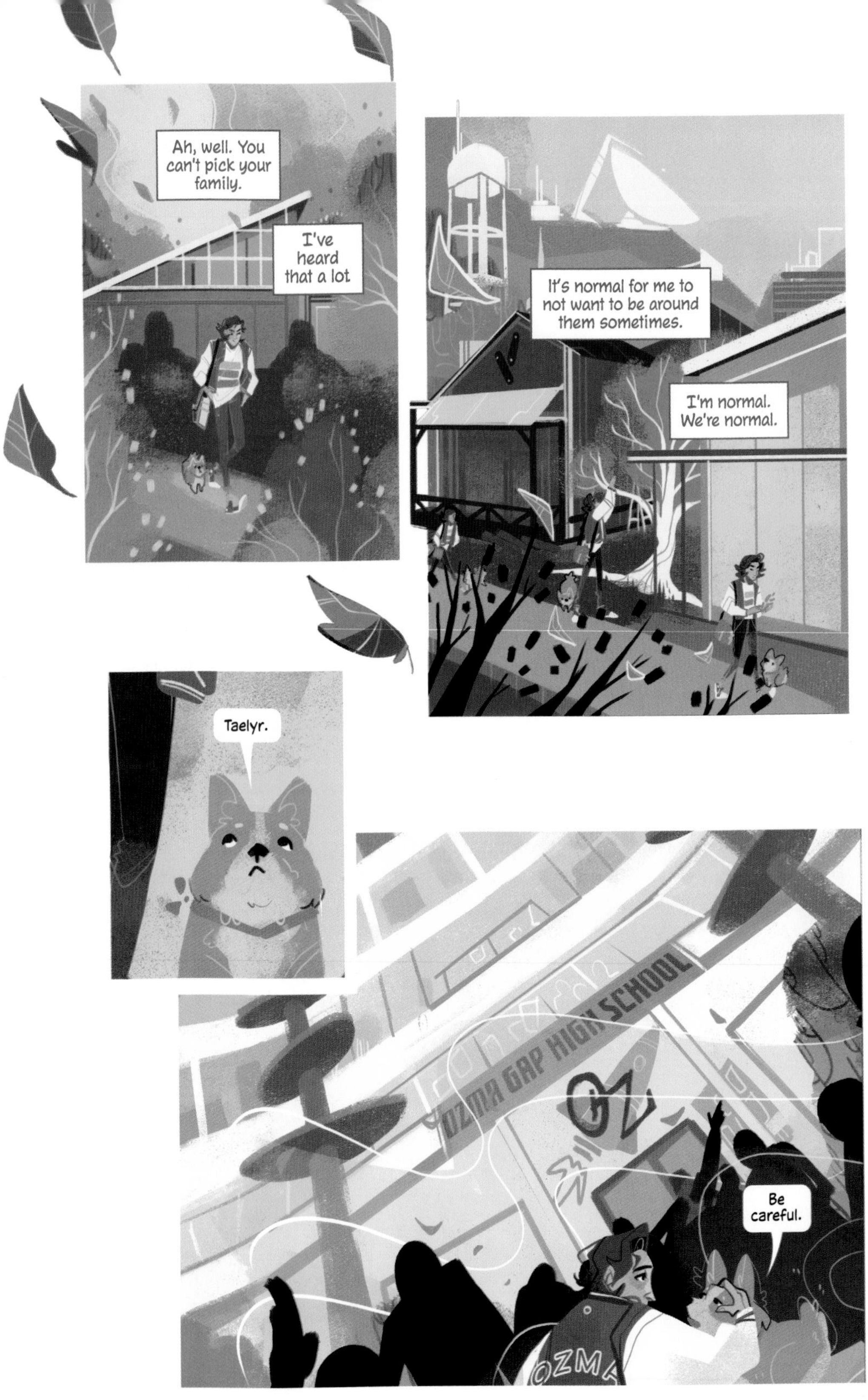
Ah, well. You can't pick your family.
I've heard that a lot
It's normal for me to not want to be around them sometimes.
I'm normal. We're normal.
Taelyr.
OZMA GAP HIGH SCHOOL
OZ
Be careful.
OZMA

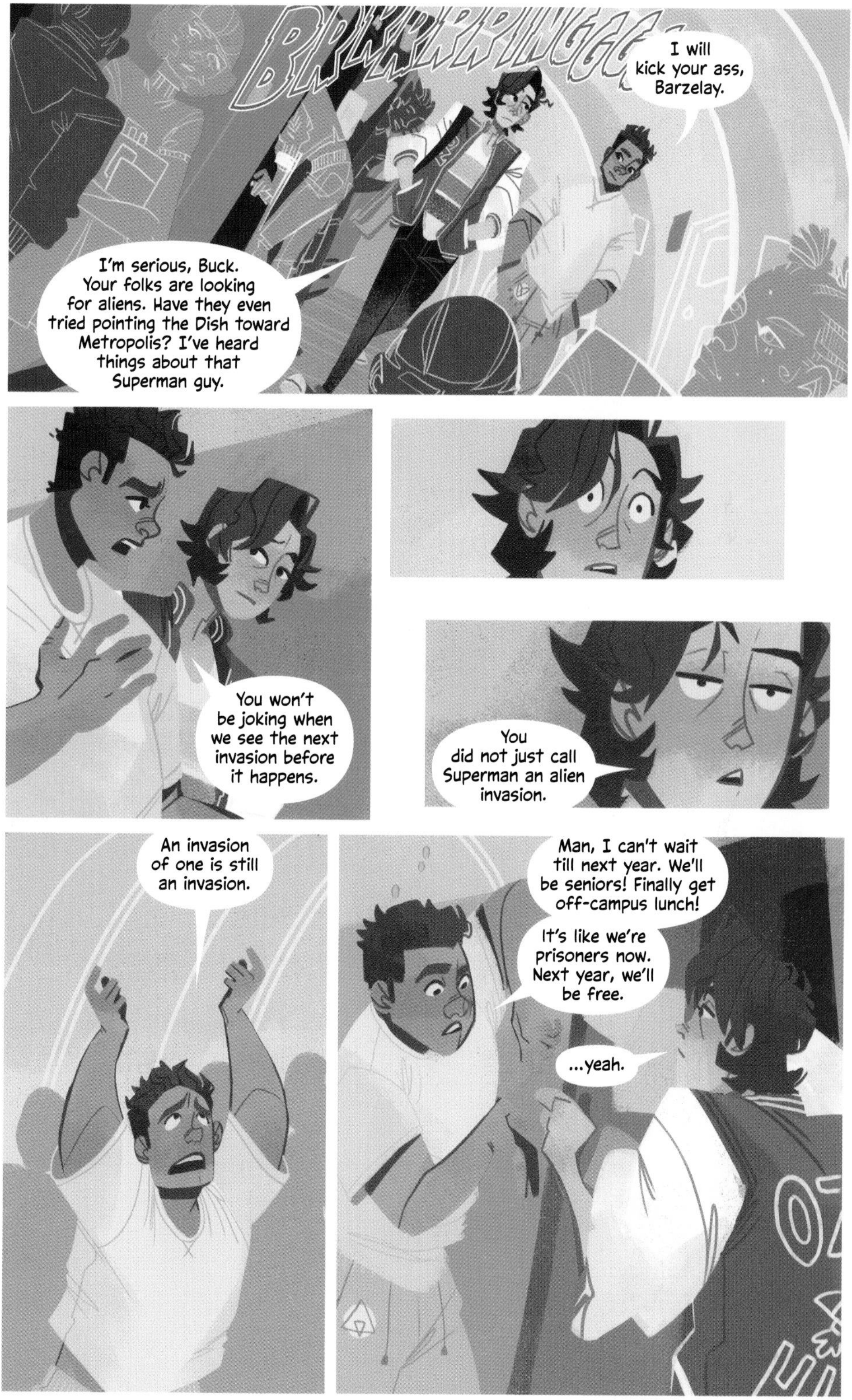

I will kick your ass, Barzelay.
I'm serious, Buck. Your folks are looking for aliens. Have they even tried pointing the Dish toward Metropolis? I've heard things about that Superman guy.
You won't be joking when we see the next invasion before it happens.
You did not just call Superman an alien invasion.
An invasion of one is still an invasion.
Man, I can't wait till next year. We'll be seniors! Finally get off-campus lunch!
It's like we're prisoners now. Next year, we'll be free.
...yeah.

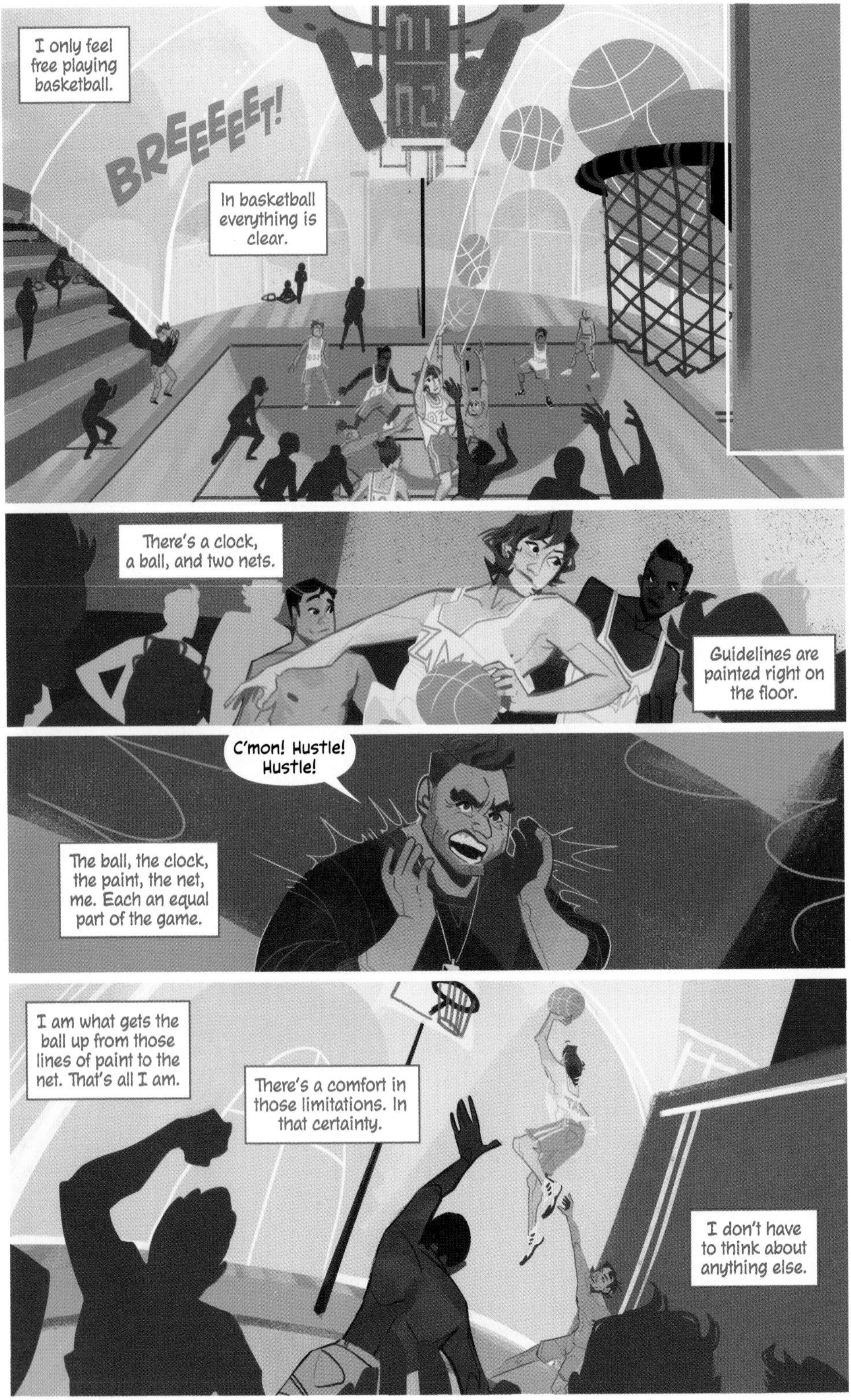
I only feel free playing basketball.
BREEEEET!
In basketball everything is clear.
There's a clock, a ball, and two nets.
Guidelines are painted right on the floor.
C'mon! Hustle! Hustle!
The ball, the clock, the paint, the net, me. Each an equal part of the game.
I am what gets the ball up from those lines of paint to the net. That's all I am.
There's a comfort in those limitations. In that certainty.
I don't have to think about anything else.

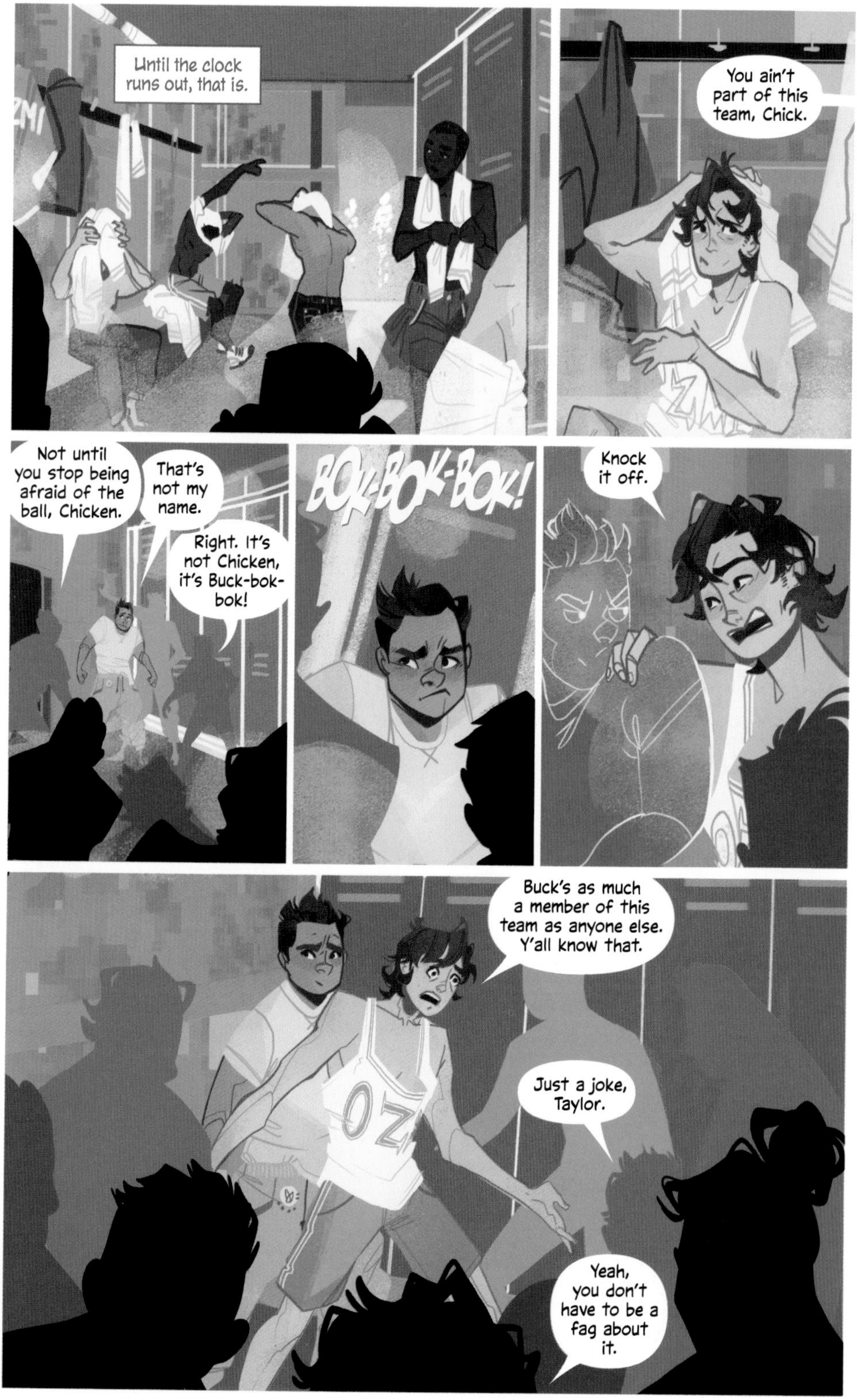
Until the clock runs out, that is.
You ain't part of this team, Chick.
Not until you stop being afraid of the ball, Chicken.
That's not my name.
Right. It's not Chicken, it's Buck-bok-bok!
BOK-BOK-BOK!
Knock it off.
Buck's as much a member of this team as anyone else. Y'all know that.
Just a joke, Taylor.
Yeah, you don't have to be a fag about it.

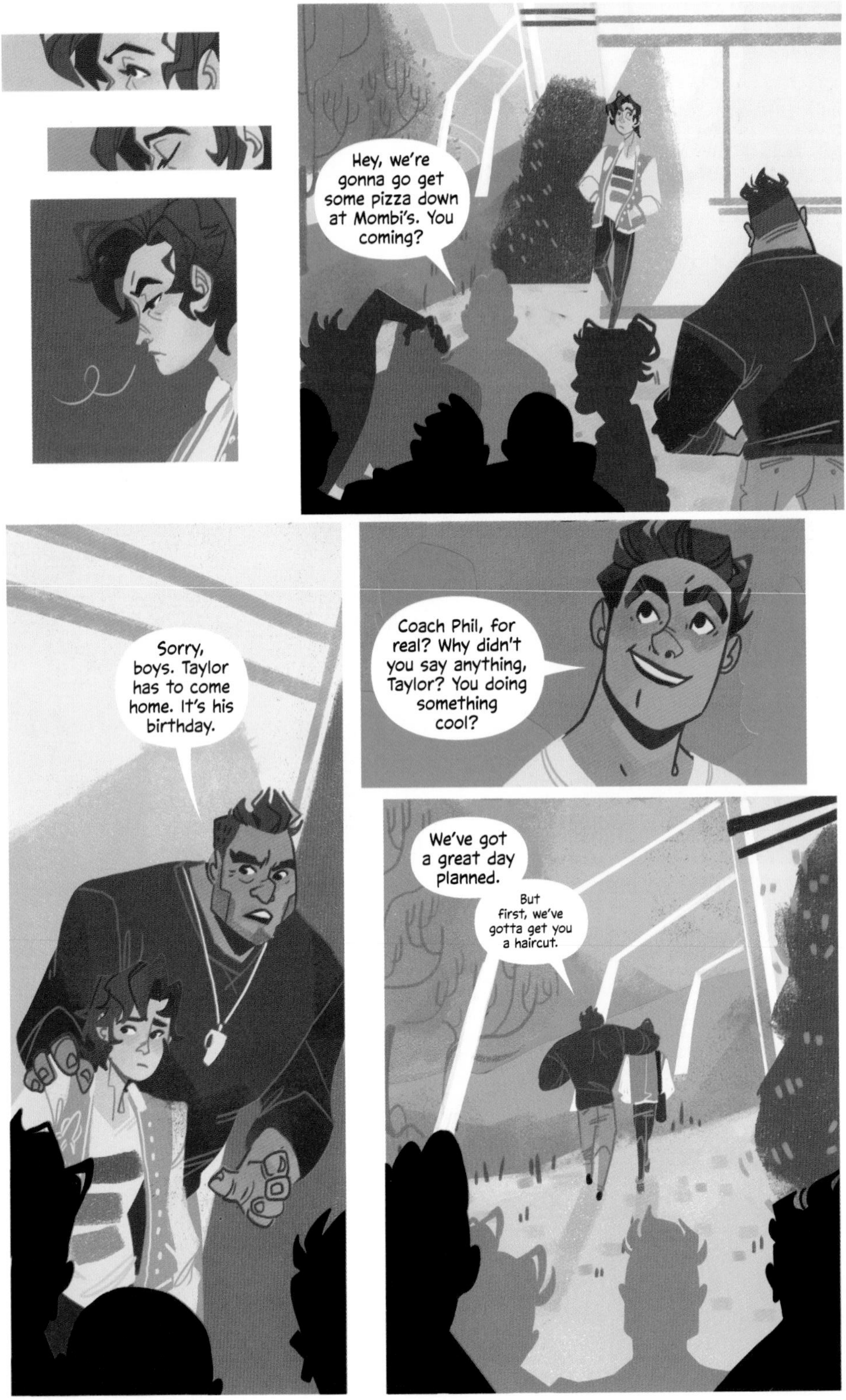
Hey, we're gonna go get some pizza down at Mombi's. You coming?
Sorry, boys. Taylor has to come home. It's his birthday.
Coach Phil, for real? Why didn't you say anything, Taylor? You doing something cool?
We've got a great day planned.
But first, we've gotta get you a haircut.

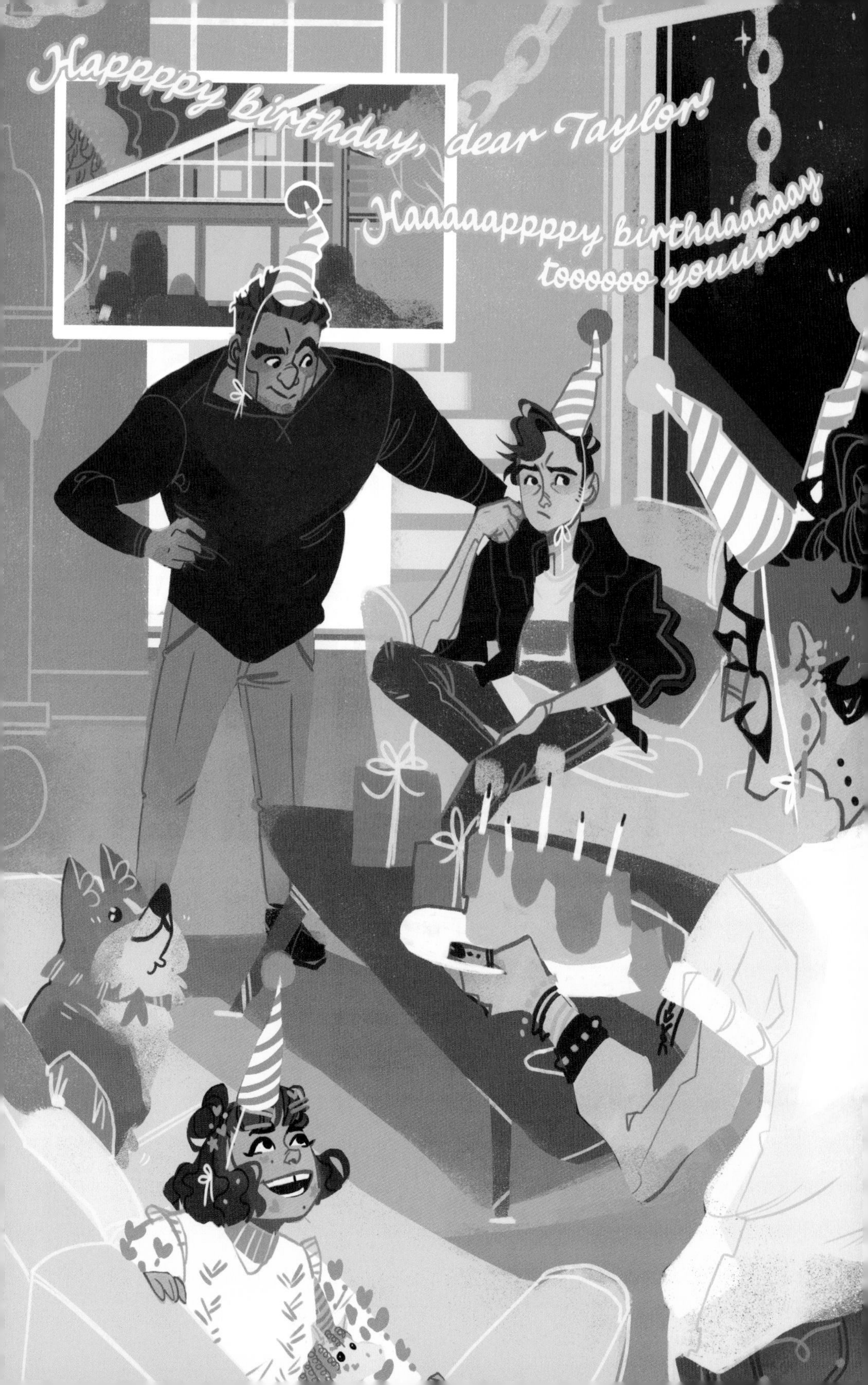
Happppy birthday, dear Taylor!
Haaaaappppy birthdaaaaay tooooooo youuuuu.

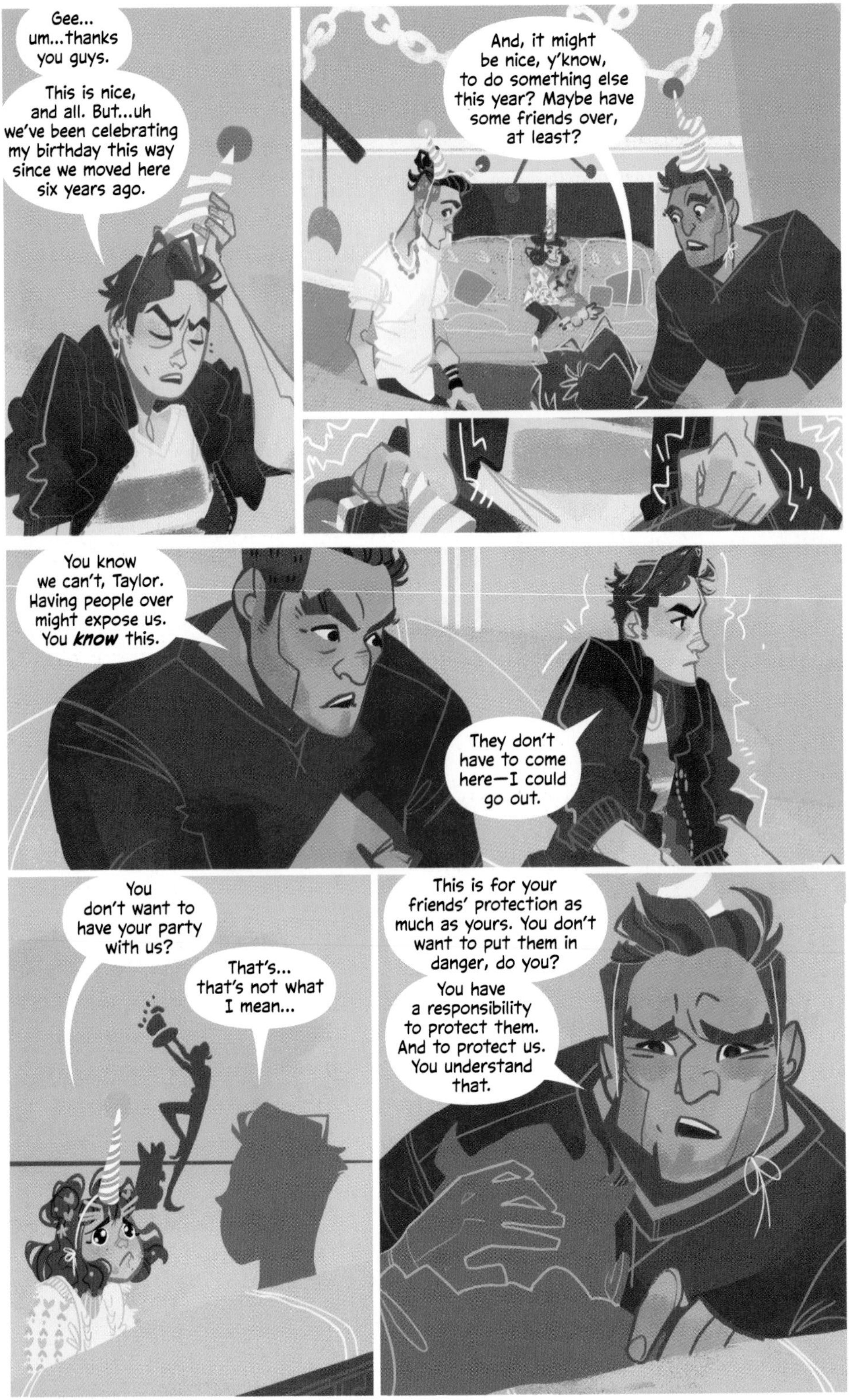
Gee... um...thanks you guys.
This is nice, and all. But...uh we've been celebrating my birthday this way since we moved here six years ago.
And, it might be nice, y'know, to do something else this year? Maybe have some friends over, at least?
You know we can't, Taylor. Having people over might expose us. You *know* this.
They don't have to come here—I could go out.
You don't want to have your party with us?
That's... that's not what I mean...
This is for your friends' protection as much as yours. You don't want to put them in danger, do you?
You have a responsibility to protect them. And to protect us. You understand that.

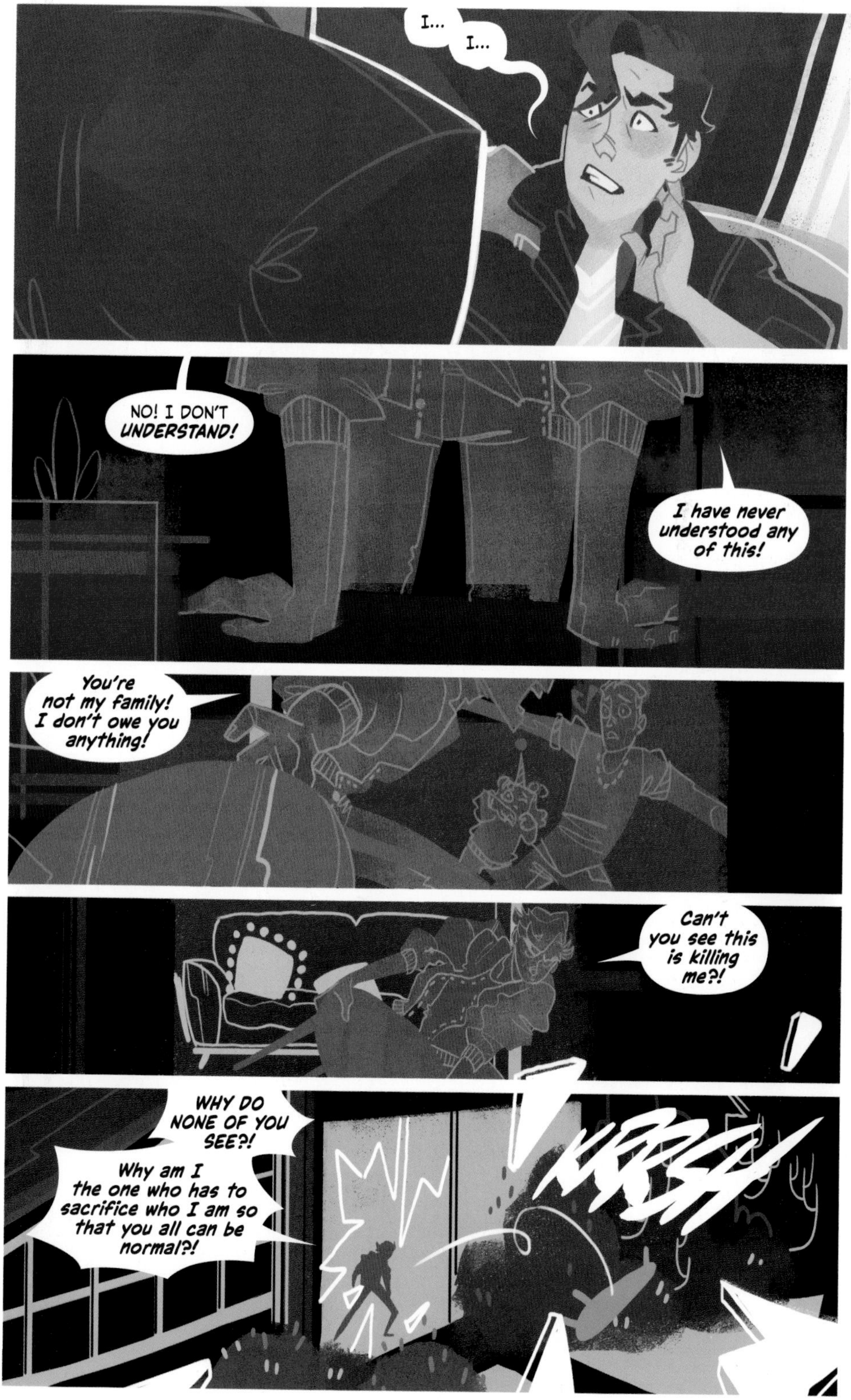
I...
I...
NO! I DON'T UNDERSTAND!
I have never understood any of this!
You're not my family! I don't owe you anything!
Can't you see this is killing me?!
WHY DO NONE OF YOU SEE?!
Why am I the one who has to sacrifice who I am so that you all can be normal?!
KRSH

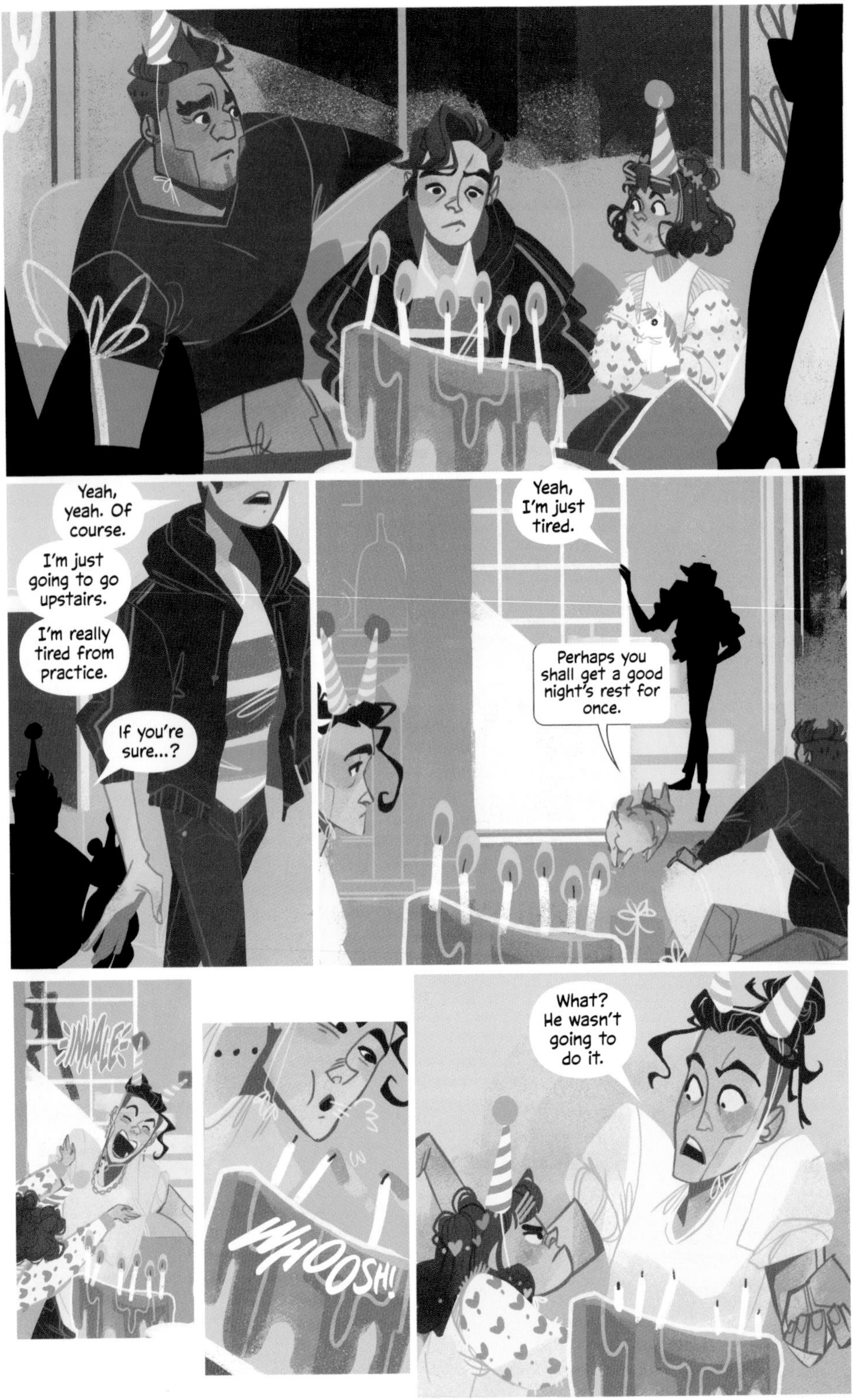

Yeah, yeah. Of course.
I'm just going to go upstairs.
I'm really tired from practice.
If you're sure...?
Yeah, I'm just tired.
Perhaps you shall get a good night's rest for once.
INHALE
...
WHOOSH!
What? He wasn't going to do it.

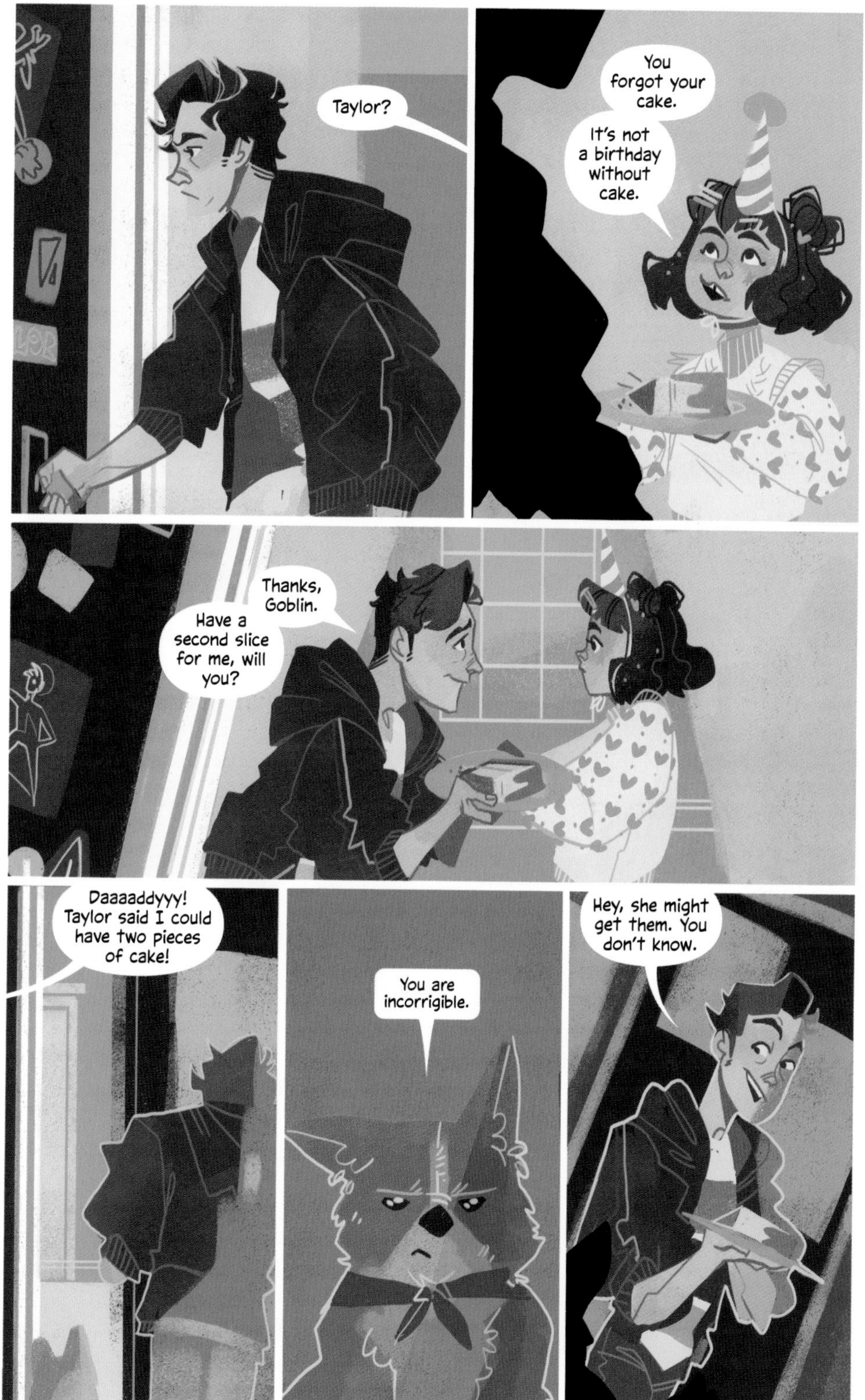
Taylor?
You forgot your cake.
It's not a birthday without cake.
Thanks, Goblin.
Have a second slice for me, will you?
Daaaaddyyy! Taylor said I could have two pieces of cake!
You are incorrigible.
Hey, she might get them. You don't know.

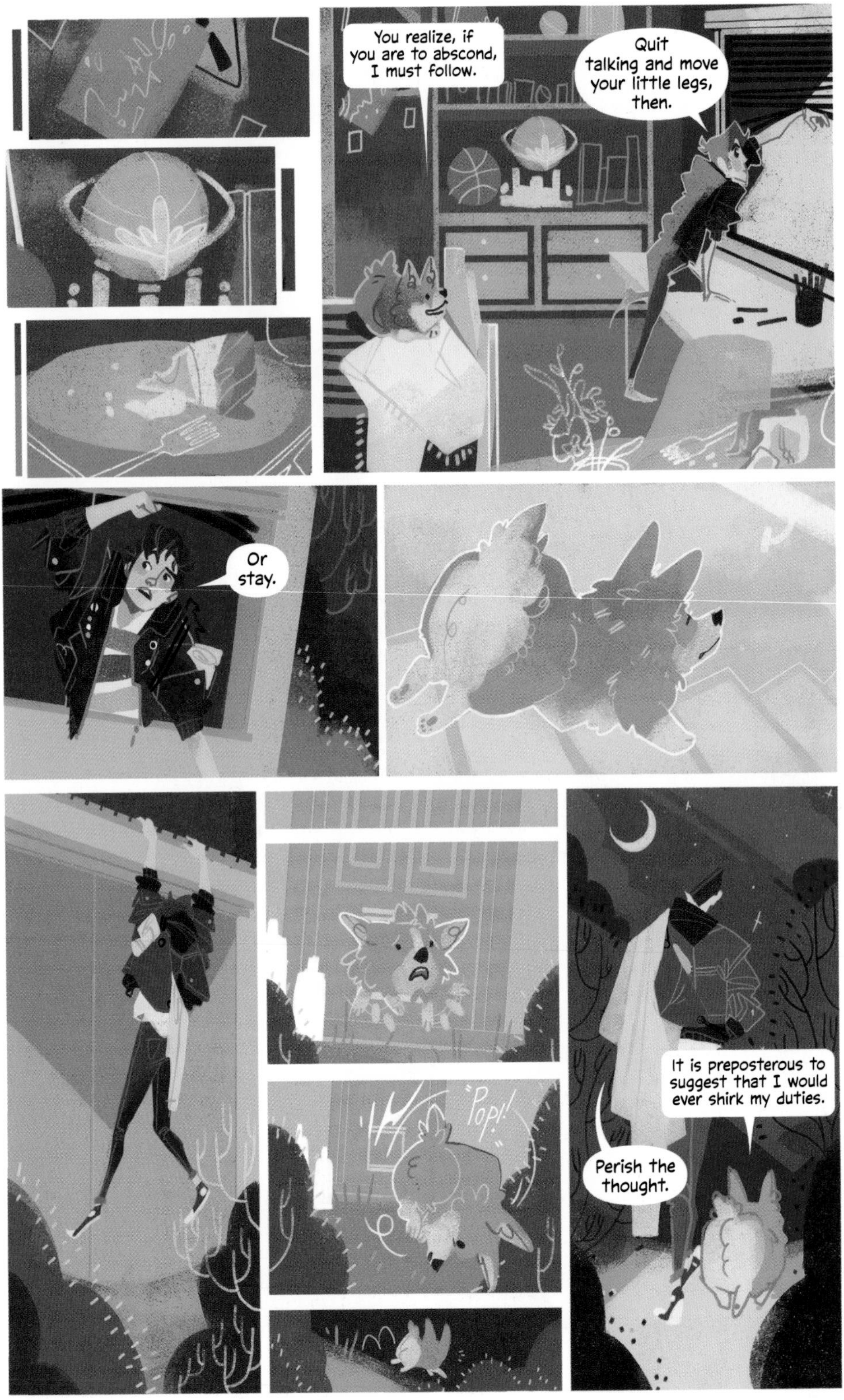
You realize, if you are to abscond, I must follow.
Quit talking and move your little legs, then.
Or stay.
POP!
It is preposterous to suggest that I would ever shirk my duties.
Perish the thought.

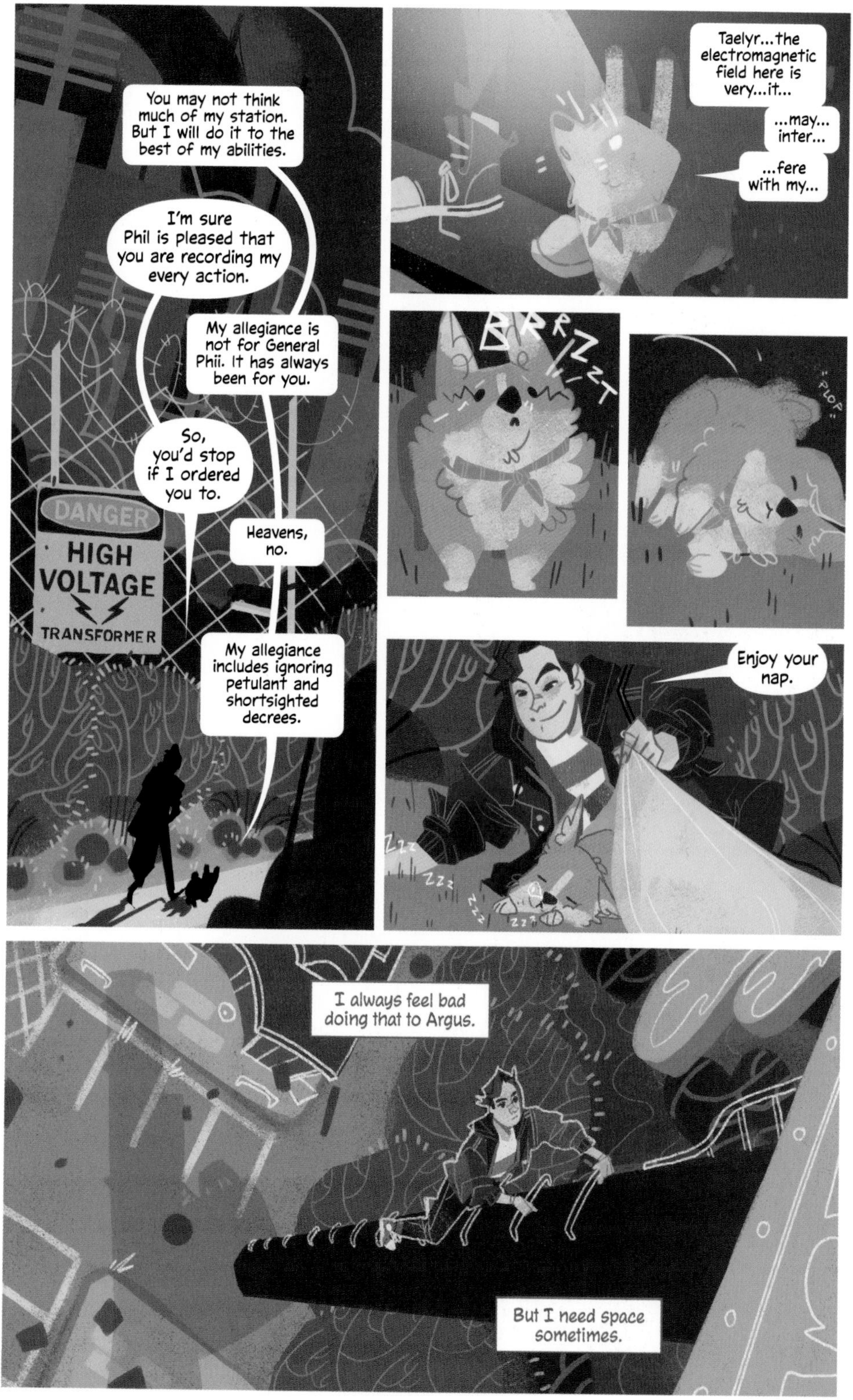

You may not think much of my station. But I will do it to the best of my abilities.
I'm sure Phil is pleased that you are recording my every action.
My allegiance is not for General Phii. It has always been for you.
So, you'd stop if I ordered you to.
Heavens, no.
My allegiance includes ignoring petulant and shortsighted decrees.
DANGER
HIGH VOLTAGE
TRANSFORMER
Taelyr...the electromagnetic field here is very...it...
...may... inter...
...fere with my...
BRRRZZZT
PLOP
Enjoy your nap.
I always feel bad doing that to Argus.
But I need space sometimes.

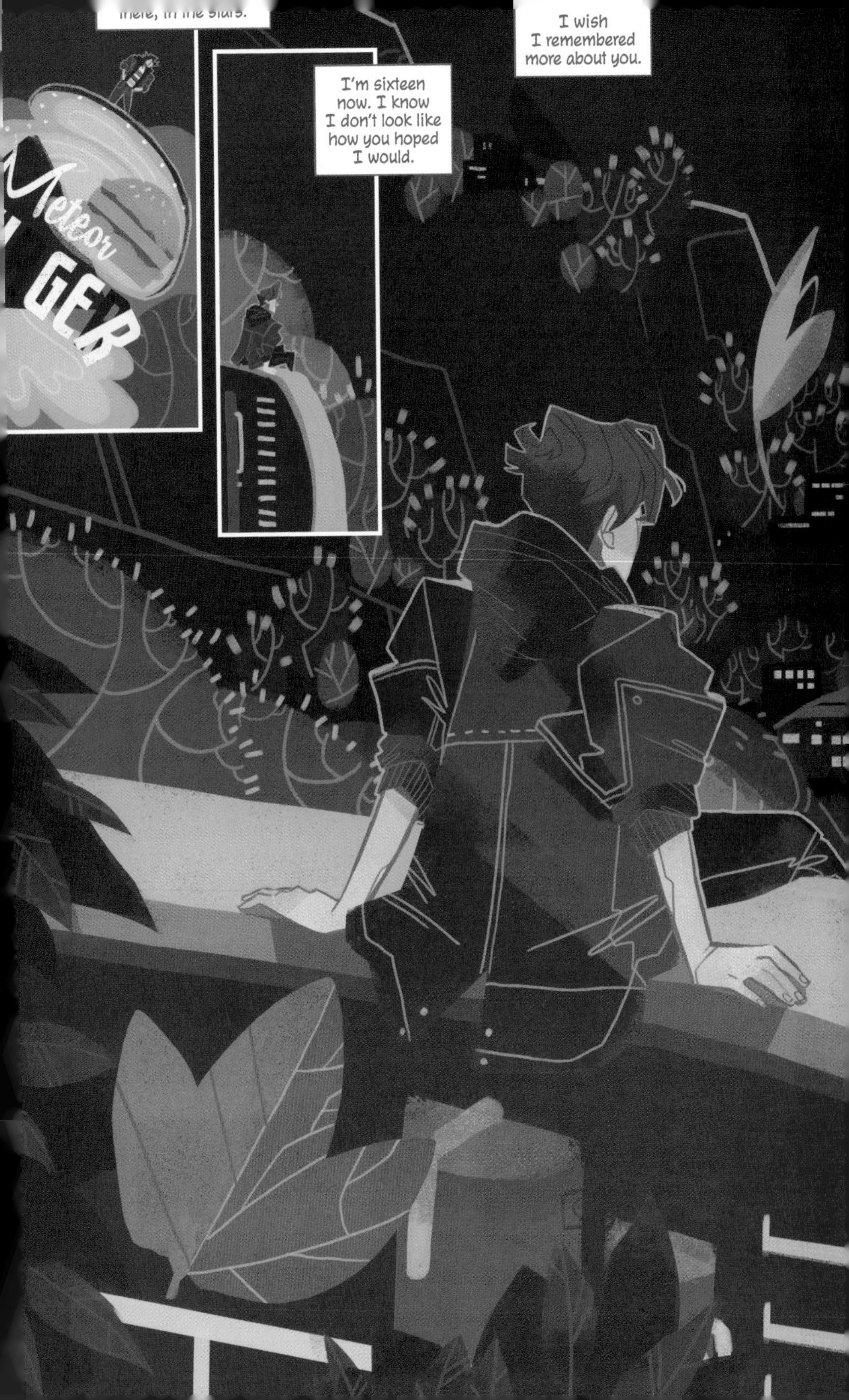
there, in the stars.
Meteor
I'm sixteen now. I know I don't look like how you hoped I would.
I wish I remembered more about you.

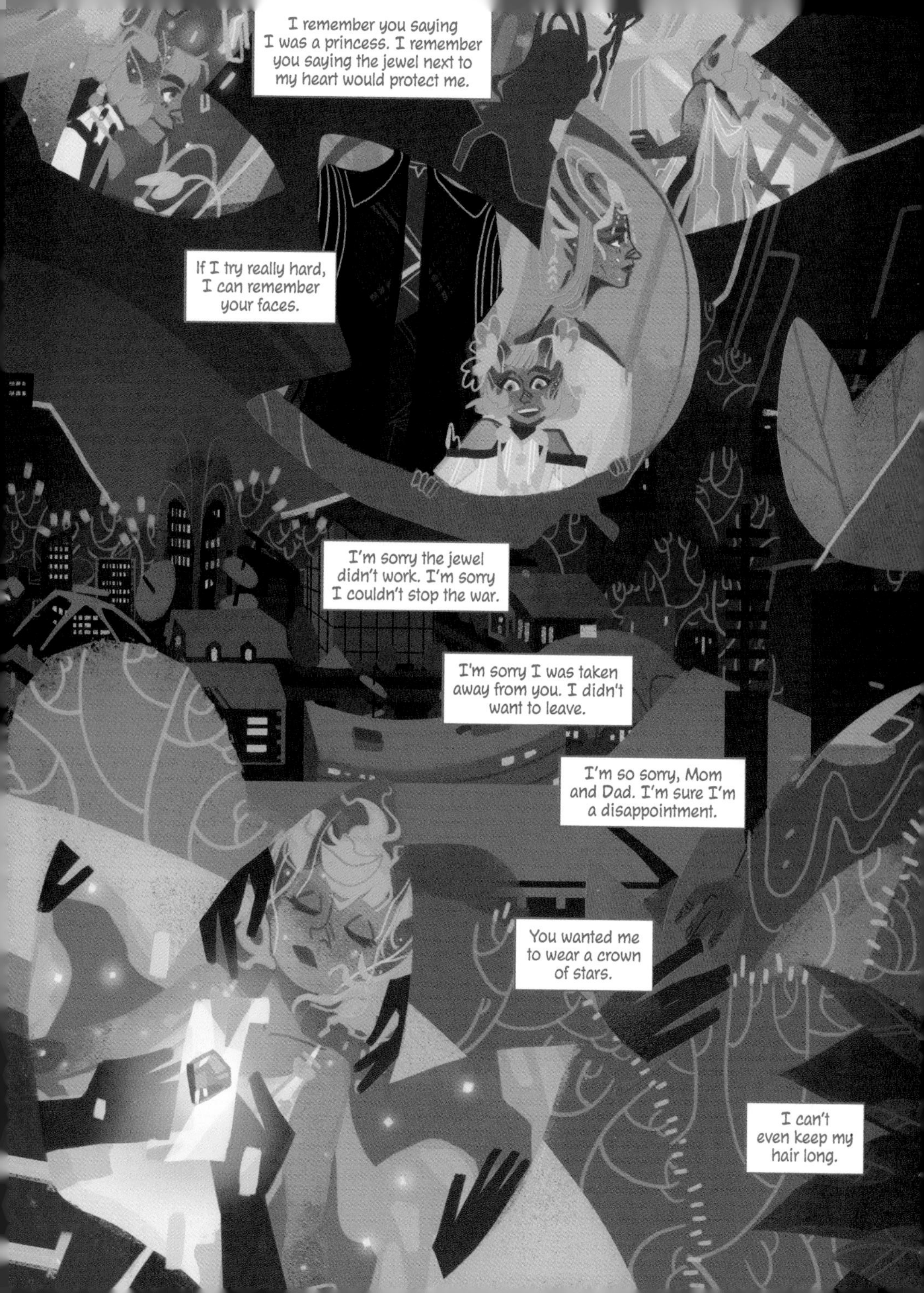
I remember you saying I was a princess. I remember you saying the jewel next to my heart would protect me.
If I try really hard, I can remember your faces.
I'm sorry the jewel didn't work. I'm sorry I couldn't stop the war.
I'm sorry I was taken away from you. I didn't want to leave.
I'm so sorry, Mom and Dad. I'm sure I'm a disappointment.
You wanted me to wear a crown of stars.
I can't even keep my hair long.

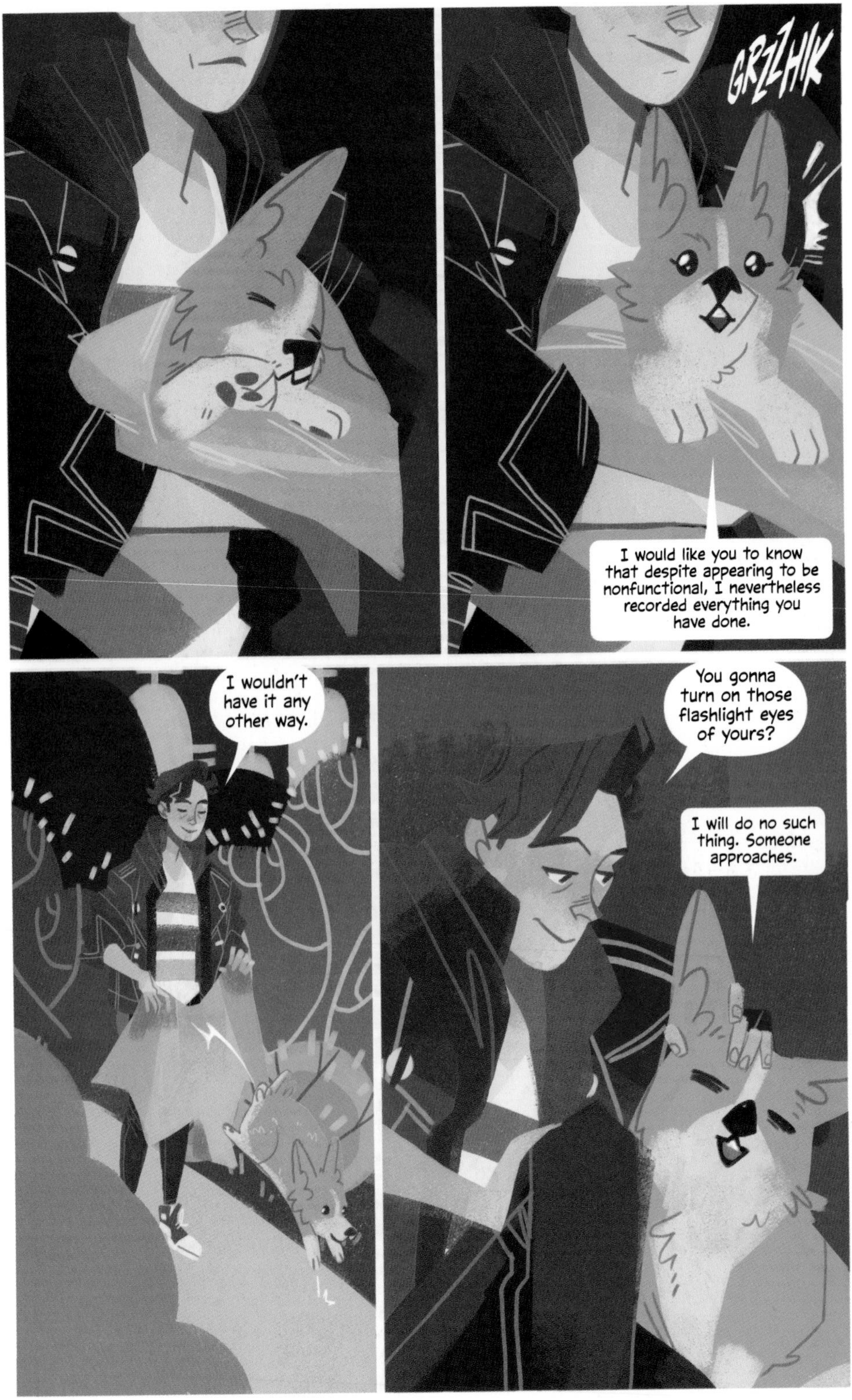
GRZZHIK
I would like you to know that despite appearing to be nonfunctional, I nevertheless recorded everything you have done.
I wouldn't have it any other way.
You gonna turn on those flashlight eyes of yours?
I will do no such thing. Someone approaches.

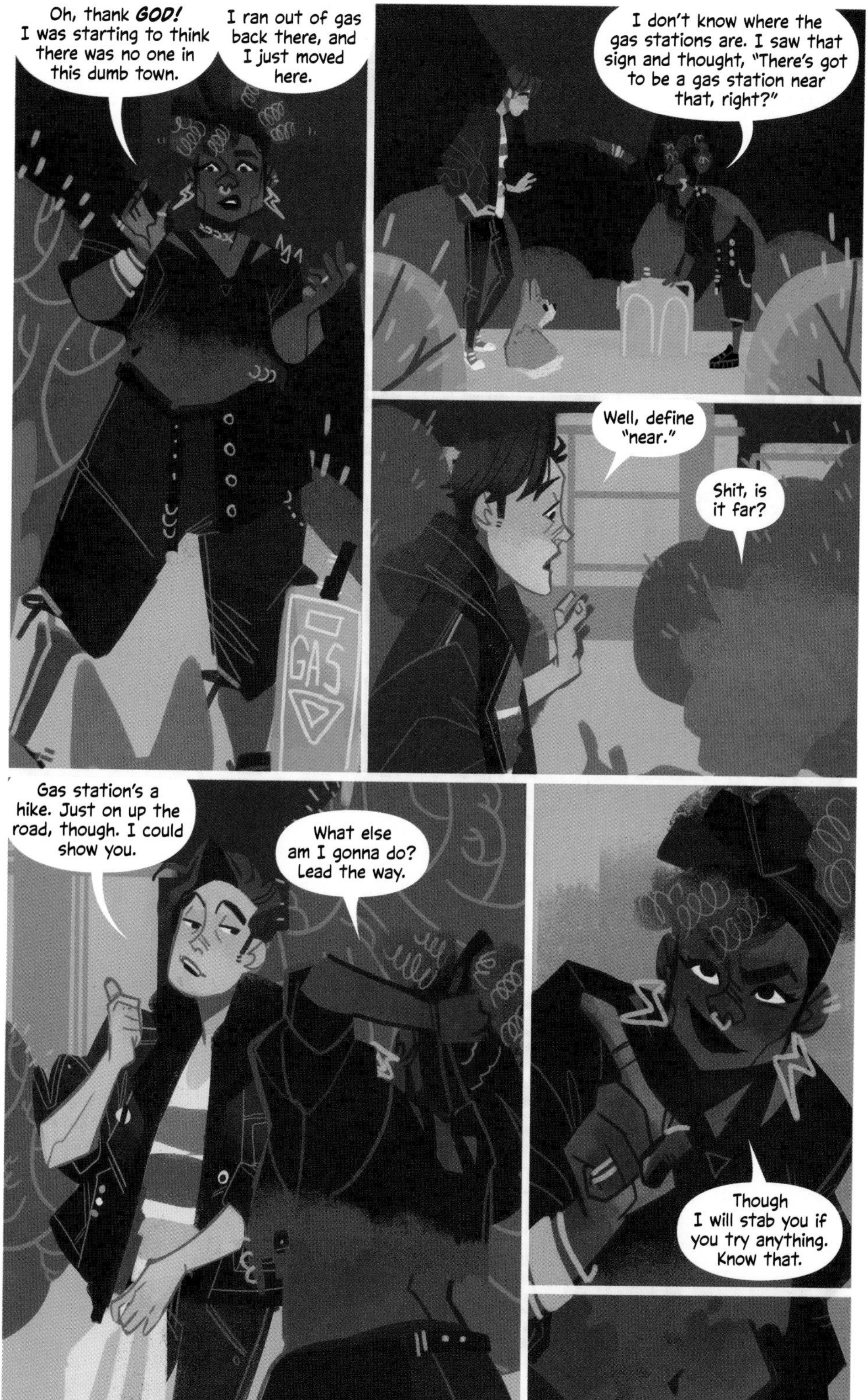

Oh, thank GOD! I was starting to think there was no one in this dumb town.
I ran out of gas back there, and I just moved here.
GAS
I don't know where the gas stations are. I saw that sign and thought, "There's got to be a gas station near that, right?"
Well, define "near."
Shit, is it far?
Gas station's a hike. Just on up the road, though. I could show you.
What else am I gonna do? Lead the way.
Though I will stab you if you try anything. Know that.

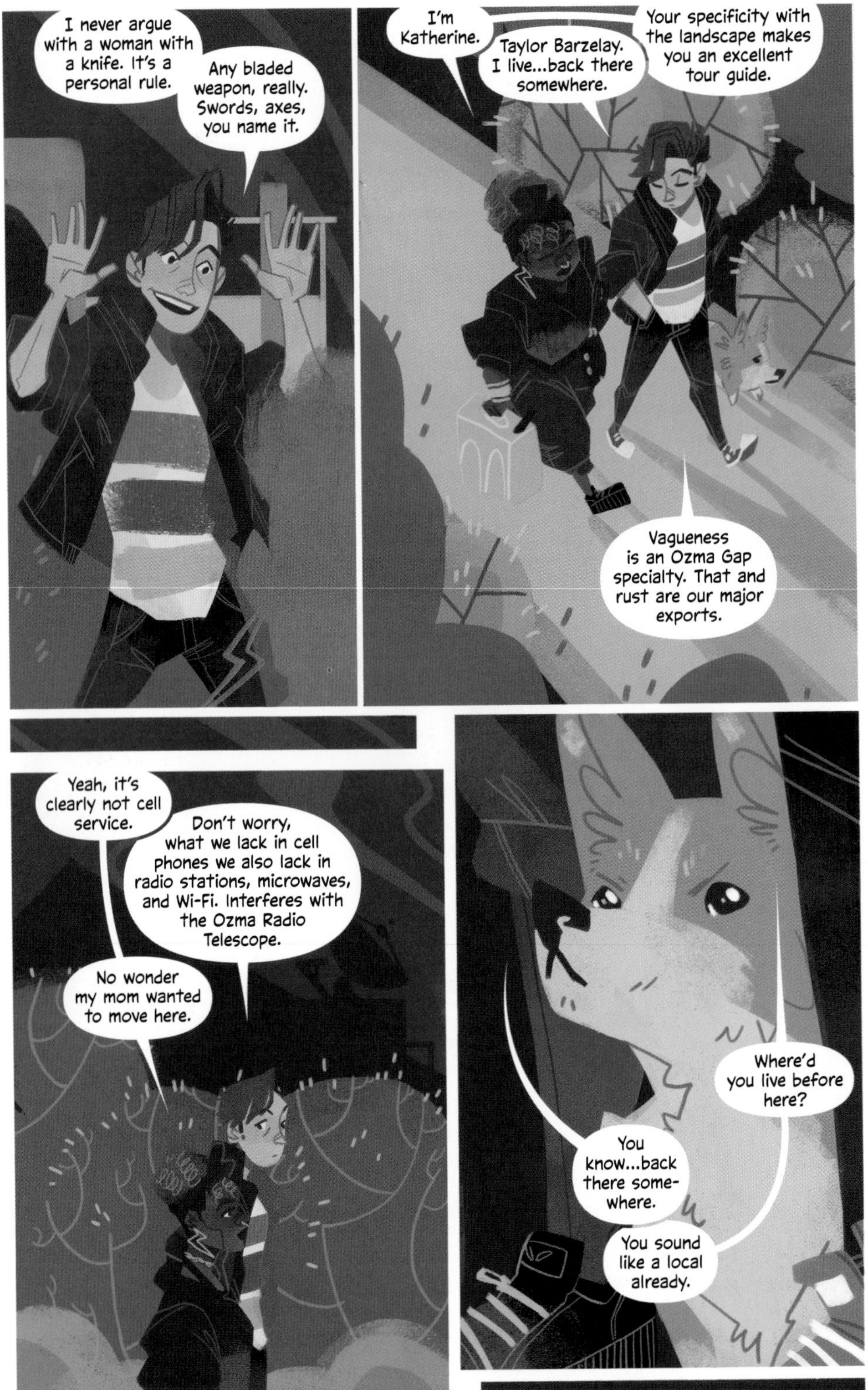

I never argue with a woman with a knife. It's a personal rule.
Any bladed weapon, really. Swords, axes, you name it.
I'm Katherine.
Taylor Barzelay. I live...back there somewhere.
Your specificity with the landscape makes you an excellent tour guide.
Vagueness is an Ozma Gap specialty. That and rust are our major exports.
Yeah, it's clearly not cell service.
Don't worry, what we lack in cell phones we also lack in radio stations, microwaves, and Wi-Fi. Interferes with the Ozma Radio Telescope.
No wonder my mom wanted to move here.
Where'd you live before here?
You know...back there some-where.
You sound like a local already.

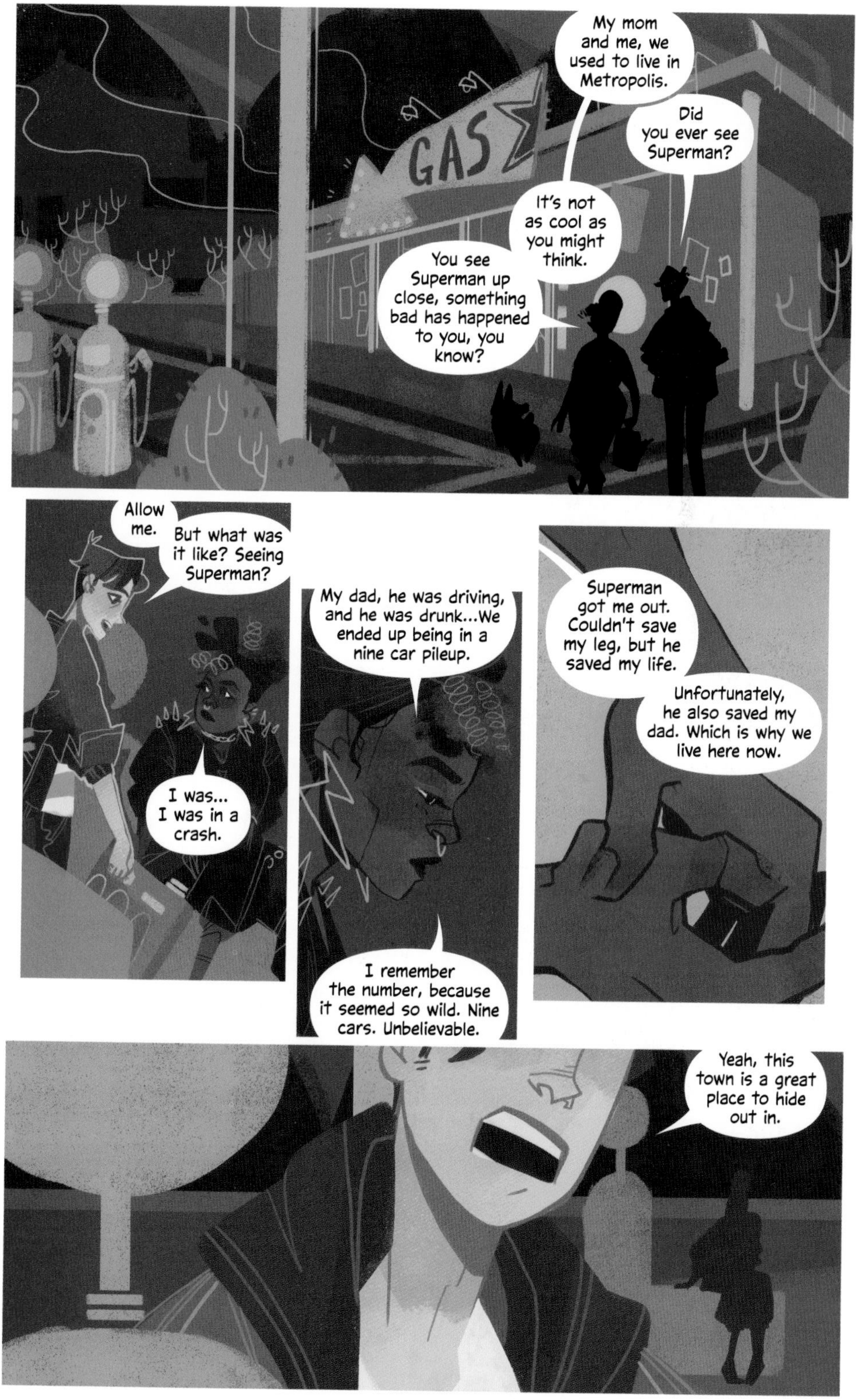
My mom and me, we used to live in Metropolis.
Did you ever see Superman?
It's not as cool as you might think.
You see Superman up close, something bad has happened to you, you know?
Allow me.
But what was it like? Seeing Superman?
I was... I was in a crash.
My dad, he was driving, and he was drunk...We ended up being in a nine car pileup.
I remember the number, because it seemed so wild. Nine cars. Unbelievable.
Superman got me out. Couldn't save my leg, but he saved my life.
Unfortunately, he also saved my dad. Which is why we live here now.
Yeah, this town is a great place to hide out in.

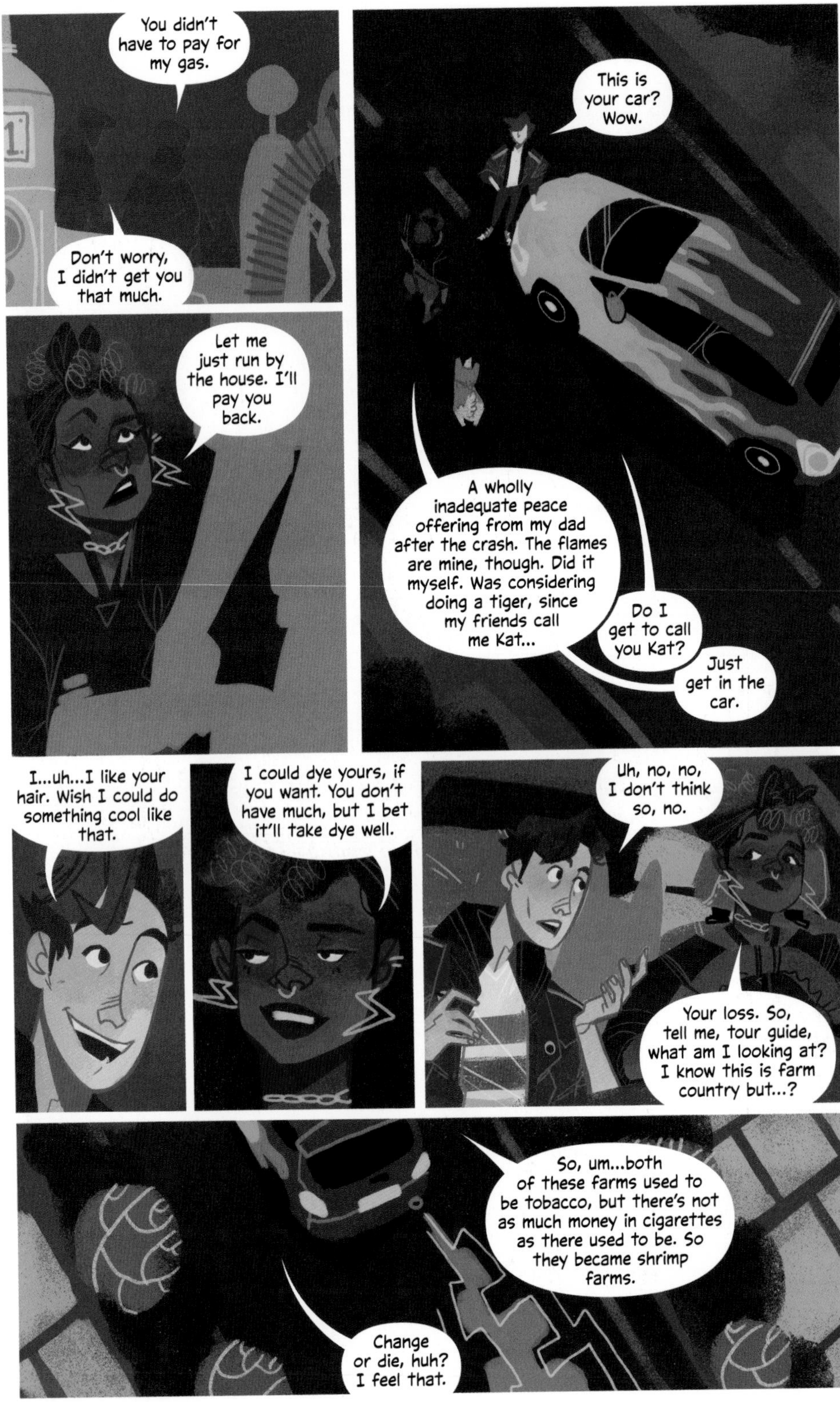
You didn't have to pay for my gas.
Don't worry, I didn't get you that much.
Let me just run by the house. I'll pay you back.
This is your car? Wow.
A wholly inadequate peace offering from my dad after the crash. The flames are mine, though. Did it myself. Was considering doing a tiger, since my friends call me Kat...
Do I get to call you Kat?
Just get in the car.
I...uh...I like your hair. Wish I could do something cool like that.
I could dye yours, if you want. You don't have much, but I bet it'll take dye well.
Uh, no, no, I don't think so, no.
Your loss. So, tell me, tour guide, what am I looking at? I know this is farm country but...?
So, um...both of these farms used to be tobacco, but there's not as much money in cigarettes as there used to be. So they became shrimp farms.
Change or die, huh? I feel that.

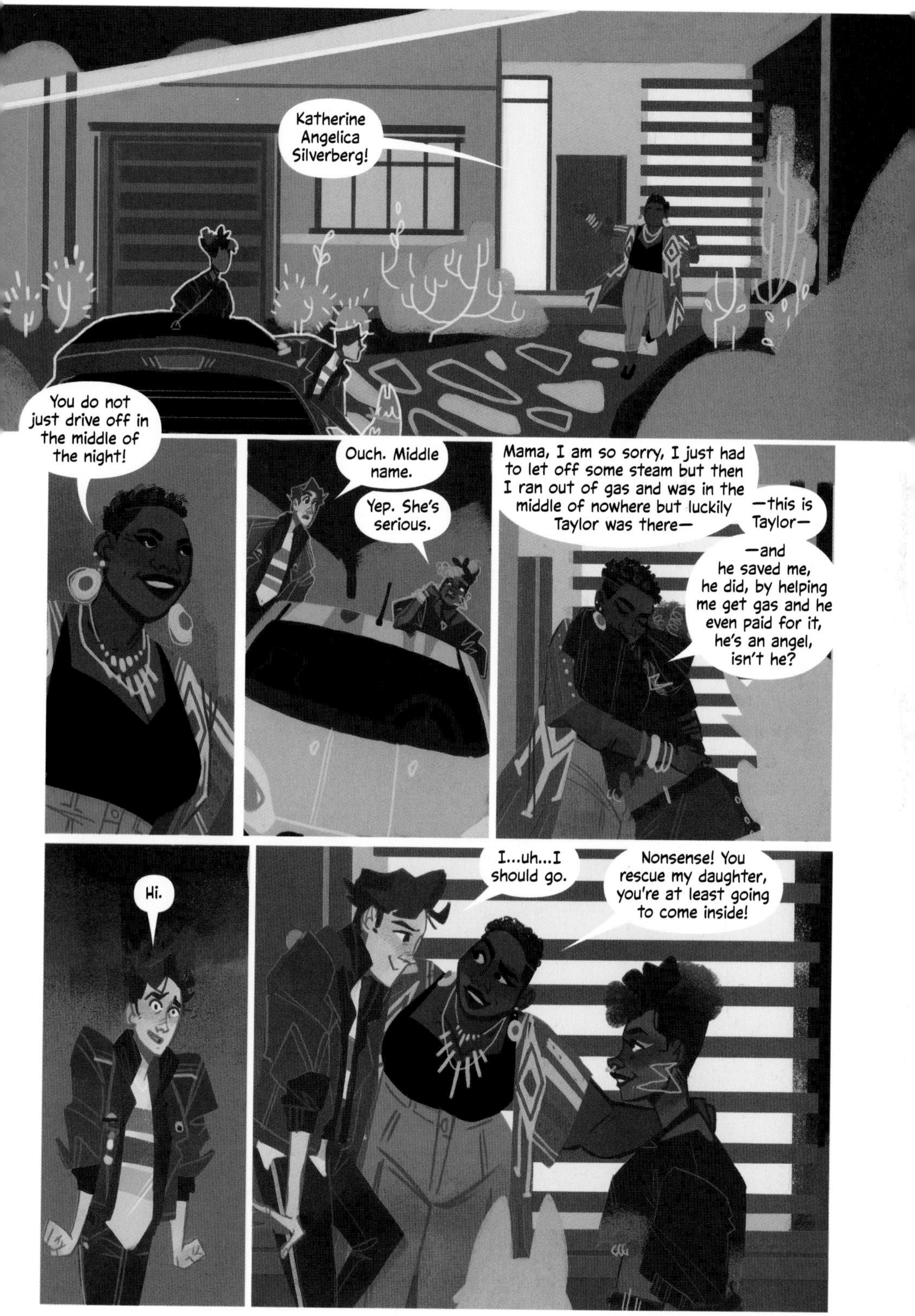
Katherine Angelica Silverberg!
You do not just drive off in the middle of the night!
Ouch. Middle name.
Yep. She's serious.
Mama, I am so sorry, I just had to let off some steam but then I ran out of gas and was in the middle of nowhere but luckily Taylor was there—
—this is Taylor—
—and he saved me, he did, by helping me get gas and he even paid for it, he's an angel, isn't he?
Hi.
I...uh...I should go.
Nonsense! You rescue my daughter, you're at least going to come inside!

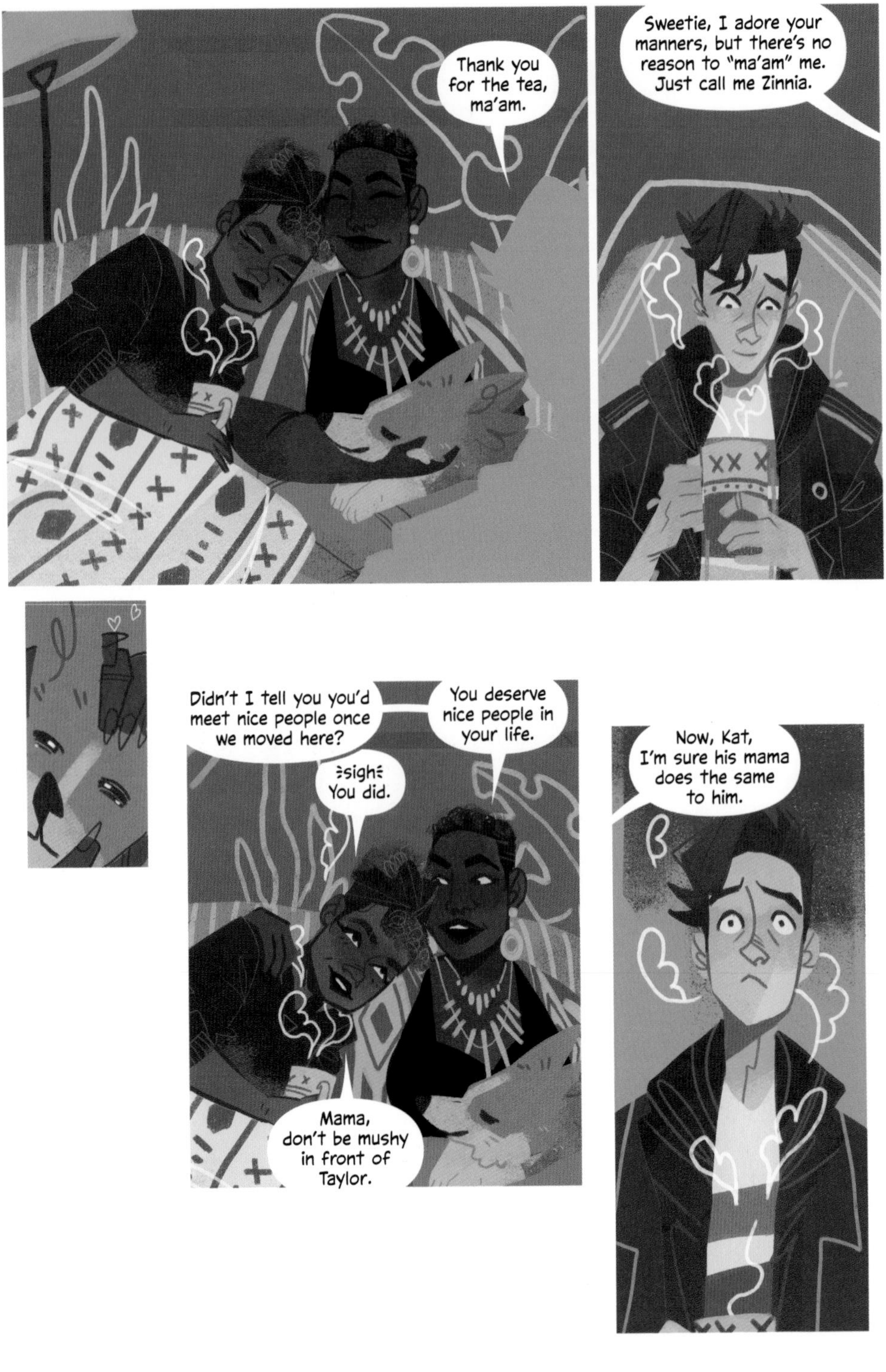
Thank you for the tea, ma'am.
Sweetie, I adore your manners, but there's no reason to "ma'am" me. Just call me Zinnia.
Didn't I tell you you'd meet nice people once we moved here?
You deserve nice people in your life.
⁝sigh⁝ You did.
Mama, don't be mushy in front of Taylor.
Now, Kat, I'm sure his mama does the same to him.

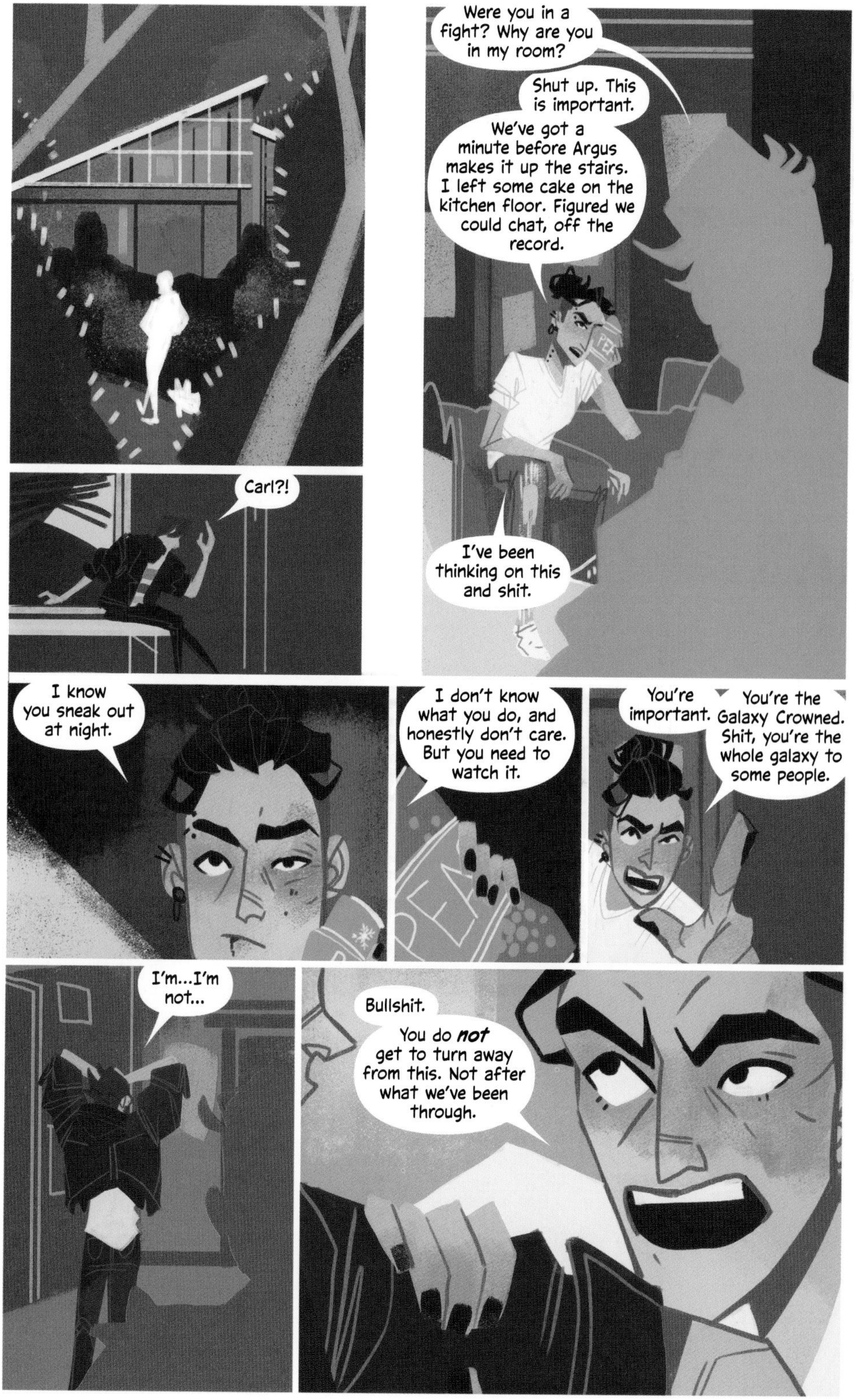
Carl?!
Were you in a fight? Why are you in my room?
Shut up. This is important.
We've got a minute before Argus makes it up the stairs. I left some cake on the kitchen floor. Figured we could chat, off the record.
I've been thinking on this and shit.
I know you sneak out at night.
I don't know what you do, and honestly don't care. But you need to watch it.
You're important.
You're the Galaxy Crowned. Shit, you're the whole galaxy to some people.
I'm...I'm not...
Bullshit.
You do ***not*** get to turn away from this. Not after what we've been through.

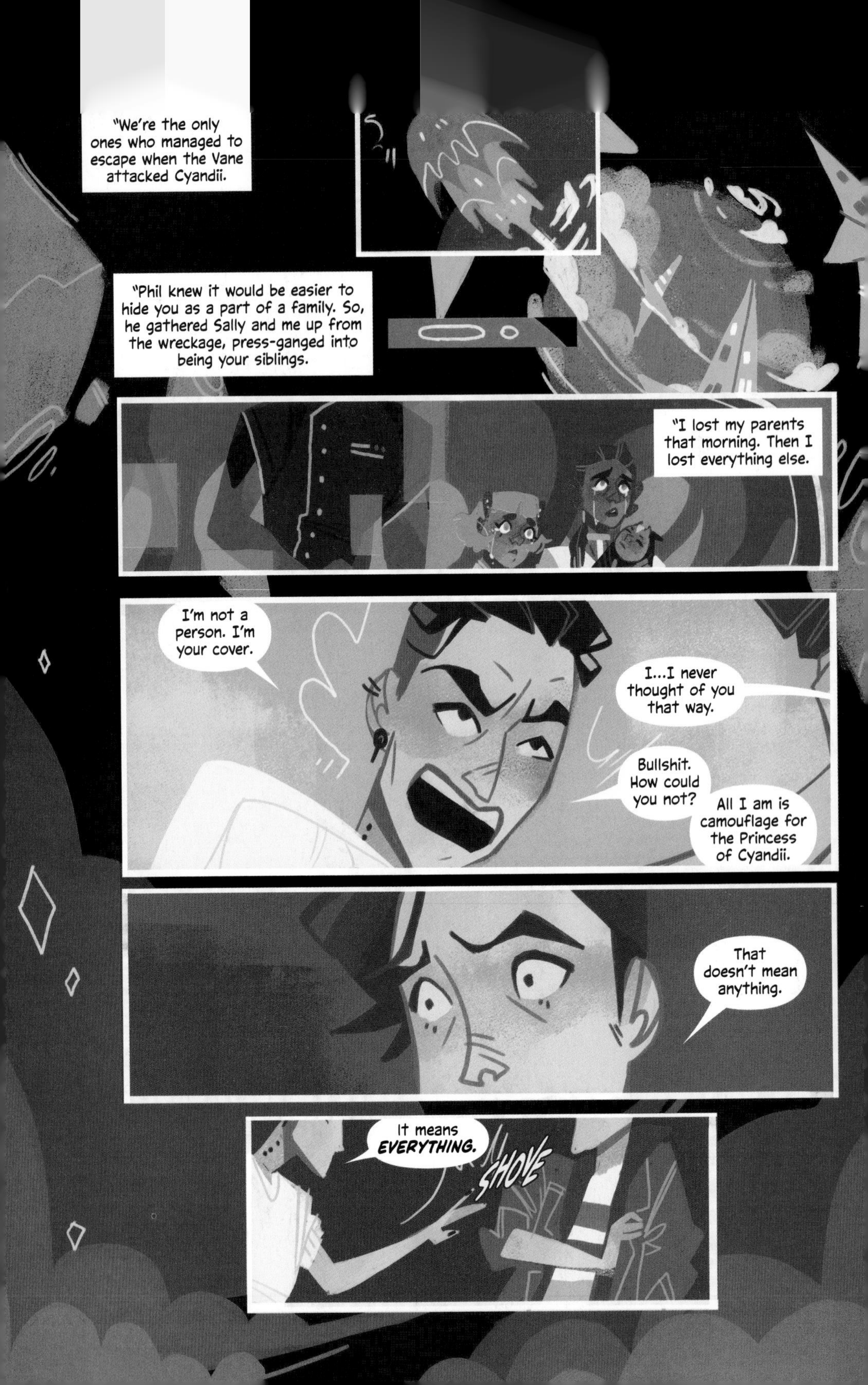
"We're the only ones who managed to escape when the Vane attacked Cyandii.
"Phil knew it would be easier to hide you as a part of a family. So, he gathered Sally and me up from the wreckage, press-ganged into being your siblings.
"I lost my parents that morning. Then I lost everything else.
I'm not a person. I'm your cover.
I...I never thought of you that way.
Bullshit. How could you not?
All I am is camouflage for the Princess of Cyandii.
That doesn't mean anything.
It means EVERYTHING.
SHOVE

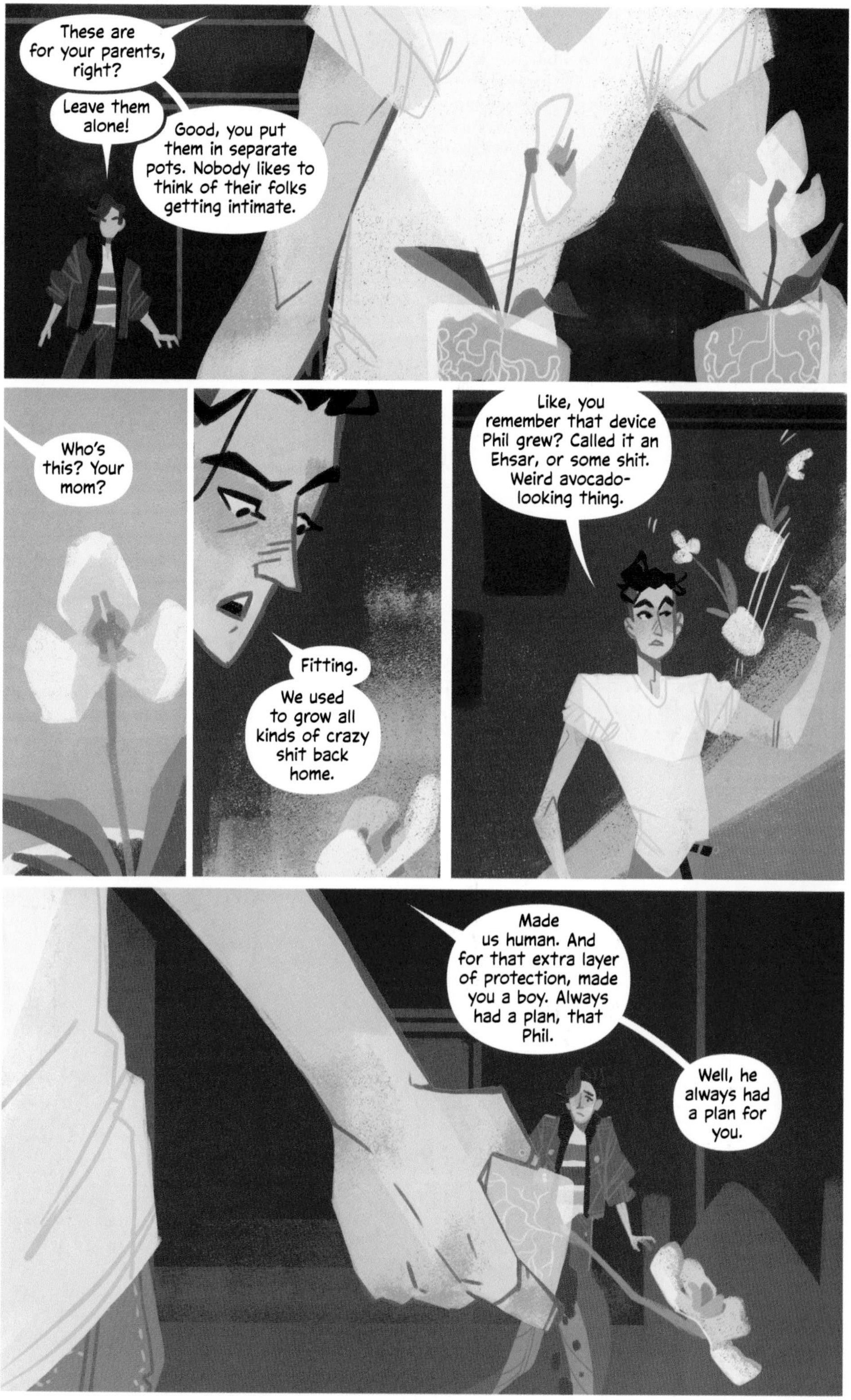
These are for your parents, right?
Leave them alone!
Good, you put them in separate pots. Nobody likes to think of their folks getting intimate.
Who's this? Your mom?
Fitting.
We used to grow all kinds of crazy shit back home.
Like, you remember that device Phil grew? Called it an Ehsar, or some shit. Weird avocado-looking thing.
Made us human. And for that extra layer of protection, made you a boy. Always had a plan, that Phil.
Well, he always had a plan for you.

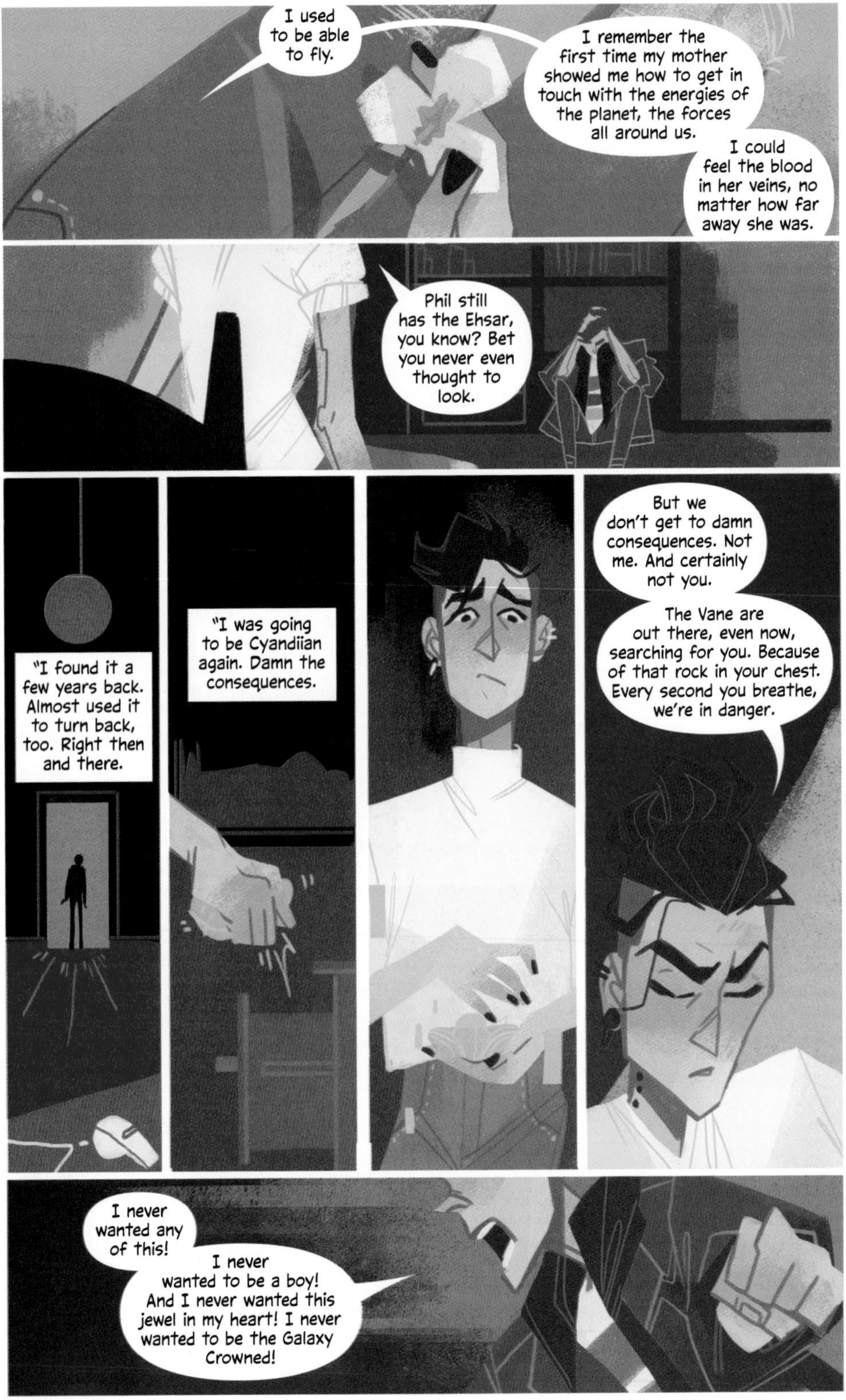
I used to be able to fly.
I remember the first time my mother showed me how to get in touch with the energies of the planet, the forces all around us.
I could feel the blood in her veins, no matter how far away she was.
Phil still has the Ehsar, you know? Bet you never even thought to look.
"I found it a few years back. Almost used it to turn back, too. Right then and there.
"I was going to be Cyandiian again. Damn the consequences.
But we don't get to damn consequences. Not me. And certainly not you.
The Vane are out there, even now, searching for you. Because of that rock in your chest. Every second you breathe, we're in danger.
I never wanted any of this!
I never wanted to be a boy! And I never wanted this jewel in my heart! I never wanted to be the Galaxy Crowned!

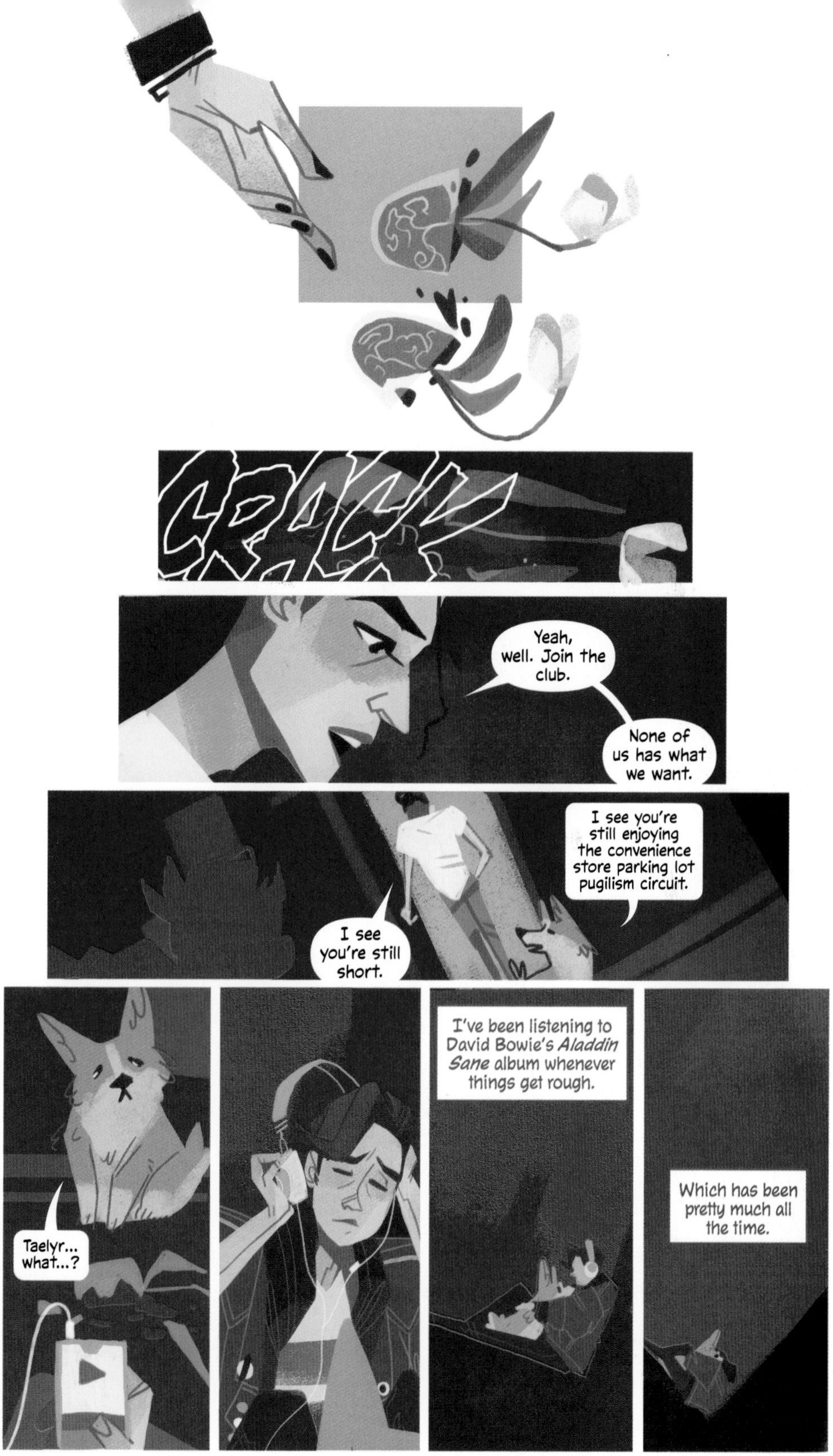
CRACK
Yeah, well. Join the club.
None of us has what we want.
I see you're still enjoying the convenience store parking lot pugilism circuit.
I see you're still short.
Taelyr... what...?
I've been listening to David Bowie's *Aladdin Sane* album whenever things get rough.
Which has been pretty much all the time.

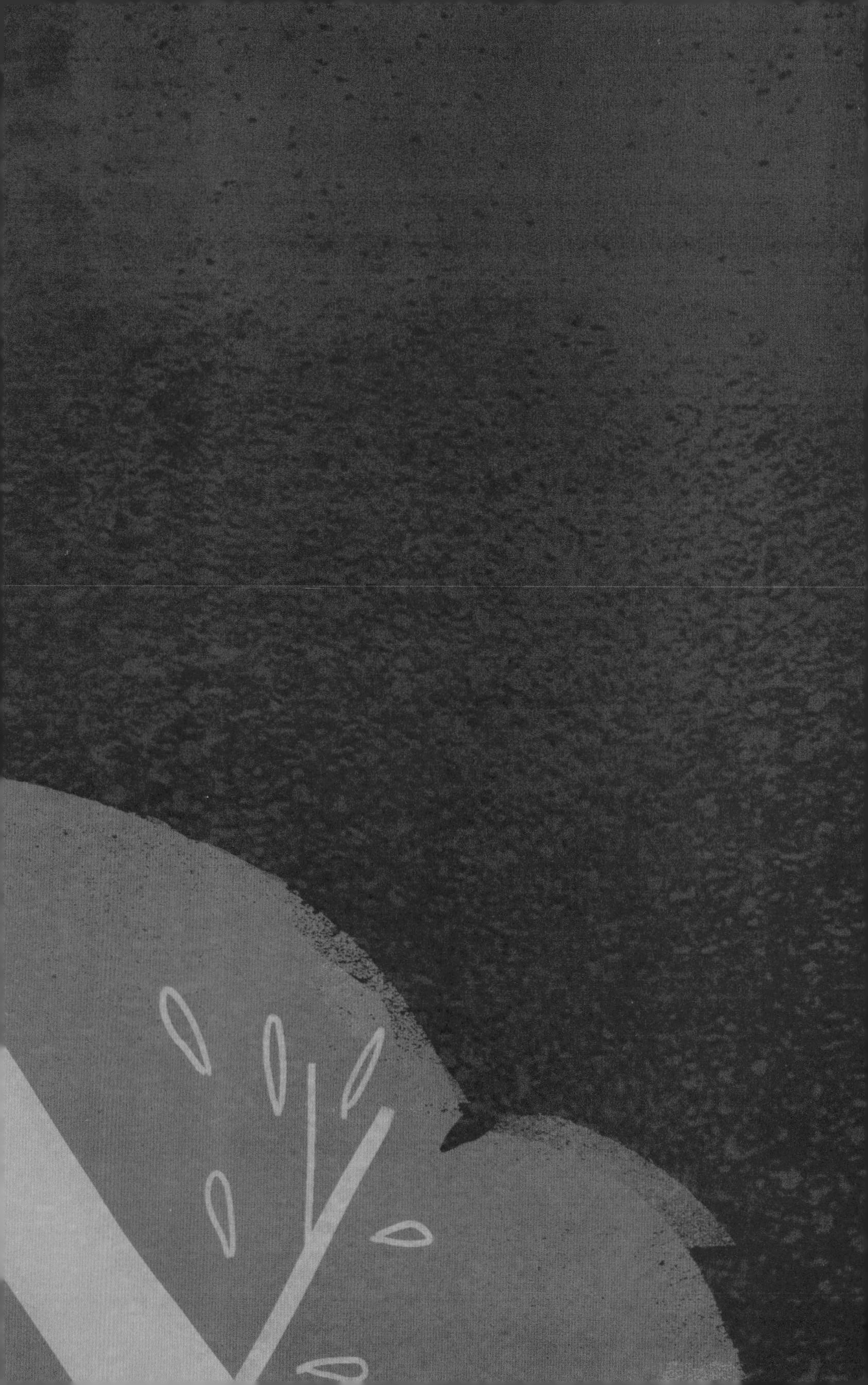

chapter 2

Cracked Actor

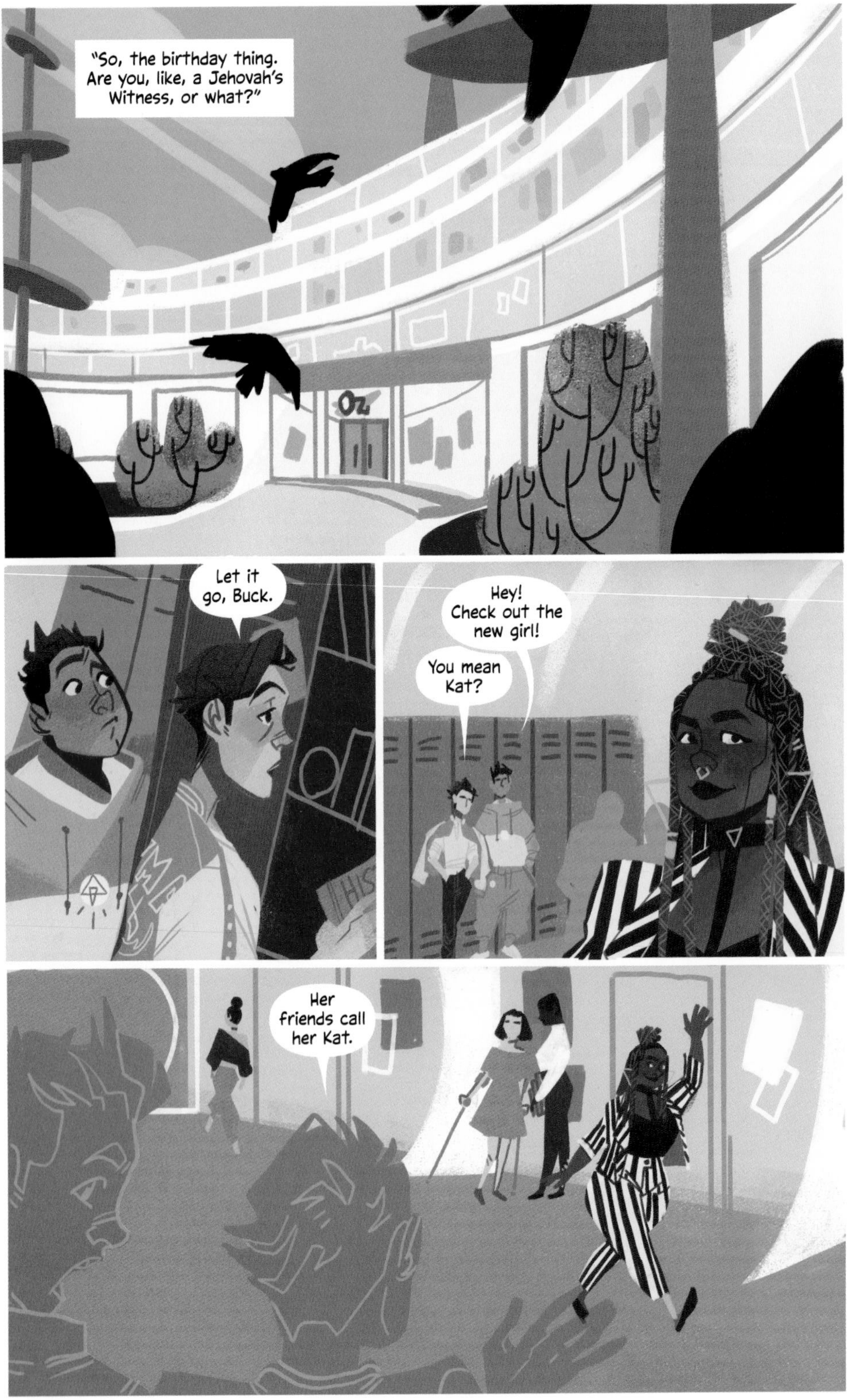
"So, the birthday thing. Are you, like, a Jehovah's Witness, or what?"
Oz
Let it go, Buck.
Hey! Check out the new girl!
You mean Kat?
Her friends call her Kat.

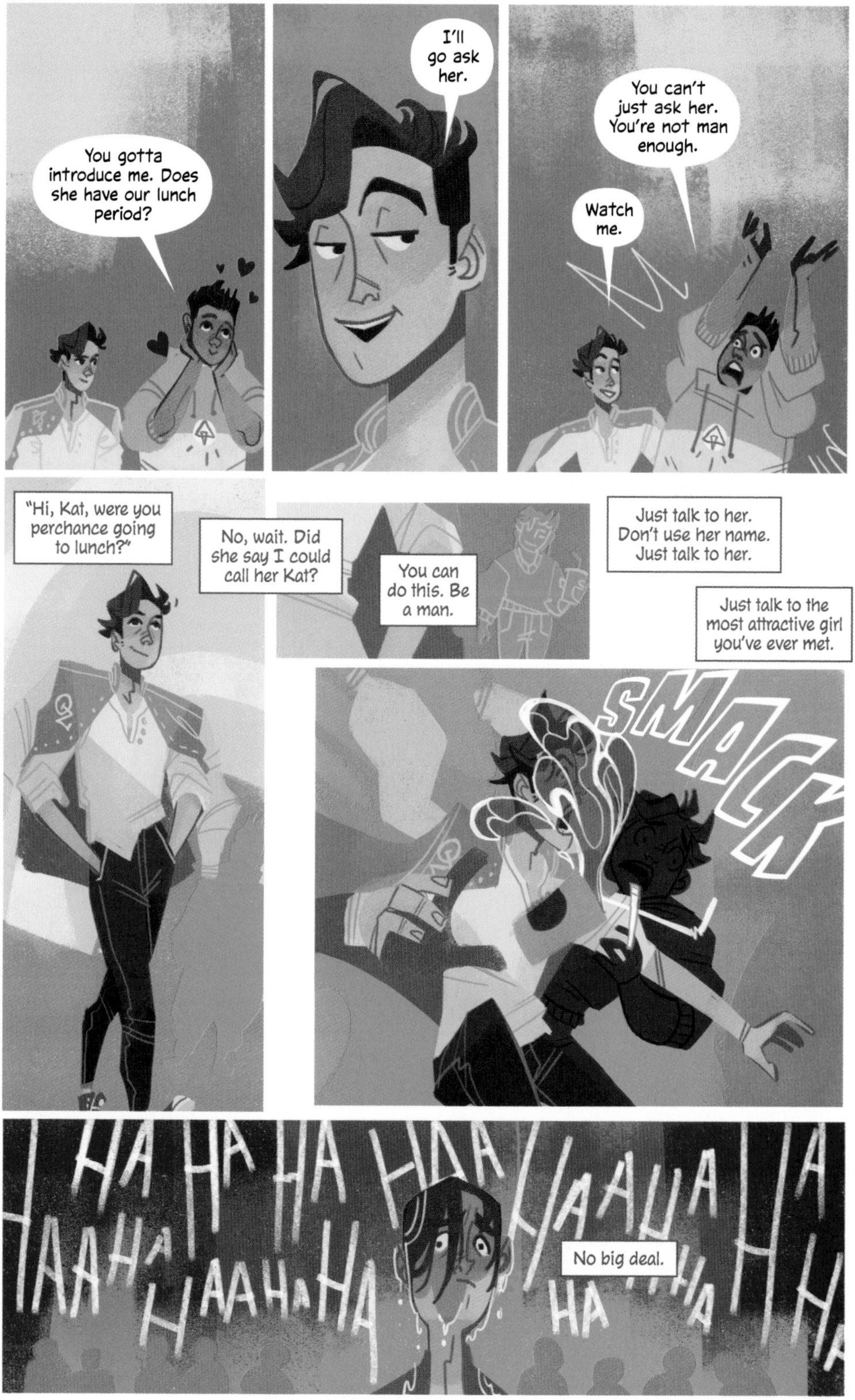
You gotta introduce me. Does she have our lunch period?
I'll go ask her.
You can't just ask her. You're not man enough.
Watch me.
"Hi, Kat, were you perchance going to lunch?"
No, wait. Did she say I could call her Kat?
You can do this. Be a man.
Just talk to her. Don't use her name. Just talk to her.
Just talk to the most attractive girl you've ever met.
SMACK
HA HA HA HA HA HA
No big deal.

I hate this.

I hate this school.

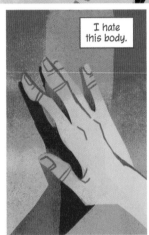

I hate this body.

I hate this face!

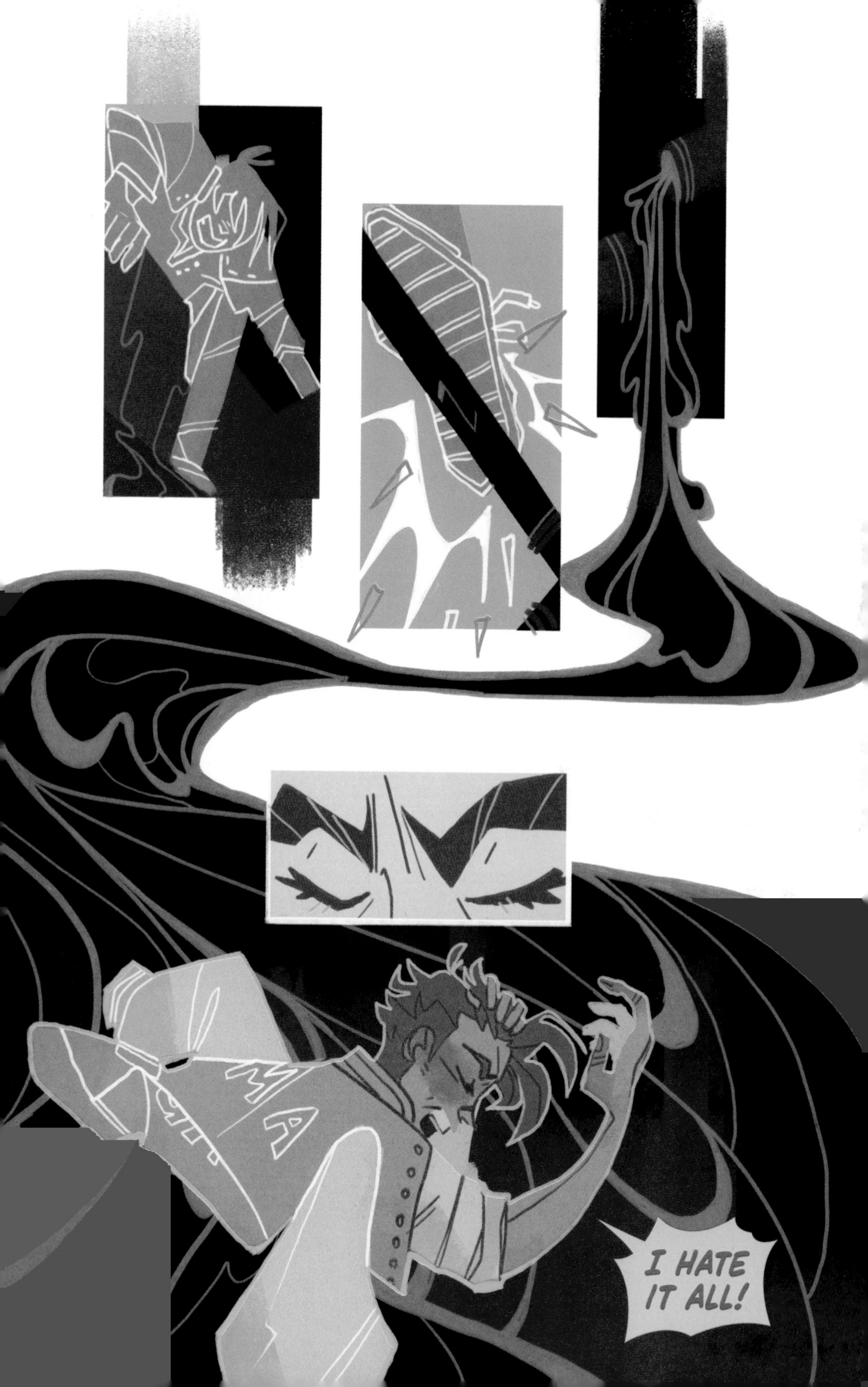
I HATE IT ALL!

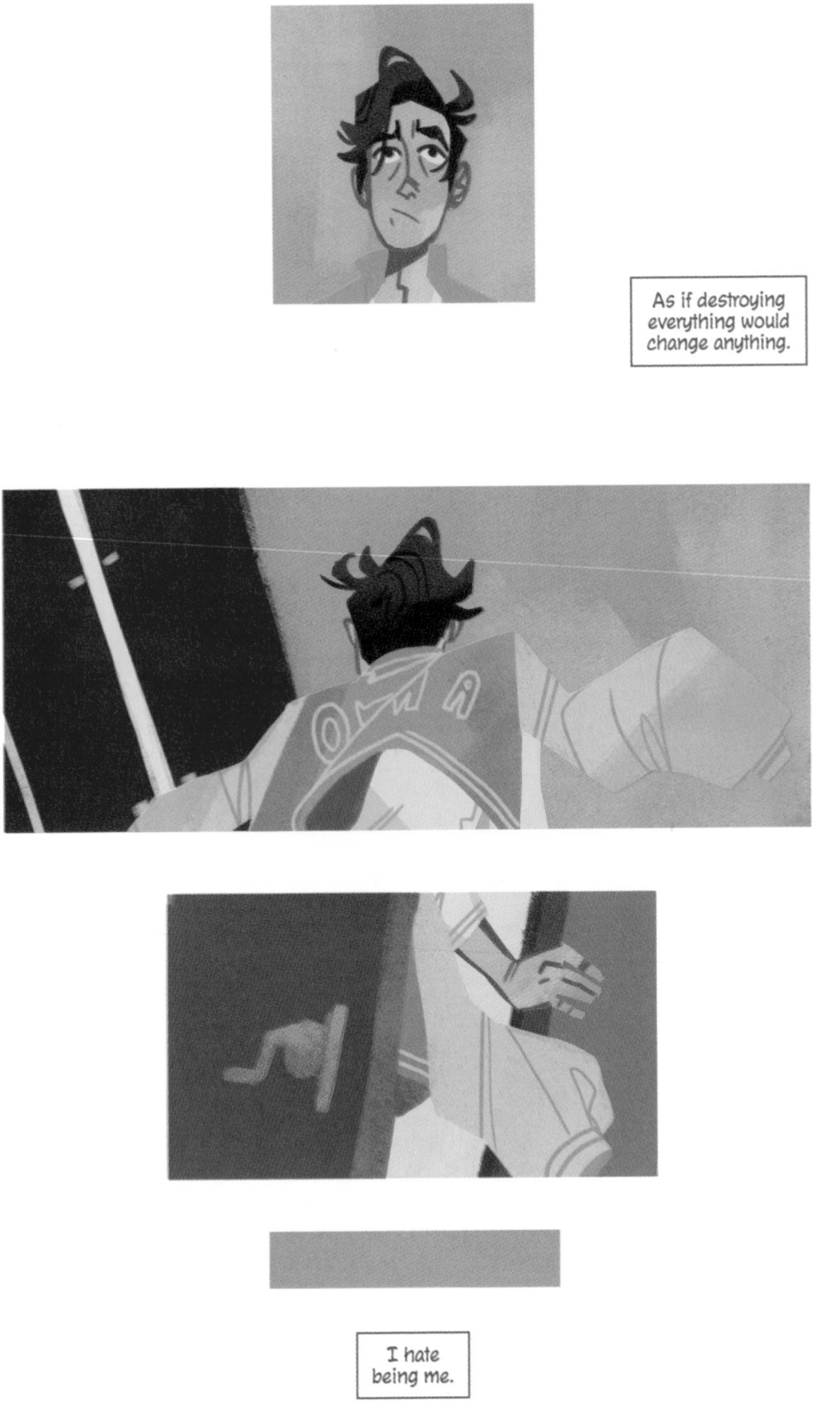
As if destroying everything would change anything.
I hate being me.

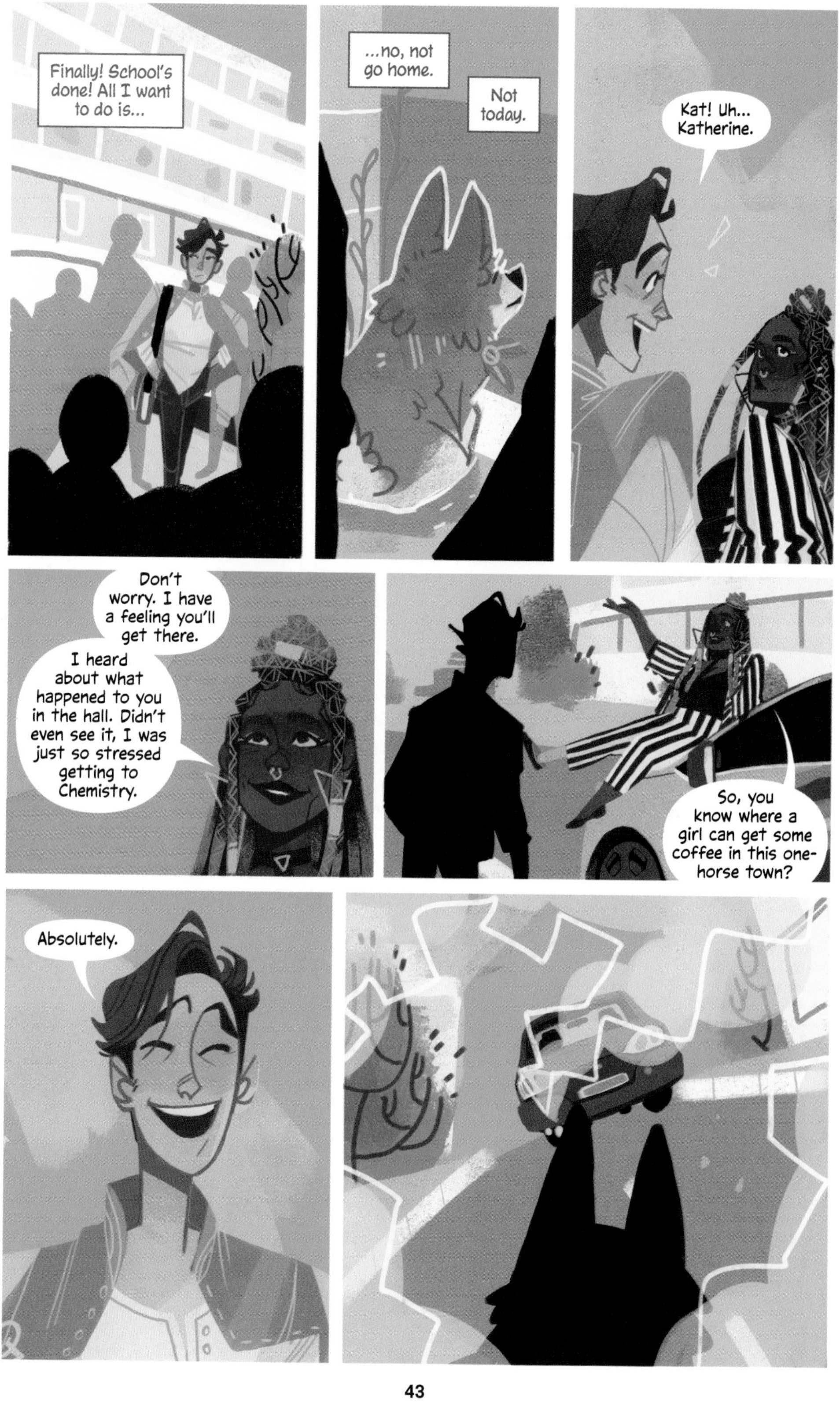
Finally! School's done! All I want to do is...
...no, not go home.
Not today.
Kat! Uh... Katherine.
Don't worry. I have a feeling you'll get there.
I heard about what happened to you in the hall. Didn't even see it, I was just so stressed getting to Chemistry.
So, you know where a girl can get some coffee in this one-horse town?
Absolutely.

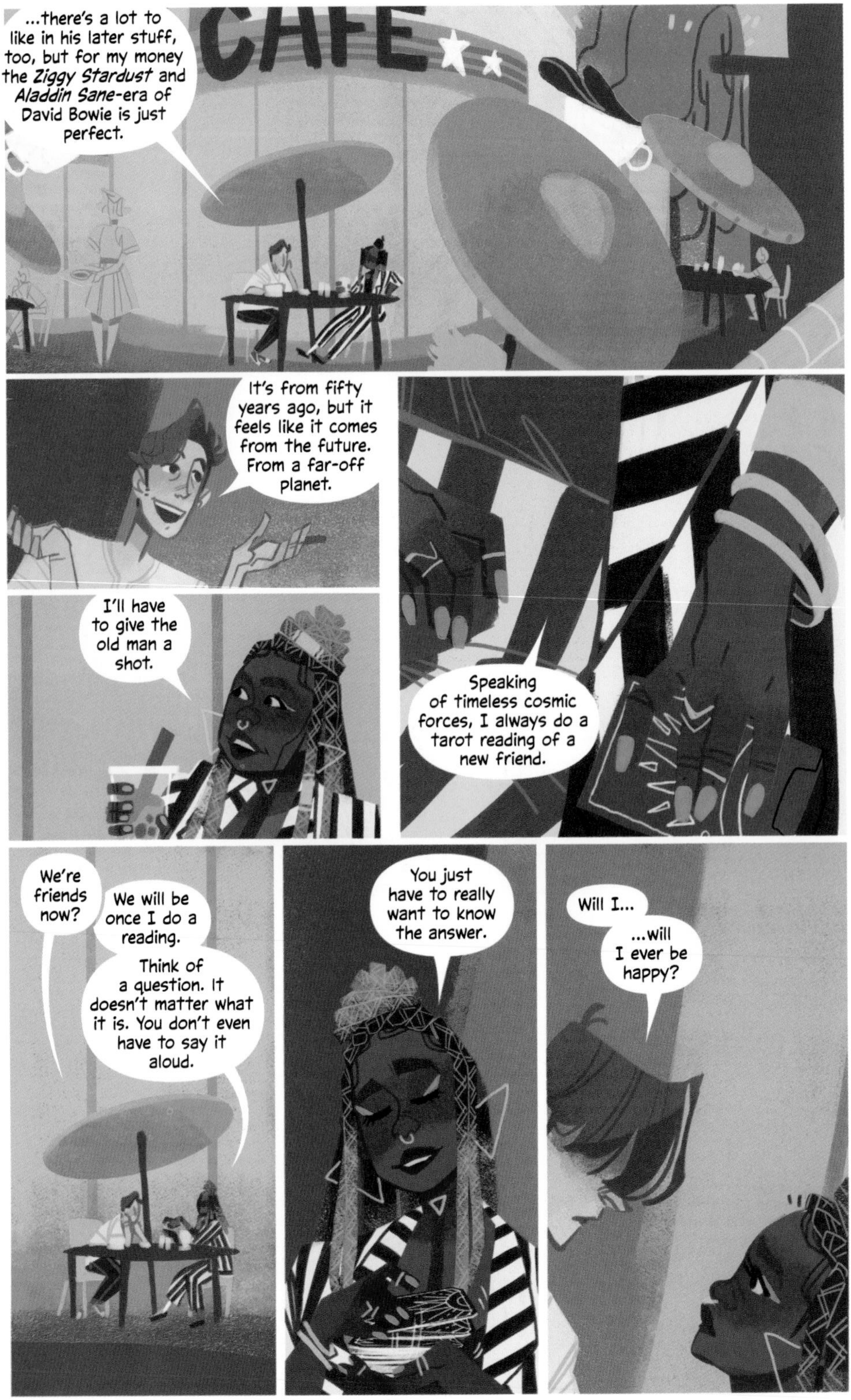
...there's a lot to like in his later stuff, too, but for my money the *Ziggy Stardust* and *Aladdin Sane*-era of David Bowie is just perfect.
CAFE
It's from fifty years ago, but it feels like it comes from the future. From a far-off planet.
I'll have to give the old man a shot.
Speaking of timeless cosmic forces, I always do a tarot reading of a new friend.
We're friends now?
We will be once I do a reading.
Think of a question. It doesn't matter what it is. You don't even have to say it aloud.
You just have to really want to know the answer.
Will I...
...will I ever be happy?

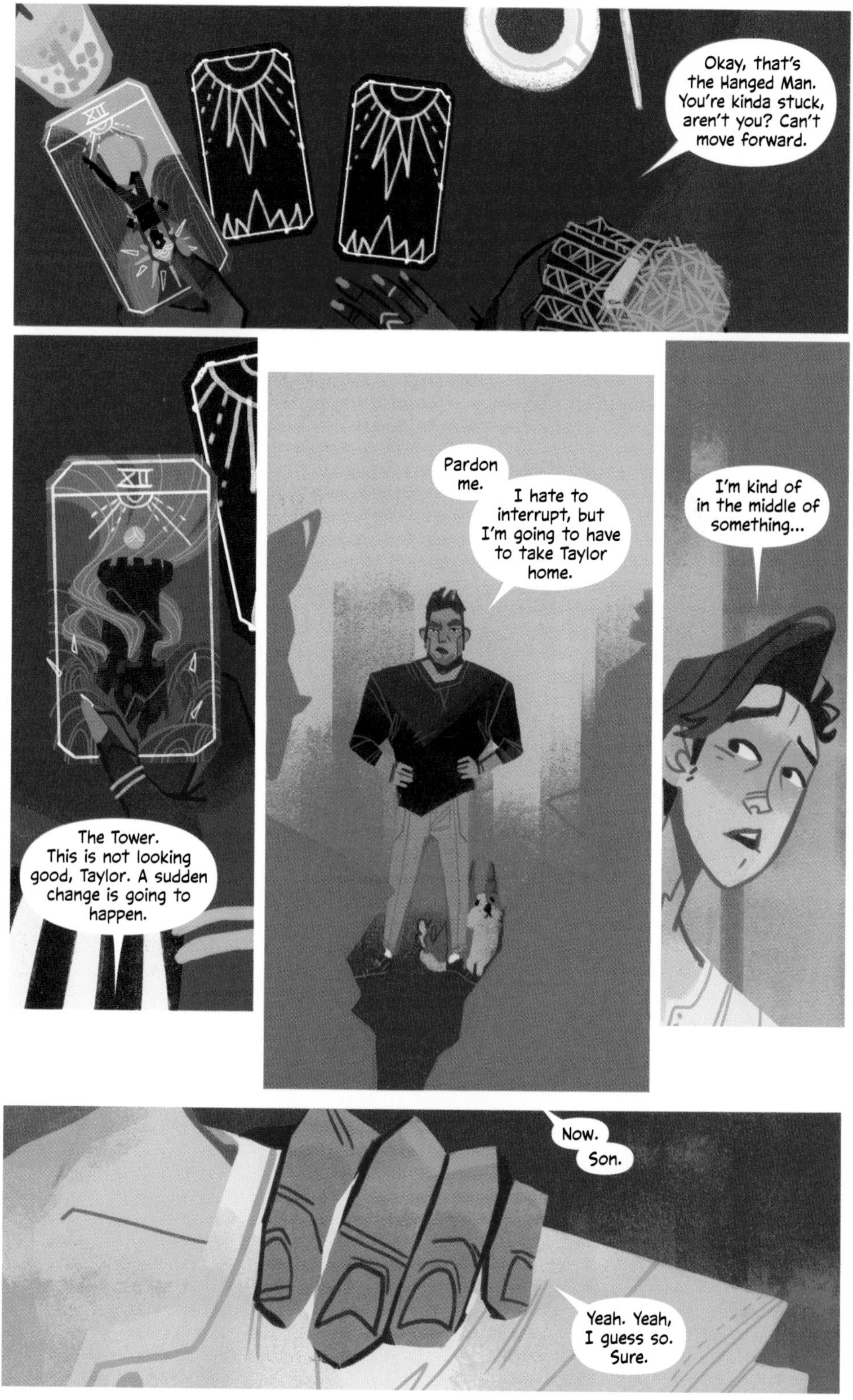
Okay, that's the Hanged Man. You're kinda stuck, aren't you? Can't move forward.
The Tower. This is not looking good, Taylor. A sudden change is going to happen.
Pardon me.
I hate to interrupt, but I'm going to have to take Taylor home.
I'm kind of in the middle of something...
Now.
Son.
Yeah. Yeah, I guess so. Sure.

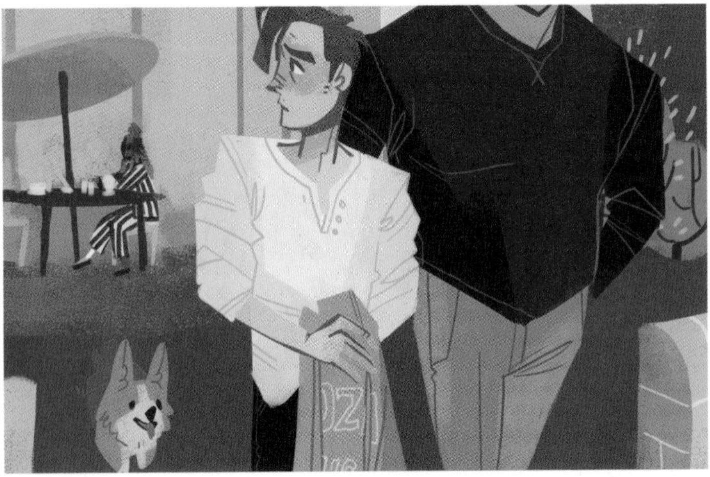

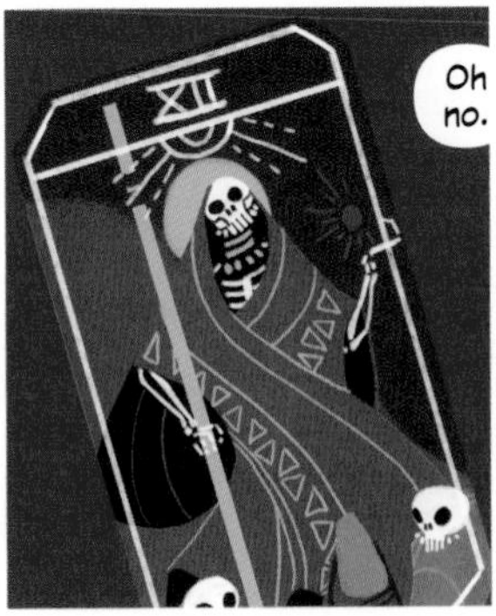
Oh no.

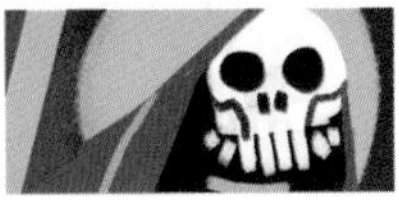

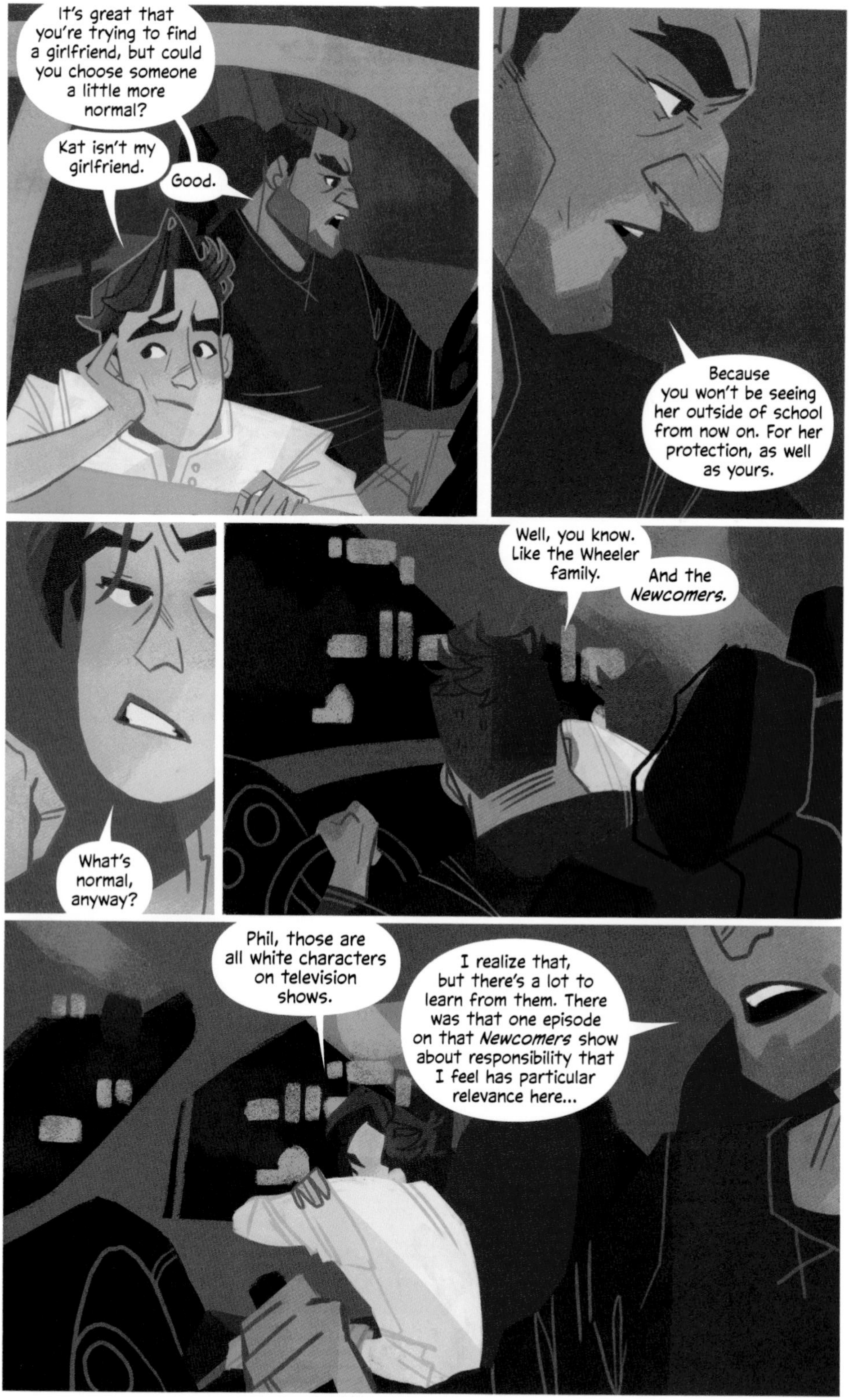
It's great that you're trying to find a girlfriend, but could you choose someone a little more normal?
Kat isn't my girlfriend.
Good.
Because you won't be seeing her outside of school from now on. For her protection, as well as yours.
What's normal, anyway?
Well, you know. Like the Wheeler family.
And the *Newcomers.*
Phil, those are all white characters on television shows.
I realize that, but there's a lot to learn from them. There was that one episode on that *Newcomers* show about responsibility that I feel has particular relevance here...

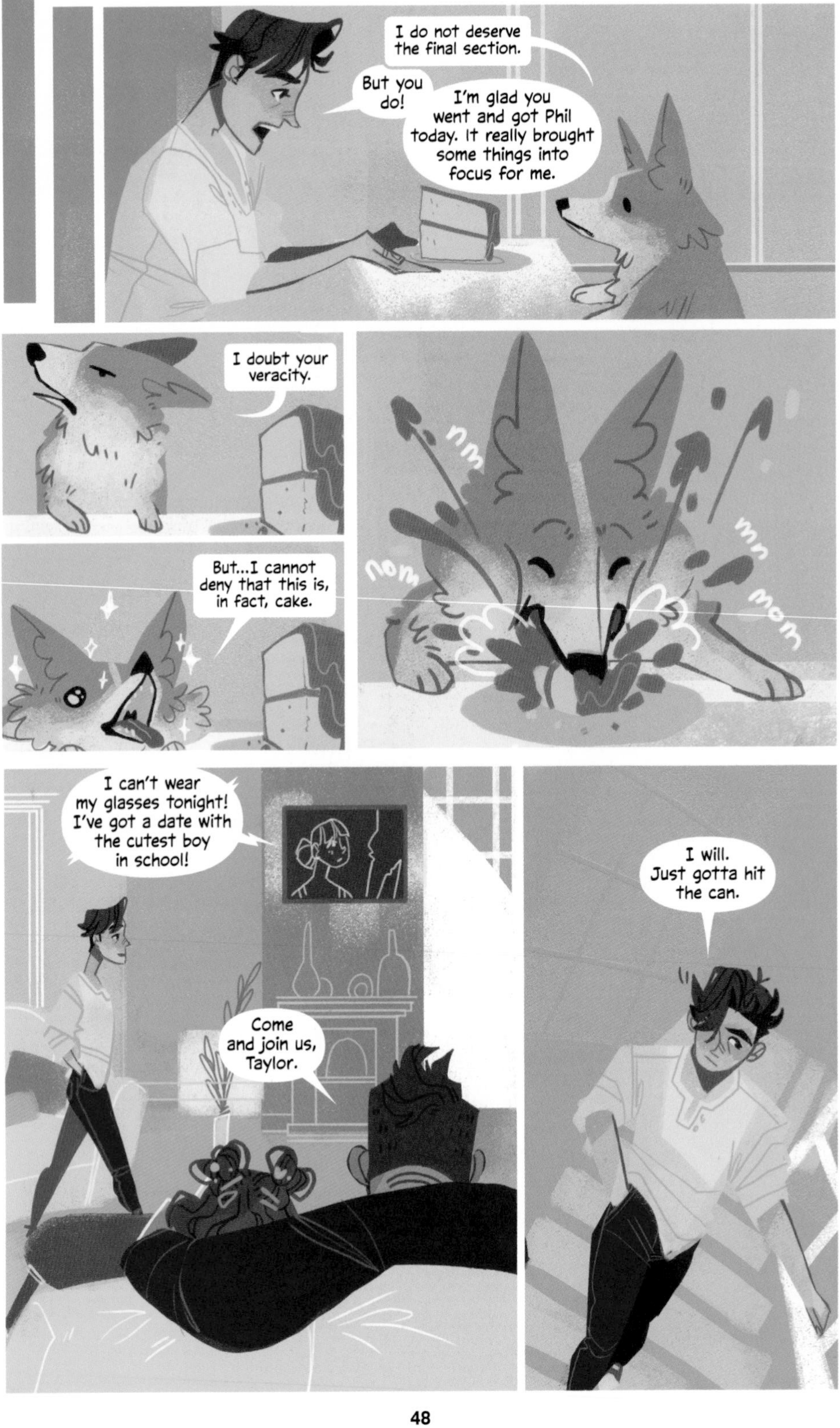
I do not deserve the final section.
But you do!
I'm glad you went and got Phil today. It really brought some things into focus for me.
I doubt your veracity.
But...I cannot deny that this is, in fact, cake.
nom
nom
nom
nom
I can't wear my glasses tonight! I've got a date with the cutest boy in school!
Come and join us, Taylor.
I will. Just gotta hit the can.

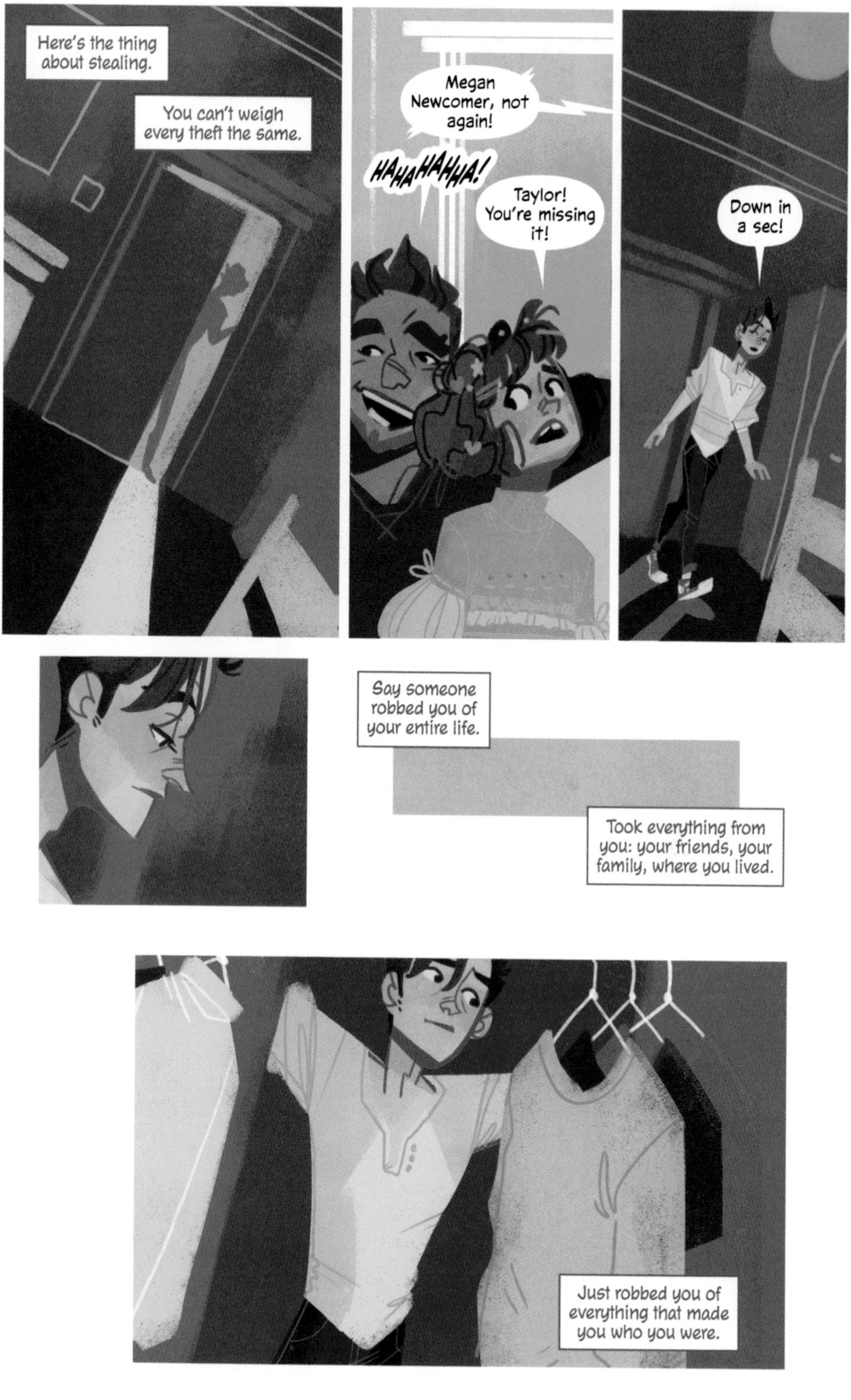
Here's the thing about stealing.
You can't weigh every theft the same.
Megan Newcomer, not again!
HAHAHAHHA!
Taylor! You're missing it!
Down in a sec!
Say someone robbed you of your entire life.
Took everything from you: your friends, your family, where you lived.
Just robbed you of everything that made you who you were.

Well, considering all that...

...some might say you deserve a little avocado.

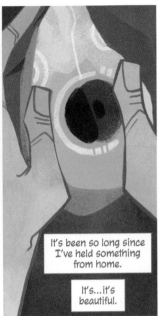

It's been so long since I've held something from home.

It's...it's beautiful.

I never want to let it go.

I should put it back.

What am I even going to do with this?

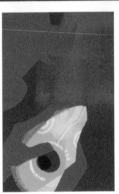

I have a responsibility...

No.

Not to thieves, I don't.

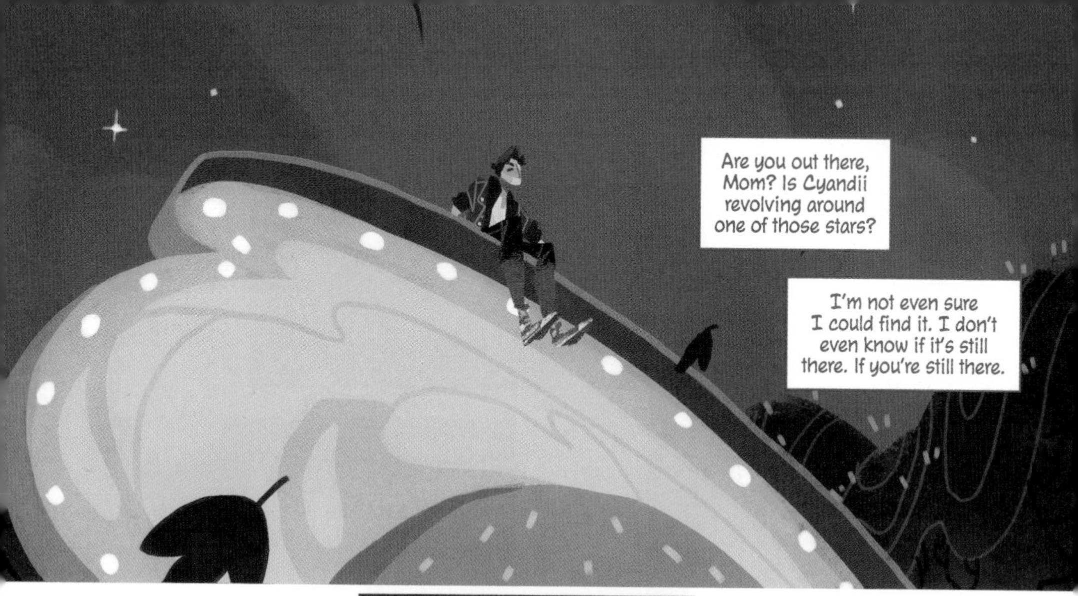
Are you out there, Mom? Is Cyandii revolving around one of those stars?
I'm not even sure I could find it. I don't even know if it's still there. If you're still there.

This could be all that remains.

This... and me.

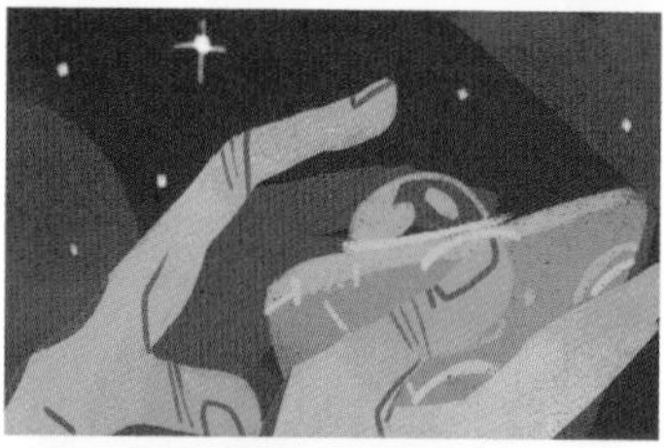

I should change back. Damn the consequences.

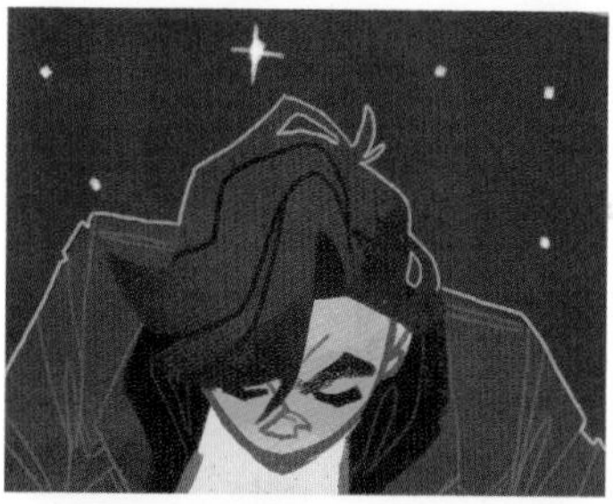

I can't. I know the Vane are out there. Even if they don't attack, it's not like this planet has a history of welcoming aliens.

We can't all be Superman.

I could ruin my life.

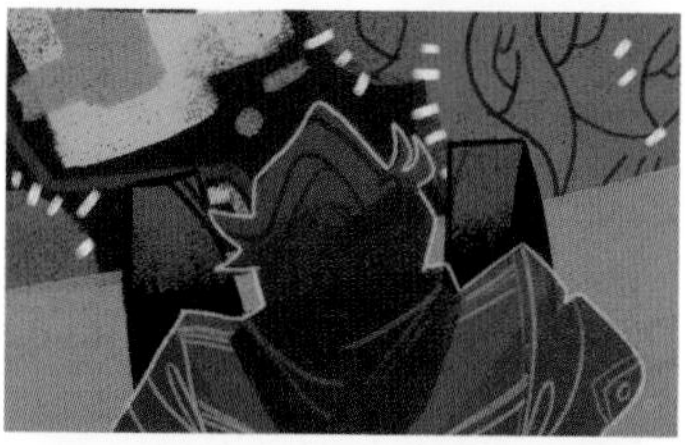

I could ruin everyone's lives. Sure, Carl and Phil, fine. But Sally? Sally deserves a normal life.

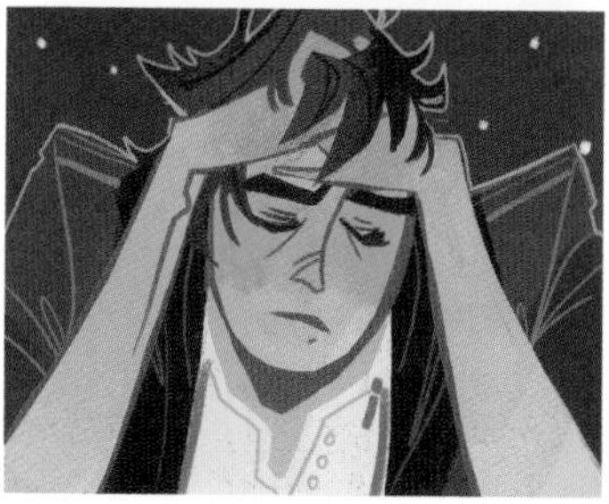

All I want to do is turn it on, Mom. I've never wanted anything more.

But I can't.

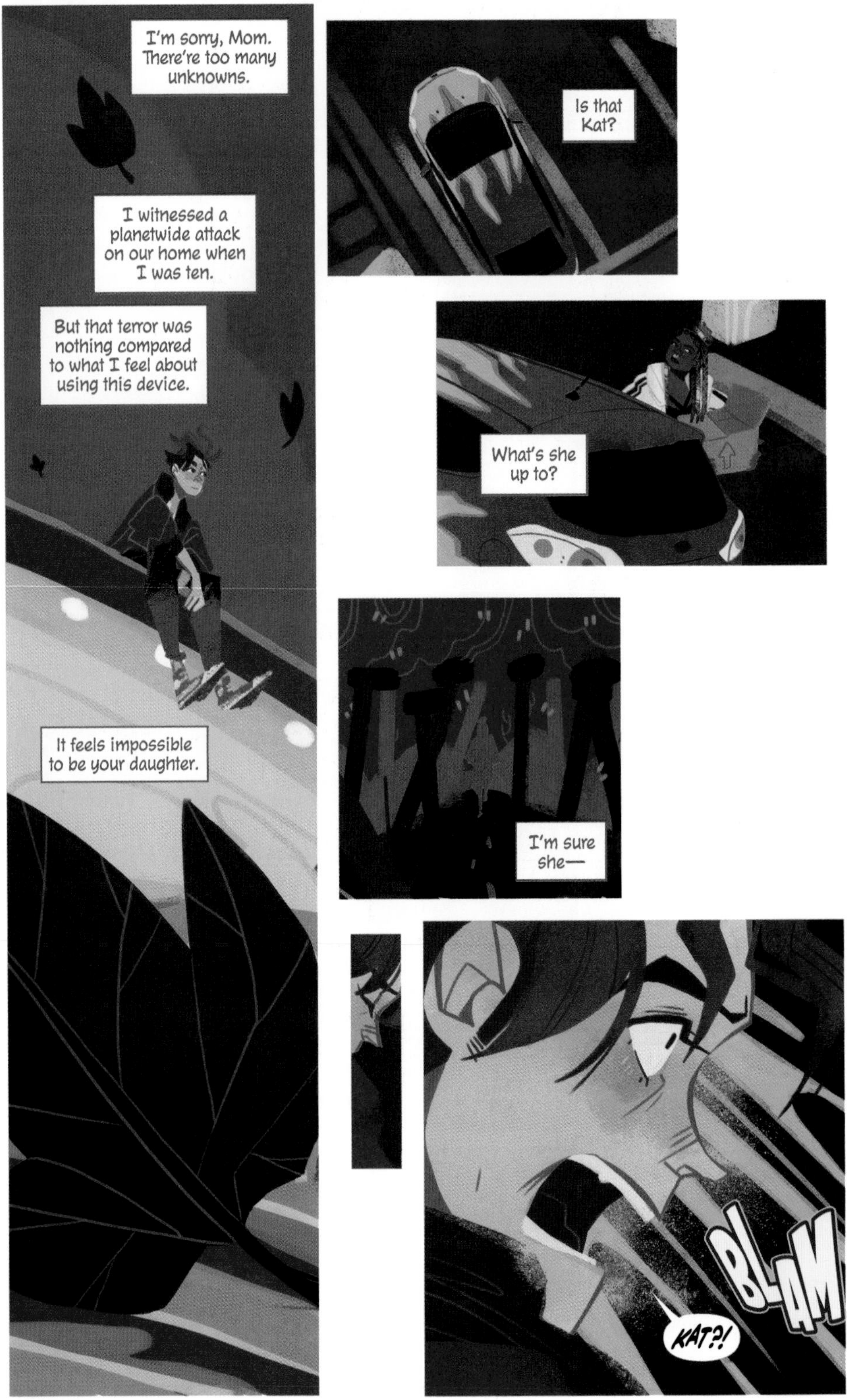
I'm sorry, Mom. There're too many unknowns.
I witnessed a planetwide attack on our home when I was ten.
But that terror was nothing compared to what I feel about using this device.
It feels impossible to be your daughter.
Is that Kat?
What's she up to?
I'm sure she—
BLAM
KAT?!

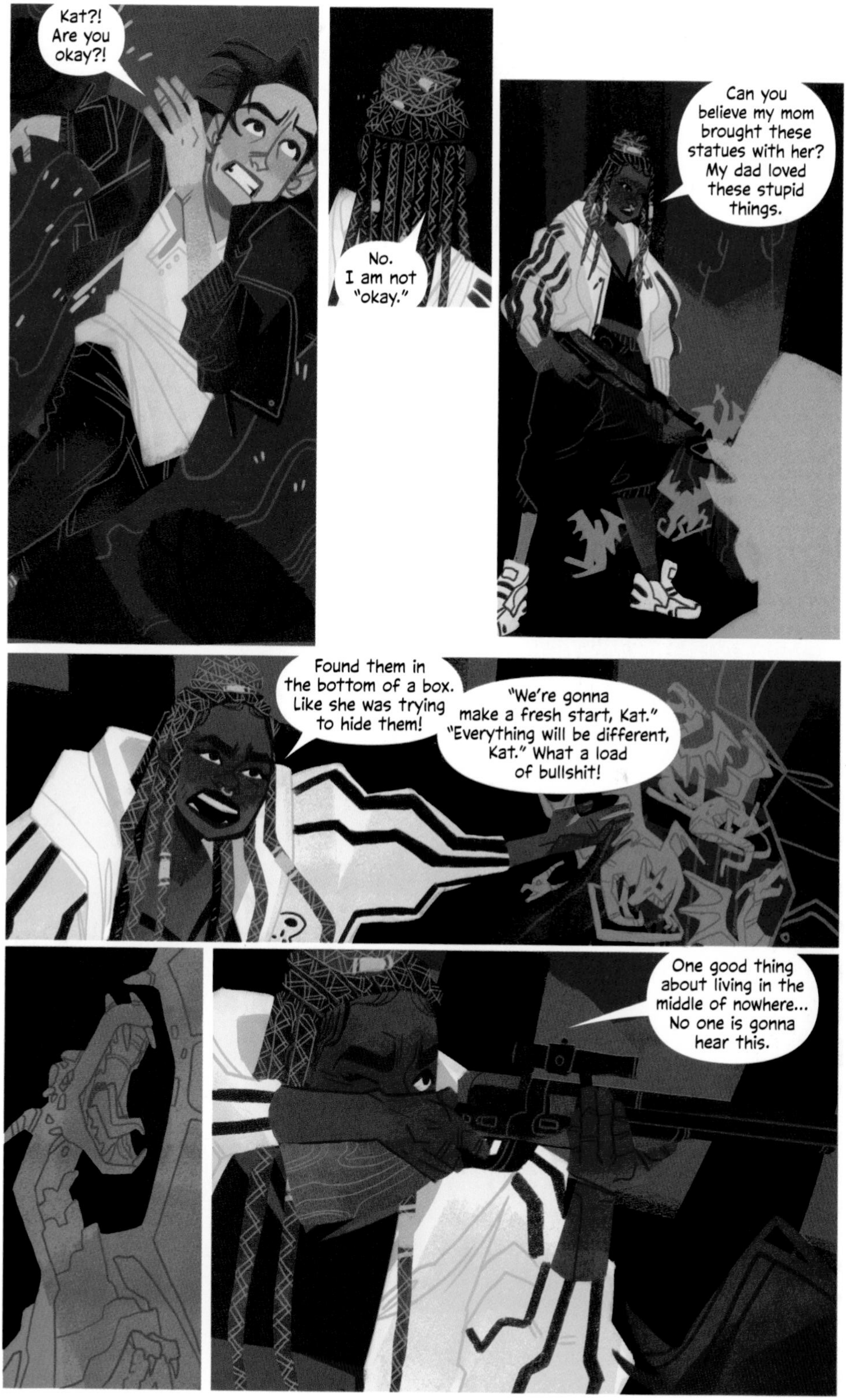
Kat?! Are you okay?!
No. I am not "okay."
Can you believe my mom brought these statues with her? My dad loved these stupid things.
Found them in the bottom of a box. Like she was trying to hide them!
"We're gonna make a fresh start, Kat." "Everything will be different, Kat." What a load of bullshit!
One good thing about living in the middle of nowhere... No one is gonna hear this.

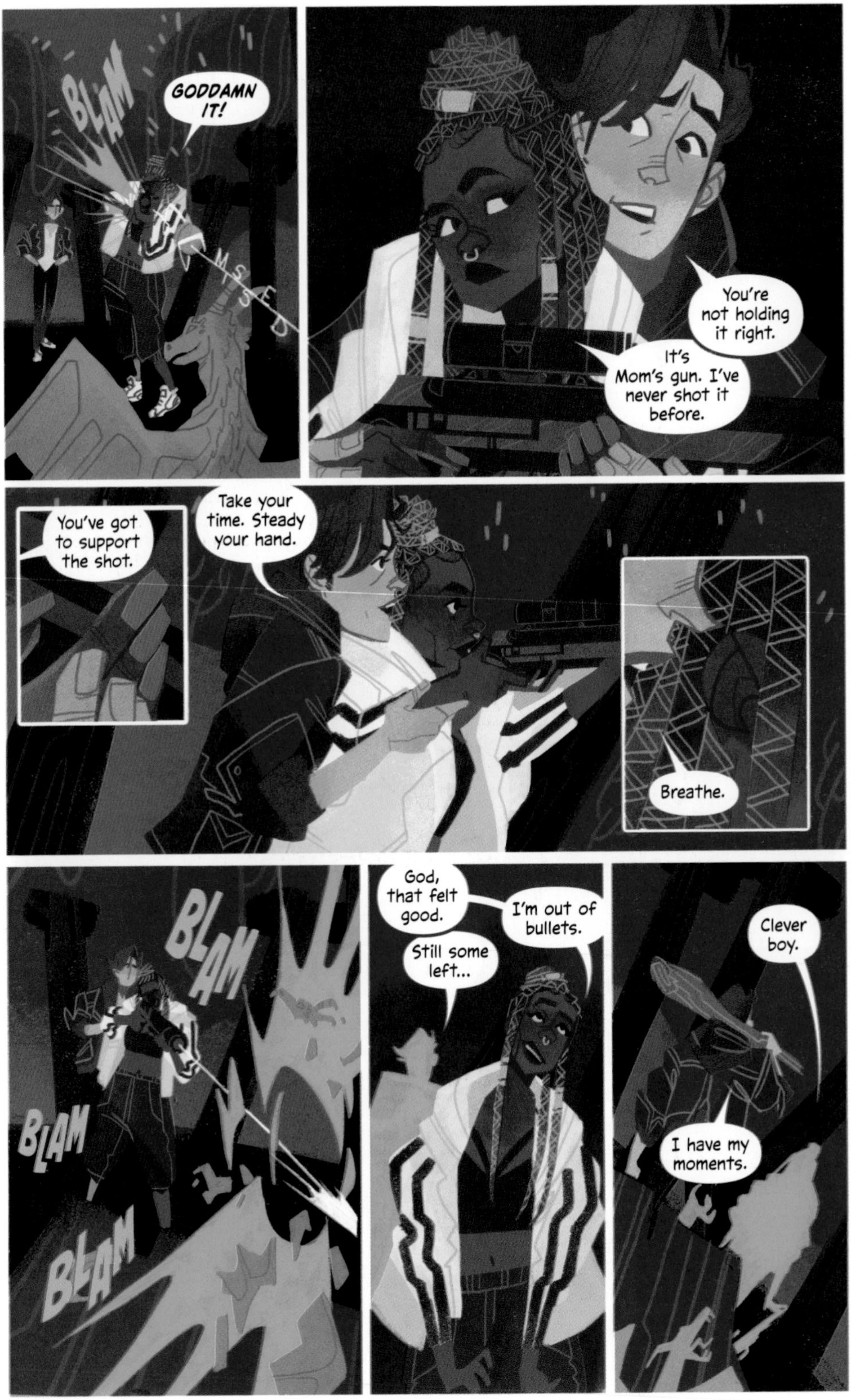
BLAM
GODDAMN IT!
MISSED
You're not holding it right.
It's Mom's gun. I've never shot it before.
You've got to support the shot.
Take your time. Steady your hand.
Breathe.
BLAM
BLAM
BLAM
God, that felt good.
I'm out of bullets.
Still some left...
Clever boy.
I have my moments.

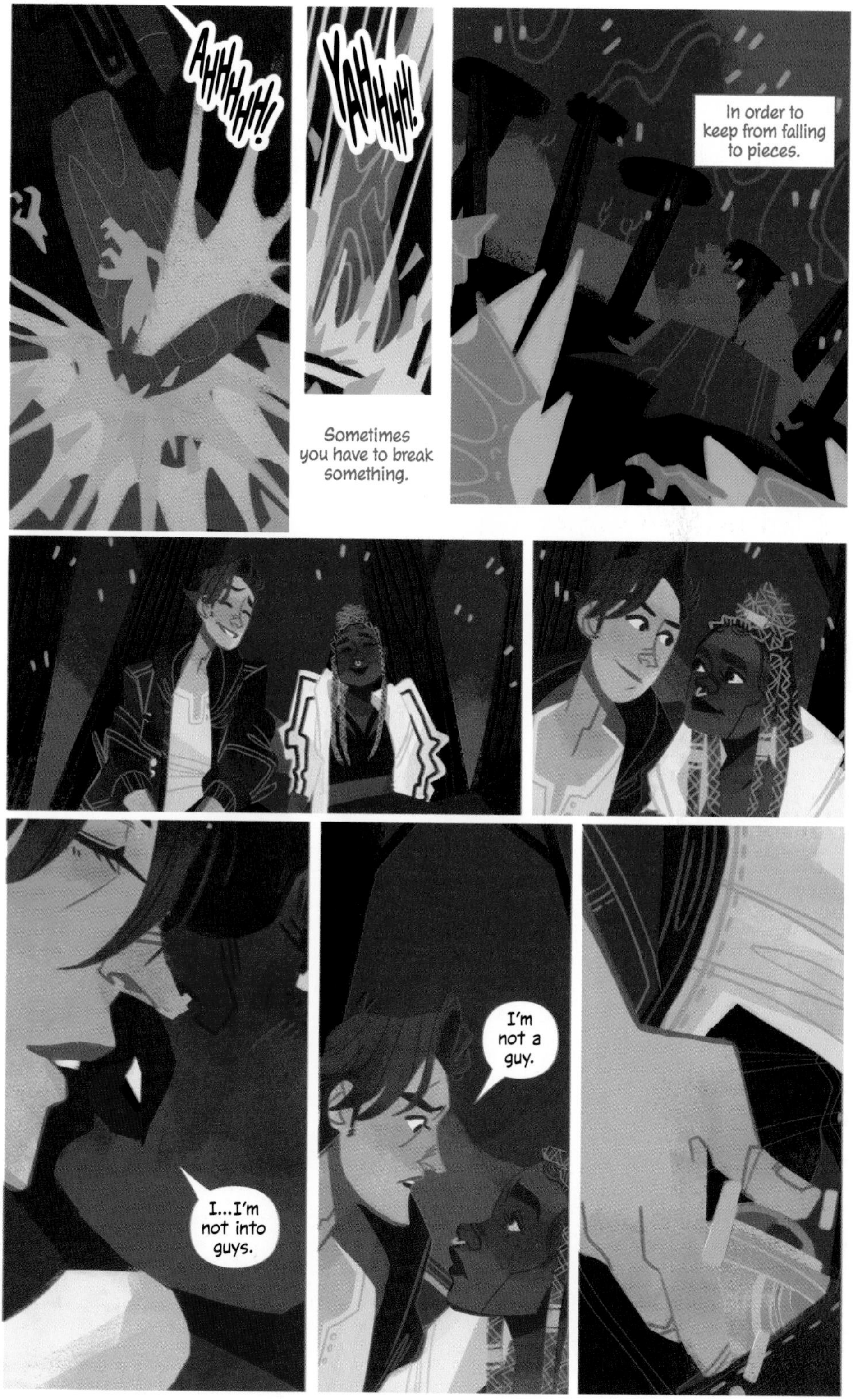
AHHHHH!
YAHHHHH!
Sometimes you have to break something.
In order to keep from falling to pieces.
I...I'm not into guys.
I'm not a guy.

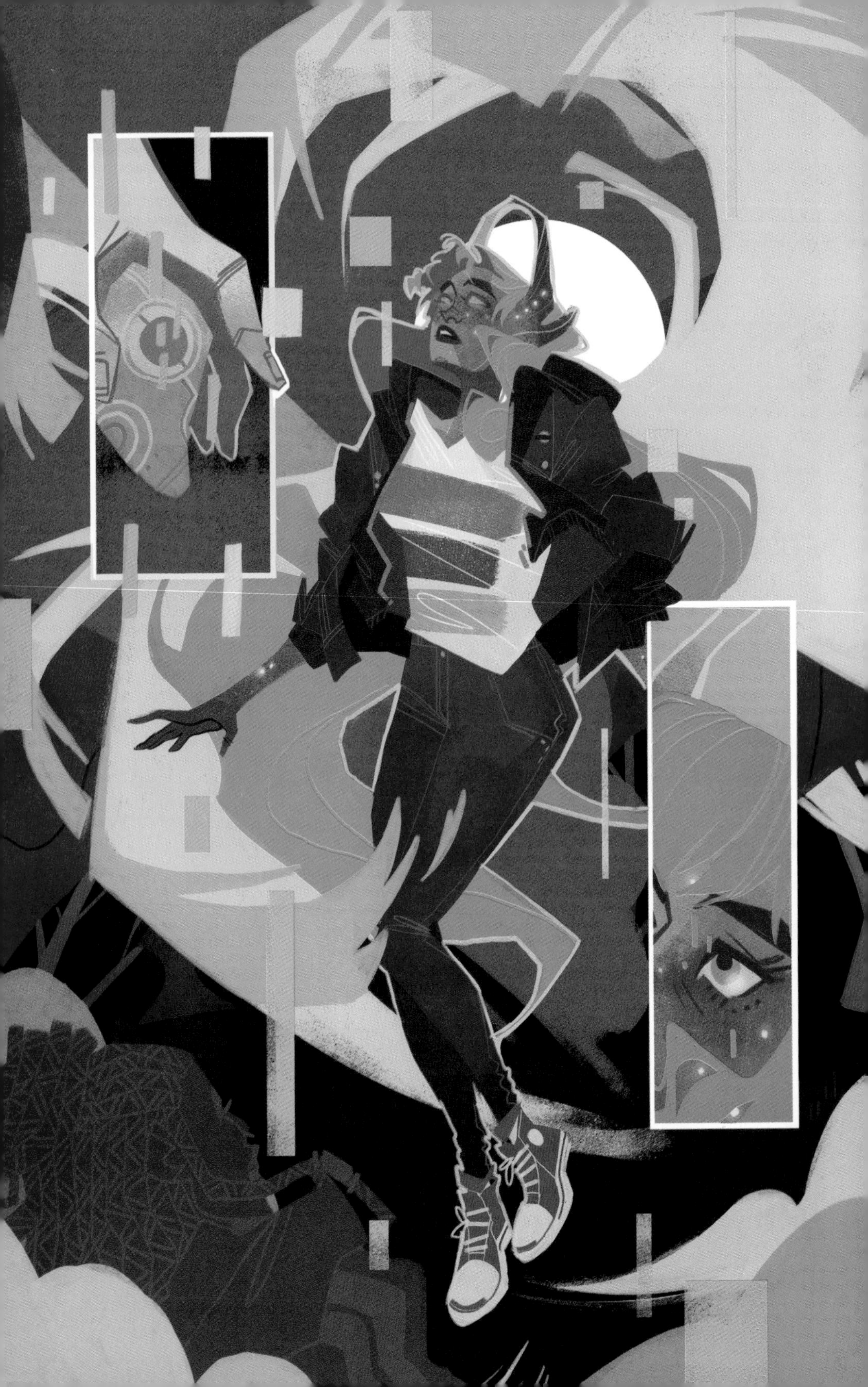

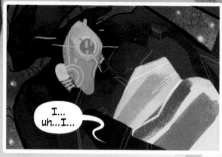

I... uh...I...

Taylor... are...are you?

No...I... no...

Taylor! Wait!

Stupid! Stupid!

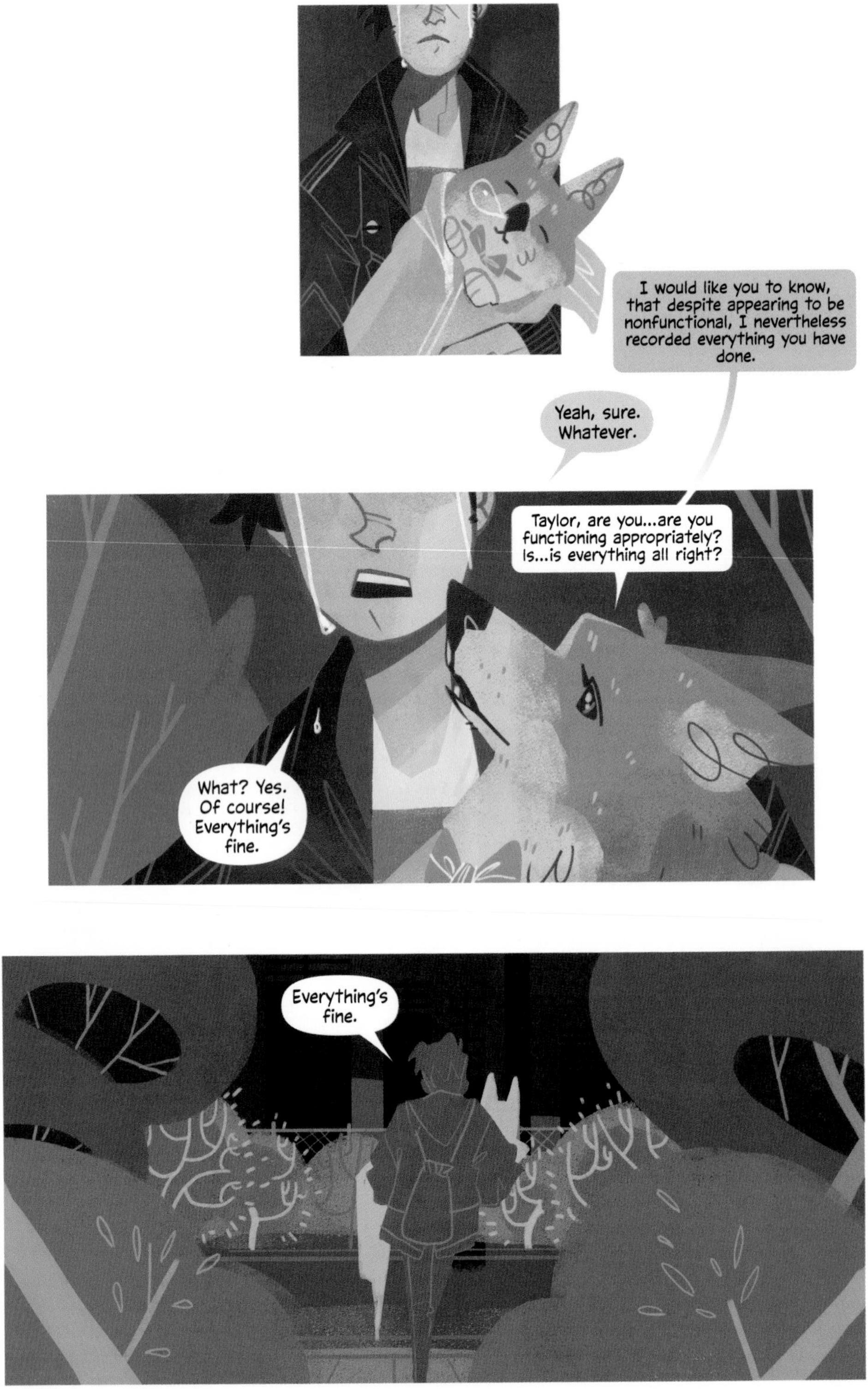
I would like you to know, that despite appearing to be nonfunctional, I nevertheless recorded everything you have done.
Yeah, sure. Whatever.
Taylor, are you...are you functioning appropriately? Is...is everything all right?
What? Yes. Of course! Everything's fine.
Everything's fine.

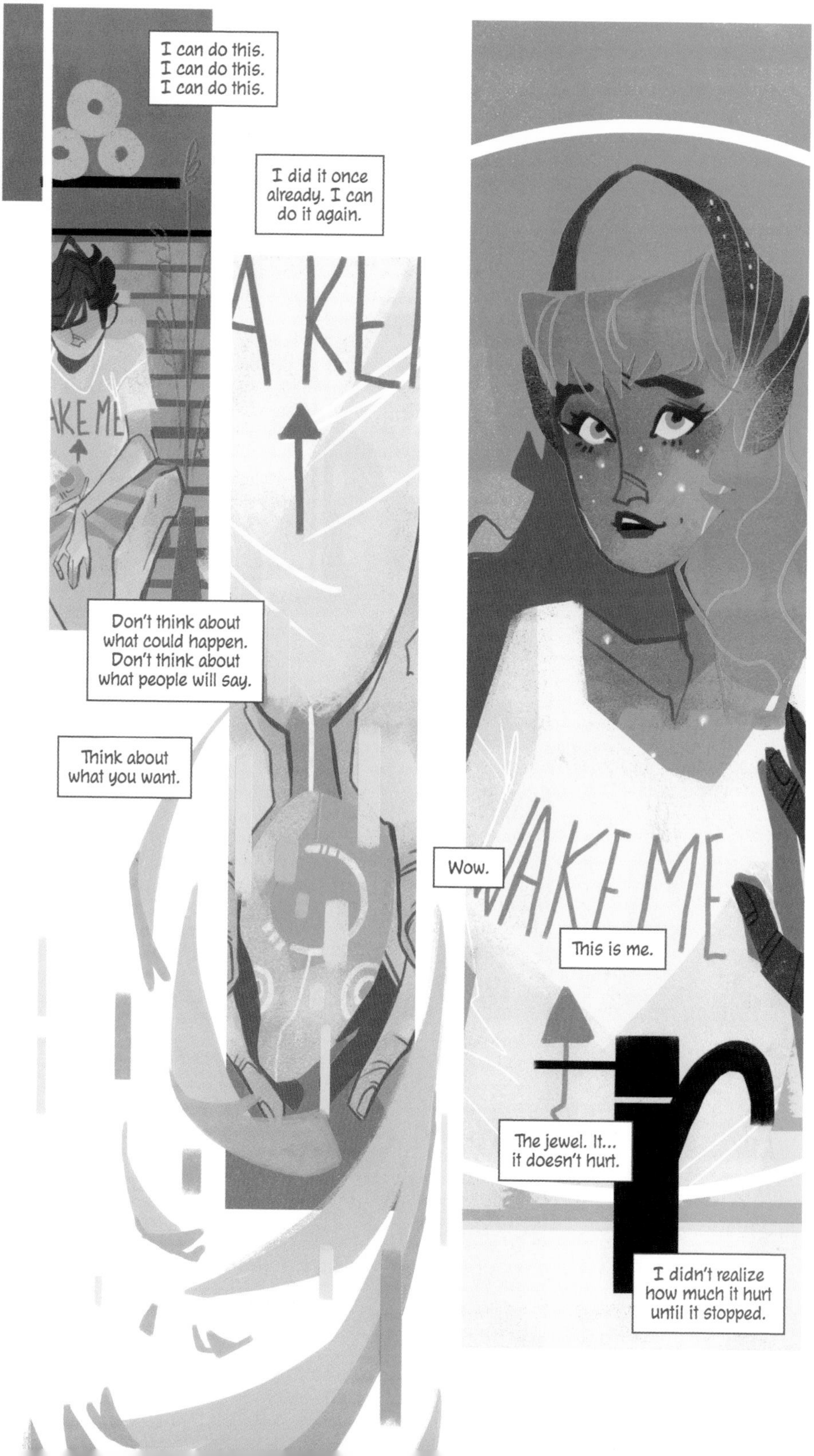
I can do this.
I can do this.
I can do this.
I did it once already. I can do it again.
WAKE ME
Don't think about what could happen. Don't think about what people will say.
Think about what you want.
Wow.
WAKE ME
This is me.
The jewel. It... it doesn't hurt.
I didn't realize how much it hurt until it stopped.

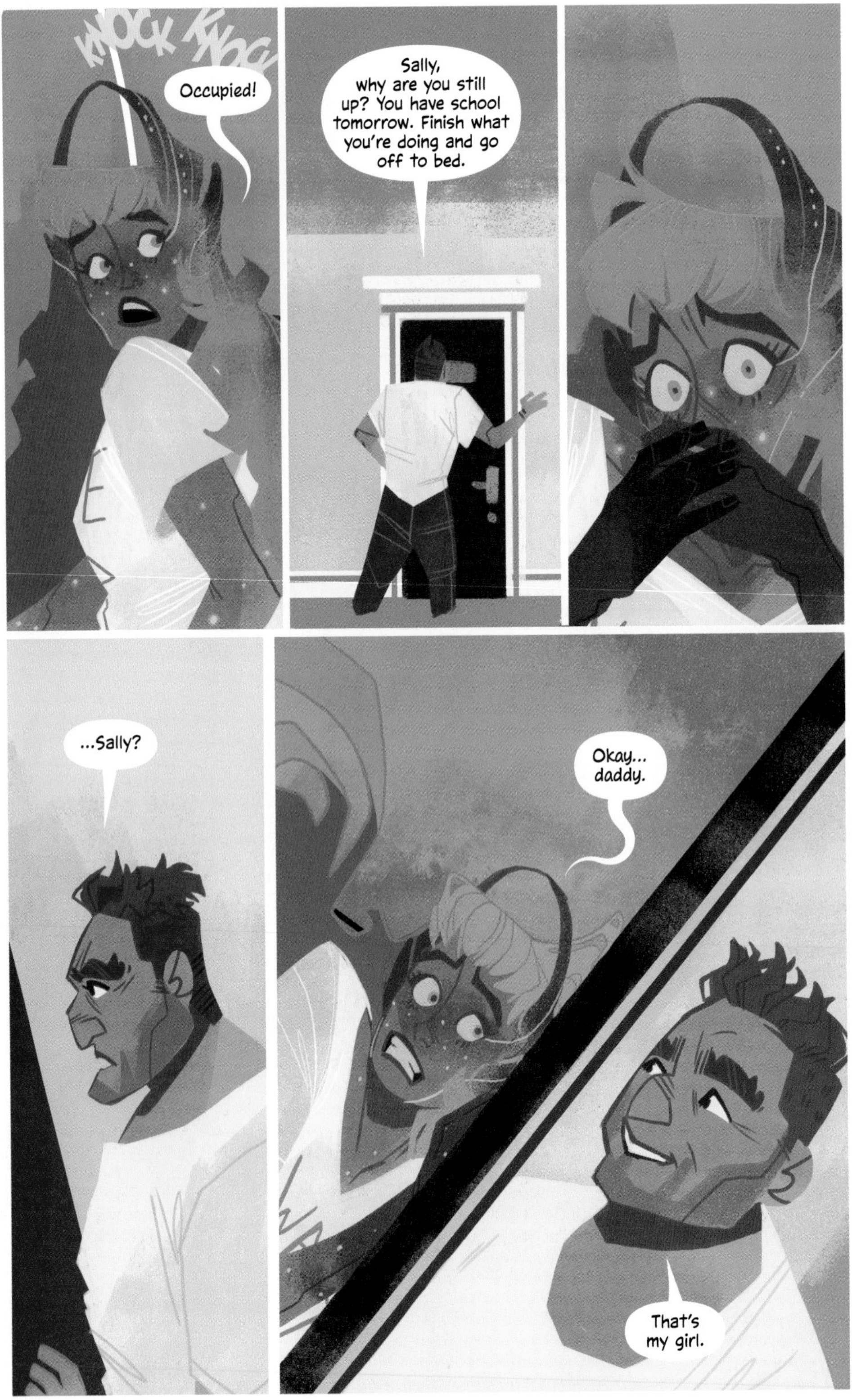
KNOCK KNOCK
Occupied!
Sally, why are you still up? You have school tomorrow. Finish what you're doing and go off to bed.
...Sally?
Okay... daddy.
That's my girl.

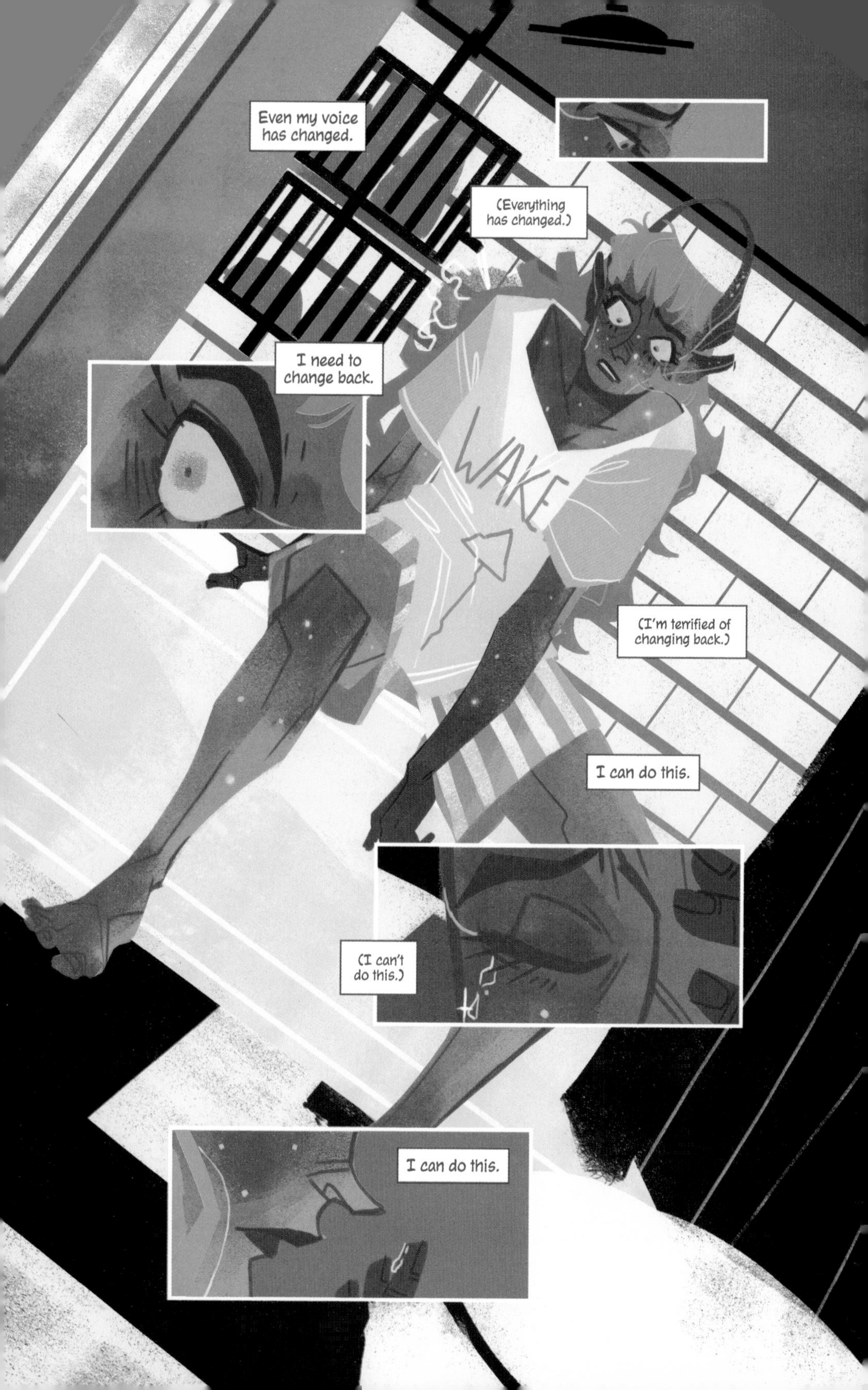
Even my voice has changed.
(Everything has changed.)
I need to change back.
WAKE
(I'm terrified of changing back.)
I can do this.
(I can't do this.)
I can do this.

chapter 3
Moonage Daydream

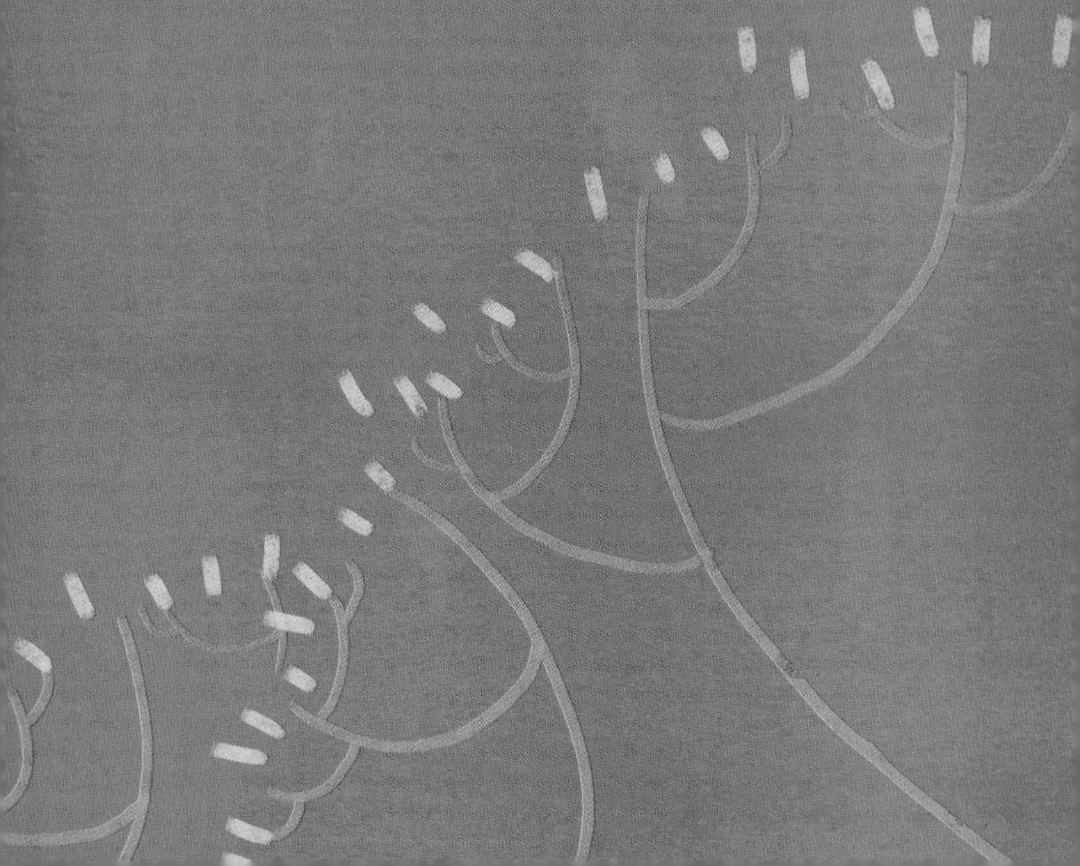

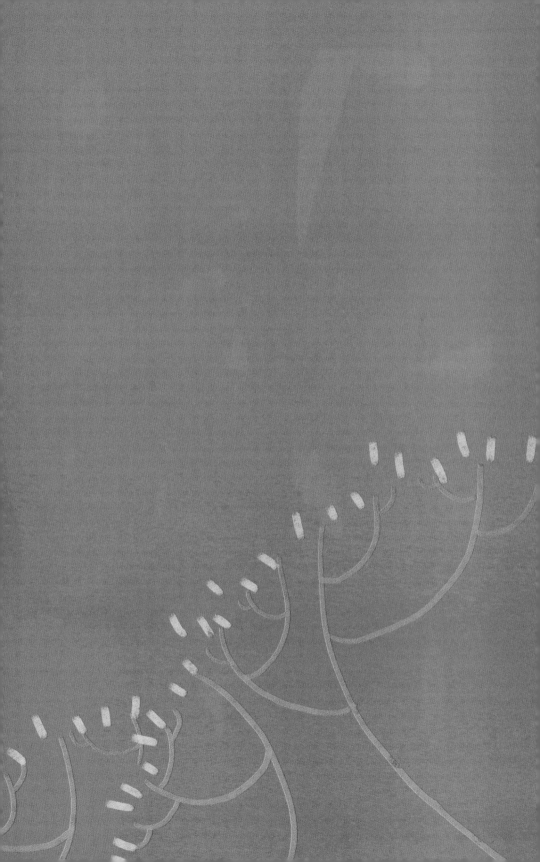

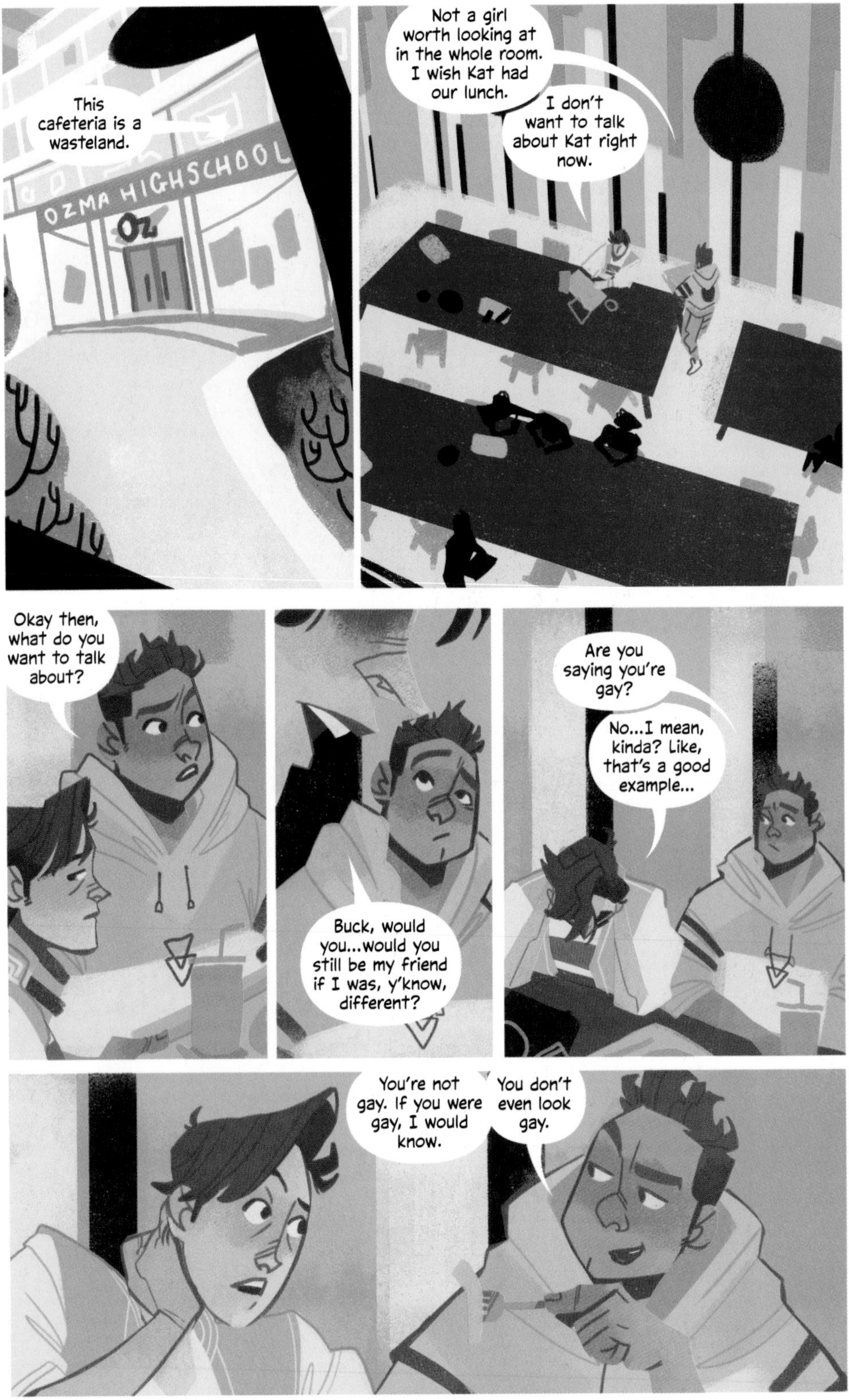
This cafeteria is a wasteland.
OZMA HIGHSCHOOL
Oz
Not a girl worth looking at in the whole room. I wish Kat had our lunch.
I don't want to talk about Kat right now.
Okay then, what do you want to talk about?
Buck, would you...would you still be my friend if I was, y'know, different?
Are you saying you're gay?
No...I mean, kinda? Like, that's a good example...
You're not gay. If you were gay, I would know.
You don't even look gay.

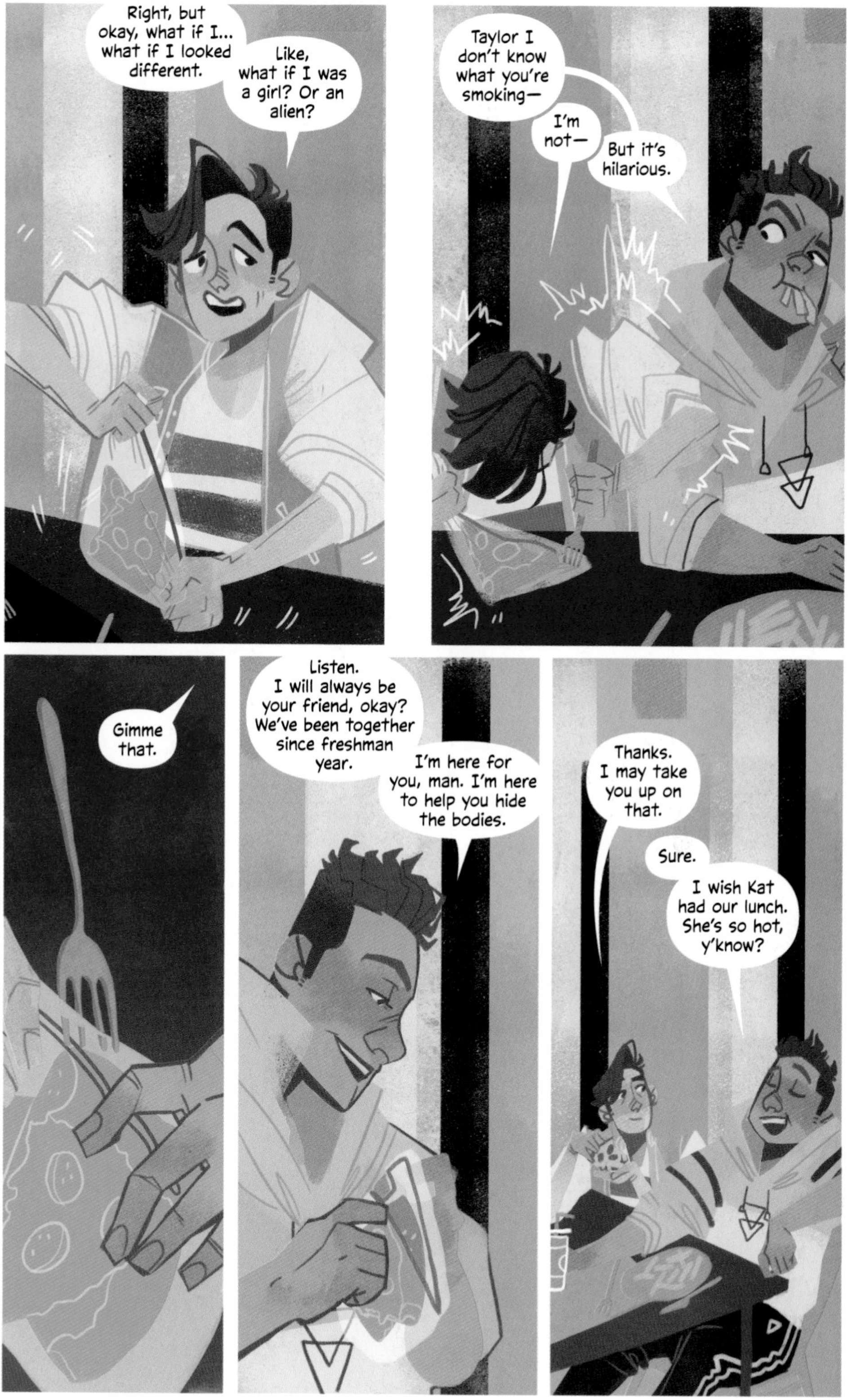
Right, but okay, what if I... what if I looked different.
Like, what if I was a girl? Or an alien?
Taylor I don't know what you're smoking—
I'm not—
But it's hilarious.
Gimme that.
Listen. I will always be your friend, okay? We've been together since freshman year.
I'm here for you, man. I'm here to help you hide the bodies.
Thanks. I may take you up on that.
Sure.
I wish Kat had our lunch. She's so hot, y'know?

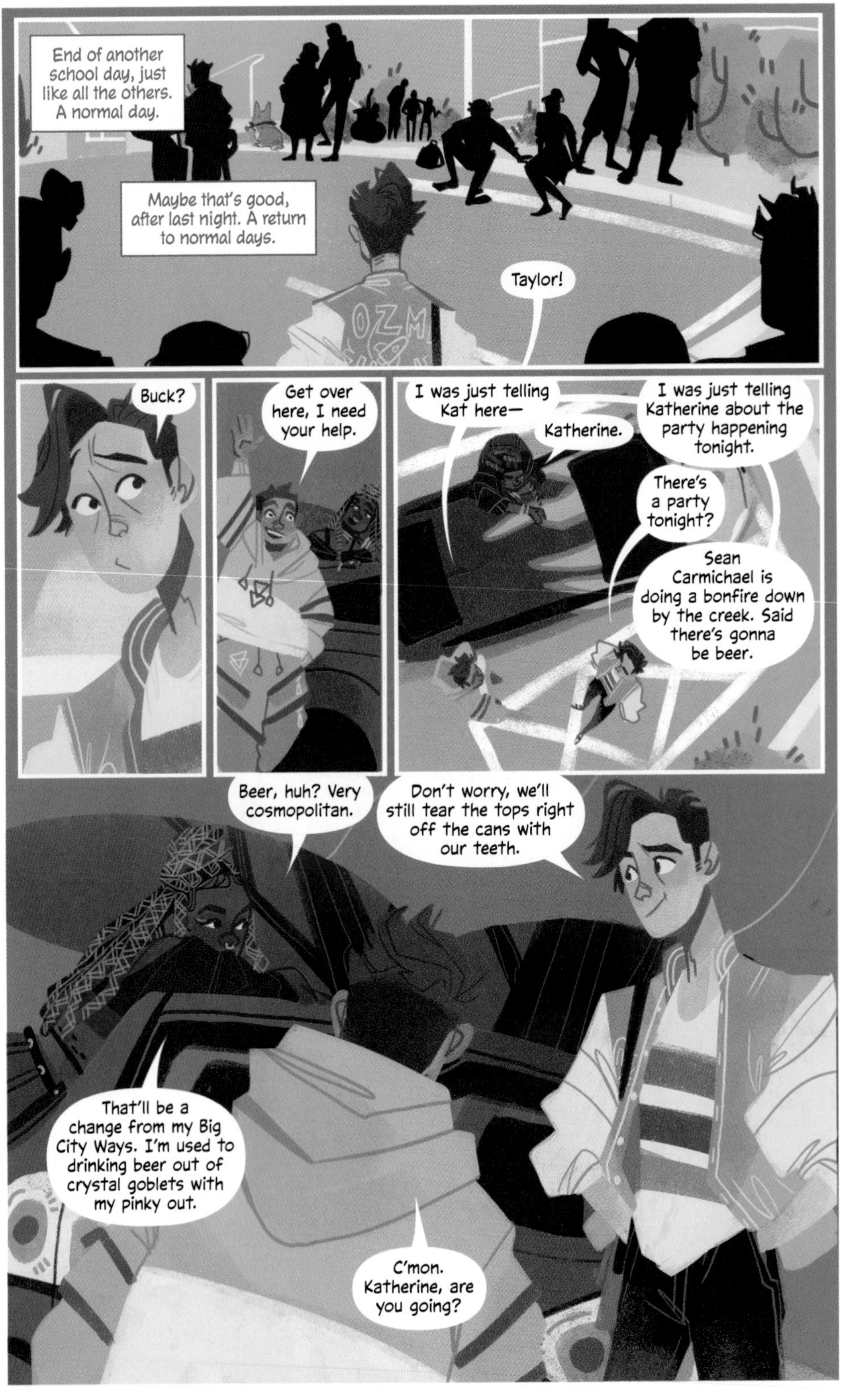
End of another school day, just like all the others. A normal day.
Maybe that's good, after last night. A return to normal days.
Taylor!
Buck?
Get over here, I need your help.
I was just telling Kat here—
Katherine.
I was just telling Katherine about the party happening tonight.
There's a party tonight?
Sean Carmichael is doing a bonfire down by the creek. Said there's gonna be beer.
Beer, huh? Very cosmopolitan.
Don't worry, we'll still tear the tops right off the cans with our teeth.
That'll be a change from my Big City Ways. I'm used to drinking beer out of crystal goblets with my pinky out.
C'mon. Katherine, are you going?

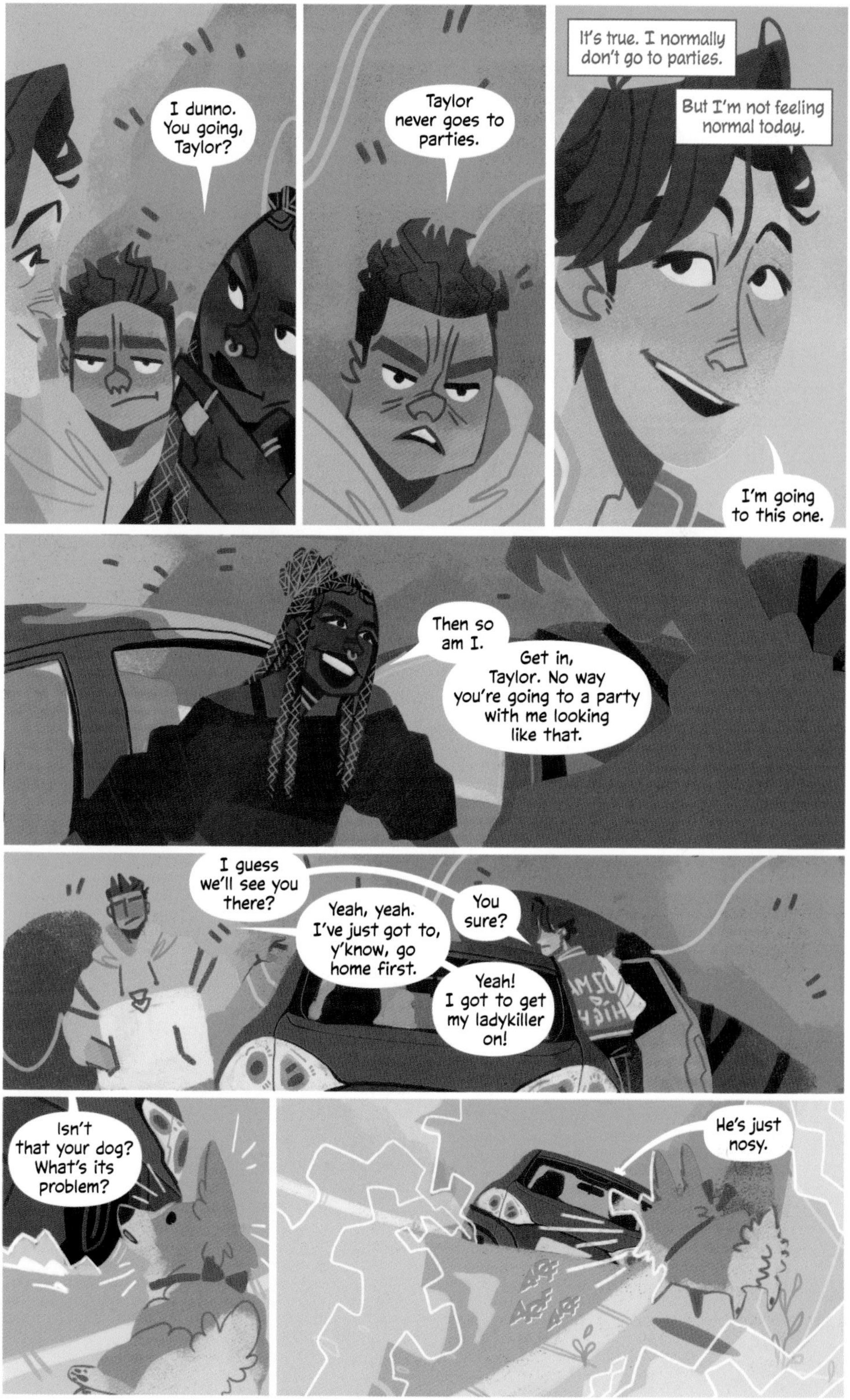

I dunno. You going, Taylor?
Taylor never goes to parties.
It's true. I normally don't go to parties.
But I'm not feeling normal today.
I'm going to this one.
Then so am I.
Get in, Taylor. No way you're going to a party with me looking like that.
I guess we'll see you there?
You sure?
Yeah, yeah. I've just got to, y'know, go home first.
Yeah! I got to get my ladykiller on!
Isn't that your dog? What's its problem?
He's just nosy.

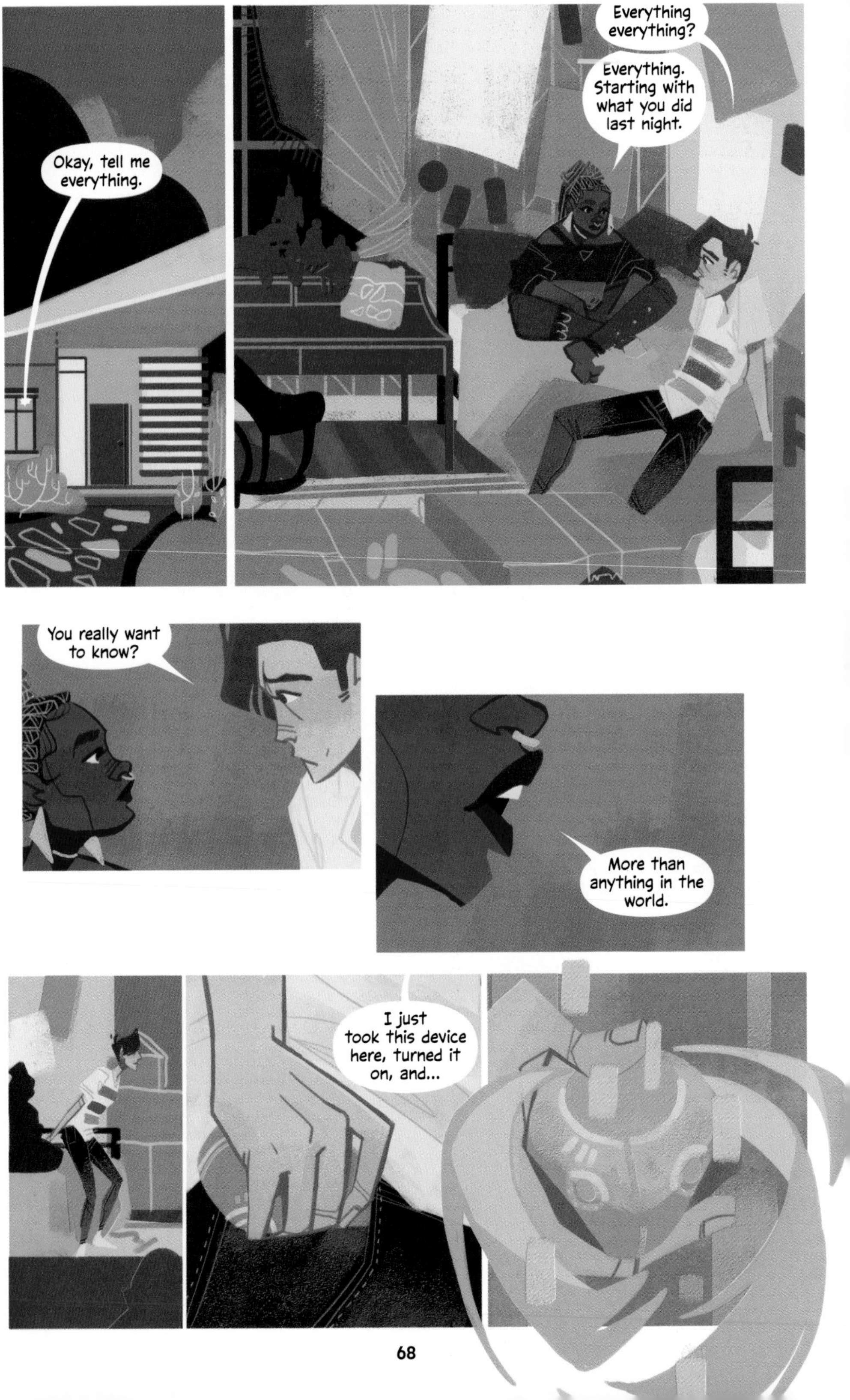
Okay, tell me everything.
Everything everything?
Everything. Starting with what you did last night.
You really want to know?
More than anything in the world.
I just took this device here, turned it on, and...

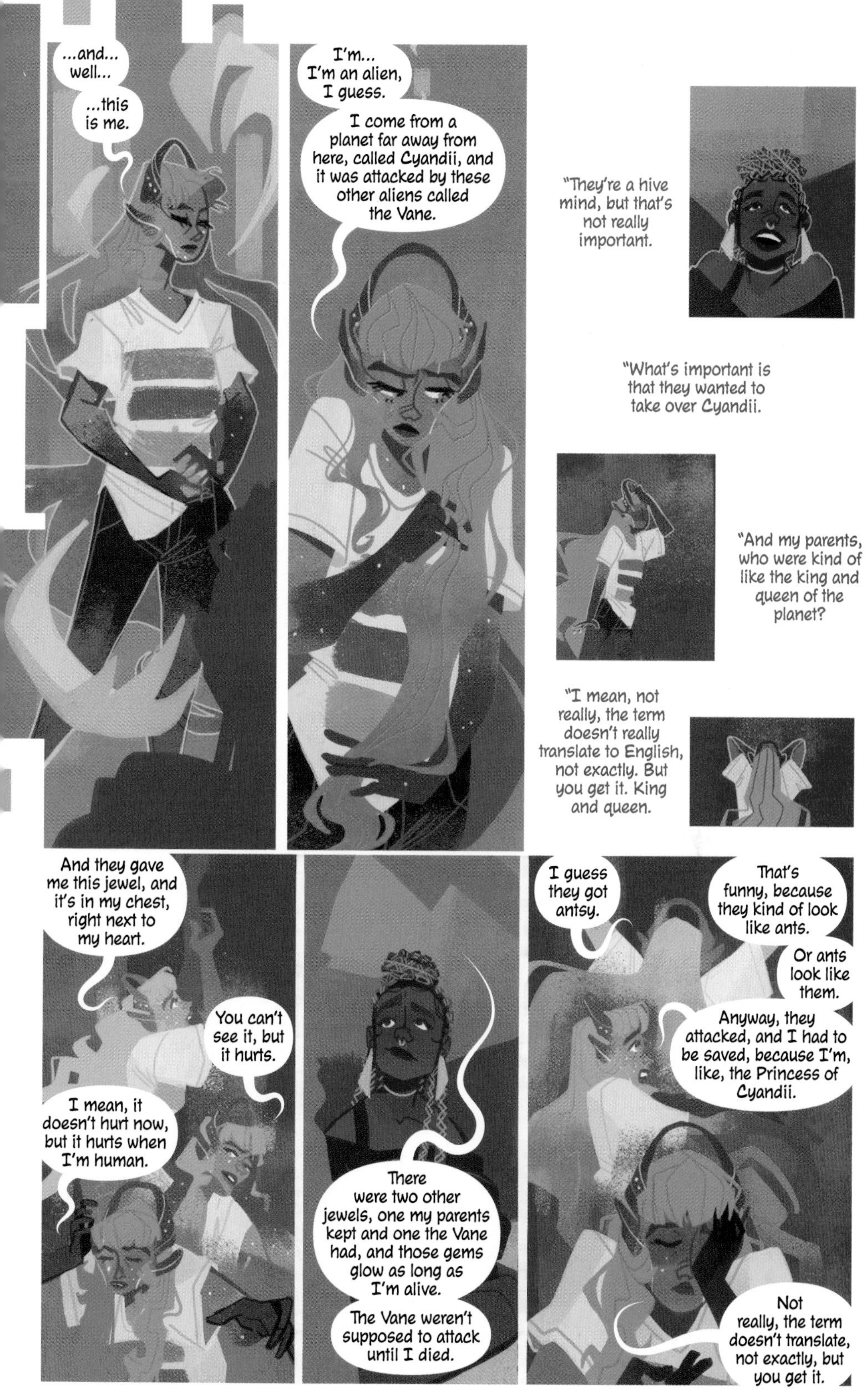
...and... well...
...this is me.
I'm... I'm an alien, I guess.
I come from a planet far away from here, called Cyandii, and it was attacked by these other aliens called the Vane.
"They're a hive mind, but that's not really important.
"What's important is that they wanted to take over Cyandii.
"And my parents, who were kind of like the king and queen of the planet?
"I mean, not really, the term doesn't really translate to English, not exactly. But you get it. King and queen.
And they gave me this jewel, and it's in my chest, right next to my heart.
You can't see it, but it hurts.
I mean, it doesn't hurt now, but it hurts when I'm human.
There were two other jewels, one my parents kept and one the Vane had, and those gems glow as long as I'm alive.
The Vane weren't supposed to attack until I died.
I guess they got antsy.
That's funny, because they kind of look like ants.
Or ants look like them.
Anyway, they attacked, and I had to be saved, because I'm, like, the Princess of Cyandii.
Not really, the term doesn't translate, not exactly, but you get it.

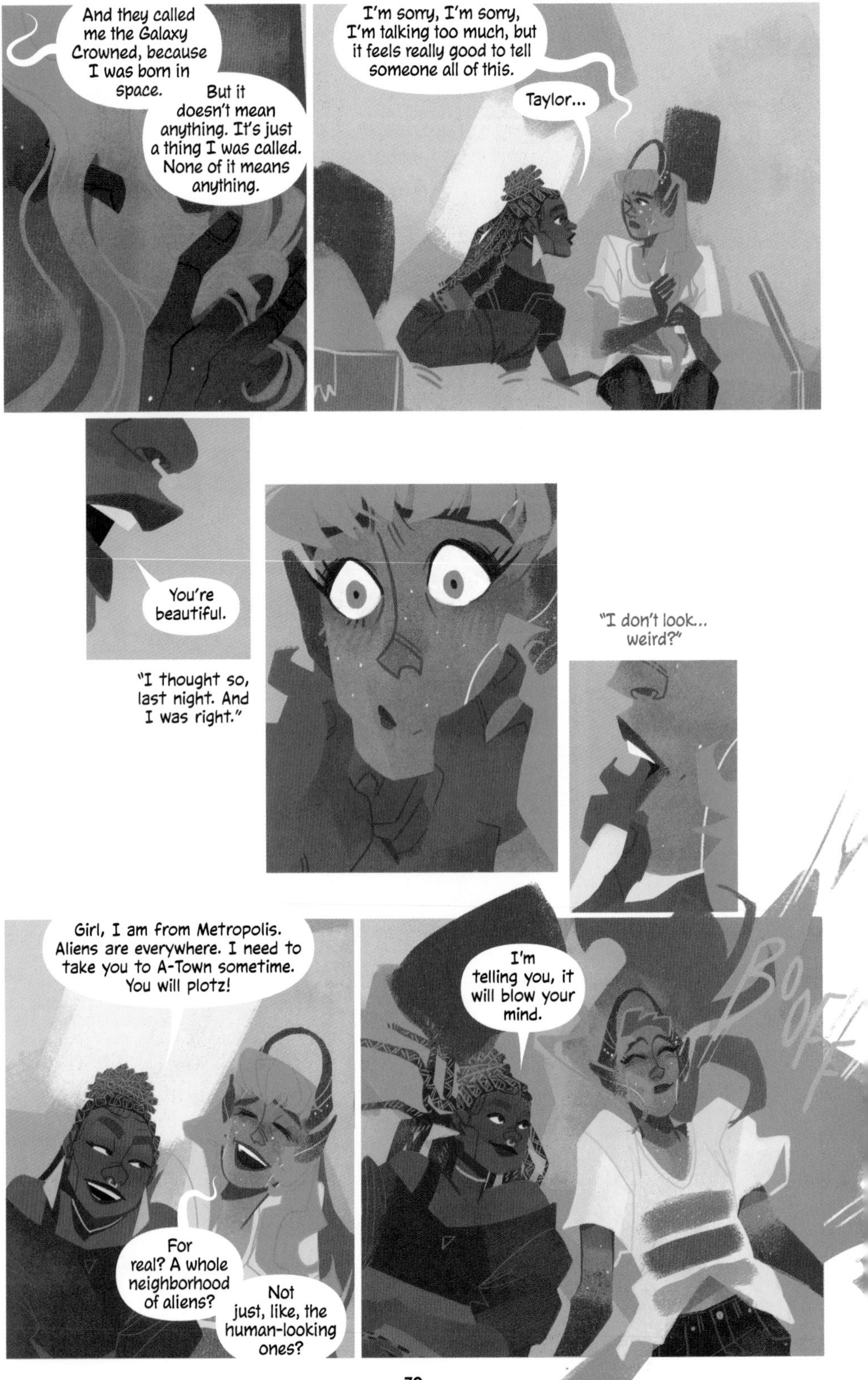
And they called me the Galaxy Crowned, because I was born in space.
But it doesn't mean anything. It's just a thing I was called. None of it means anything.
I'm sorry, I'm sorry, I'm talking too much, but it feels really good to tell someone all of this.
Taylor...
You're beautiful.
"I thought so, last night. And I was right."
"I don't look... weird?"
Girl, I am from Metropolis. Aliens are everywhere. I need to take you to A-Town sometime. You will plotz!
For real? A whole neighborhood of aliens?
Not just, like, the human-looking ones?
I'm telling you, it will blow your mind.
BOOF

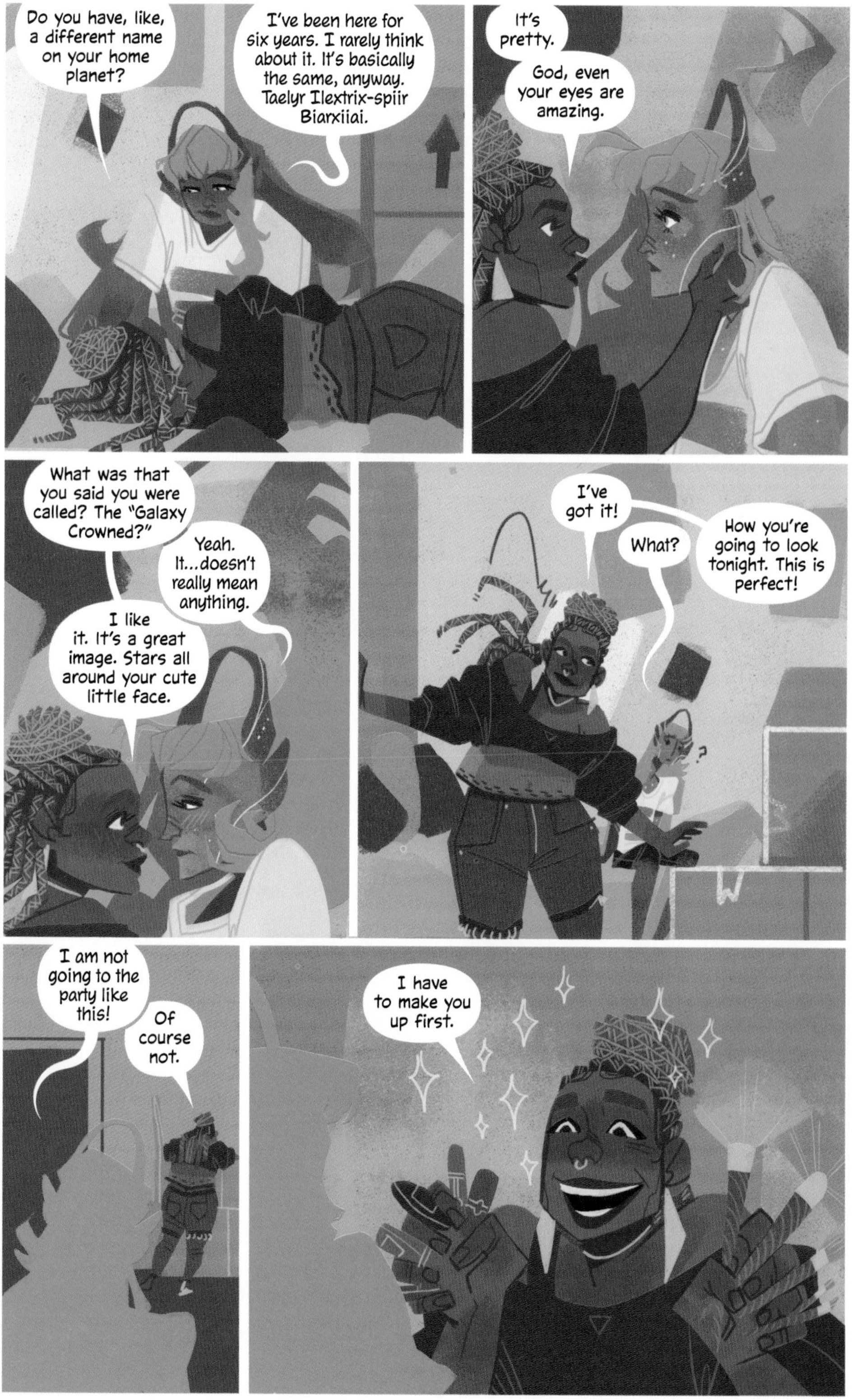
Do you have, like, a different name on your home planet?
I've been here for six years. I rarely think about it. It's basically the same, anyway. Taelyr Ilextrix-spiir Biarxiiai.
It's pretty.
God, even your eyes are amazing.
What was that you said you were called? The "Galaxy Crowned?"
Yeah. It...doesn't really mean anything.
I like it. It's a great image. Stars all around your cute little face.
I've got it!
What?
How you're going to look tonight. This is perfect!
I am not going to the party like this!
Of course not.
I have to make you up first.

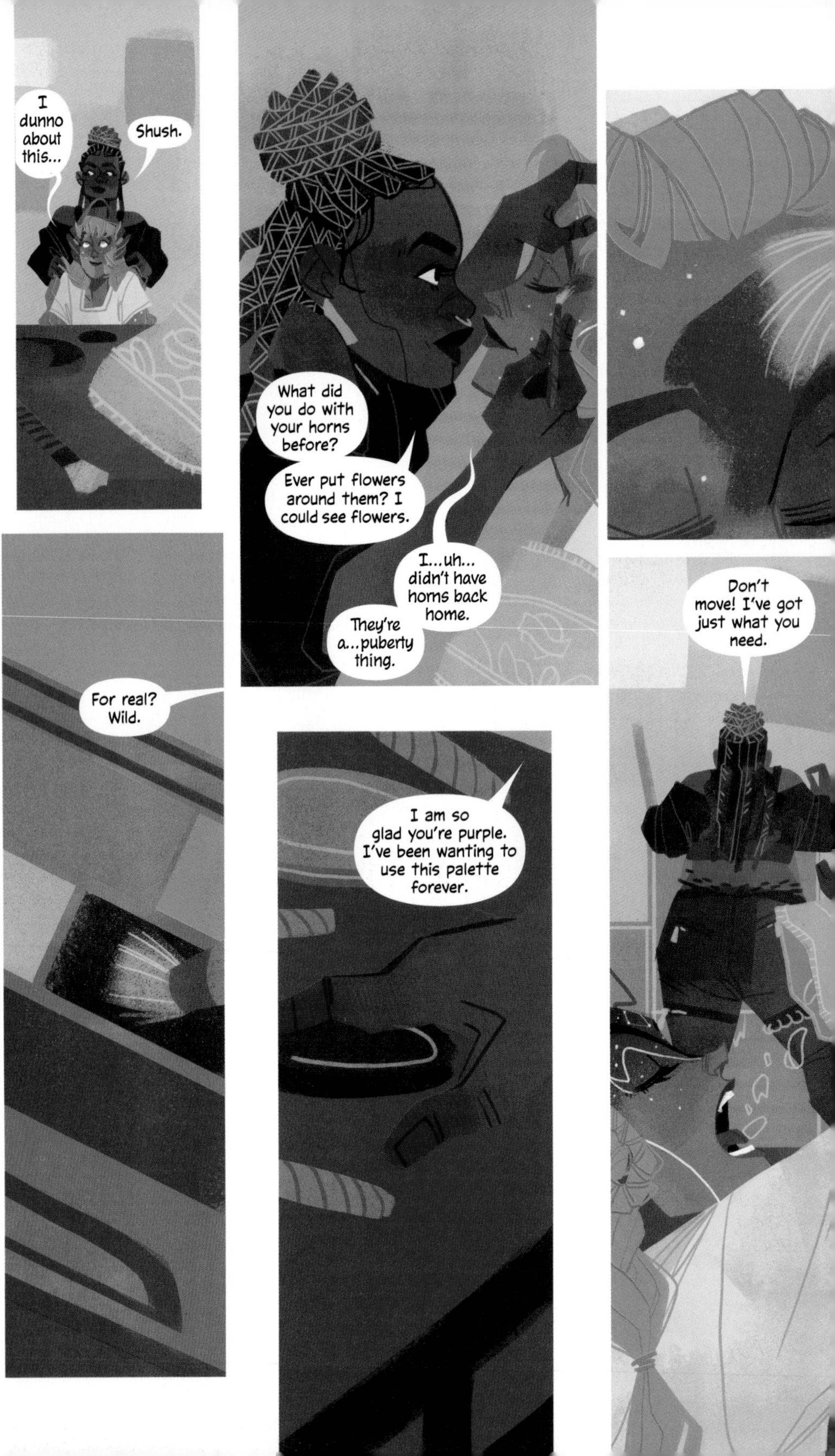
I dunno about this...
Shush.
What did you do with your horns before?
Ever put flowers around them? I could see flowers.
I...uh... didn't have horns back home.
They're a...puberty thing.
Don't move! I've got just what you need.
For real? Wild.
I am so glad you're purple. I've been wanting to use this palette forever.

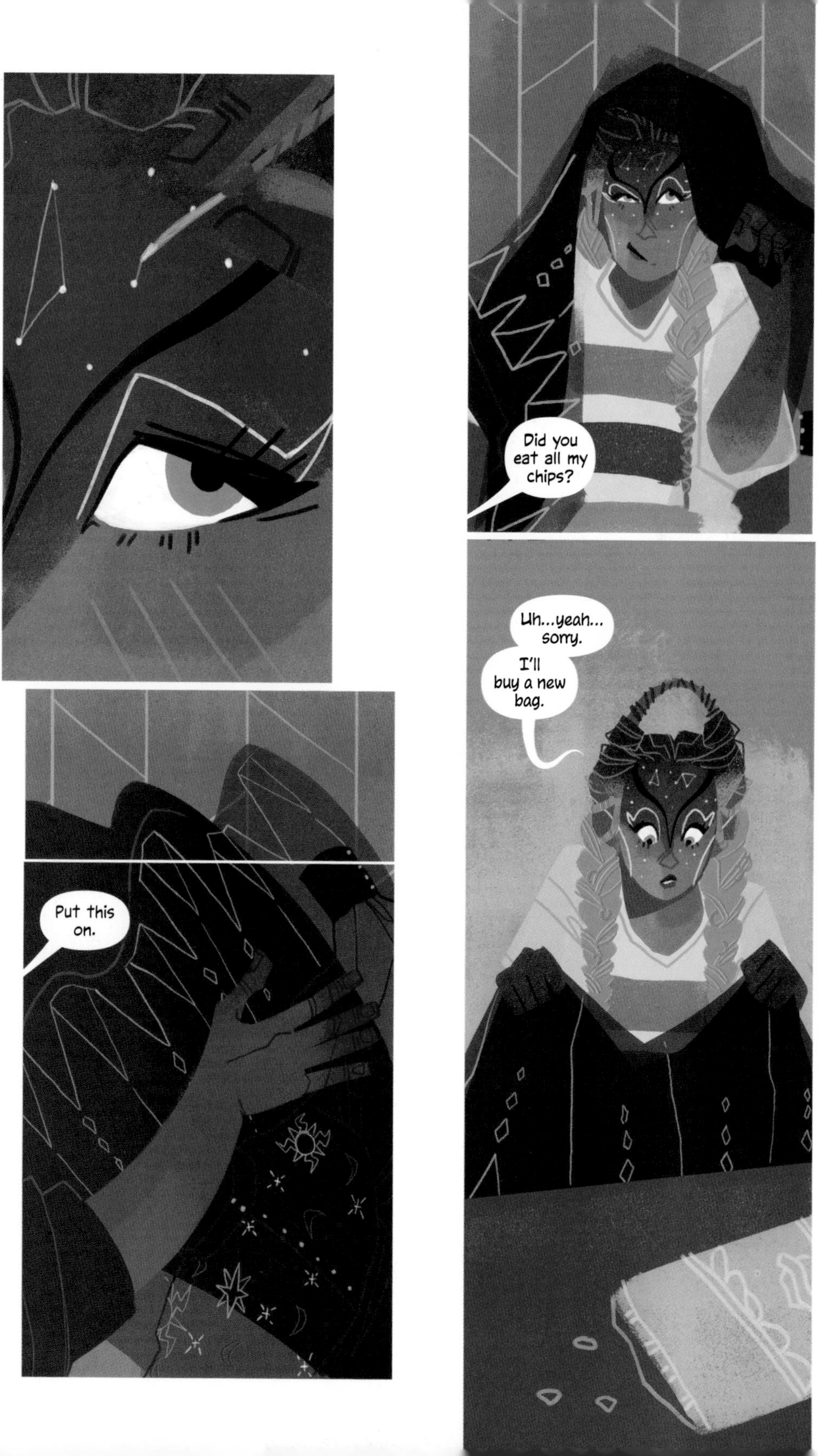
Put this on.
Did you eat all my chips?
Uh...yeah... sorry.
I'll buy a new bag.

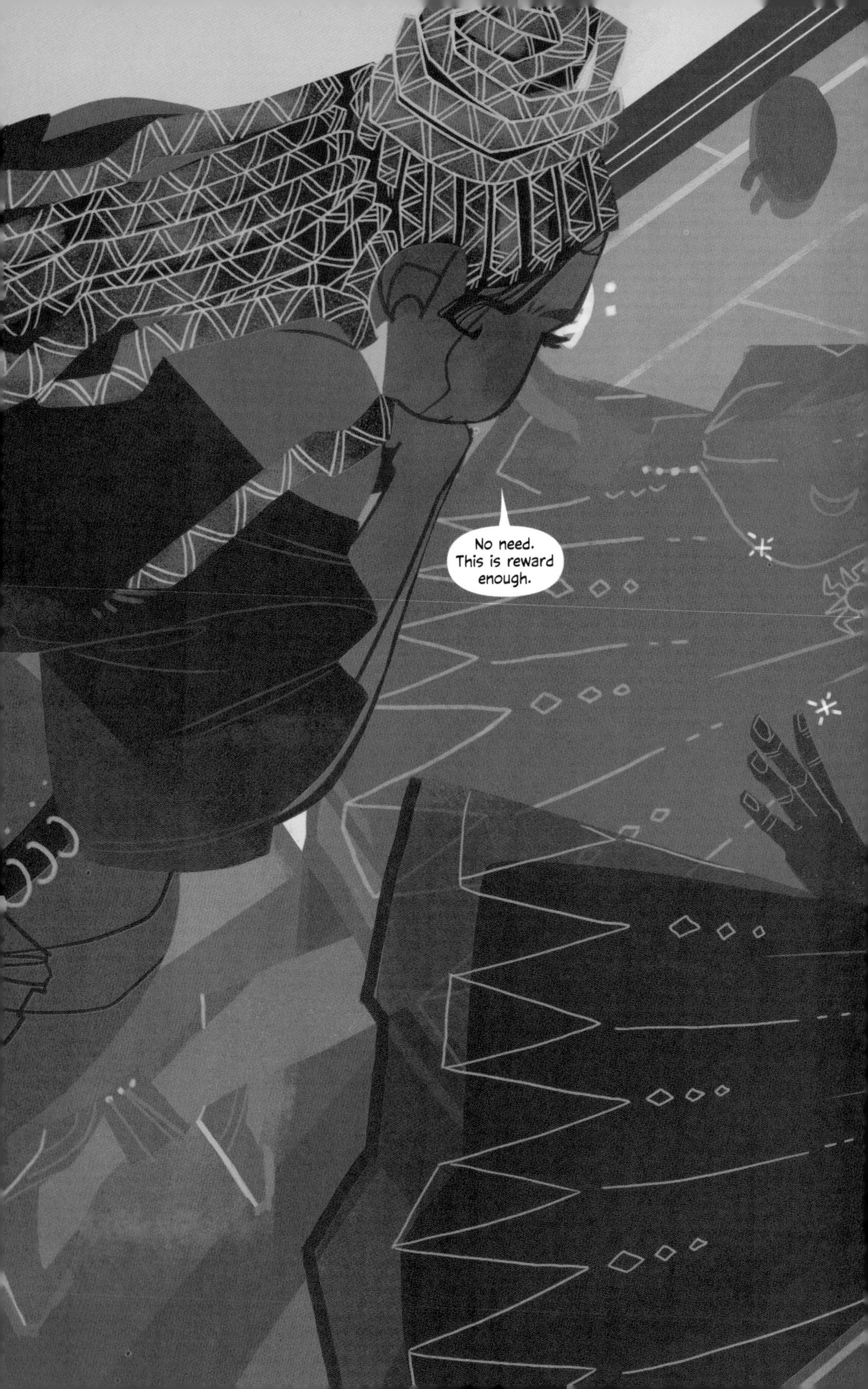
No need. This is reward enough.

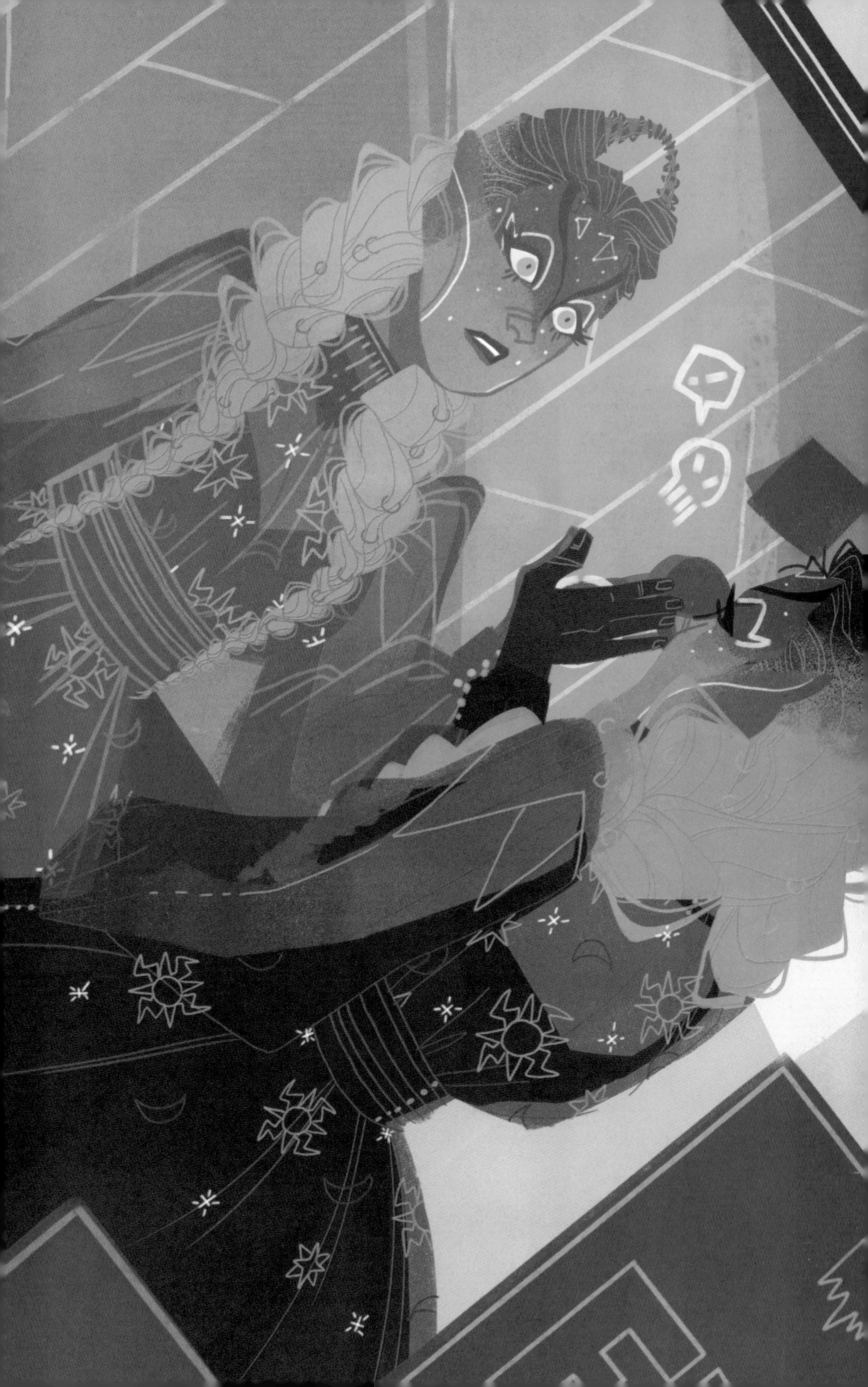

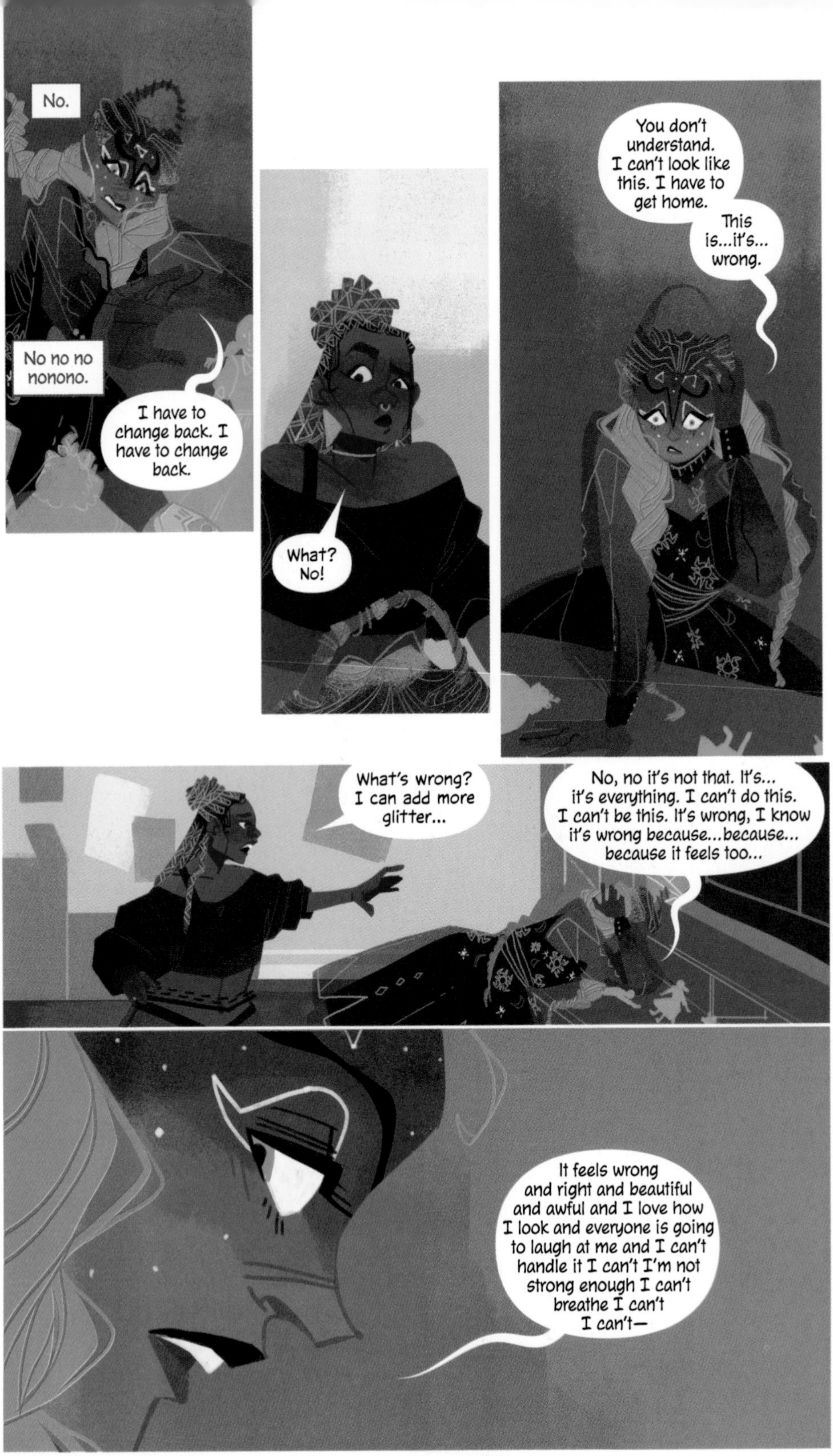
No.
No no no nonono.
I have to change back. I have to change back.
What? No!
You don't understand. I can't look like this. I have to get home.
This is...it's... wrong.
What's wrong? I can add more glitter...
No, no it's not that. It's... it's everything. I can't do this. I can't be this. It's wrong, I know it's wrong because...because... because it feels too...
It feels wrong and right and beautiful and awful and I love how I look and everyone is going to laugh at me and I can't handle it I can't I'm not strong enough I can't breathe I can't I can't—

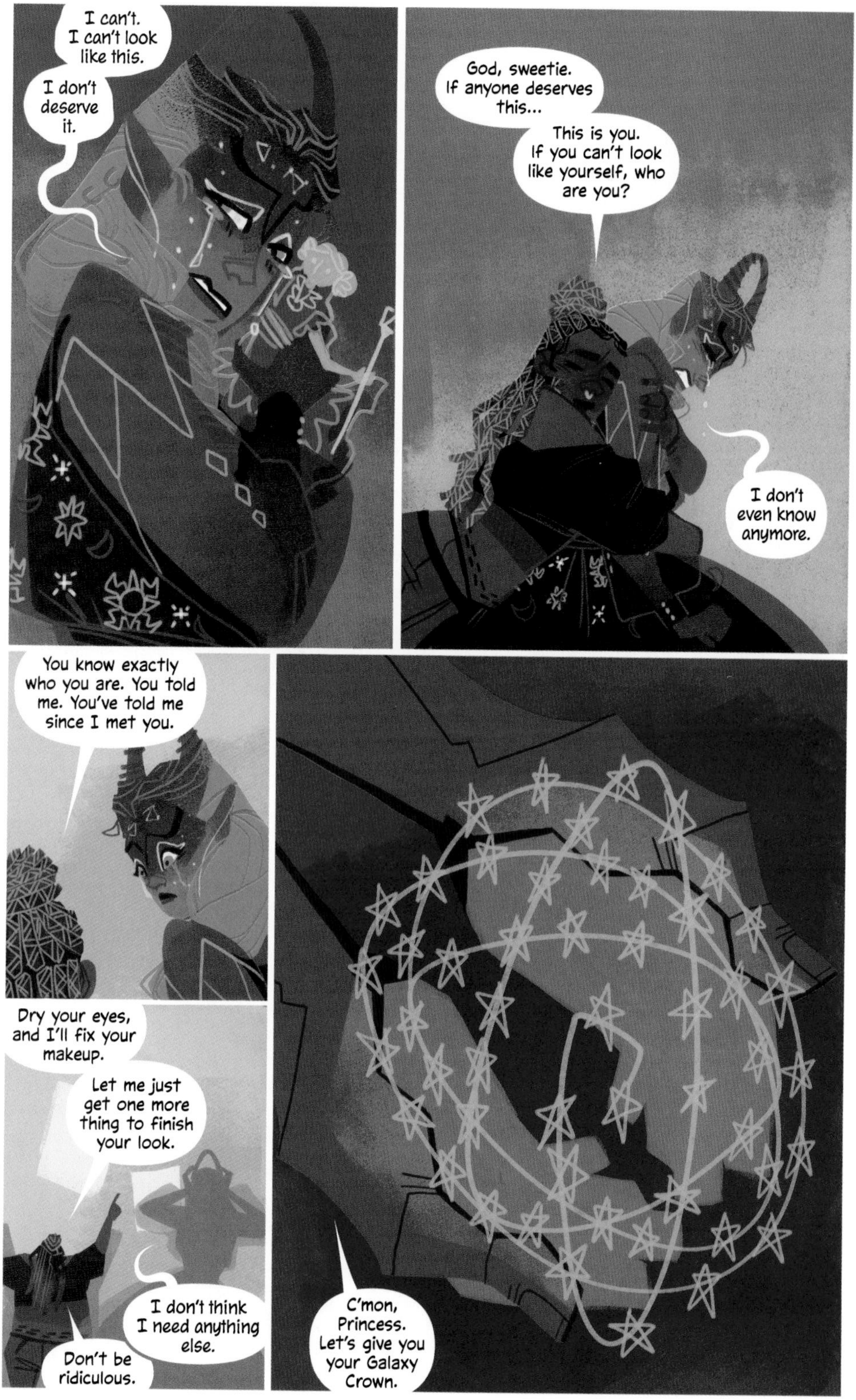
I can't. I can't look like this.
I don't deserve it.
God, sweetie. If anyone deserves this...
This is you. If you can't look like yourself, who are you?
I don't even know anymore.
You know exactly who you are. You told me. You've told me since I met you.
Dry your eyes, and I'll fix your makeup.
Let me just get one more thing to finish your look.
I don't think I need anything else.
Don't be ridiculous.
C'mon, Princess. Let's give you your Galaxy Crown.

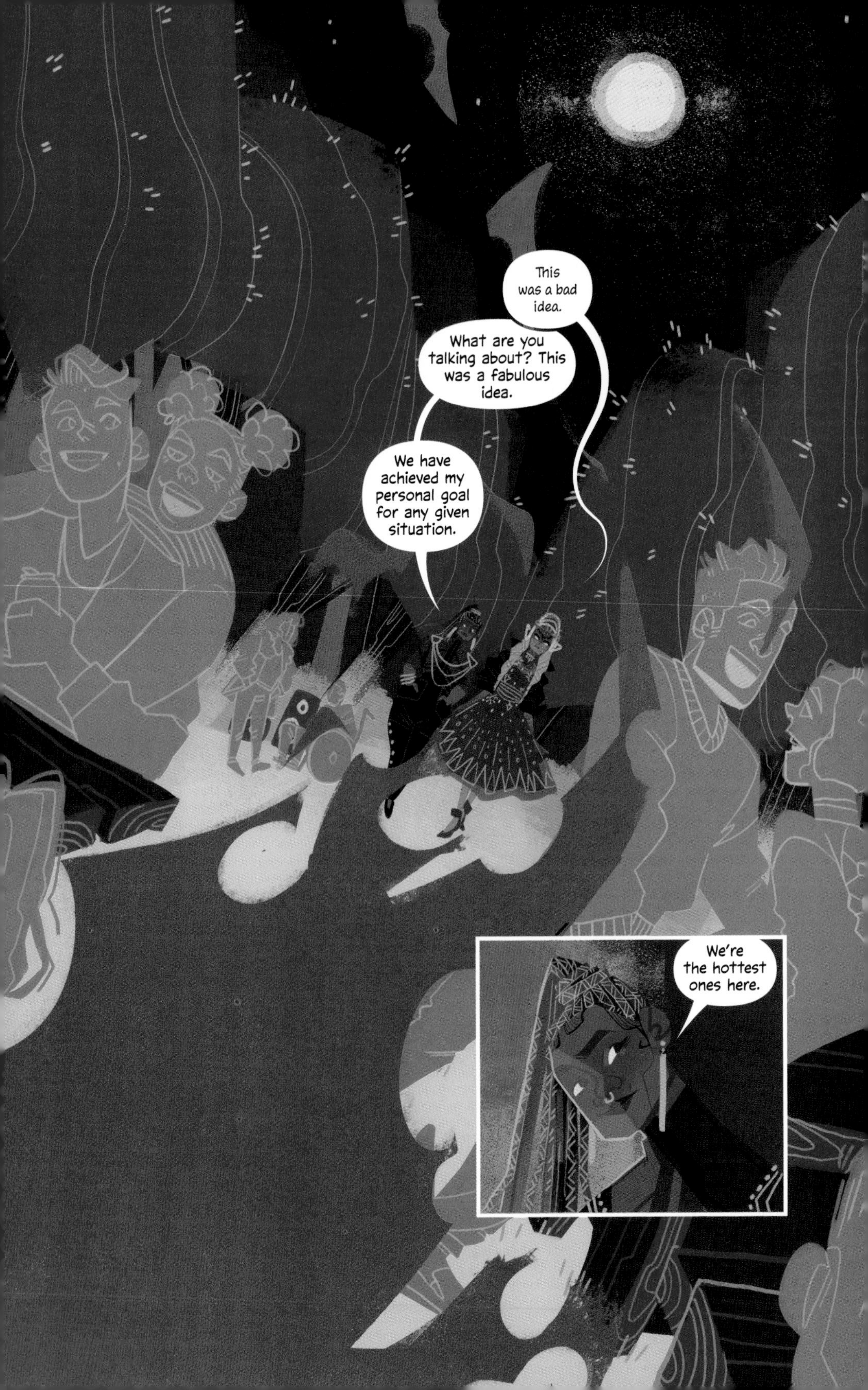
This was a bad idea.
What are you talking about? This was a fabulous idea.
We have achieved my personal goal for any given situation.
We're the hottest ones here.

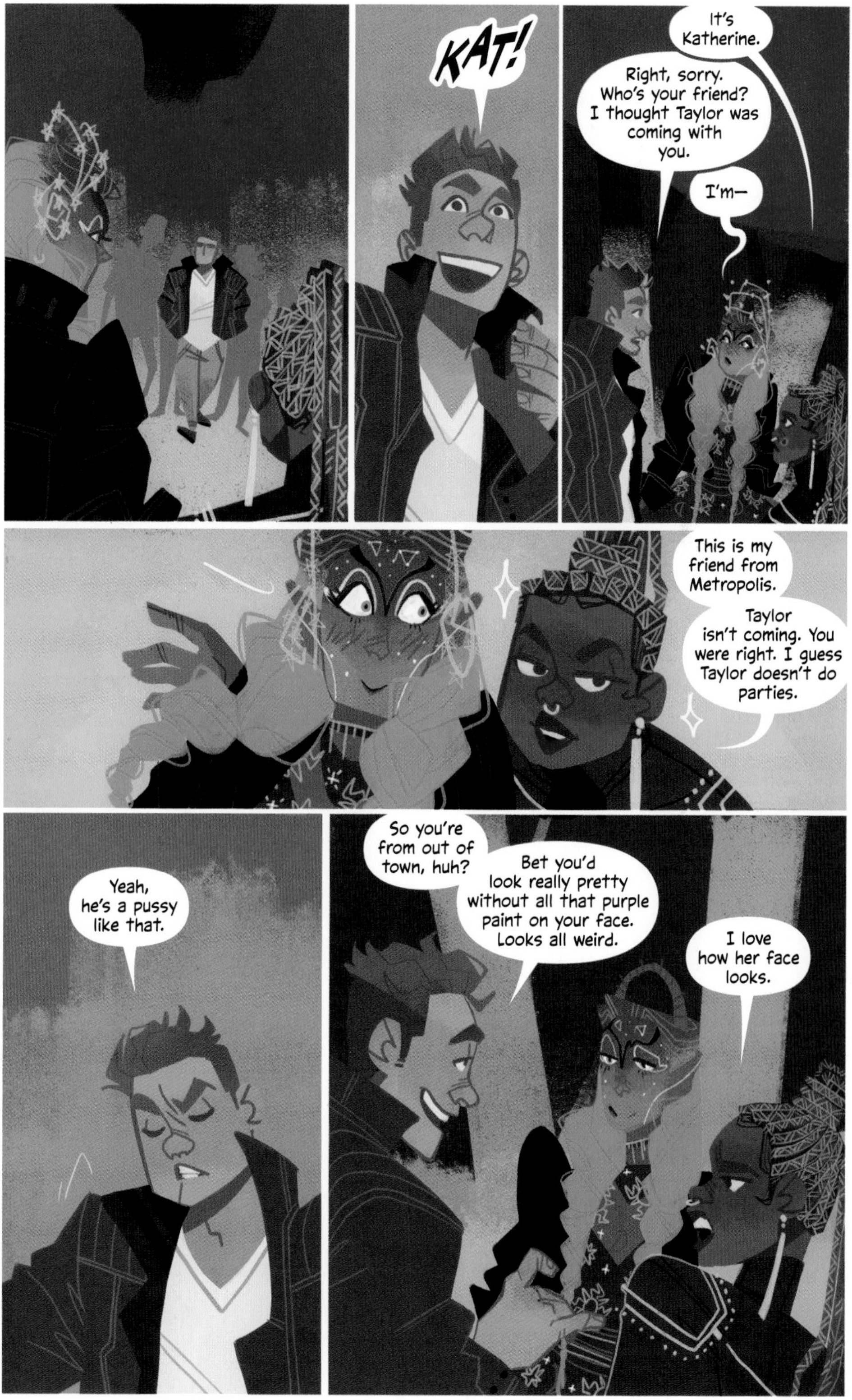
KAT!
It's Katherine.
Right, sorry. Who's your friend? I thought Taylor was coming with you.
I'm—
This is my friend from Metropolis.
Taylor isn't coming. You were right. I guess Taylor doesn't do parties.
Yeah, he's a pussy like that.
So you're from out of town, huh?
Bet you'd look really pretty without all that purple paint on your face. Looks all weird.
I love how her face looks.

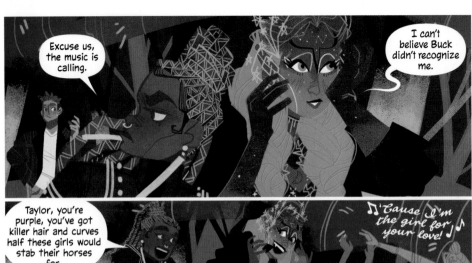

Excuse us, the music is calling.

I can't believe Buck didn't recognize me.

Taylor, you're purple, you've got killer hair and curves half these girls would stab their horses for.

Nobody's gonna recognize you.

♪'Cause I'm the girl for your love!♪

You're right.

Naturally.

I've never felt this...

What? Relaxed?

...free.

♪Wearin' that skirt you like, tight as a glove!♪

Think they've got any Bowie on that?

Only one way to find out.

I can't believe I'm doing this.

I can't believe I'm here.

I can't believe I look like this.

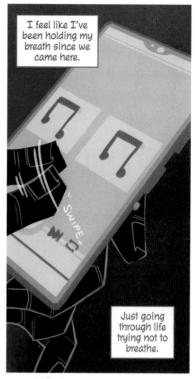

I feel like I've been holding my breath since we came here.

Just going through life trying not to breathe.

"Suffragette City"?

Oh, hell yes.

And now, I can open my mouth.

I can let the air fill my lungs.

I can do anything.

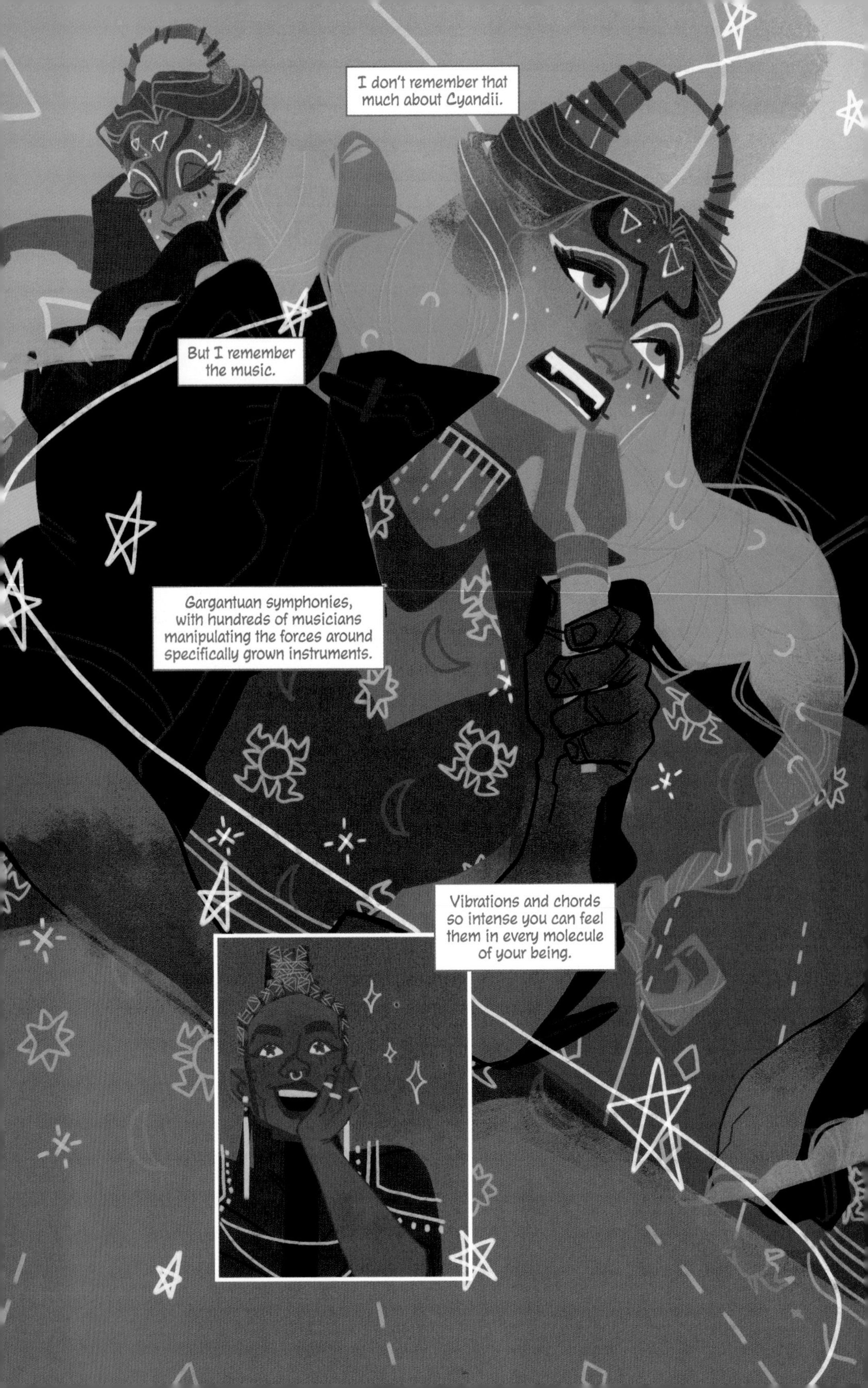
I don't remember that much about Cyandii.
But I remember the music.
Gargantuan symphonies, with hundreds of musicians manipulating the forces around specifically grown instruments.
Vibrations and chords so intense you can feel them in every molecule of your being.

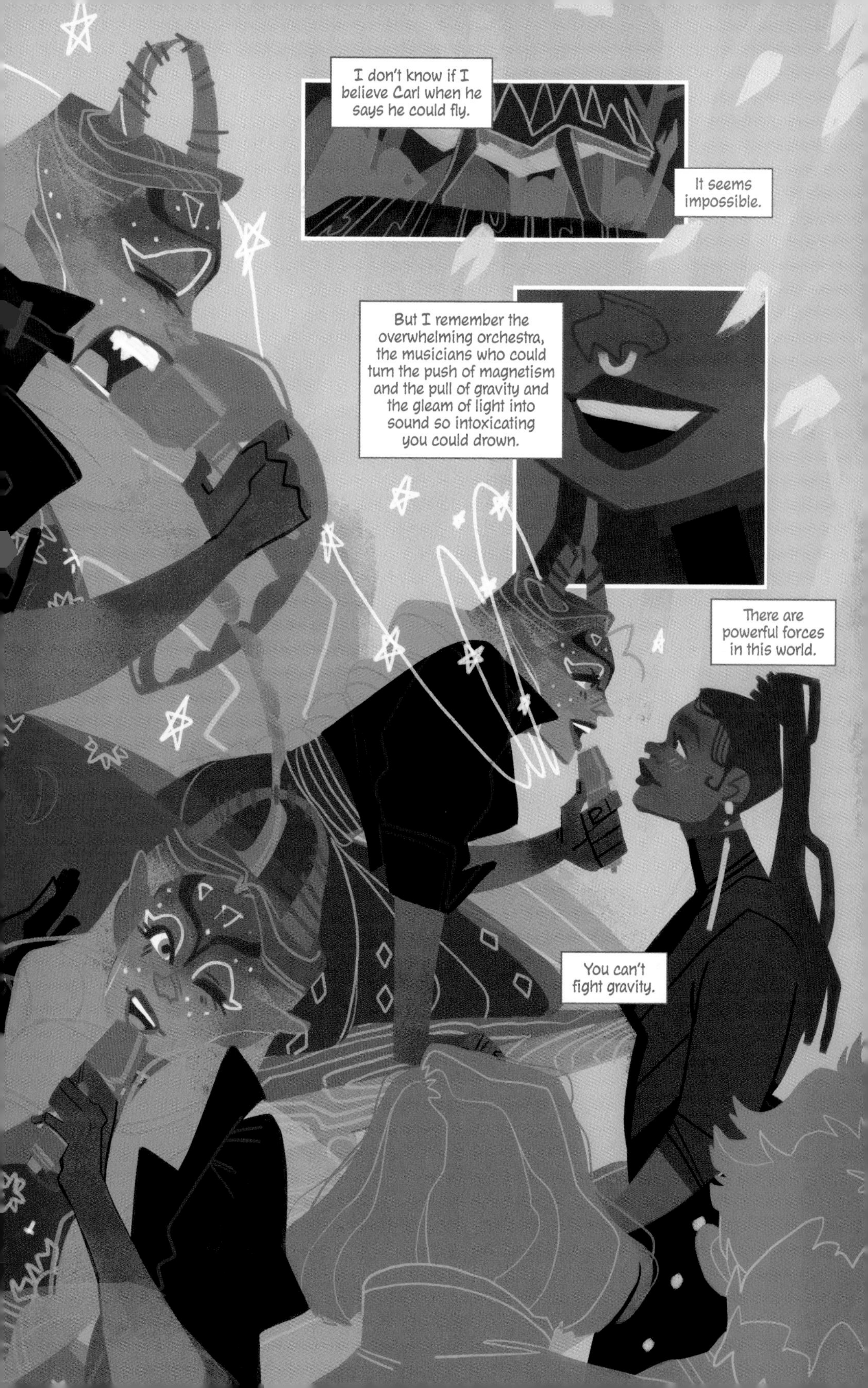
I don't know if I believe Carl when he says he could fly.
It seems impossible.
But I remember the overwhelming orchestra, the musicians who could turn the push of magnetism and the pull of gravity and the gleam of light into sound so intoxicating you could drown.
There are powerful forces in this world.
You can't fight gravity.

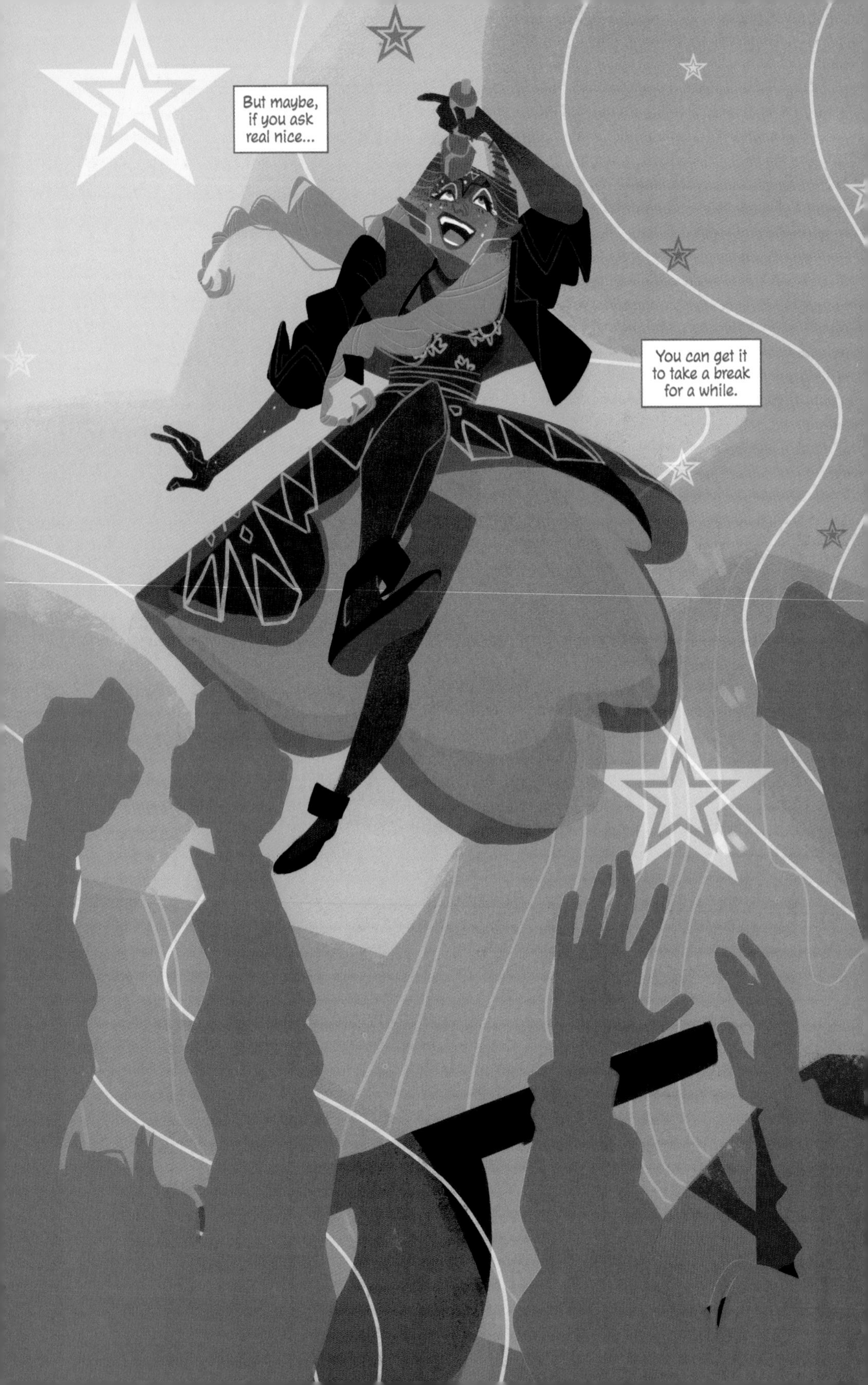
But maybe, if you ask real nice...
You can get it to take a break for a while.

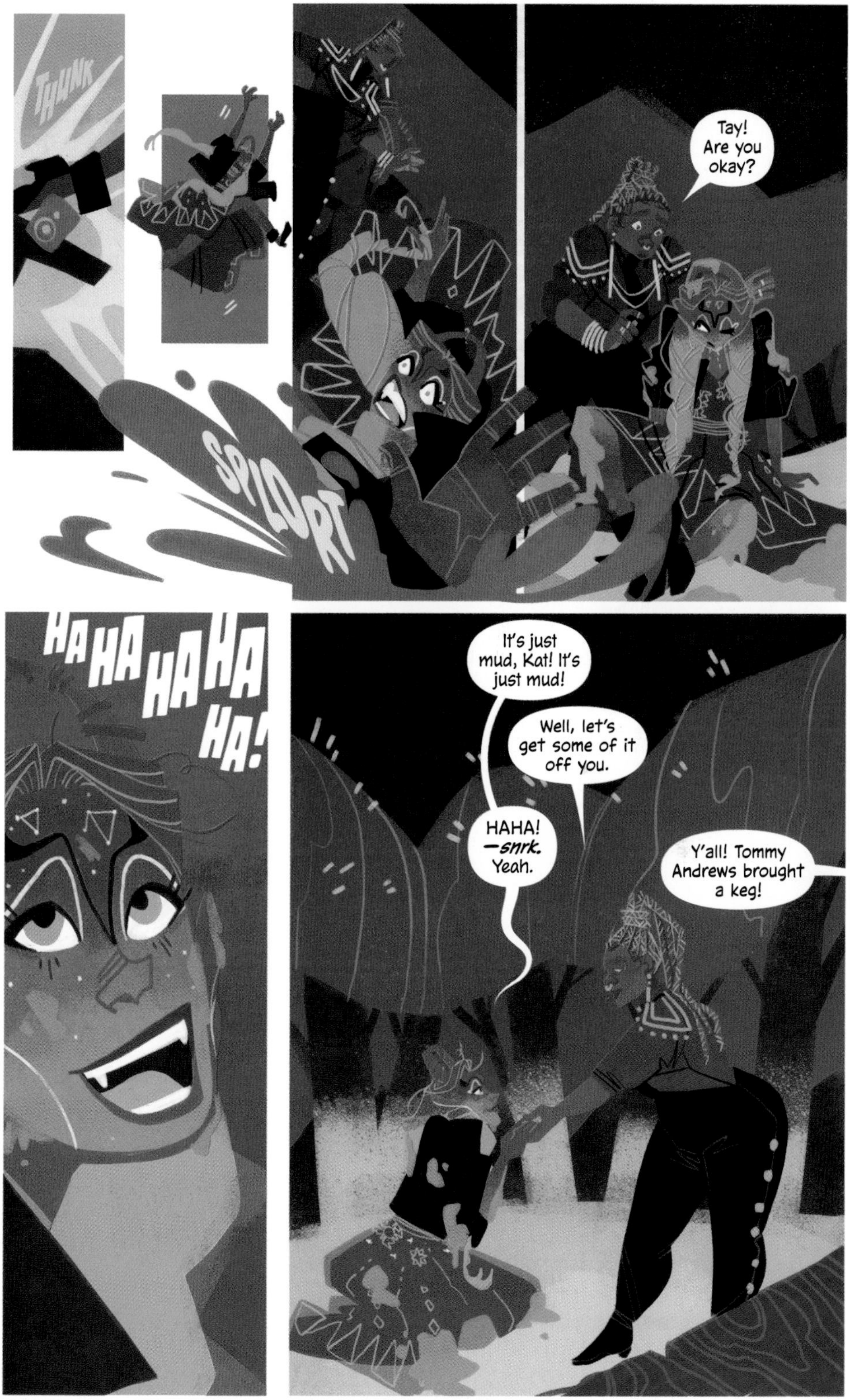
THUNK
SPLORT
Tay! Are you okay?
HAHAHAHAHAHA!
It's just mud, Kat! It's just mud!
Well, let's get some of it off you.
HAHA! —snrk. Yeah.
Y'all! Tommy Andrews brought a keg!

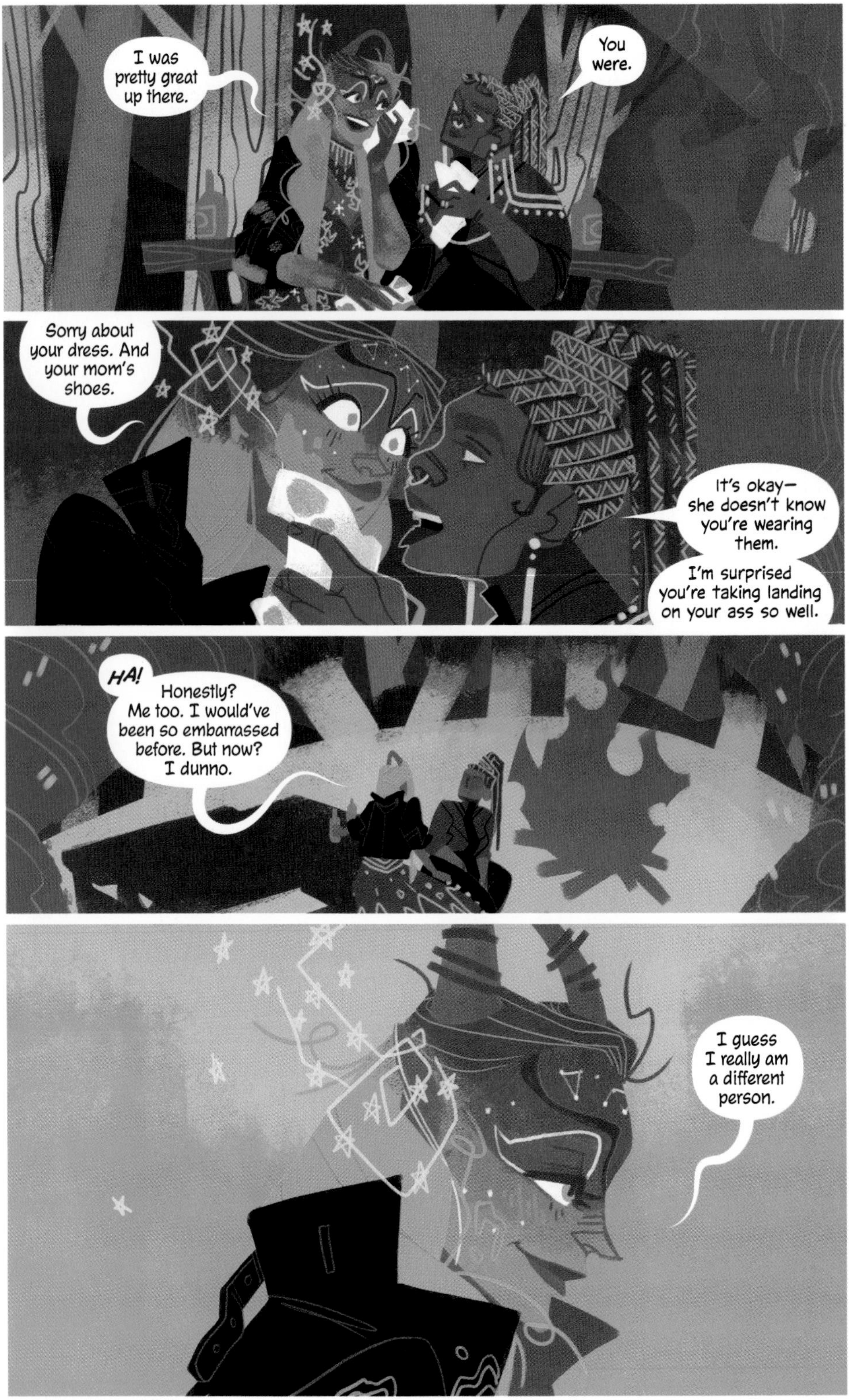
I was pretty great up there.
You were.
Sorry about your dress. And your mom's shoes.
It's okay— she doesn't know you're wearing them.
I'm surprised you're taking landing on your ass so well.
HA!
Honestly? Me too. I would've been so embarrassed before. But now? I dunno.
I guess I really am a different person.

GLUG GLUG

Is that hot sauce?

It smelled so good as I walked by! And it doesn't taste hot, it tastes like... flowers?

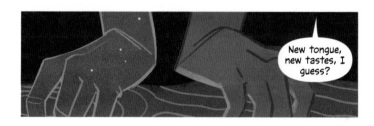

New tongue, new tastes, I guess?

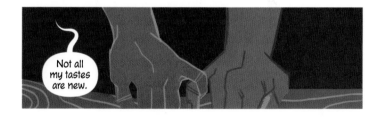

Not all my tastes are new.

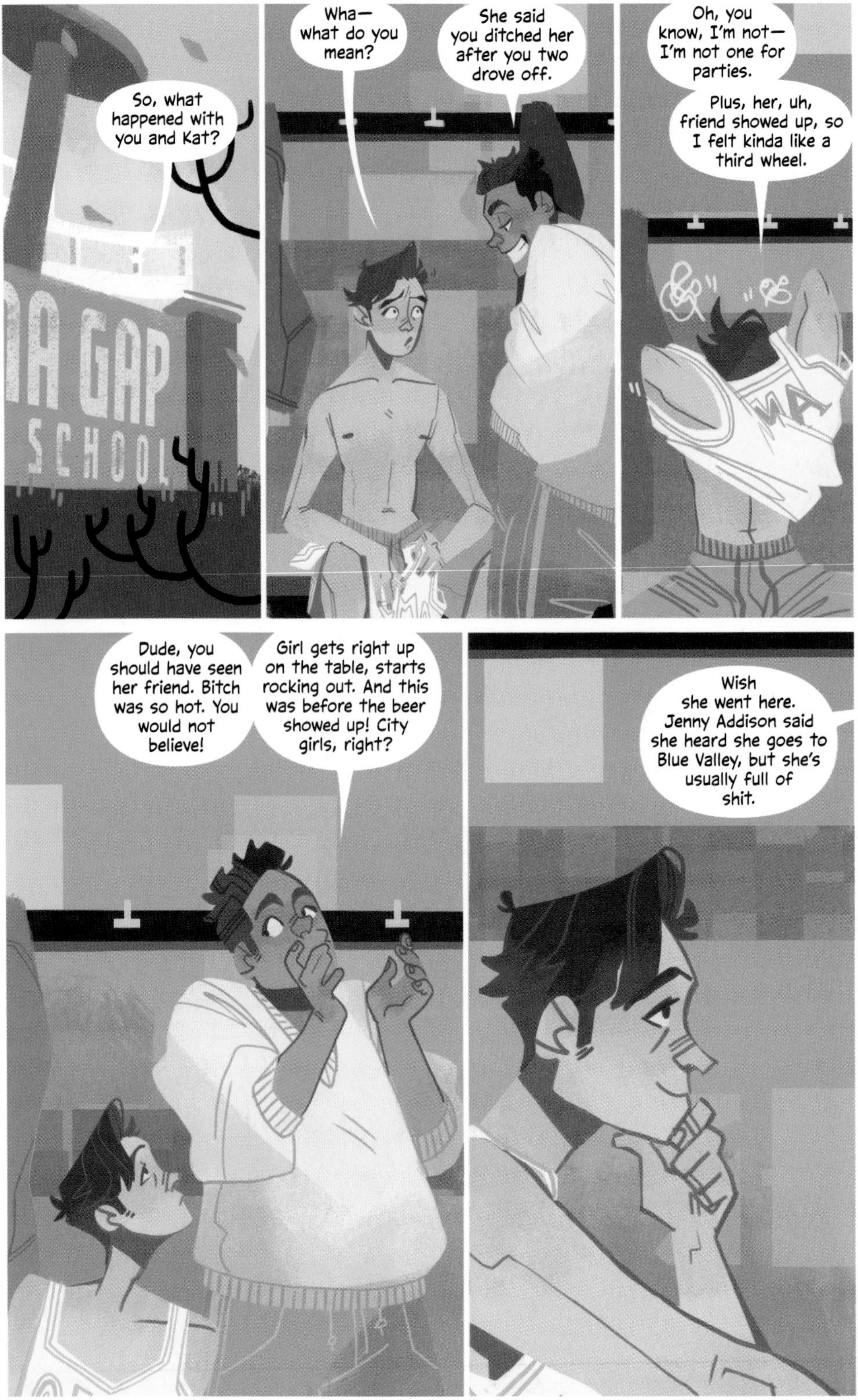
So, what happened with you and Kat?
Wha— what do you mean?
She said you ditched her after you two drove off.
Oh, you know, I'm not— I'm not one for parties.
Plus, her, uh, friend showed up, so I felt kinda like a third wheel.
Dude, you should have seen her friend. Bitch was so hot. You would not believe!
Girl gets right up on the table, starts rocking out. And this was before the beer showed up! City girls, right?
Wish she went here. Jenny Addison said she heard she goes to Blue Valley, but she's usually full of shit.

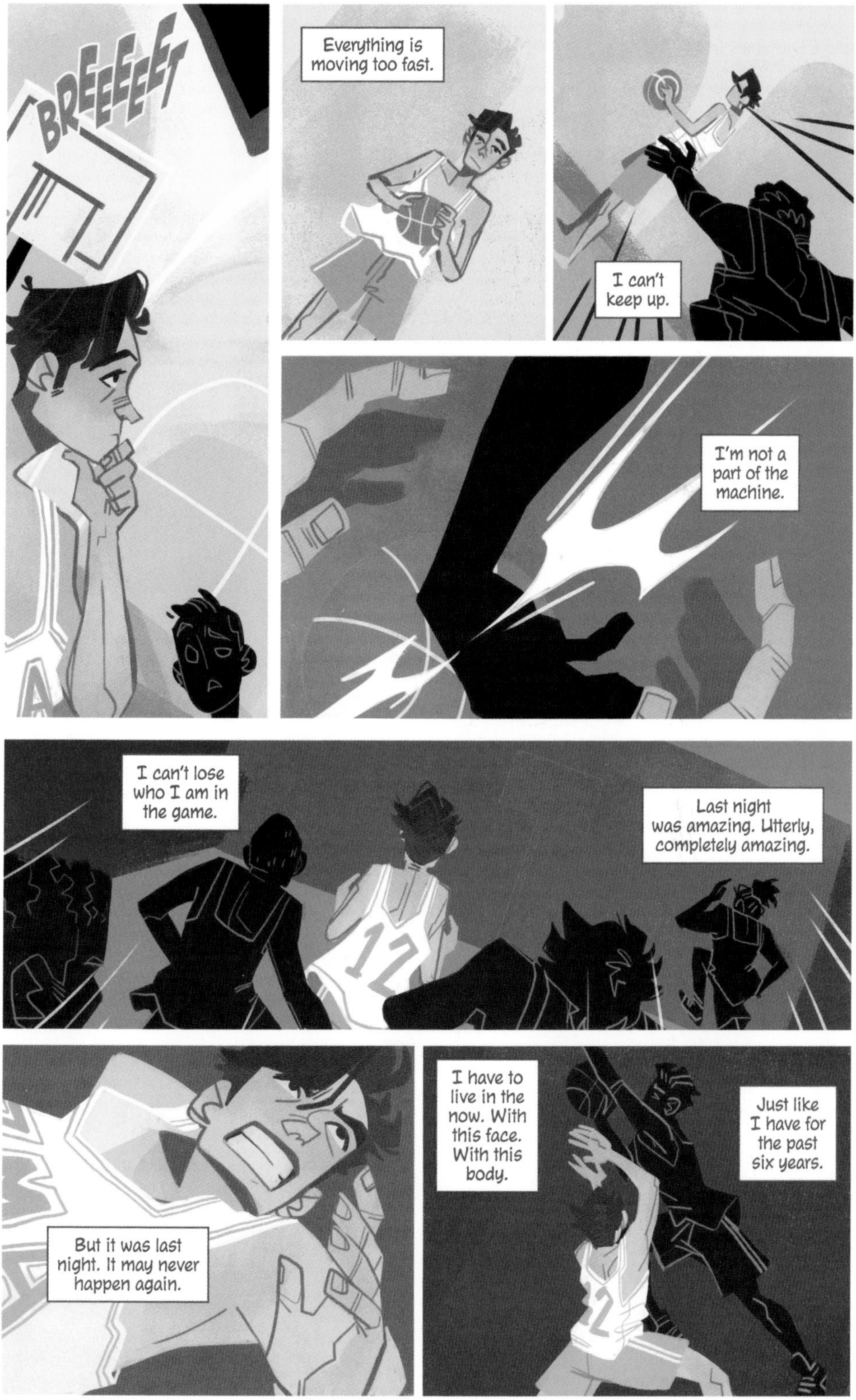
BREEEEEET
Everything is moving too fast.
I can't keep up.
I'm not a part of the machine.
I can't lose who I am in the game.
Last night was amazing. Utterly, completely amazing.
But it was last night. It may never happen again.
I have to live in the now. With this face. With this body.
Just like I have for the past six years.

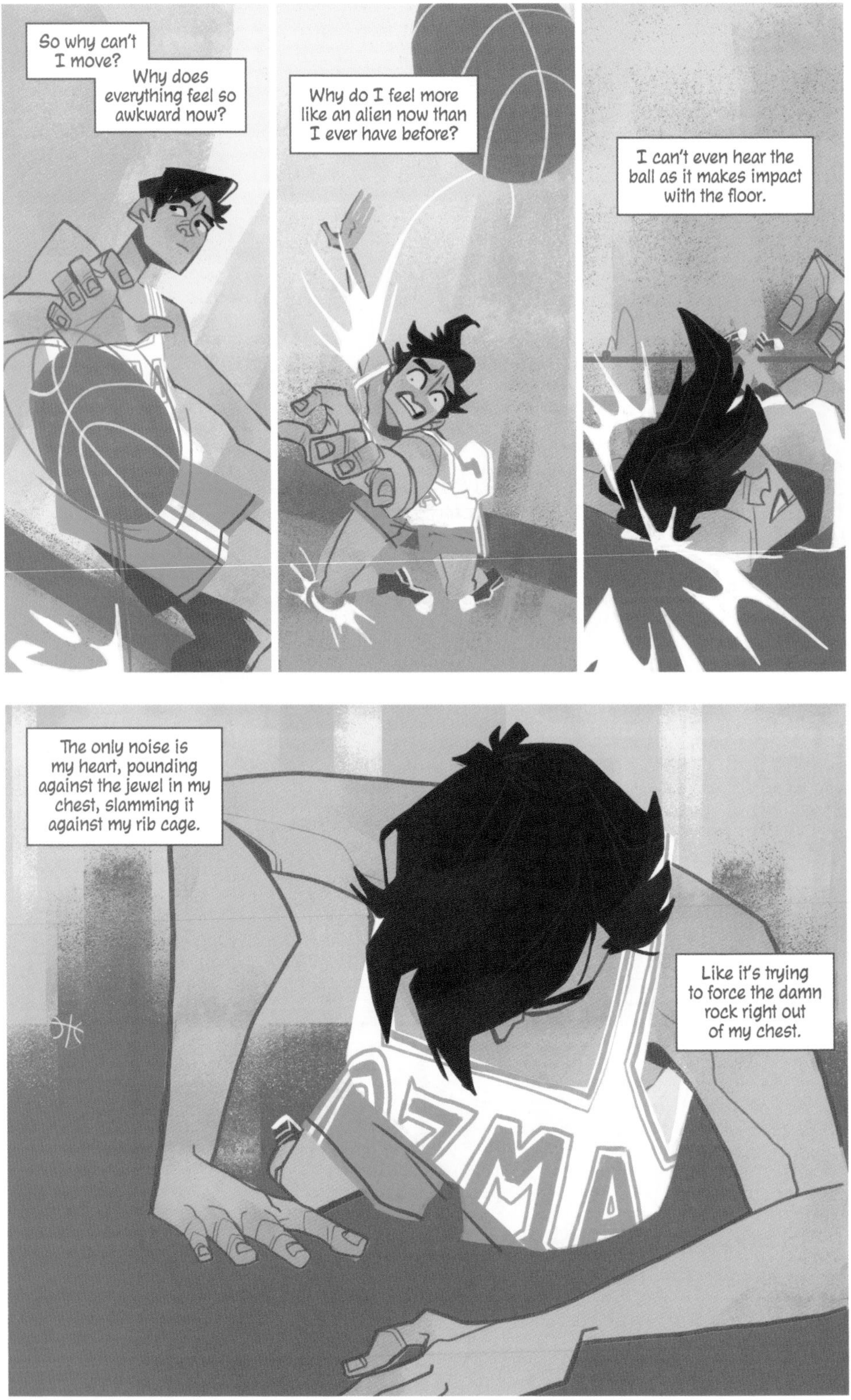
So why can't I move?
Why does everything feel so awkward now?
Why do I feel more like an alien now than I ever have before?
I can't even hear the ball as it makes impact with the floor.
The only noise is my heart, pounding against the jewel in my chest, slamming it against my rib cage.
Like it's trying to force the damn rock right out of my chest.

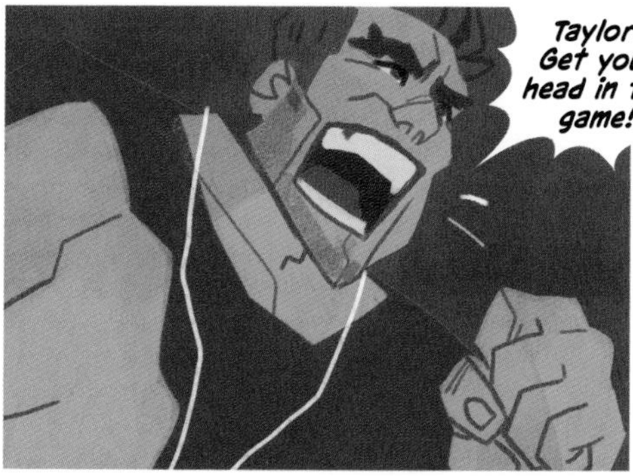
Taylor! Get your head in the game!

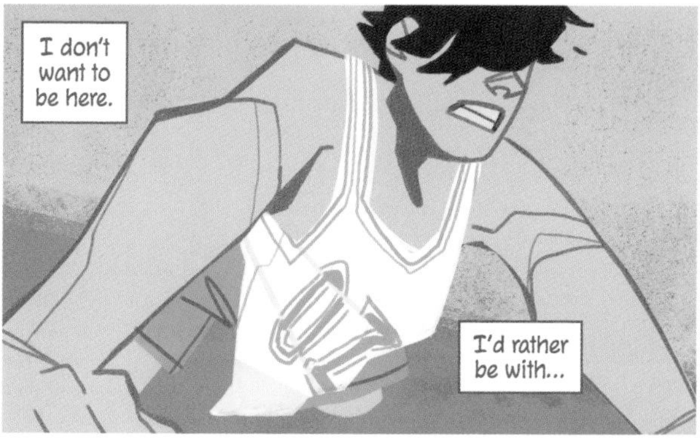
I don't want to be here.
I'd rather be with...

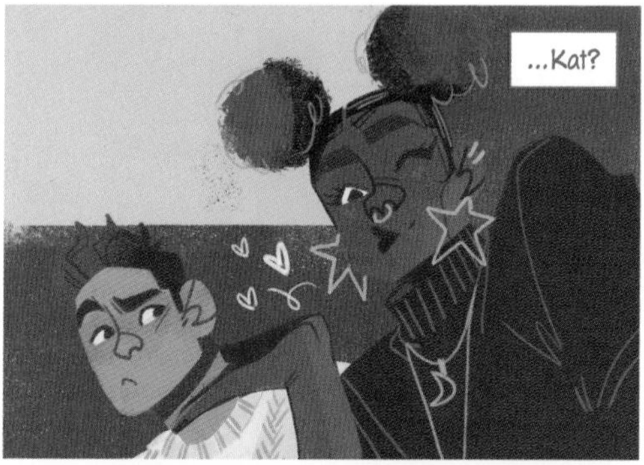
...Kat?

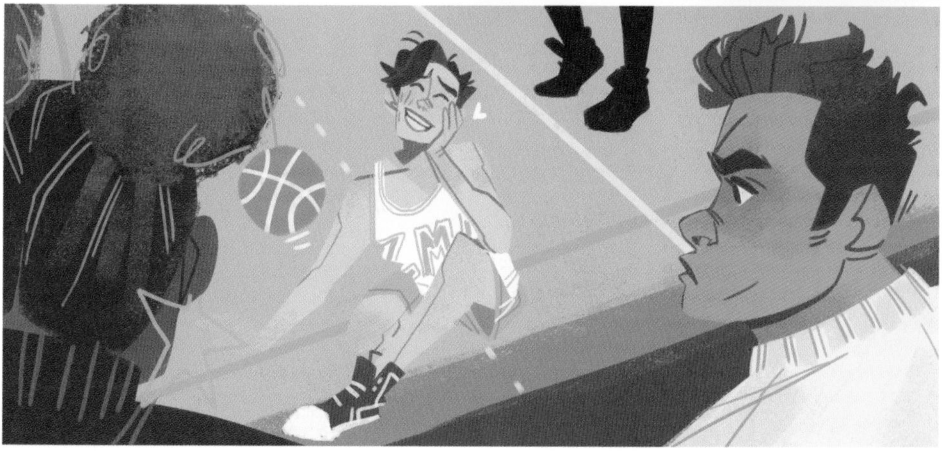

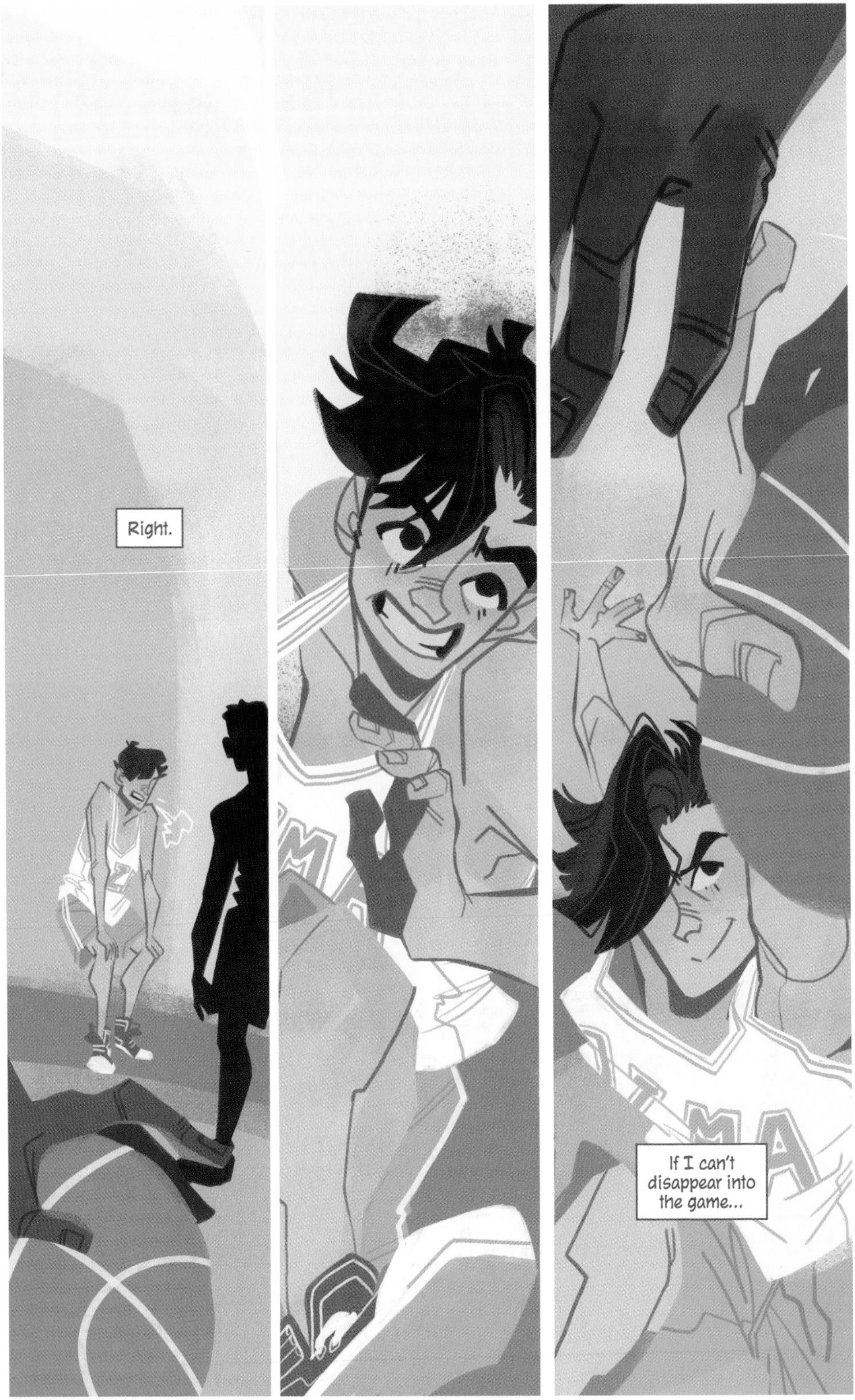
Right.
If I can't disappear into the game...

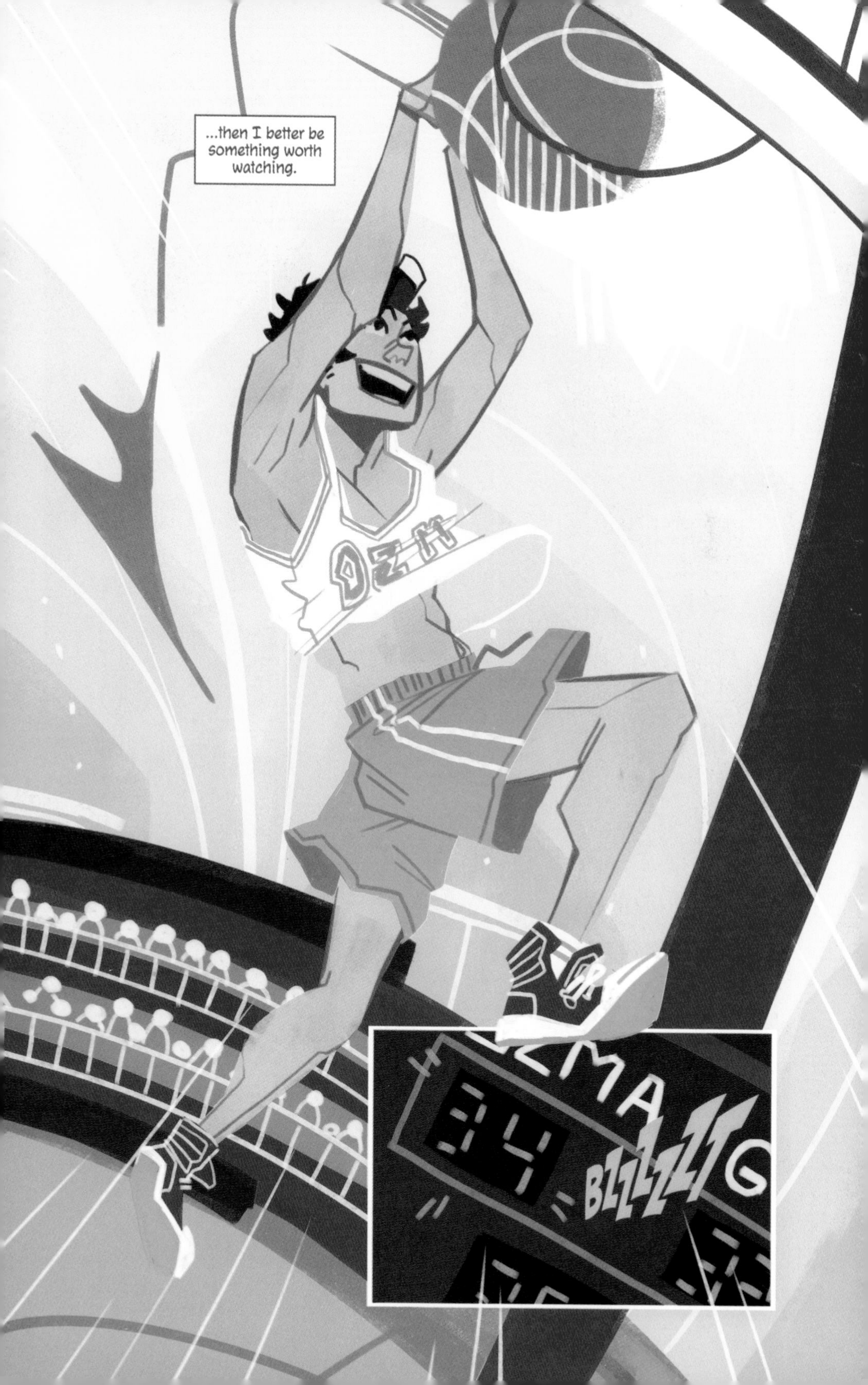
...then I better be something worth watching.
BZZZZZT

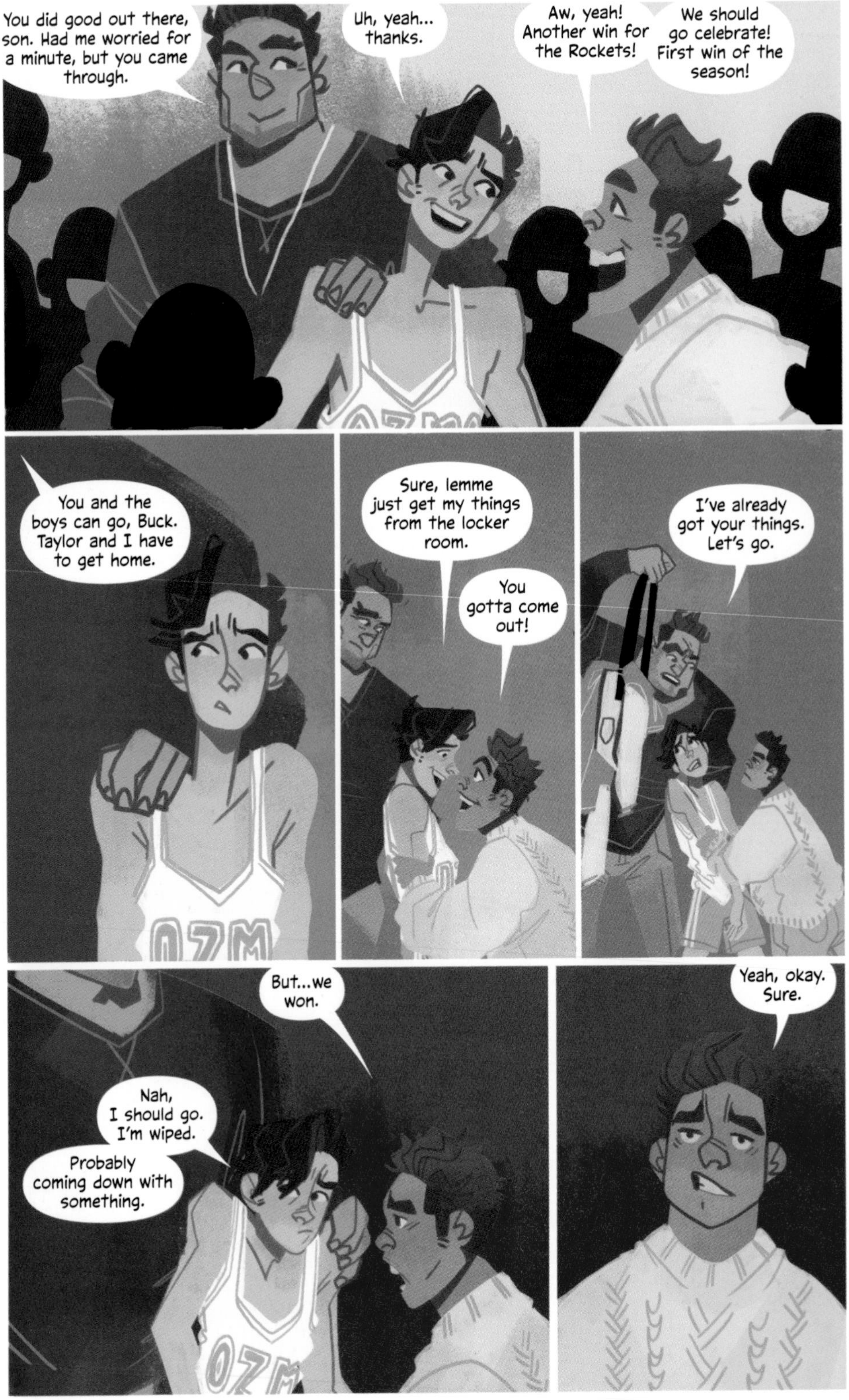
You did good out there, son. Had me worried for a minute, but you came through.
Uh, yeah... thanks.
Aw, yeah! Another win for the Rockets!
We should go celebrate! First win of the season!
You and the boys can go, Buck. Taylor and I have to get home.
Sure, lemme just get my things from the locker room.
You gotta come out!
I've already got your things. Let's go.
But...we won.
Nah, I should go. I'm wiped.
Probably coming down with something.
Yeah, okay. Sure.

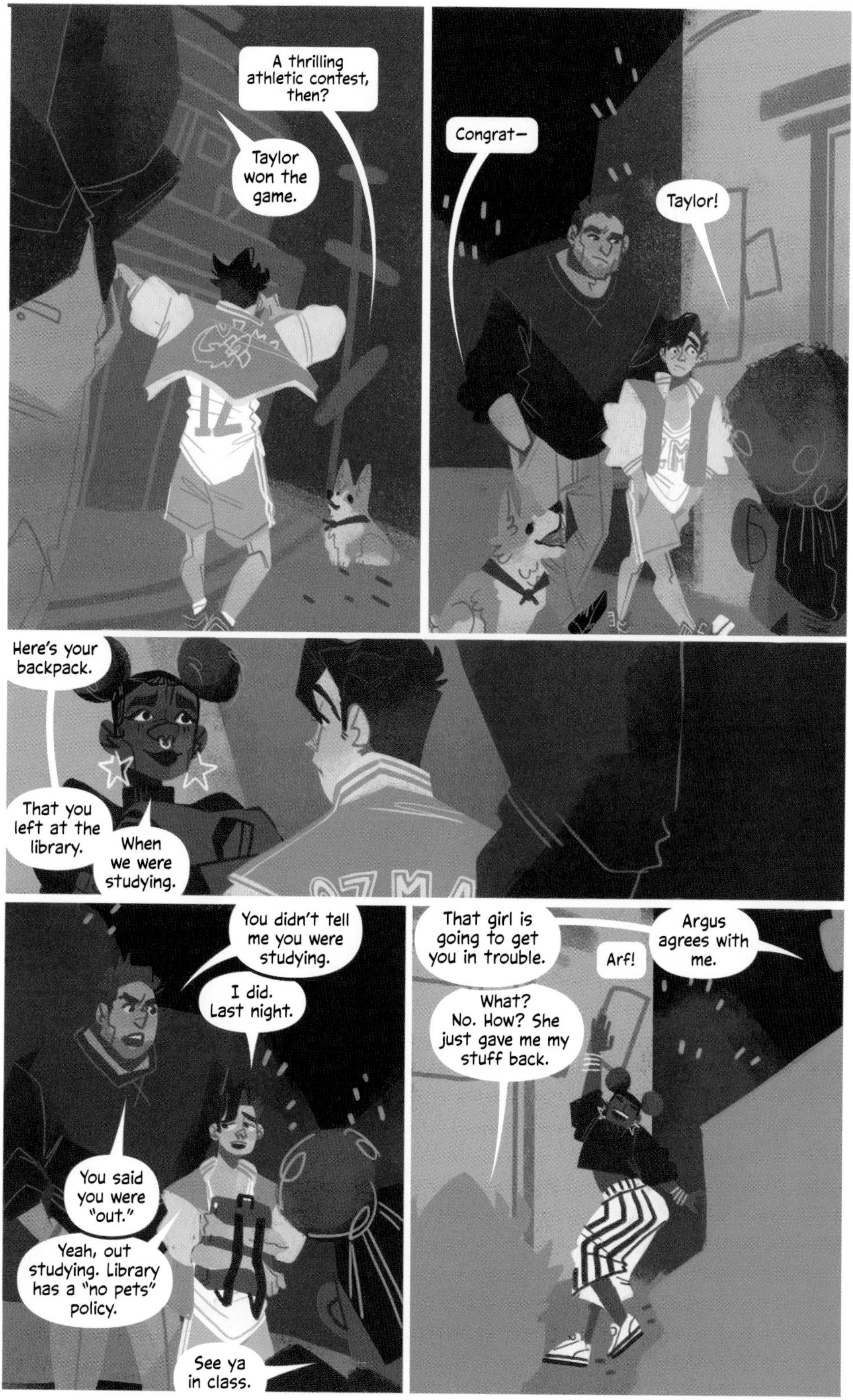
Taylor won the game.
A thrilling athletic contest, then?
Congrat—
Taylor!
Here's your backpack.
That you left at the library.
When we were studying.
You didn't tell me you were studying.
I did. Last night.
You said you were "out."
Yeah, out studying. Library has a "no pets" policy.
See ya in class.
That girl is going to get you in trouble.
Arf!
Argus agrees with me.
What? No. How? She just gave me my stuff back.

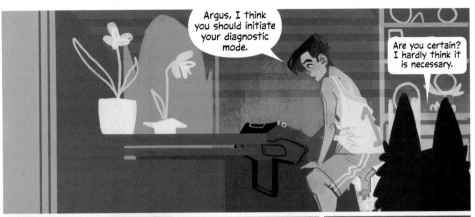

Argus, I think you should initiate your diagnostic mode.

Are you certain? I hardly think it is necessary.

You've been eating a lot of sugar recently.

I have not—

There's the birthday cake, and Sally told me about the cookies.

She offered. What was I to do?

Sally said you whined. And begged.

I won't stand for this character assassination.

I wouldn't bring it up if you hadn't spoken in front of Kat earlier. That's not like you.

It is true. I am usually far more alert to oncoming presences.

I shall run a diagnostic once you retire for the night.

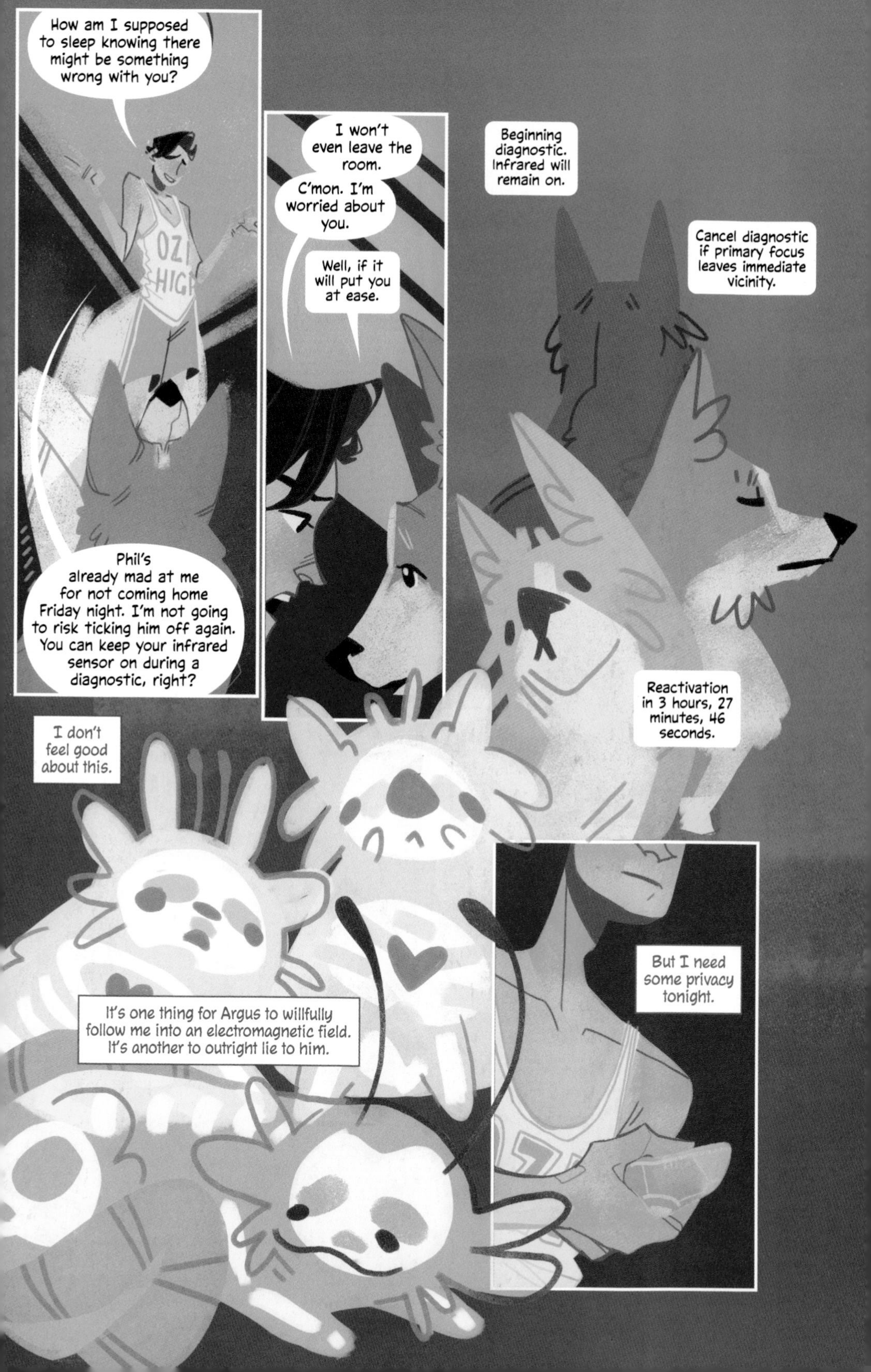
How am I supposed to sleep knowing there might be something wrong with you?
I won't even leave the room.
C'mon. I'm worried about you.
Well, if it will put you at ease.
Phil's already mad at me for not coming home Friday night. I'm not going to risk ticking him off again. You can keep your infrared sensor on during a diagnostic, right?
Beginning diagnostic. Infrared will remain on.
Cancel diagnostic if primary focus leaves immediate vicinity.
Reactivation in 3 hours, 27 minutes, 46 seconds.
I don't feel good about this.
It's one thing for Argus to willfully follow me into an electromagnetic field. It's another to outright lie to him.
But I need some privacy tonight.

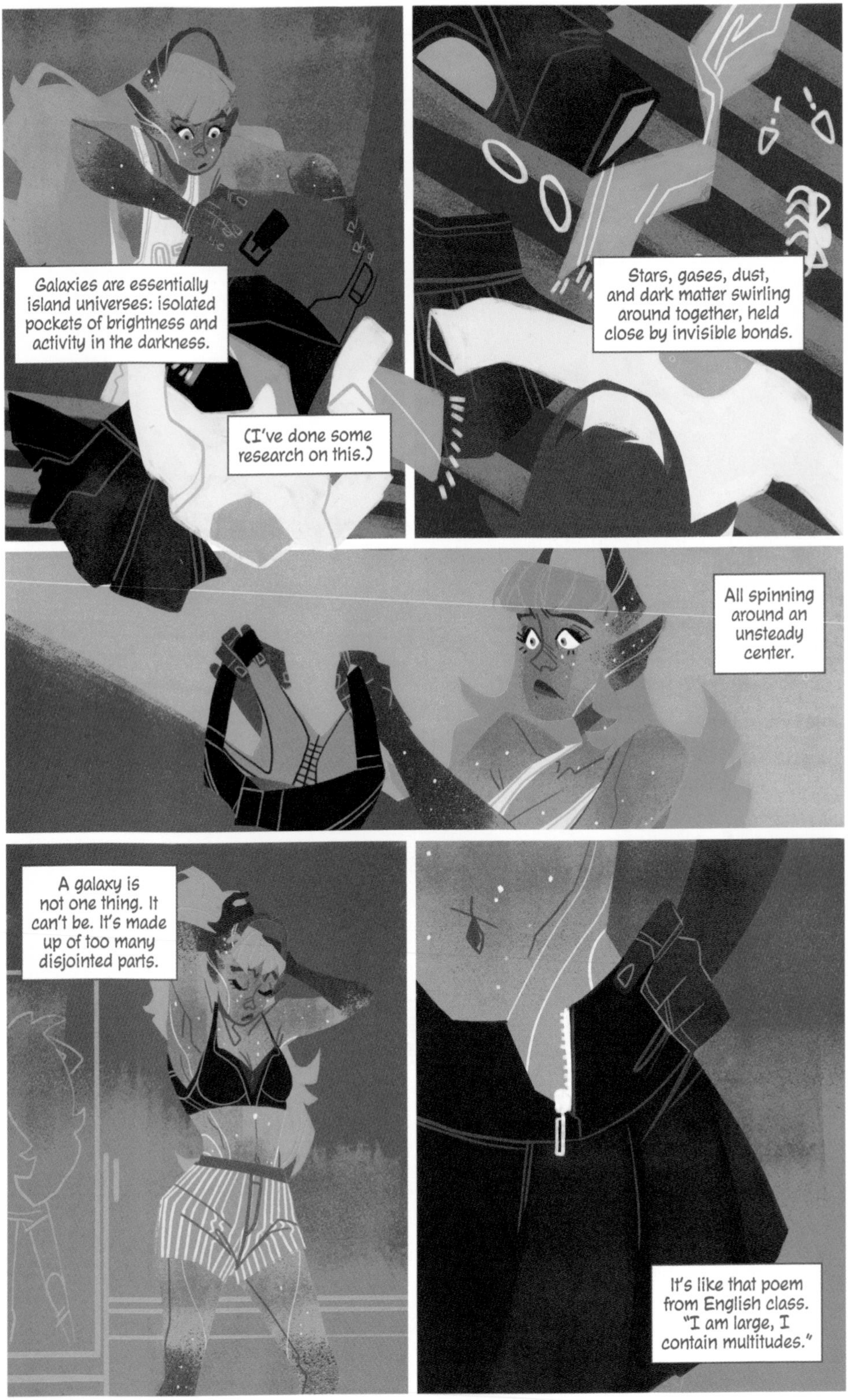
Galaxies are essentially island universes: isolated pockets of brightness and activity in the darkness.
(I've done some research on this.)
Stars, gases, dust, and dark matter swirling around together, held close by invisible bonds.
All spinning around an unsteady center.
A galaxy is not one thing. It can't be. It's made up of too many disjointed parts.
It's like that poem from English class. "I am large, I contain multitudes."

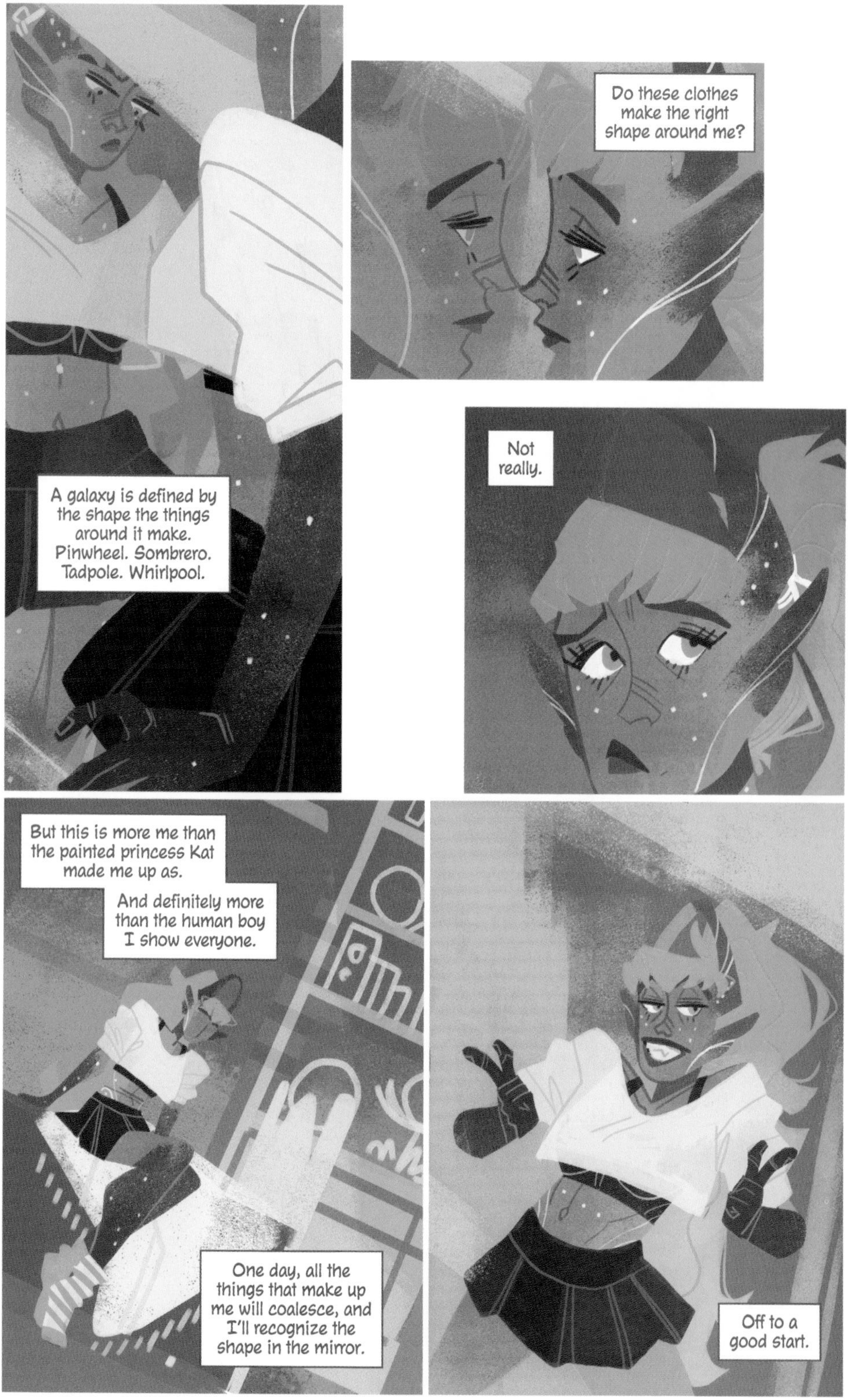
Do these clothes make the right shape around me?
A galaxy is defined by the shape the things around it make. Pinwheel. Sombrero. Tadpole. Whirlpool.
Not really.
But this is more me than the painted princess Kat made me up as.
And definitely more than the human boy I show everyone.
One day, all the things that make up me will coalesce, and I'll recognize the shape in the mirror.
Off to a good start.

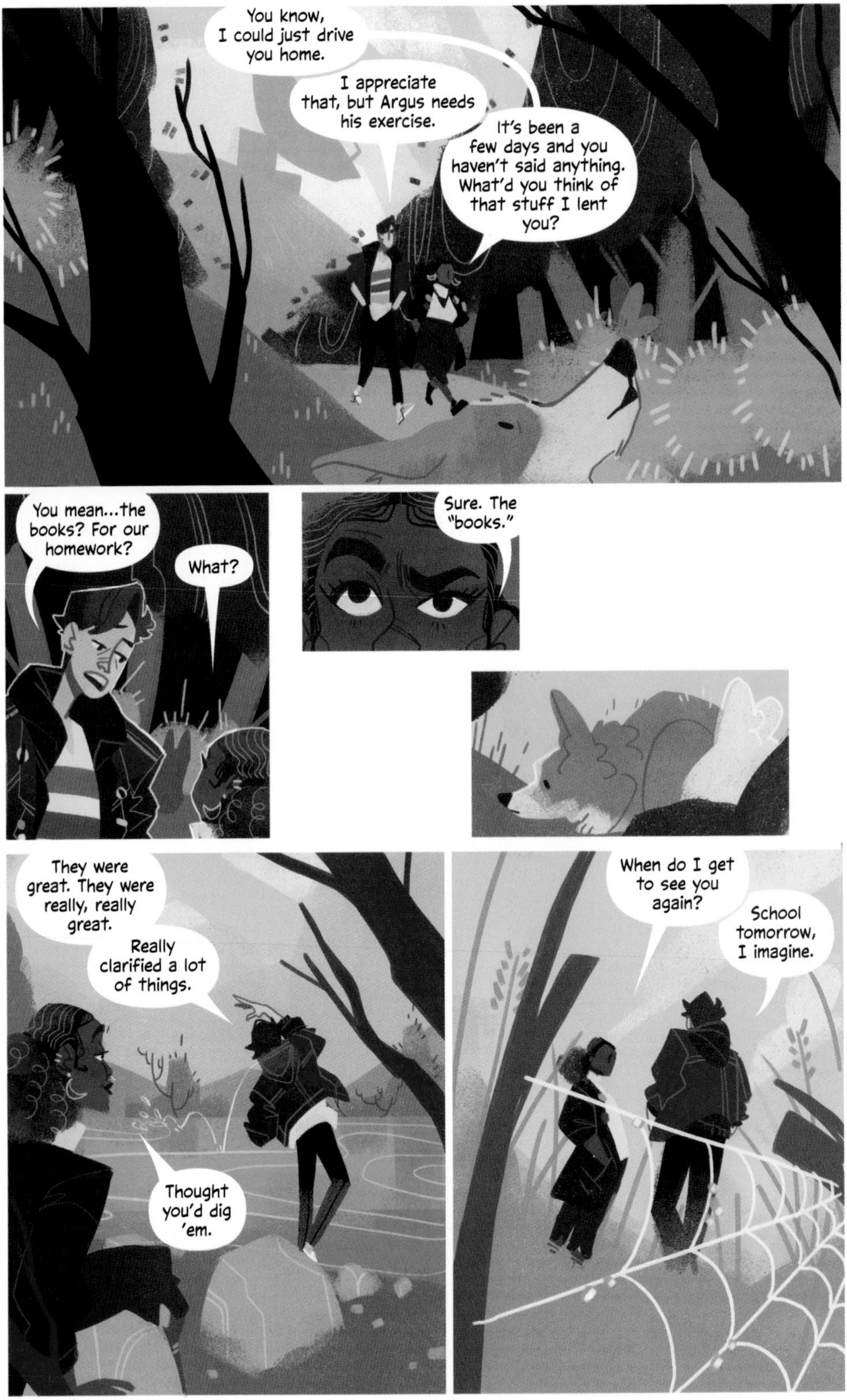
You know, I could just drive you home.
I appreciate that, but Argus needs his exercise.
It's been a few days and you haven't said anything. What'd you think of that stuff I lent you?
You mean...the books? For our homework?
What?
Sure. The "books."
They were great. They were really, really great.
Really clarified a lot of things.
Thought you'd dig 'em.
When do I get to see you again?
School tomorrow, I imagine.

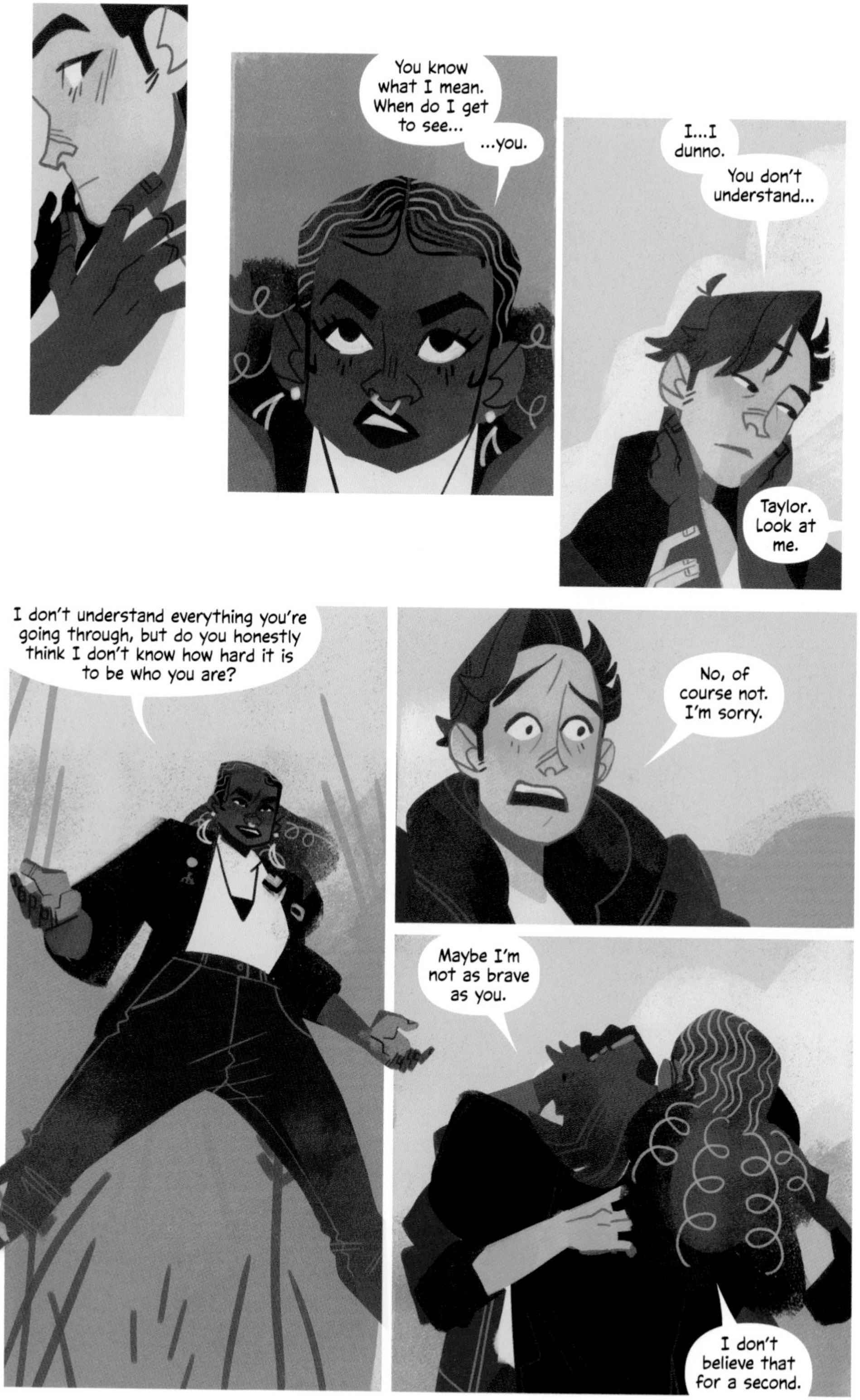
You know what I mean. When do I get to see...
...you.
I...I dunno.
You don't understand...
Taylor. Look at me.
I don't understand everything you're going through, but do you honestly think I don't know how hard it is to be who you are?
No, of course not. I'm sorry.
Maybe I'm not as brave as you.
I don't believe that for a second.

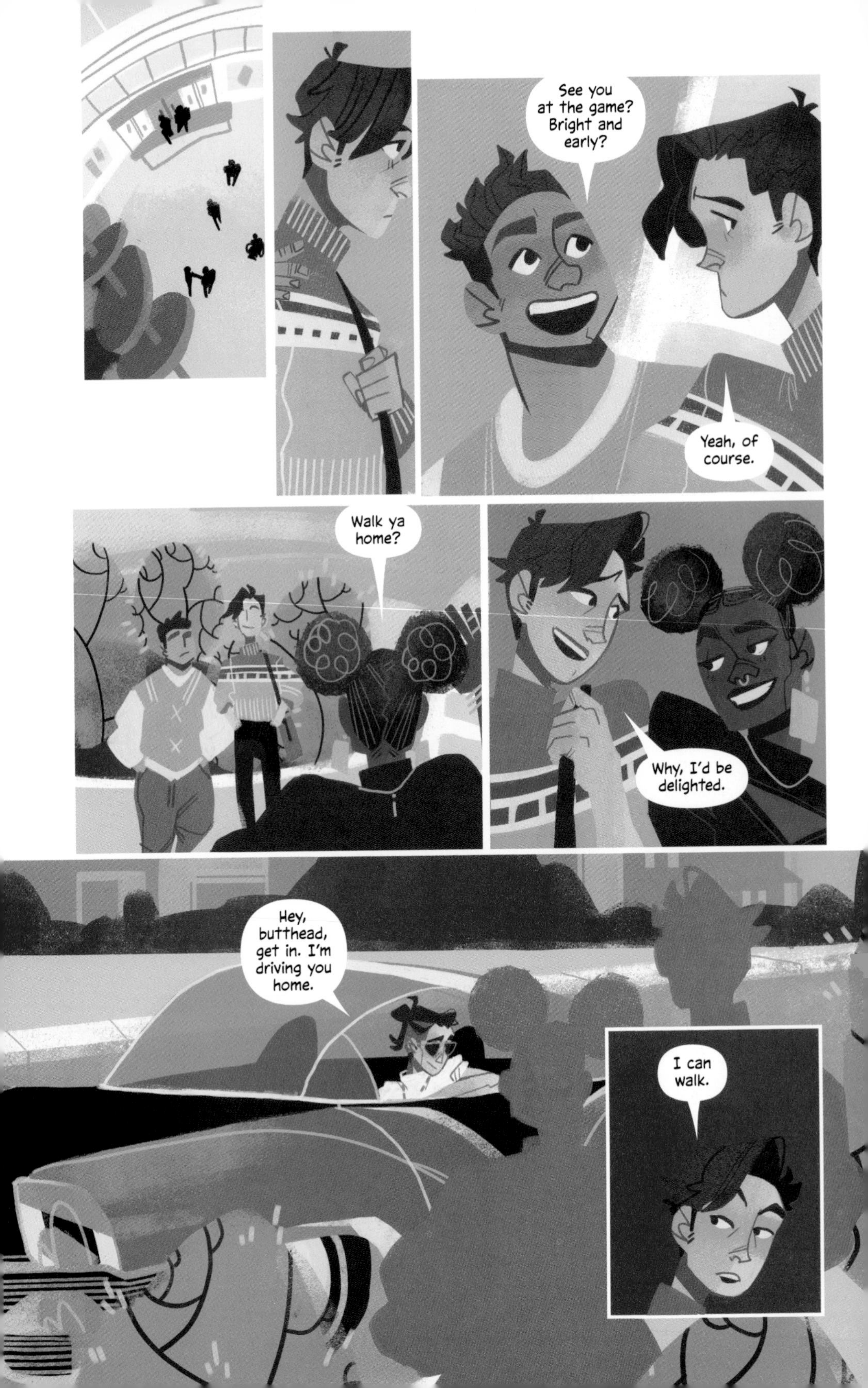
See you at the game? Bright and early?
Yeah, of course.
Walk ya home?
Why, I'd be delighted.
Hey, butthead, get in. I'm driving you home.
I can walk.

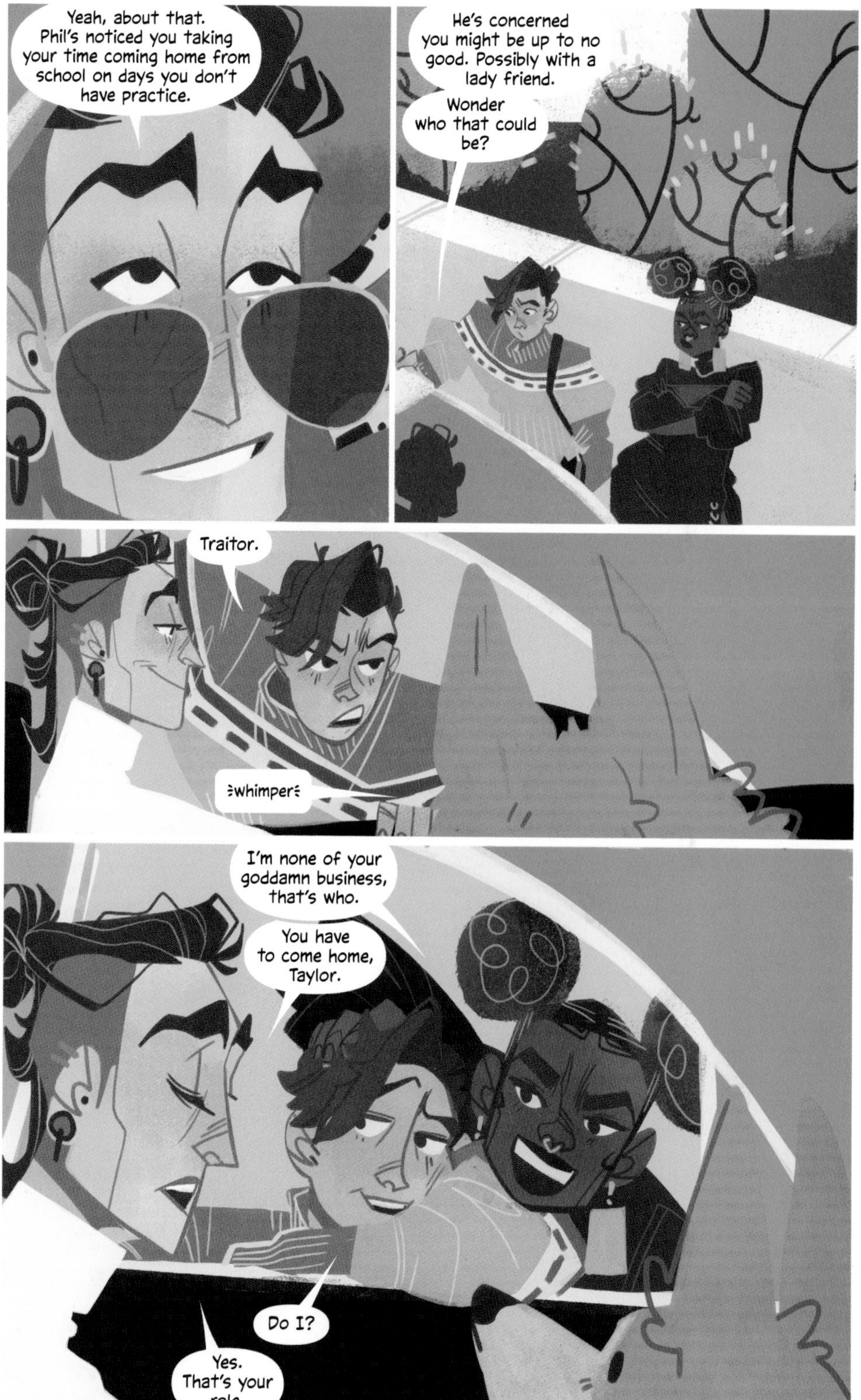
Yeah, about that. Phil's noticed you taking your time coming home from school on days you don't have practice.
He's concerned you might be up to no good. Possibly with a lady friend.
Wonder who that could be?
Traitor.
whimper
I'm none of your goddamn business, that's who.
You have to come home, Taylor.
Do I?
Yes. That's your role.

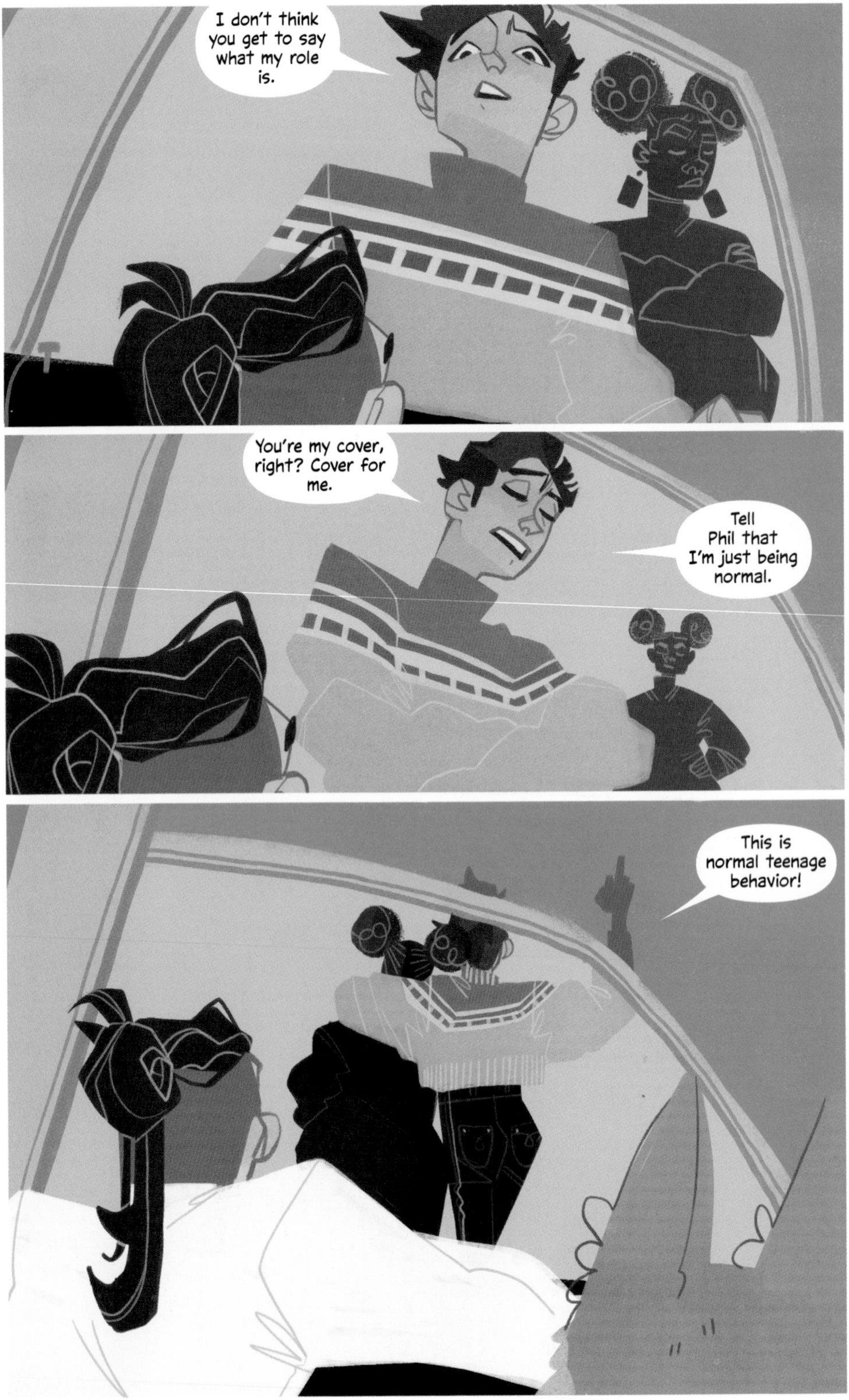
I don't think you get to say what my role is.
You're my cover, right? Cover for me.
Tell Phil that I'm just being normal.
This is normal teenage behavior!

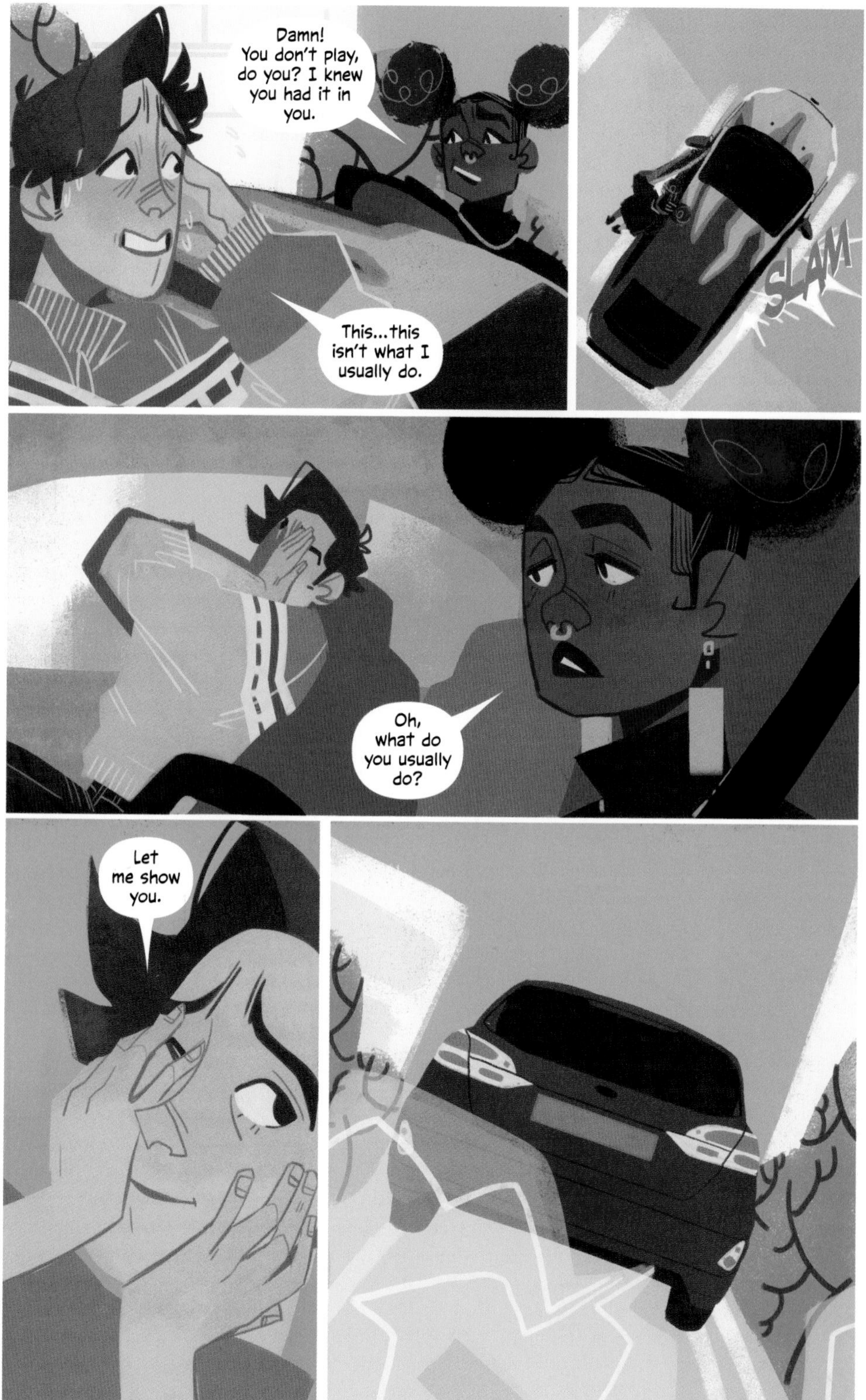
Damn! You don't play, do you? I knew you had it in you.
This...this isn't what I usually do.
SLAM
Oh, what do you usually do?
Let me show you.

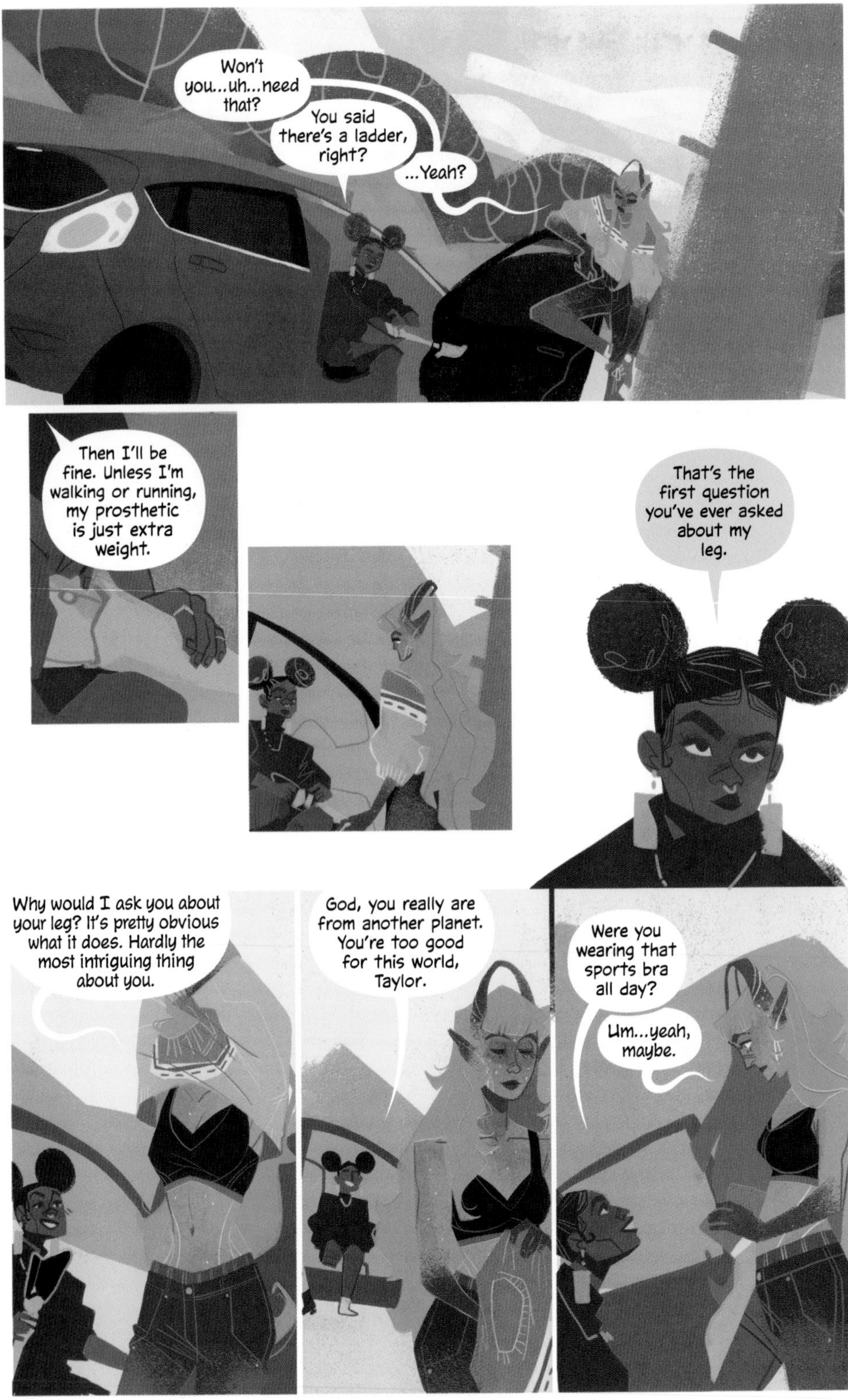
Won't you...uh...need that?
You said there's a ladder, right?
...Yeah?
Then I'll be fine. Unless I'm walking or running, my prosthetic is just extra weight.
That's the first question you've ever asked about my leg.
Why would I ask you about your leg? It's pretty obvious what it does. Hardly the most intriguing thing about you.
God, you really are from another planet. You're too good for this world, Taylor.
Were you wearing that sports bra all day?
Um...yeah, maybe.

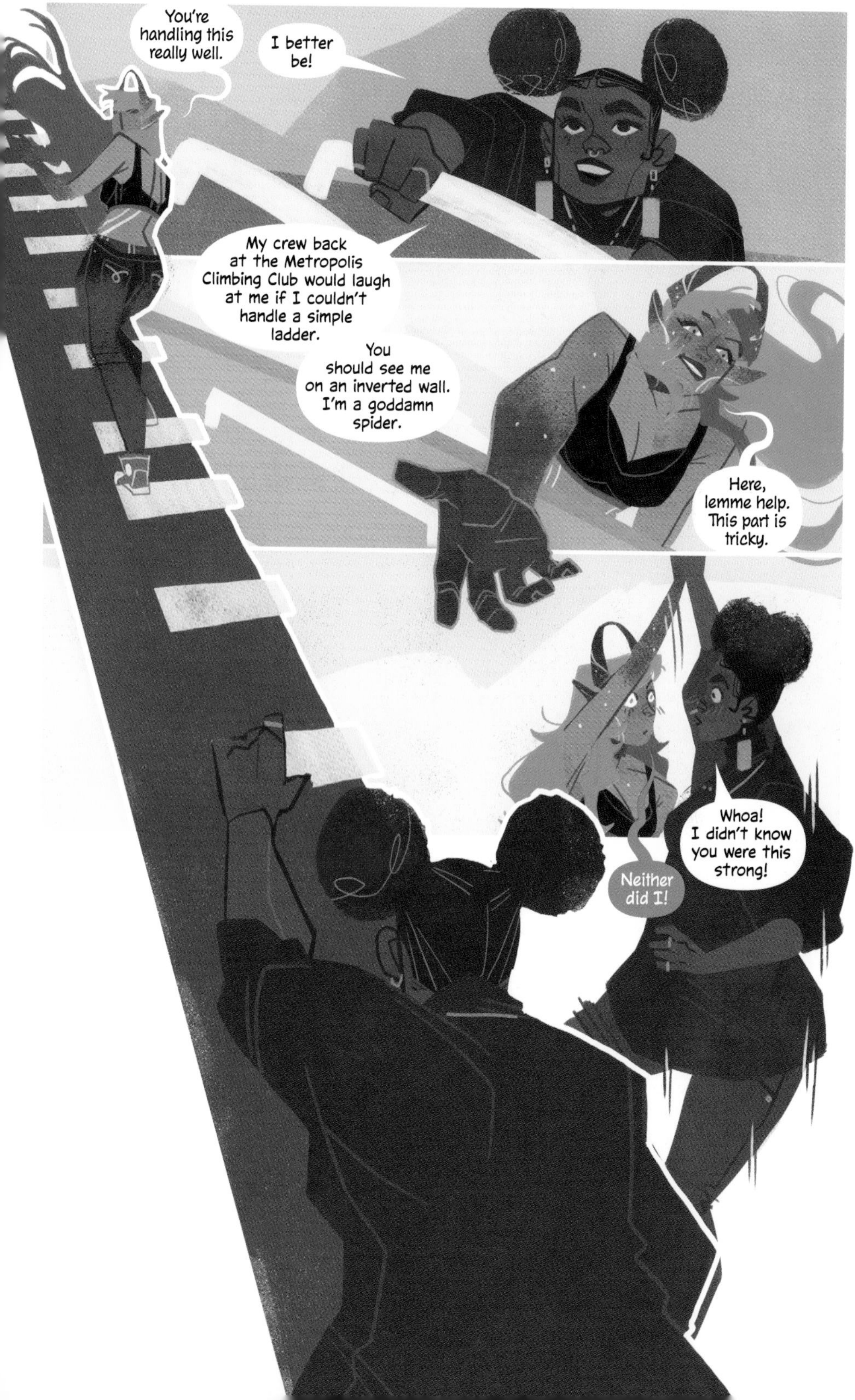
You're handling this really well.
I better be!
My crew back at the Metropolis Climbing Club would laugh at me if I couldn't handle a simple ladder.
You should see me on an inverted wall. I'm a goddamn spider.
Here, lemme help. This part is tricky.
Whoa! I didn't know you were this strong!
Neither did I!

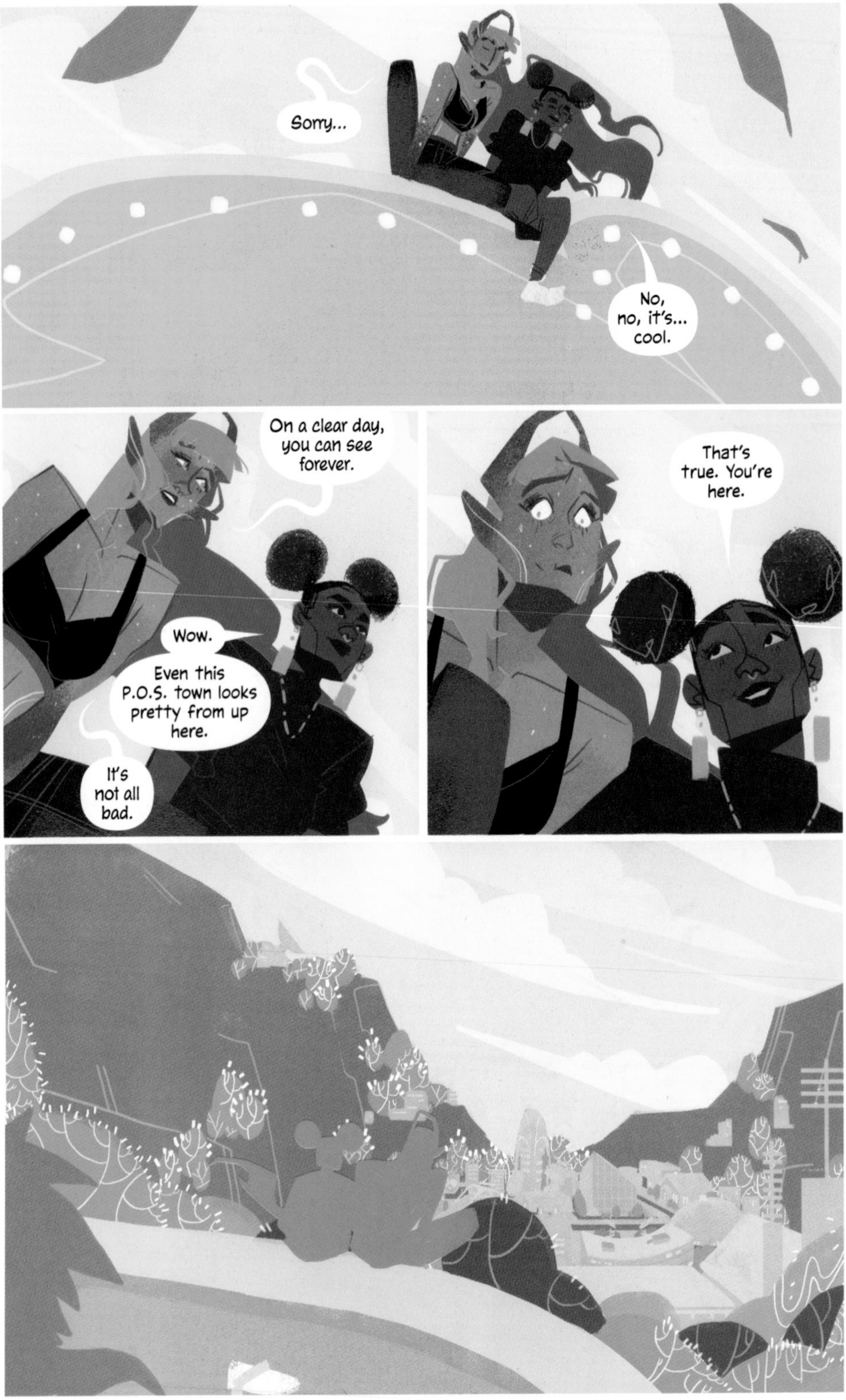
Sorry...
No, no, it's... cool.
On a clear day, you can see forever.
Wow.
Even this P.O.S. town looks pretty from up here.
It's not all bad.
That's true. You're here.

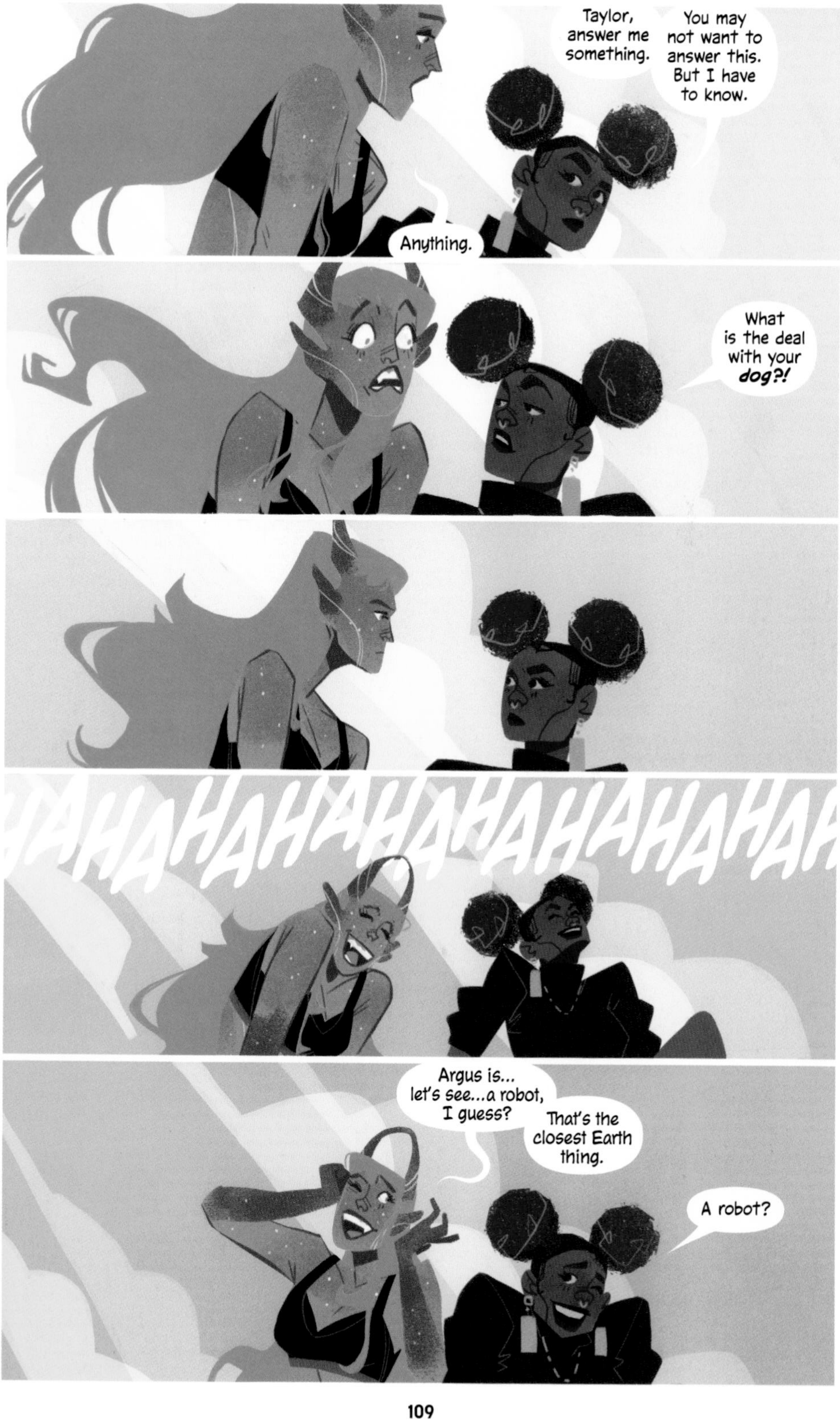
Taylor, answer me something.
You may not want to answer this. But I have to know.
Anything.
What is the deal with your *dog?!*
HAHAHAHAHAHAHAHAHAHAHAHA
Argus is... let's see...a robot, I guess?
That's the closest Earth thing.
A robot?

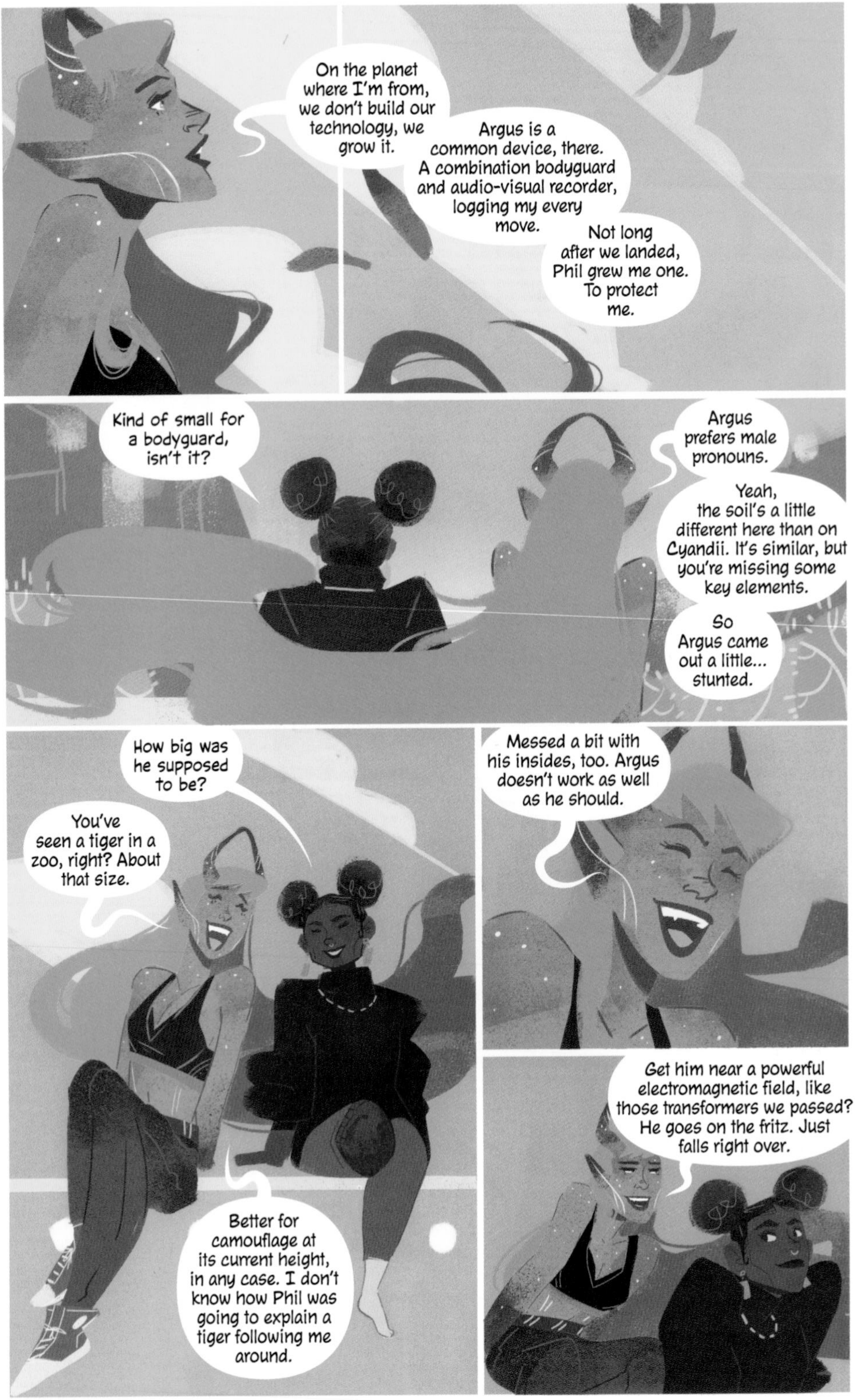
On the planet where I'm from, we don't build our technology, we grow it.
Argus is a common device, there. A combination bodyguard and audio-visual recorder, logging my every move.
Not long after we landed, Phil grew me one. To protect me.
Kind of small for a bodyguard, isn't it?
Argus prefers male pronouns.
Yeah, the soil's a little different here than on Cyandii. It's similar, but you're missing some key elements.
So Argus came out a little... stunted.
How big was he supposed to be?
You've seen a tiger in a zoo, right? About that size.
Better for camouflage at its current height, in any case. I don't know how Phil was going to explain a tiger following me around.
Messed a bit with his insides, too. Argus doesn't work as well as he should.
Get him near a powerful electromagnetic field, like those transformers we passed? He goes on the fritz. Just falls right over.

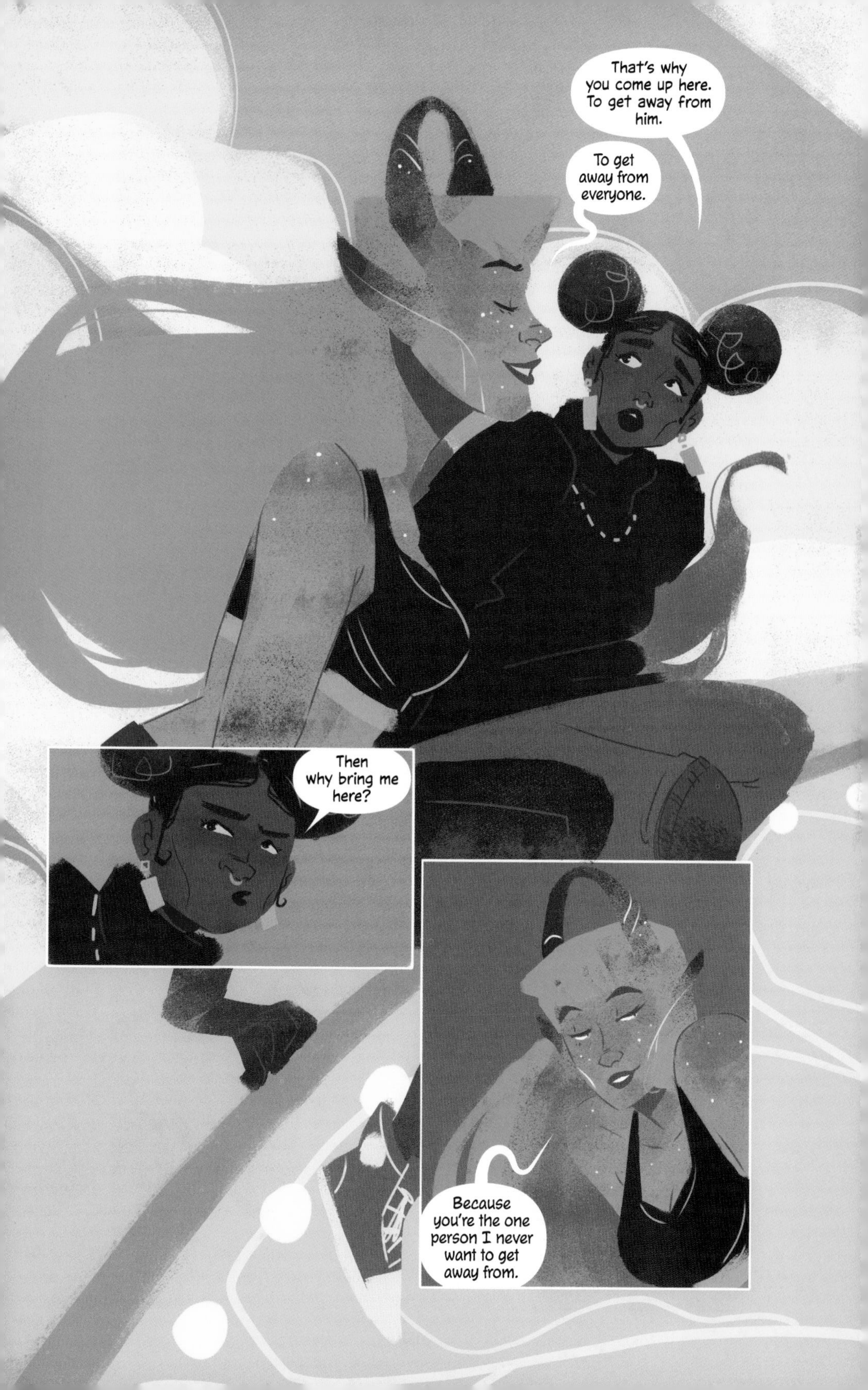
That's why you come up here. To get away from him.
To get away from everyone.
Then why bring me here?
Because you're the one person I never want to get away from.

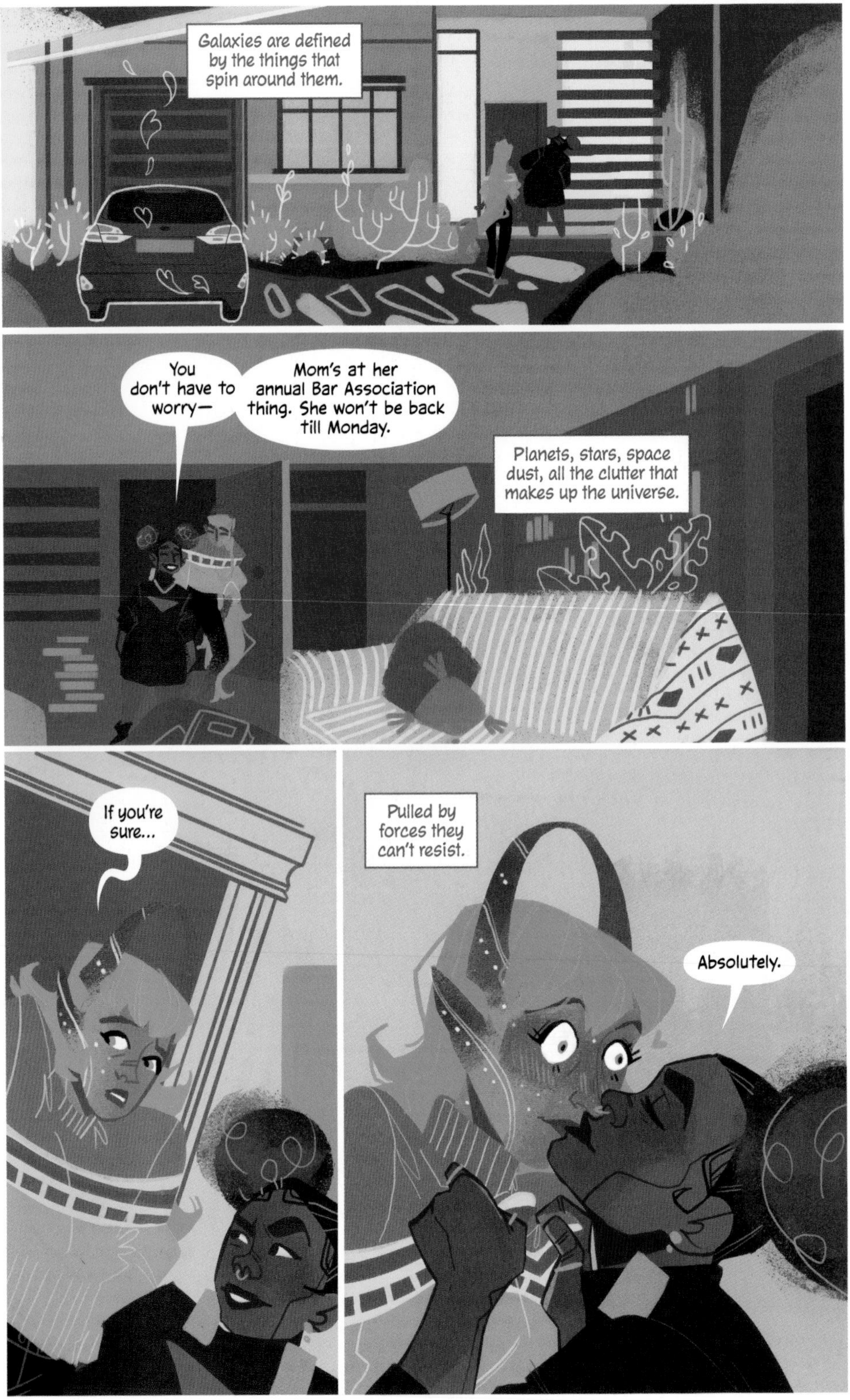
Galaxies are defined by the things that spin around them.
You don't have to worry—
Mom's at her annual Bar Association thing. She won't be back till Monday.
Planets, stars, space dust, all the clutter that makes up the universe.
If you're sure...
Pulled by forces they can't resist.
Absolutely.

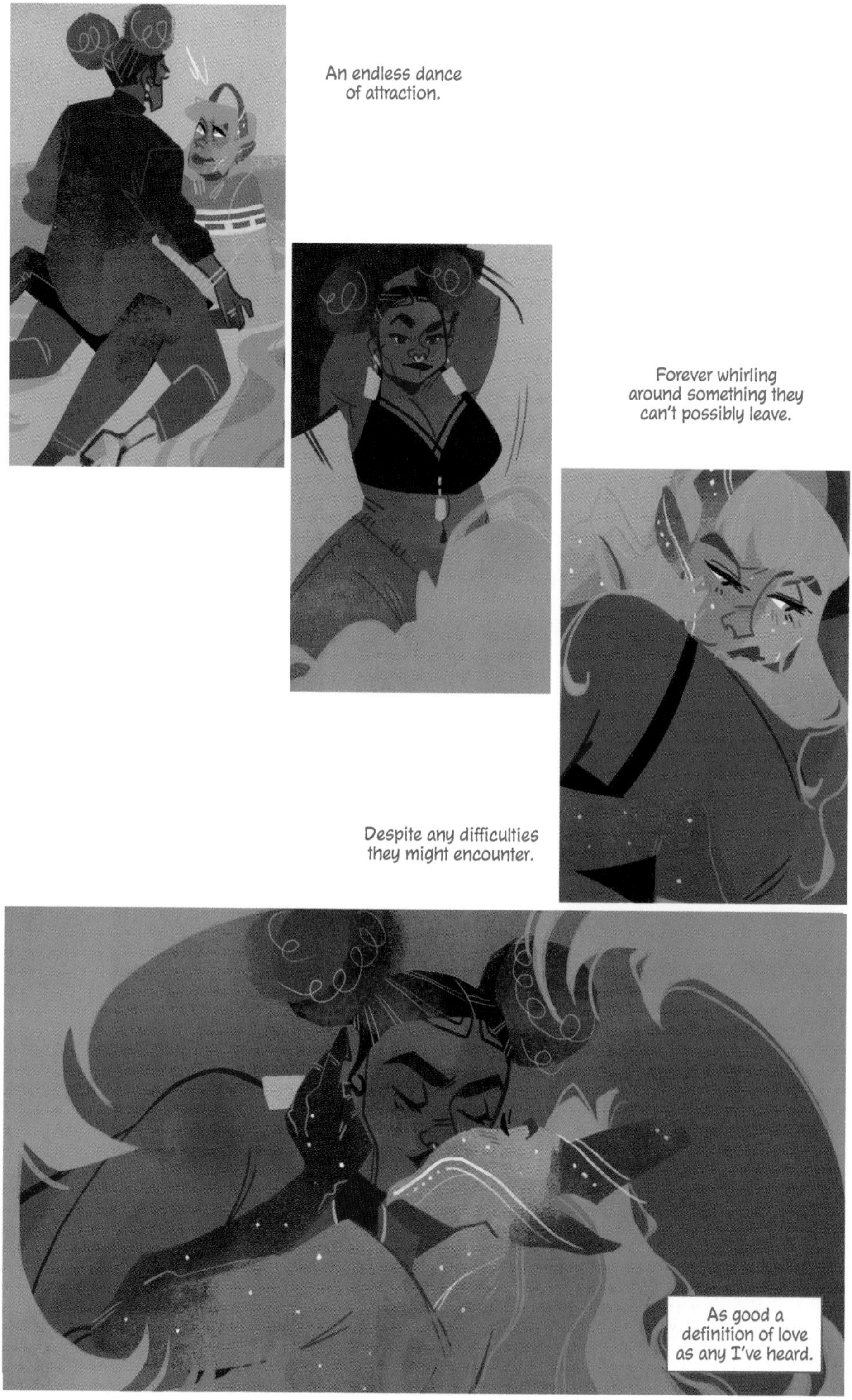
An endless dance of attraction.
Forever whirling around something they can't possibly leave.
Despite any difficulties they might encounter.
As good a definition of love as any I've heard.

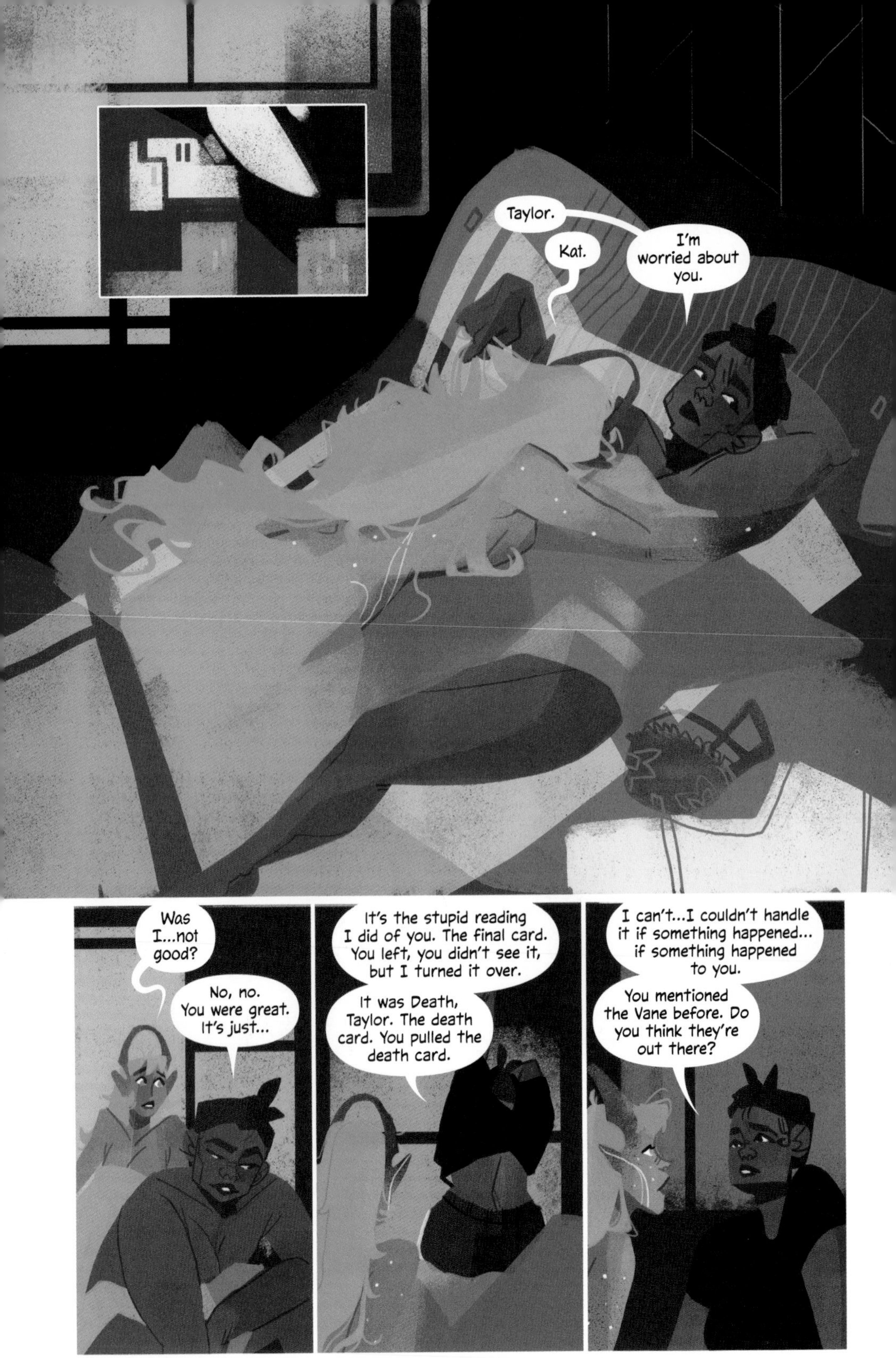
Taylor.
Kat.
I'm worried about you.
Was I...not good?
No, no. You were great. It's just...
It's the stupid reading I did of you. The final card. You left, you didn't see it, but I turned it over.
It was Death, Taylor. The death card. You pulled the death card.
I can't...I couldn't handle it if something happened... if something happened to you.
You mentioned the Vane before. Do you think they're out there?

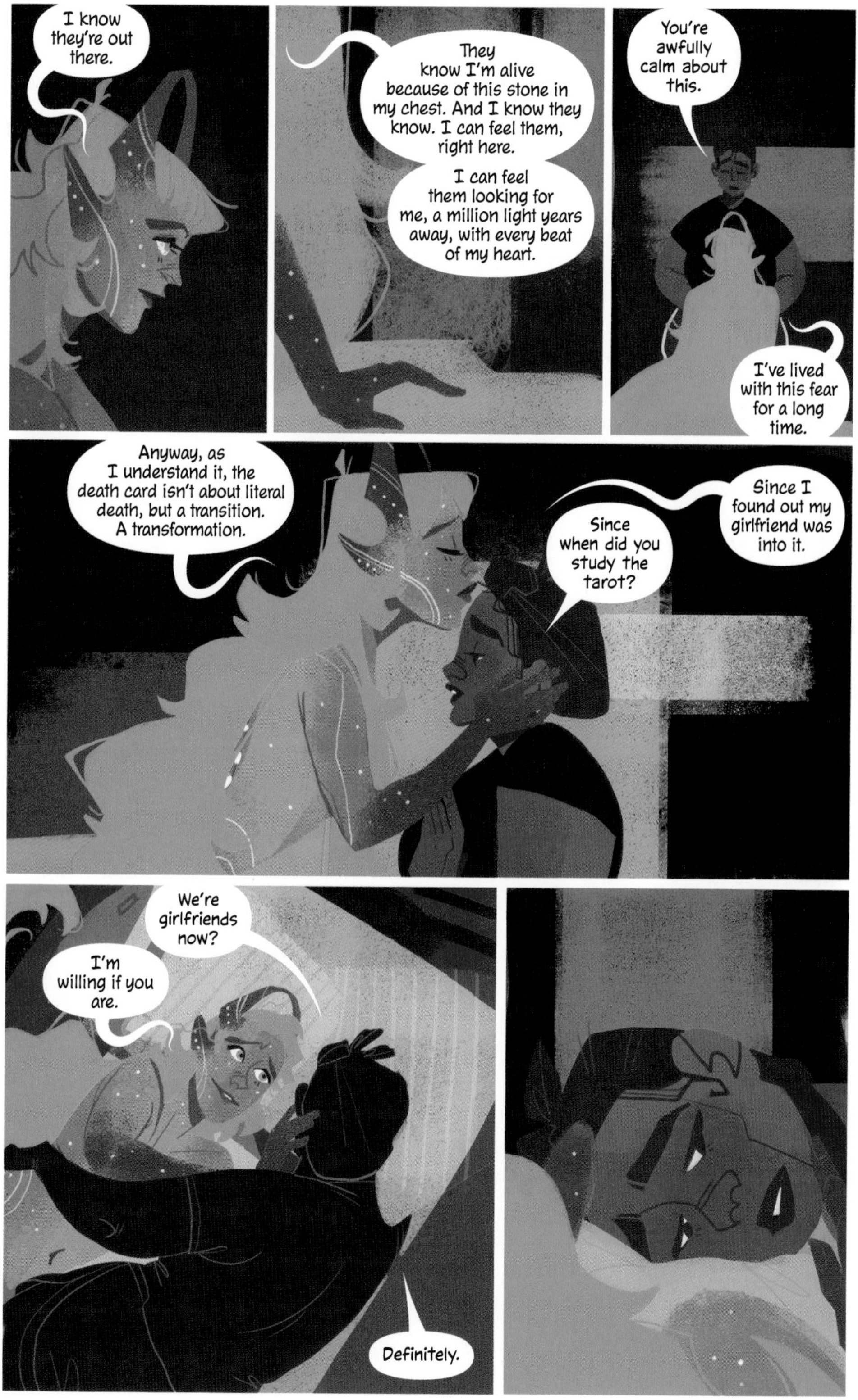
I know they're out there.
They know I'm alive because of this stone in my chest. And I know they know. I can feel them, right here.
I can feel them looking for me, a million light years away, with every beat of my heart.
You're awfully calm about this.
I've lived with this fear for a long time.
Anyway, as I understand it, the death card isn't about literal death, but a transition. A transformation.
Since when did you study the tarot?
Since I found out my girlfriend was into it.
We're girlfriends now?
I'm willing if you are.
Definitely.

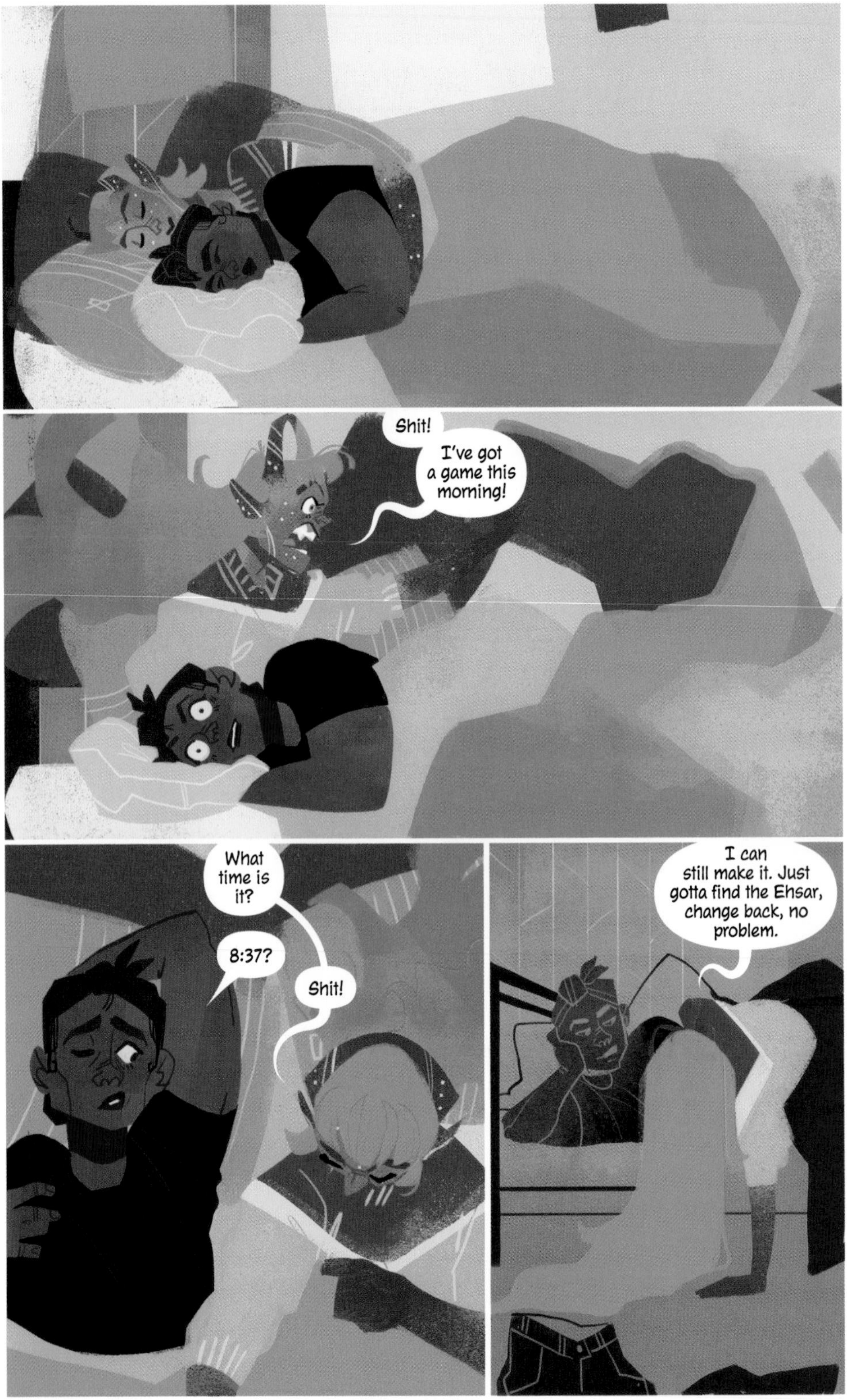
Shit!
I've got a game this morning!
What time is it?
8:37?
Shit!
I can still make it. Just gotta find the Ehsar, change back, no problem.

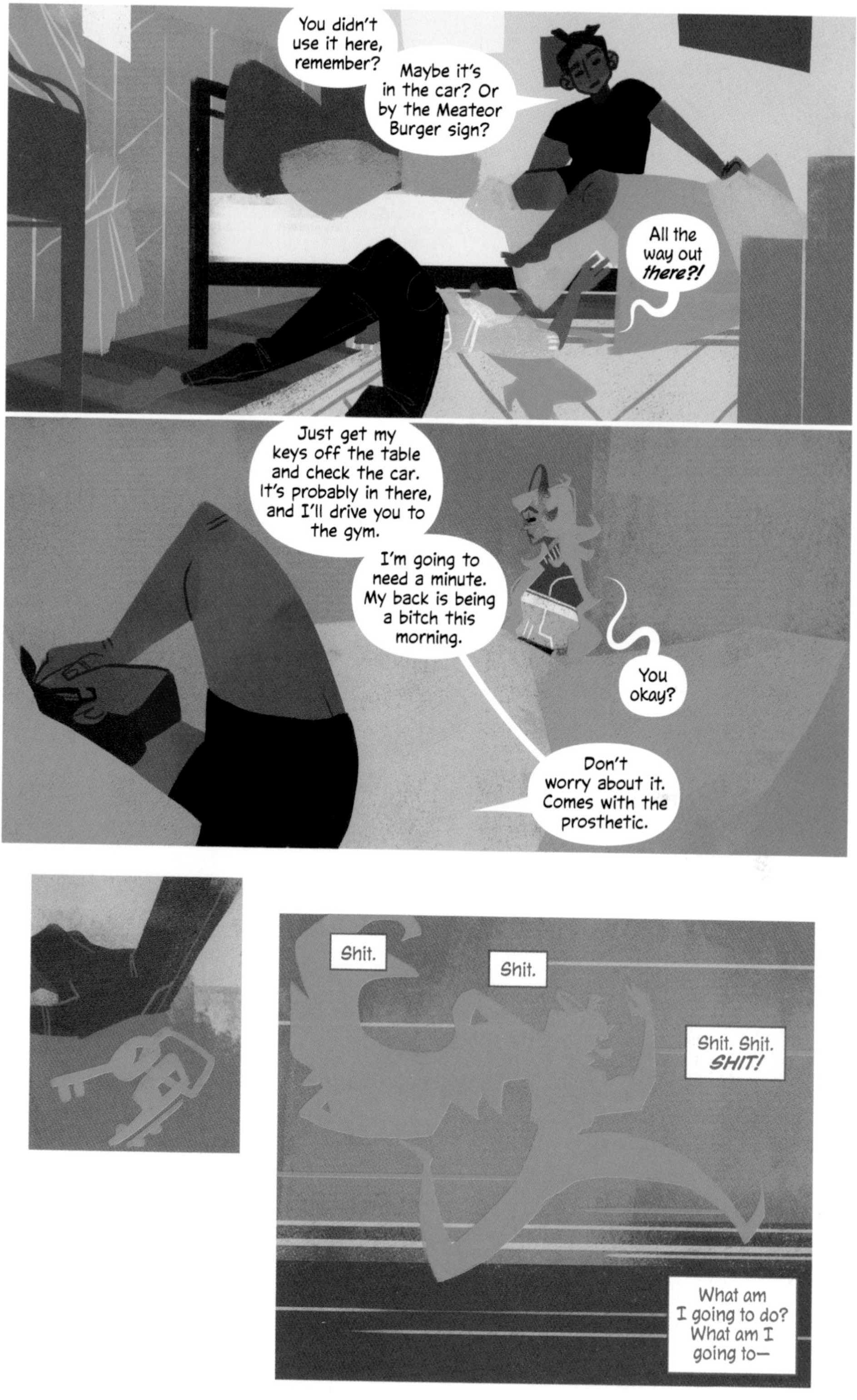
You didn't use it here, remember?
Maybe it's in the car? Or by the Meateor Burger sign?
All the way out *there?!*
Just get my keys off the table and check the car. It's probably in there, and I'll drive you to the gym.
I'm going to need a minute. My back is being a bitch this morning.
You okay?
Don't worry about it. Comes with the prosthetic.
Shit.
Shit.
Shit. Shit. *SHIT!*
What am I going to do? What am I going to—

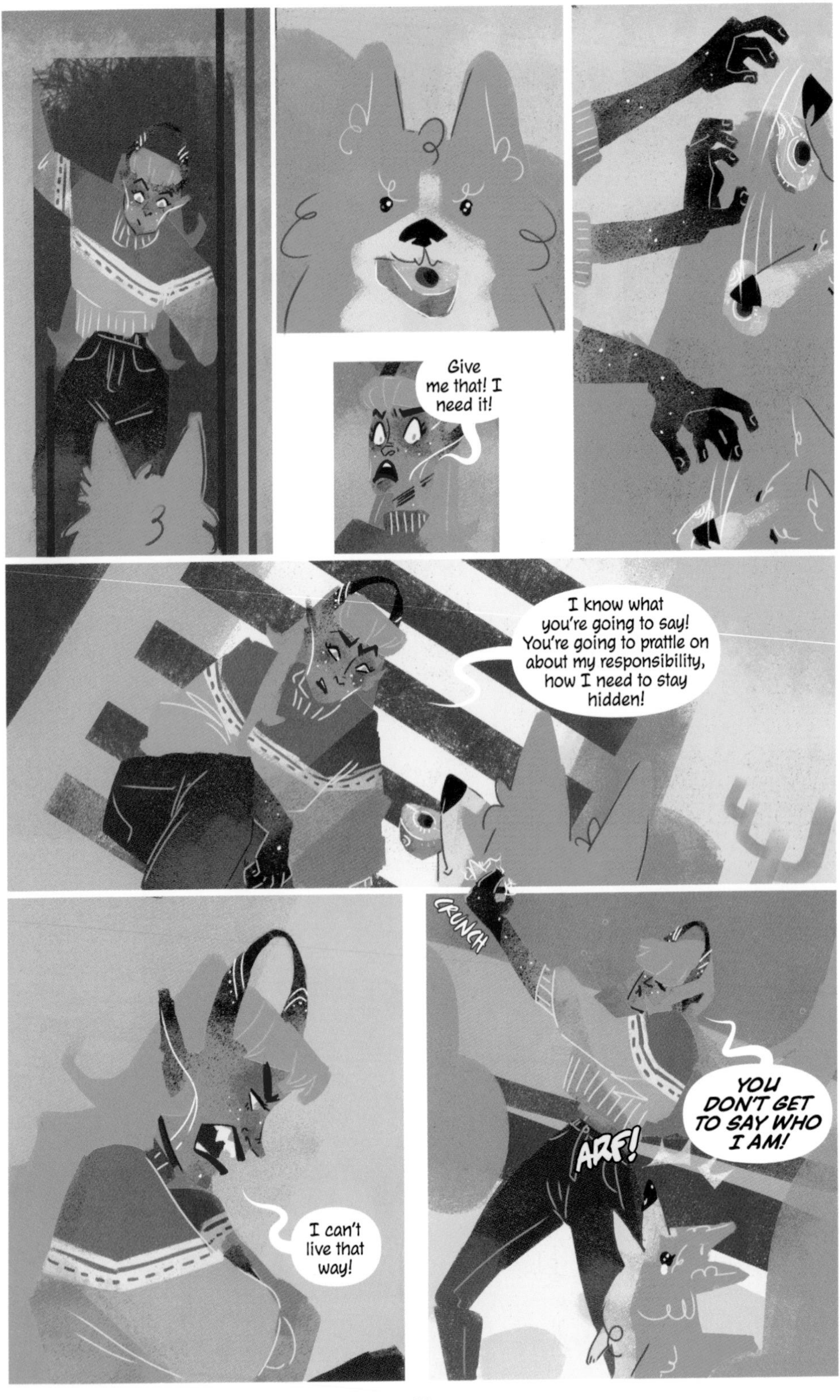
Give me that! I need it!
I know what you're going to say! You're going to prattle on about my responsibility, how I need to stay hidden!
I can't live that way!
CRUNCH
YOU DON'T GET TO SAY WHO I AM!
ARF!

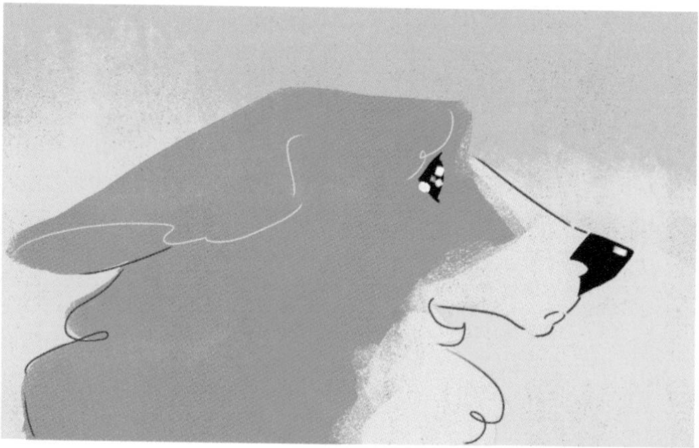

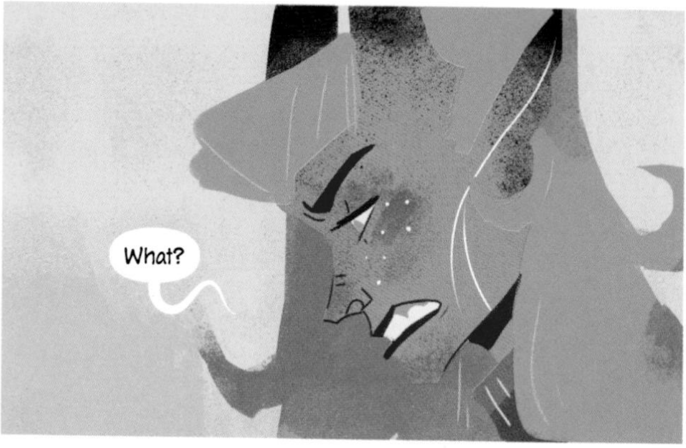
What?

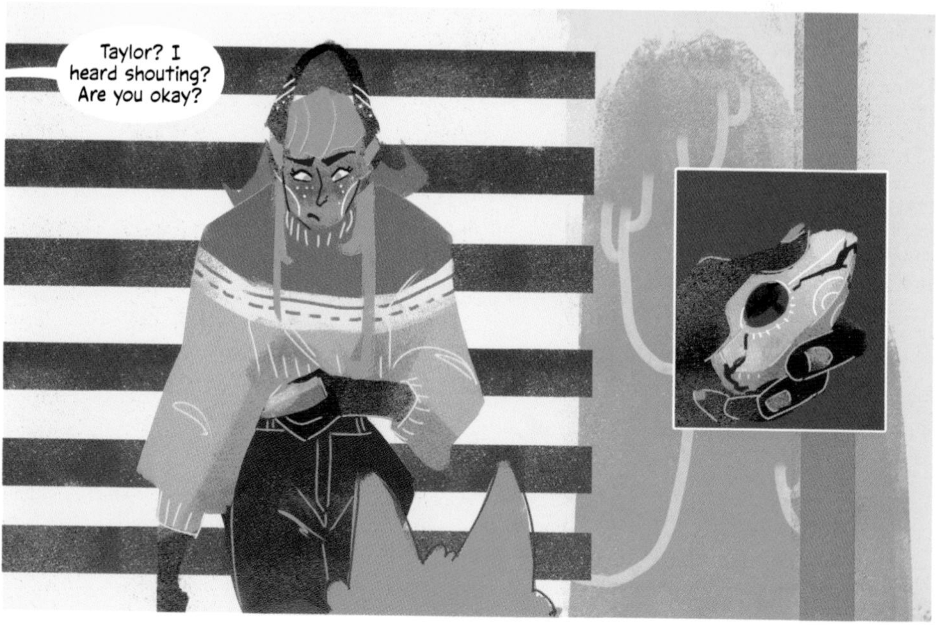
Taylor? I heard shouting? Are you okay?

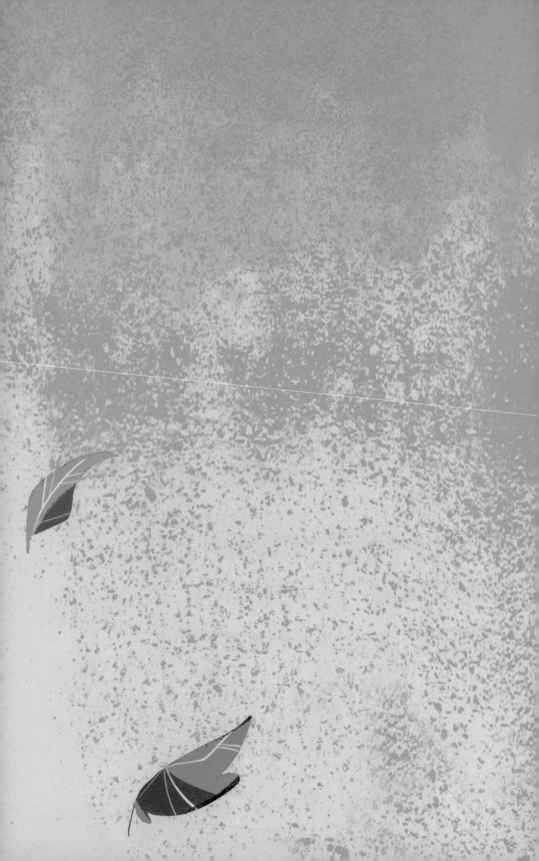

chapter 4
Space Oddity

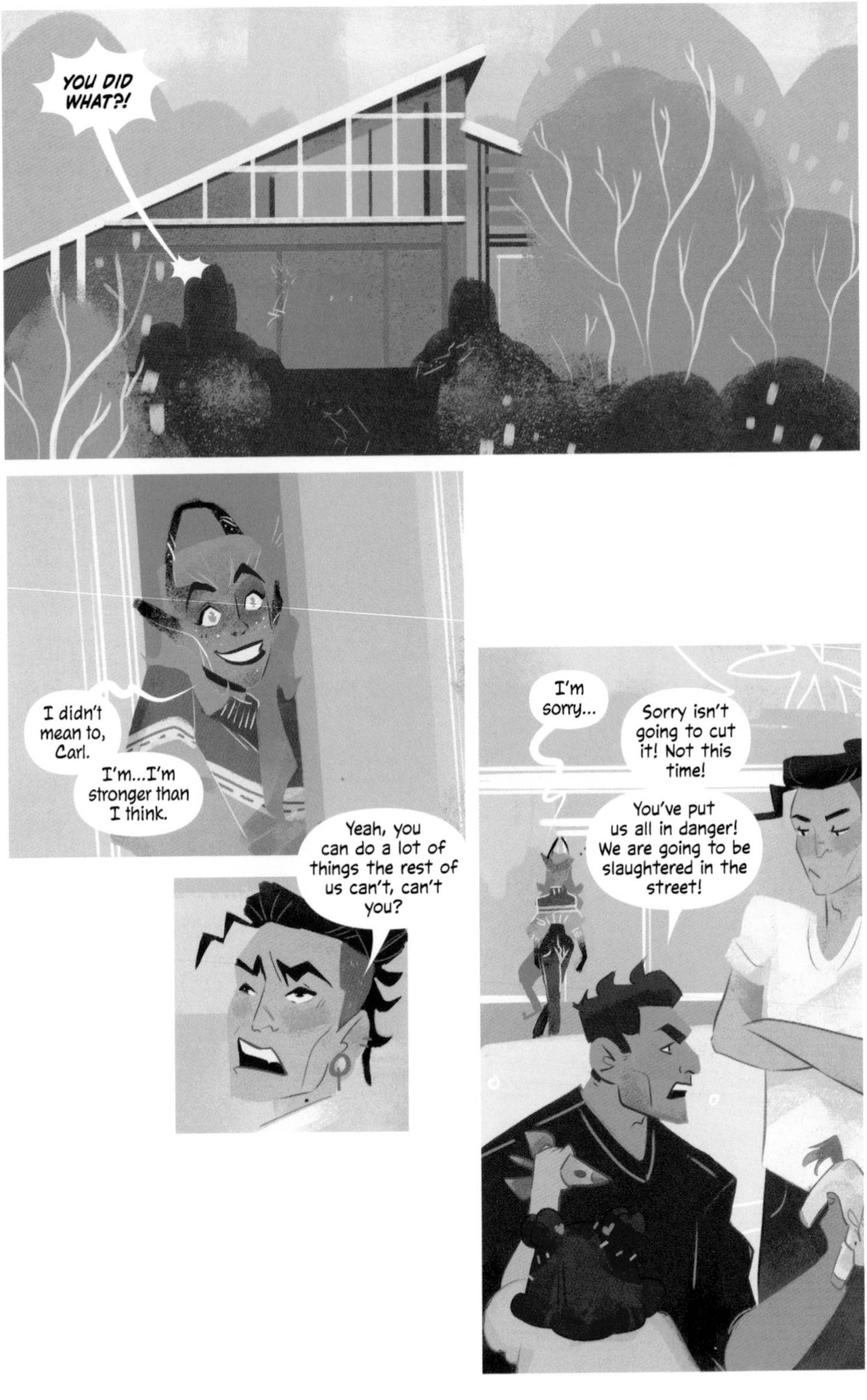
YOU DID WHAT?!
I didn't mean to, Carl.
I'm...I'm stronger than I think.
Yeah, you can do a lot of things the rest of us can't, can't you?
I'm sorry...
Sorry isn't going to cut it! Not this time!
You've put us all in danger! We are going to be slaughtered in the street!

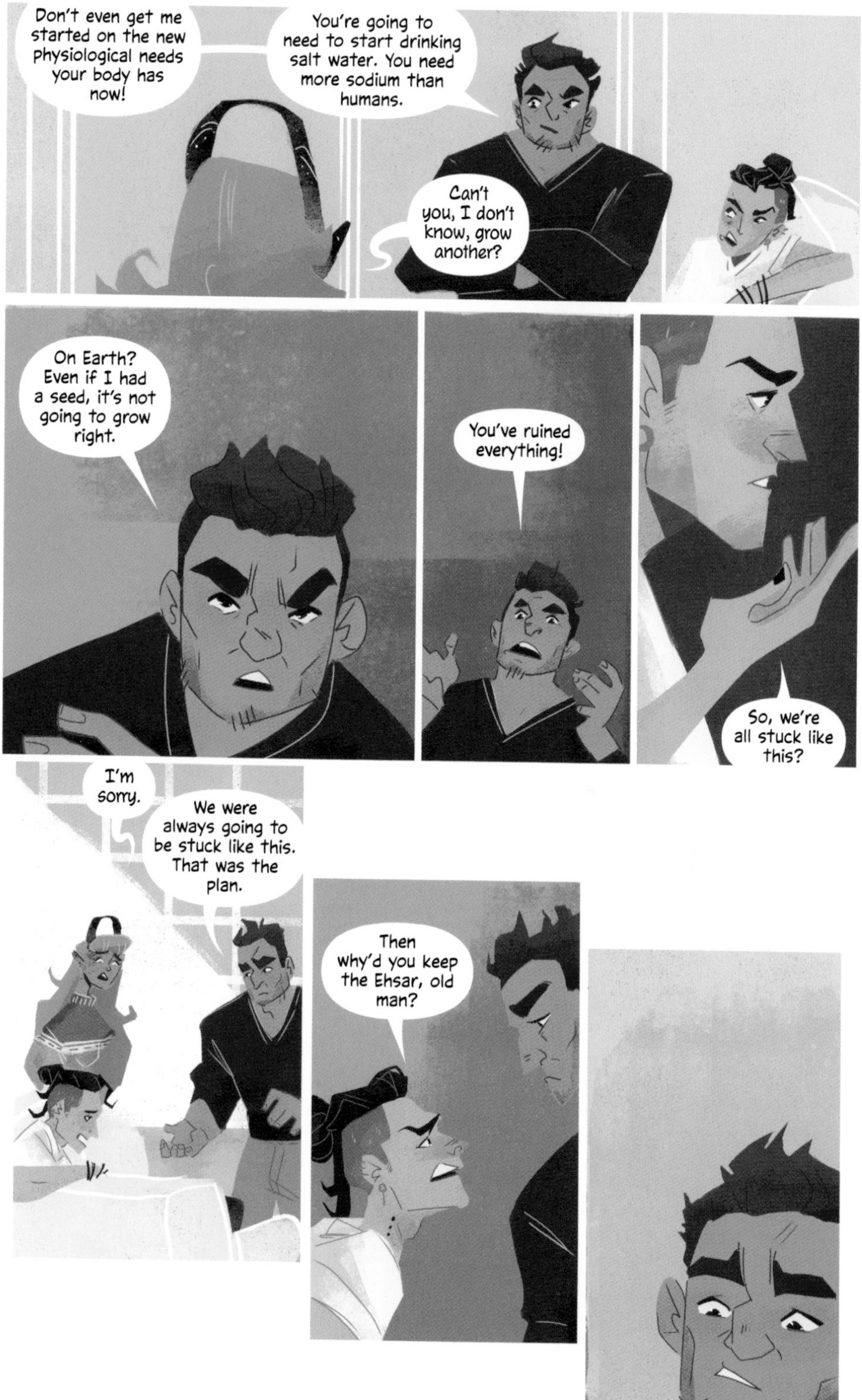
Don't even get me started on the new physiological needs your body has now!
You're going to need to start drinking salt water. You need more sodium than humans.
Can't you, I don't know, grow another?
On Earth? Even if I had a seed, it's not going to grow right.
You've ruined everything!
So, we're all stuck like this?
I'm sorry.
We were always going to be stuck like this. That was the plan.
Then why'd you keep the Ehsar, old man?

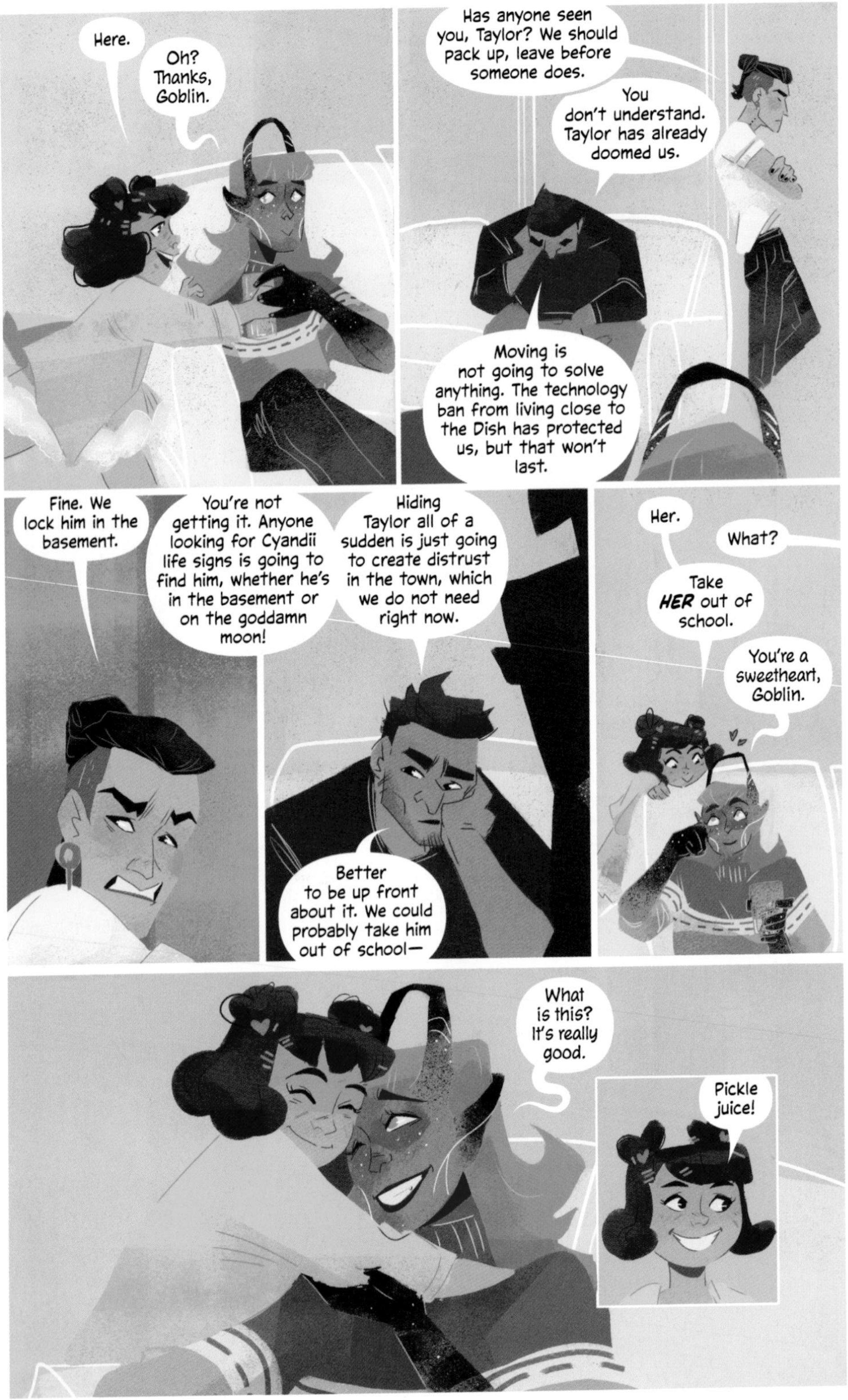
Here.
Oh? Thanks, Goblin.
Has anyone seen you, Taylor? We should pack up, leave before someone does.
You don't understand. Taylor has already doomed us.
Moving is not going to solve anything. The technology ban from living close to the Dish has protected us, but that won't last.
Fine. We lock him in the basement.
You're not getting it. Anyone looking for Cyandii life signs is going to find him, whether he's in the basement or on the goddamn moon!
Hiding Taylor all of a sudden is just going to create distrust in the town, which we do not need right now.
Better to be up front about it. We could probably take him out of school—
Her.
What?
Take ***HER*** out of school.
You're a sweetheart, Goblin.
What is this? It's really good.
Pickle juice!

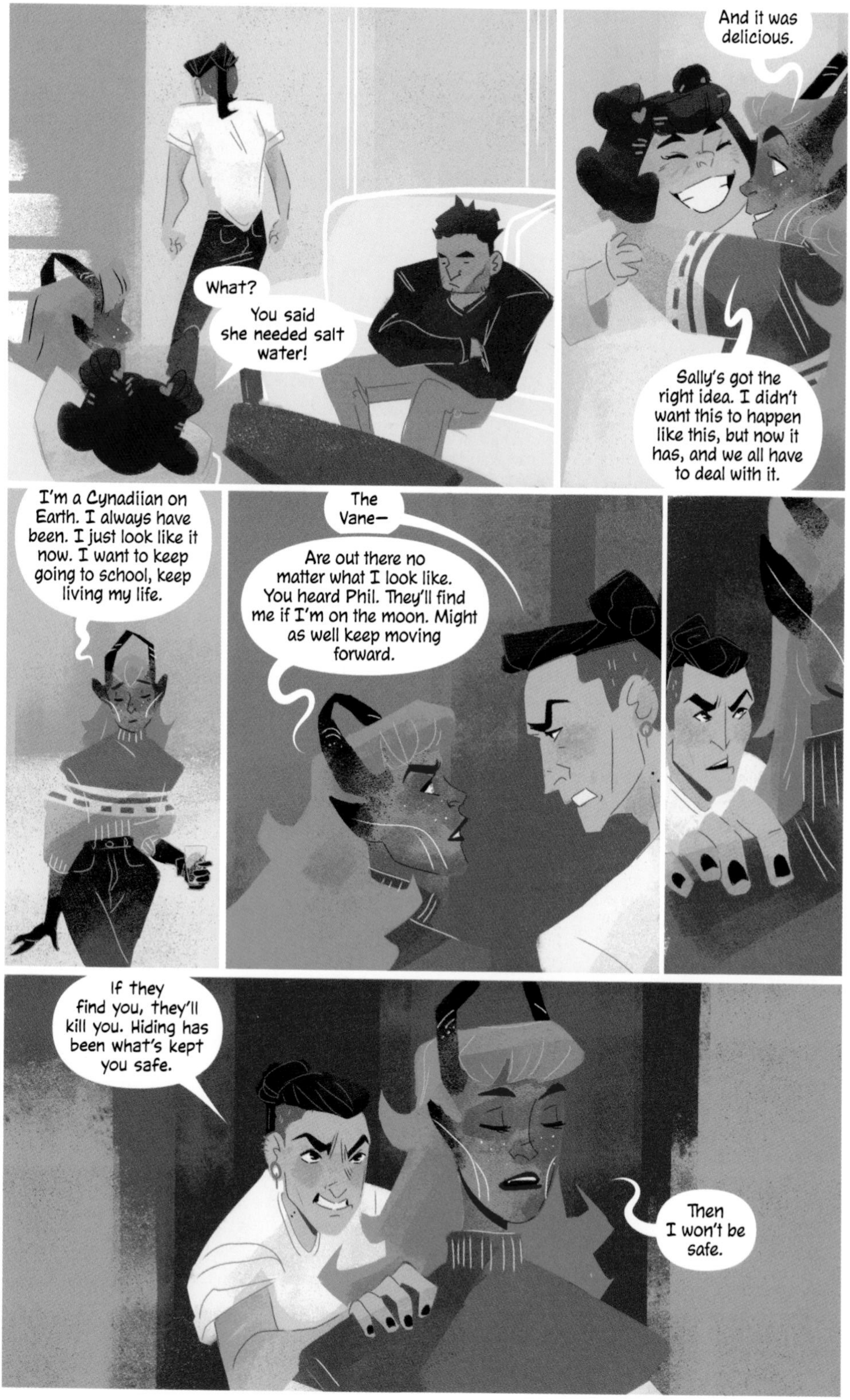
What?
You said she needed salt water!
And it was delicious.
Sally's got the right idea. I didn't want this to happen like this, but now it has, and we all have to deal with it.
I'm a Cynadiian on Earth. I always have been. I just look like it now. I want to keep going to school, keep living my life.
The Vane—
Are out there no matter what I look like. You heard Phil. They'll find me if I'm on the moon. Might as well keep moving forward.
If they find you, they'll kill you. Hiding has been what's kept you safe.
Then I won't be safe.

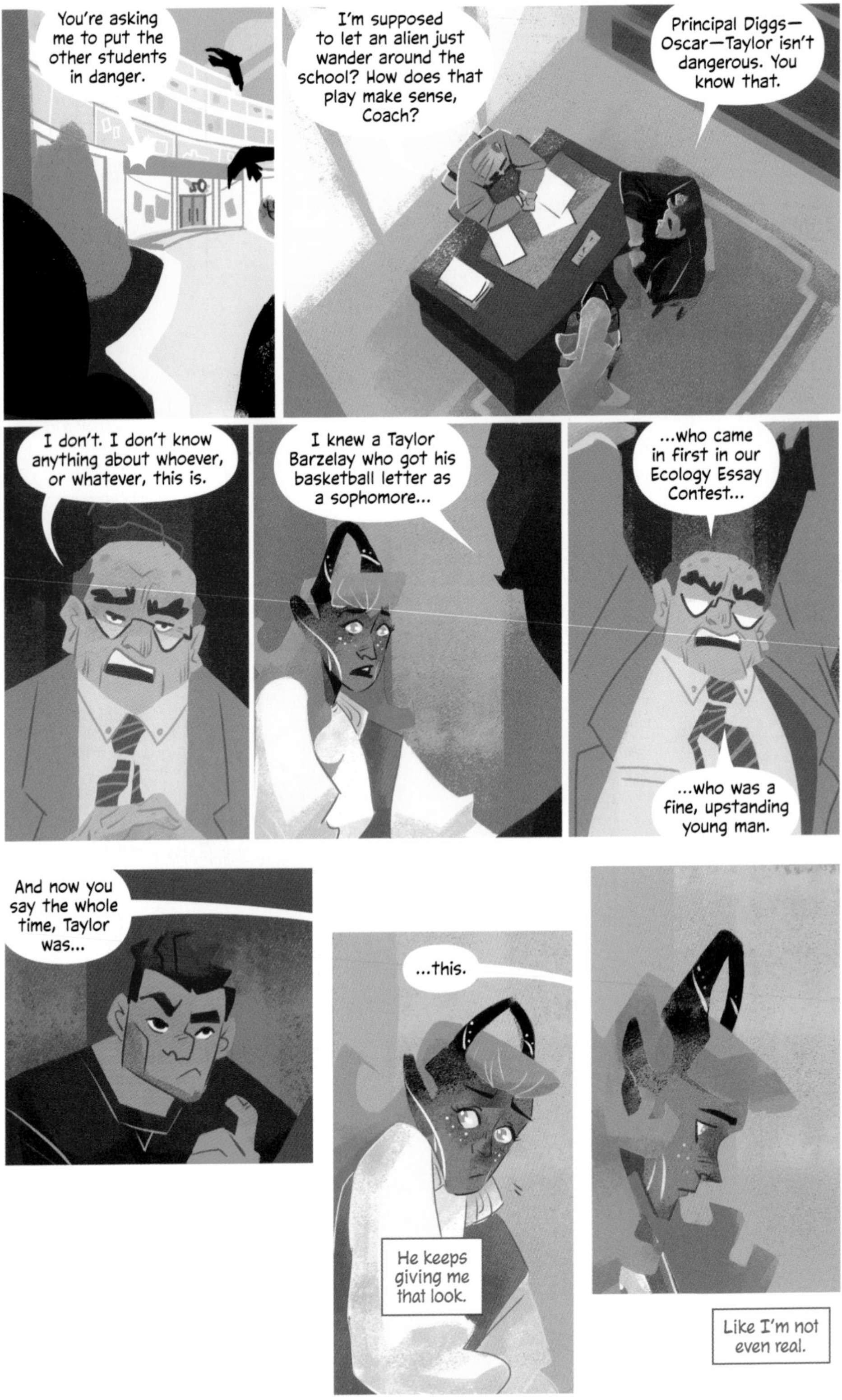
You're asking me to put the other students in danger.
I'm supposed to let an alien just wander around the school? How does that play make sense, Coach?
Principal Diggs—Oscar—Taylor isn't dangerous. You know that.
I don't. I don't know anything about whoever, or whatever, this is.
I knew a Taylor Barzelay who got his basketball letter as a sophomore...
...who came in first in our Ecology Essay Contest...
...who was a fine, upstanding young man.
And now you say the whole time, Taylor was...
...this.
He keeps giving me that look.
Like I'm not even real.

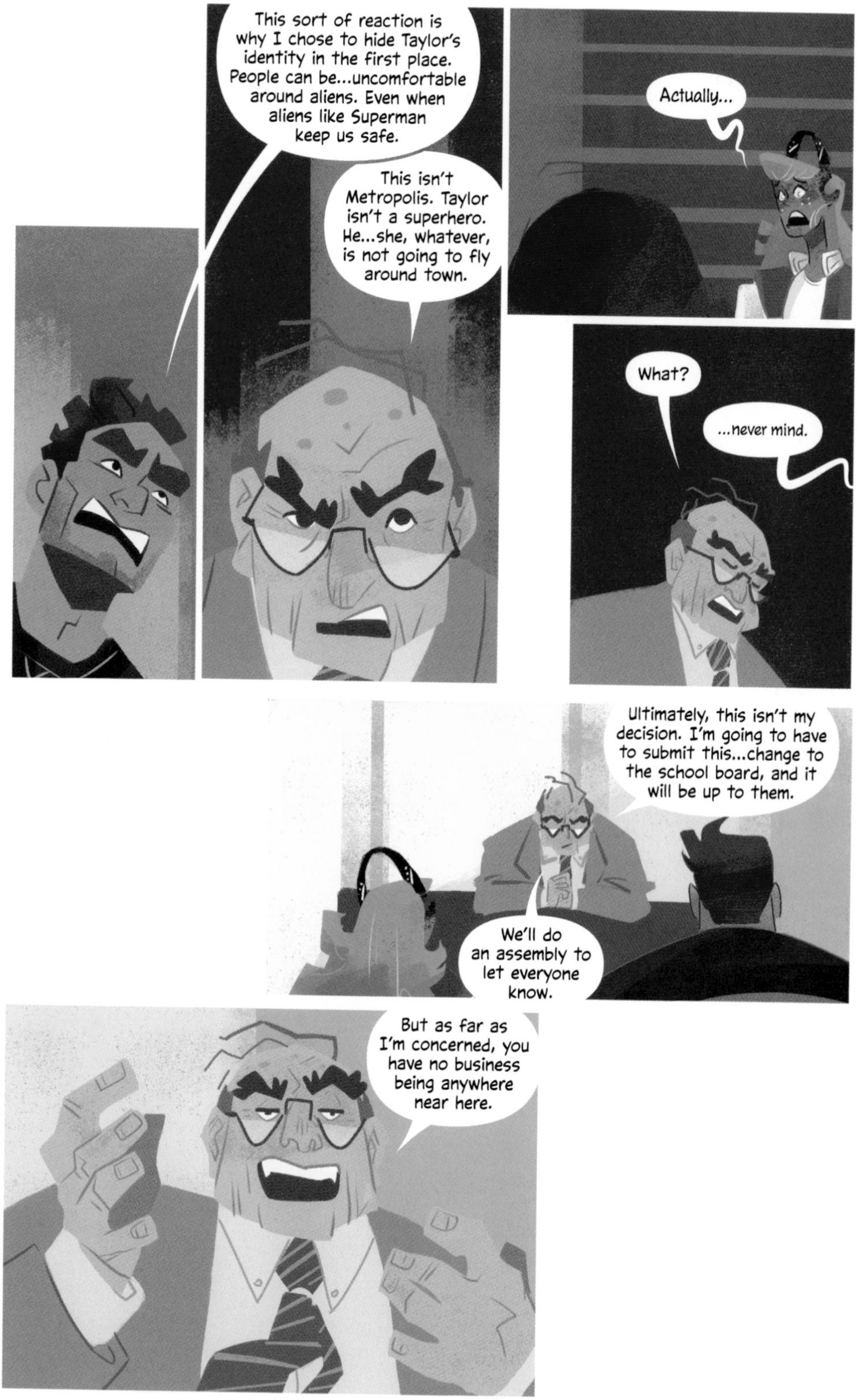
This sort of reaction is why I chose to hide Taylor's identity in the first place. People can be...uncomfortable around aliens. Even when aliens like Superman keep us safe.
This isn't Metropolis. Taylor isn't a superhero. He...she, whatever, is not going to fly around town.
Actually...
What?
...never mind.
Ultimately, this isn't my decision. I'm going to have to submit this...change to the school board, and it will be up to them.
We'll do an assembly to let everyone know.
But as far as I'm concerned, you have no business being anywhere near here.

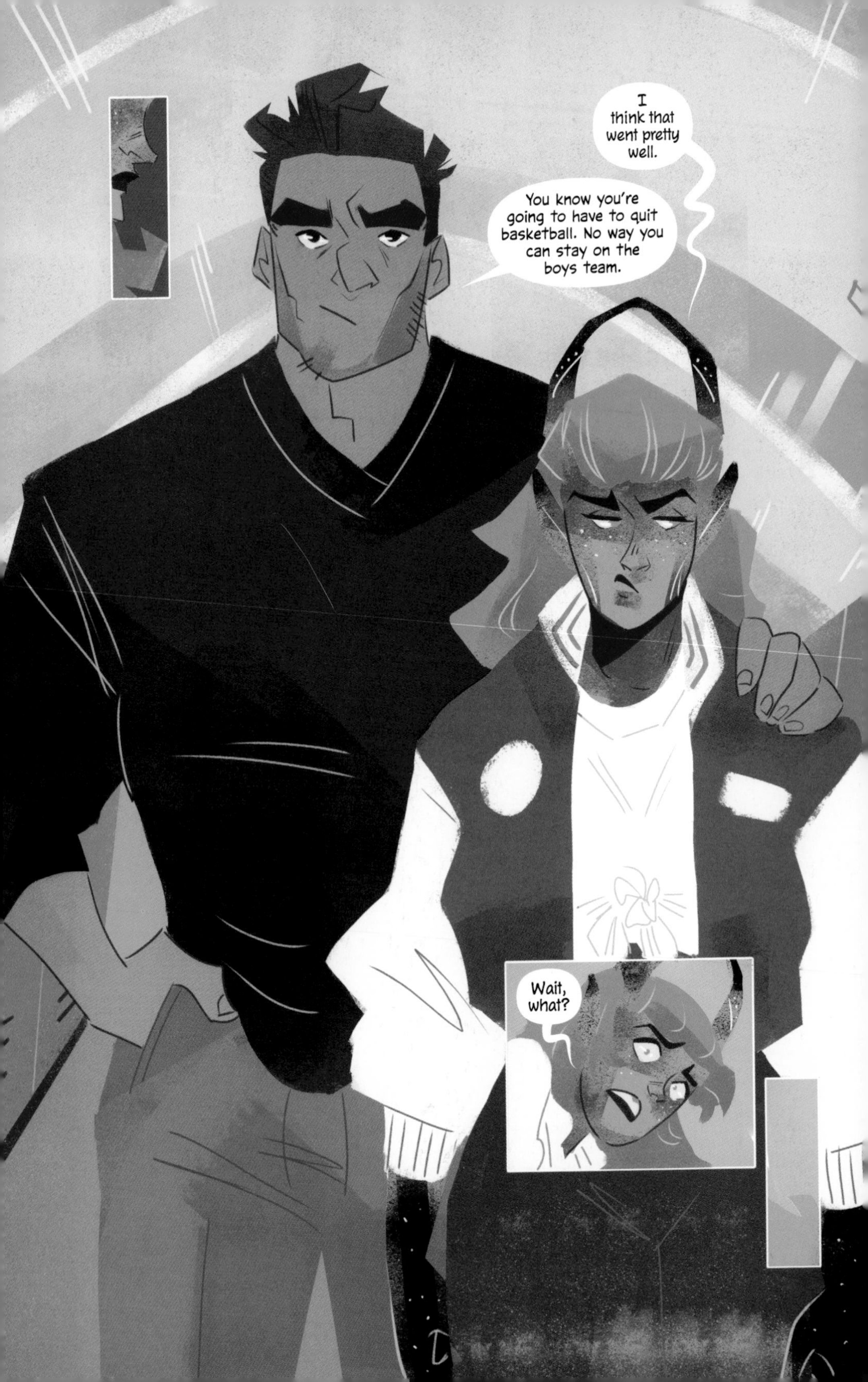
I think that went pretty well.
You know you're going to have to quit basketball. No way you can stay on the boys team.
Wait, what?

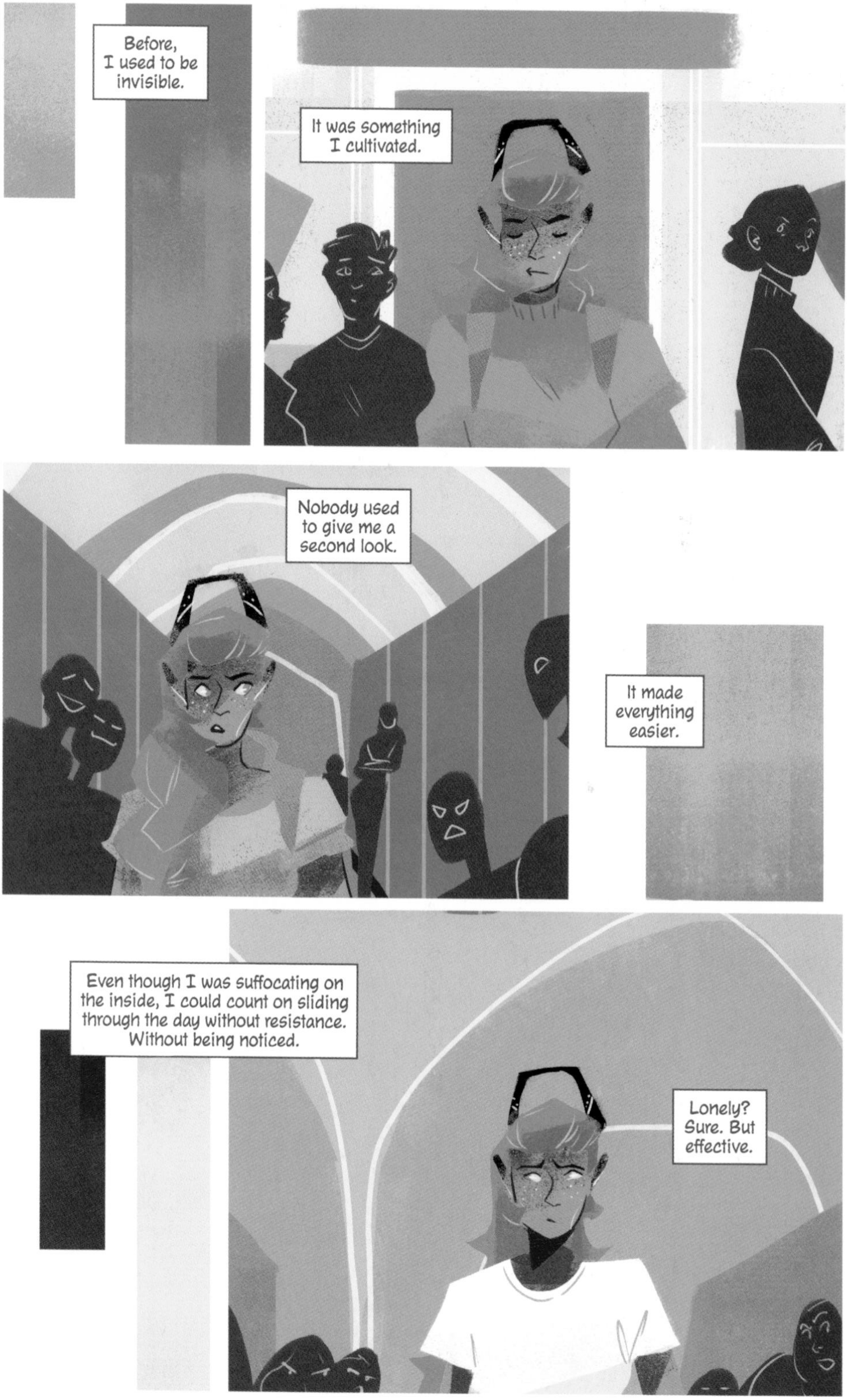
Before, I used to be invisible.
It was something I cultivated.
Nobody used to give me a second look.
It made everything easier.
Even though I was suffocating on the inside, I could count on sliding through the day without resistance. Without being noticed.
Lonely? Sure. But effective.

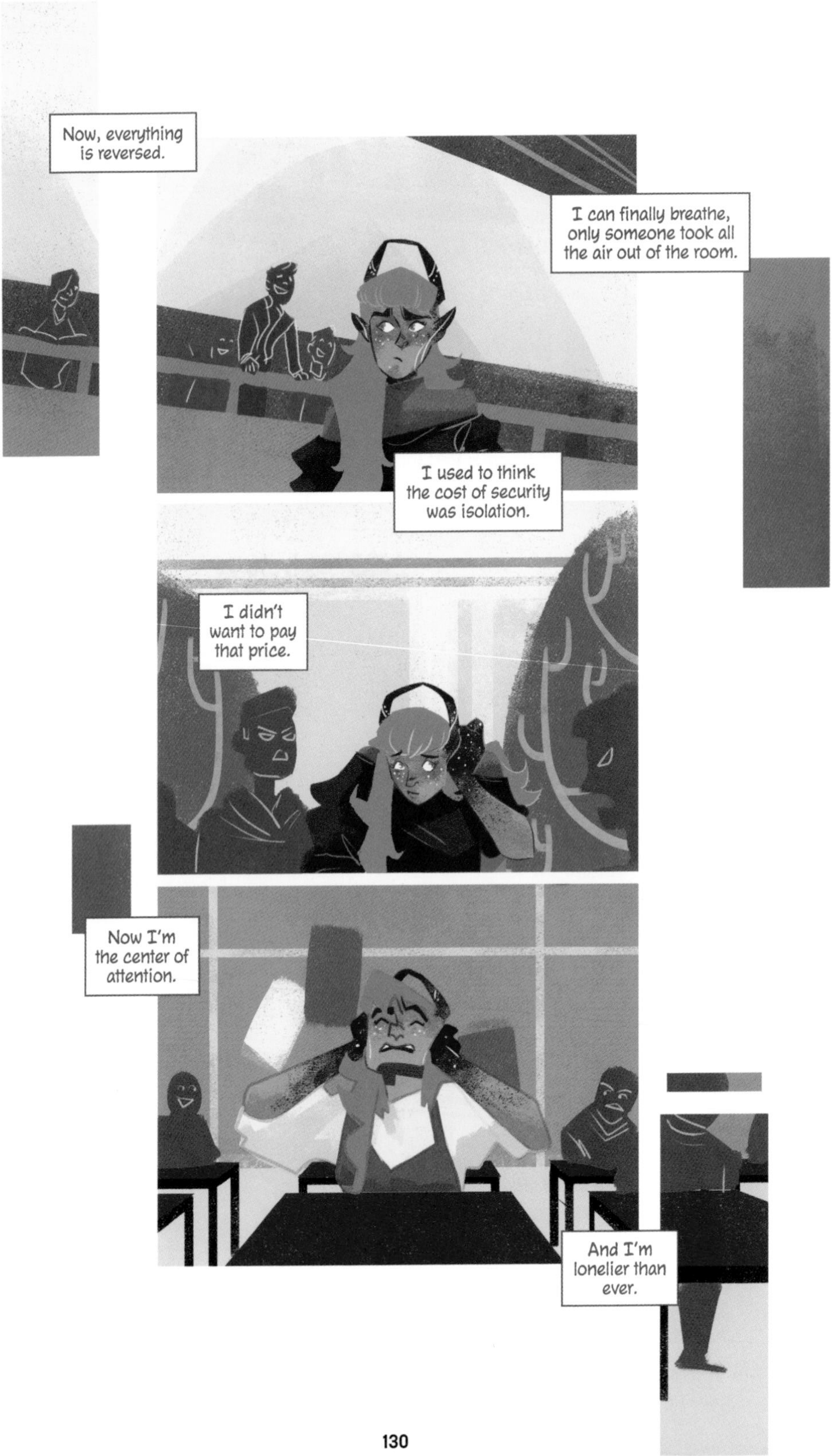
Now, everything is reversed.
I can finally breathe, only someone took all the air out of the room.
I used to think the cost of security was isolation.
I didn't want to pay that price.
Now I'm the center of attention.
And I'm lonelier than ever.

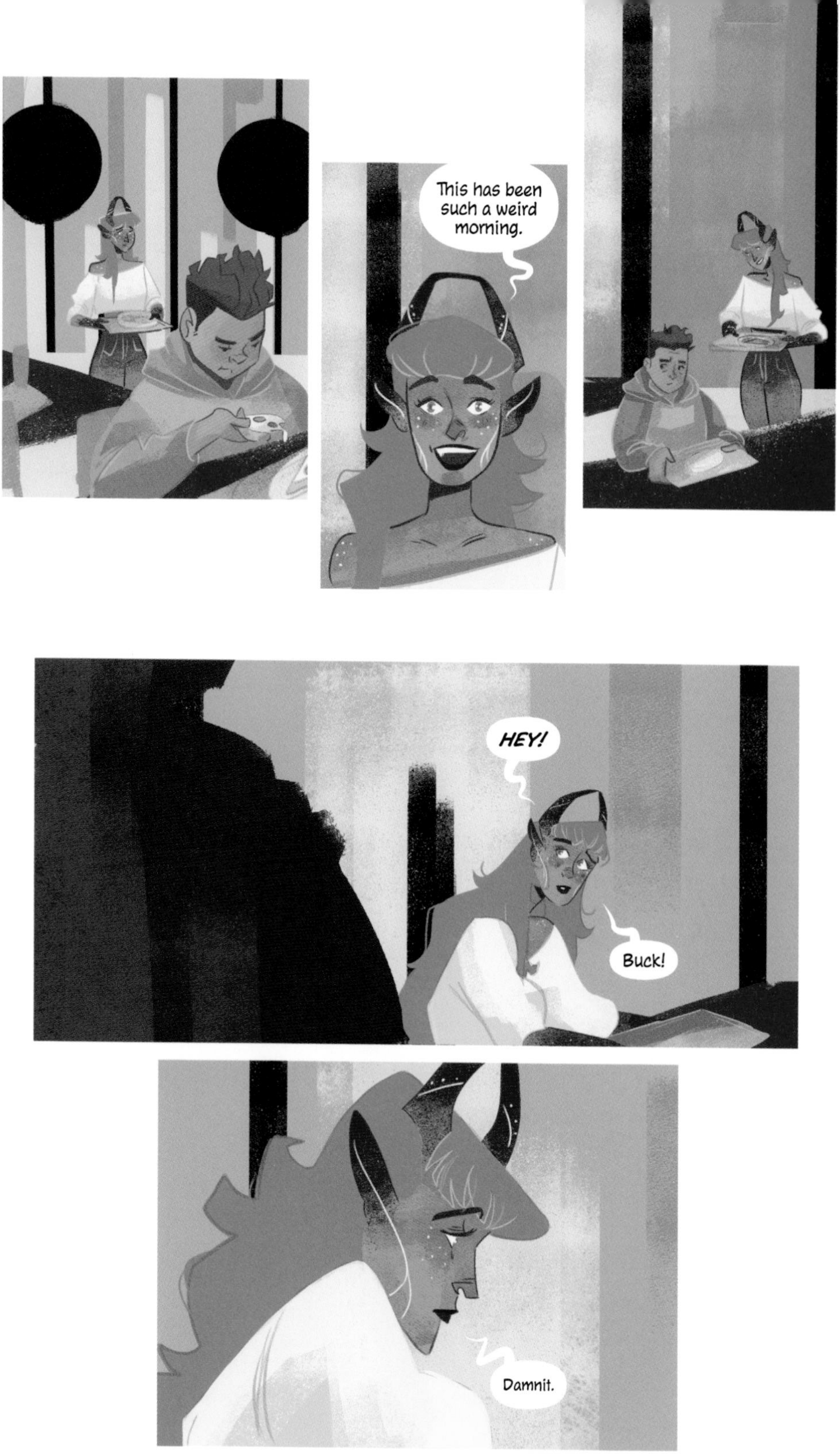
This has been such a weird morning.
HEY!
Buck!
Damnit.

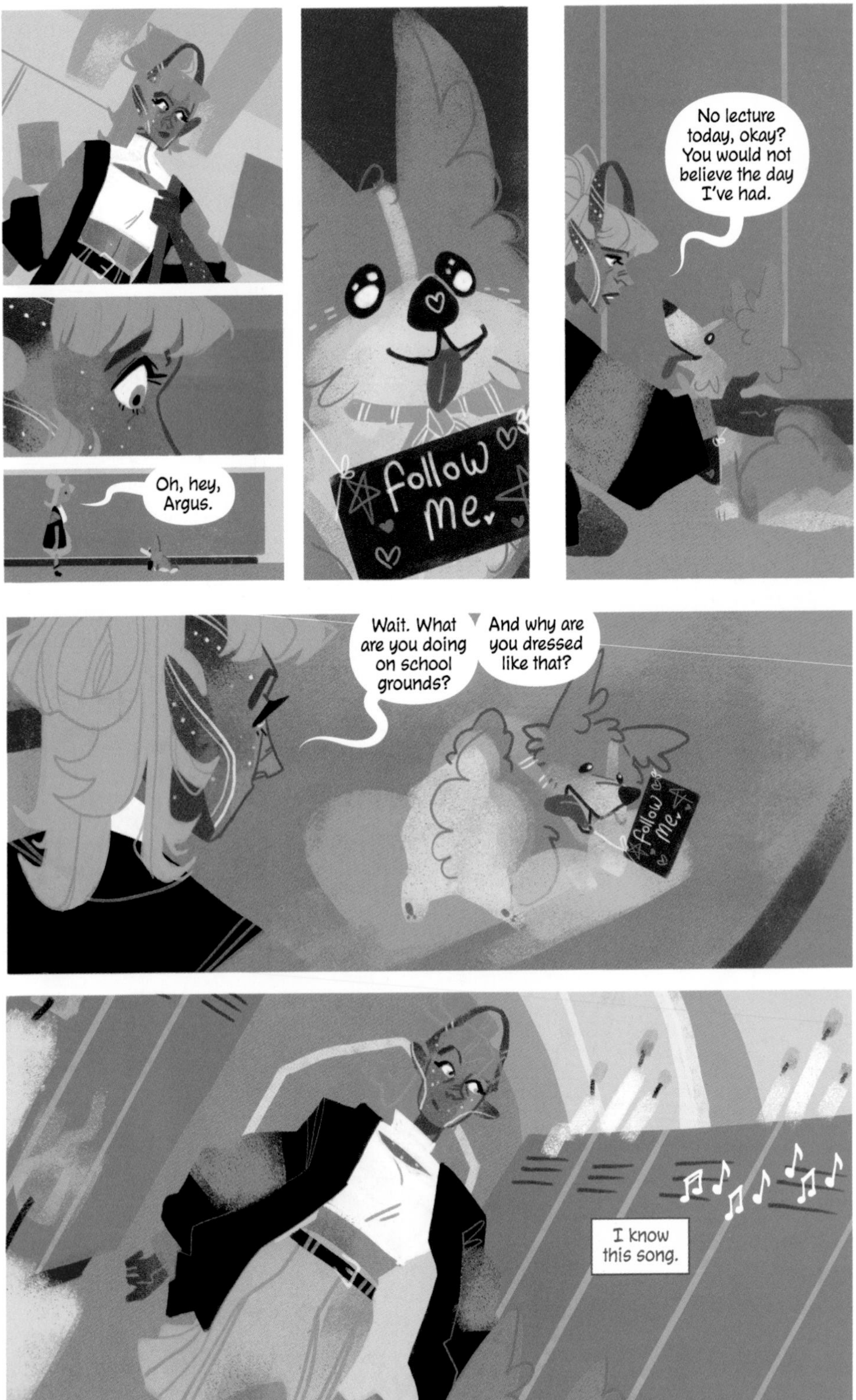

follow me
No lecture today, okay? You would not believe the day I've had.
Oh, hey, Argus.
Wait. What are you doing on school grounds?
And why are you dressed like that?
follow me
I know this song.

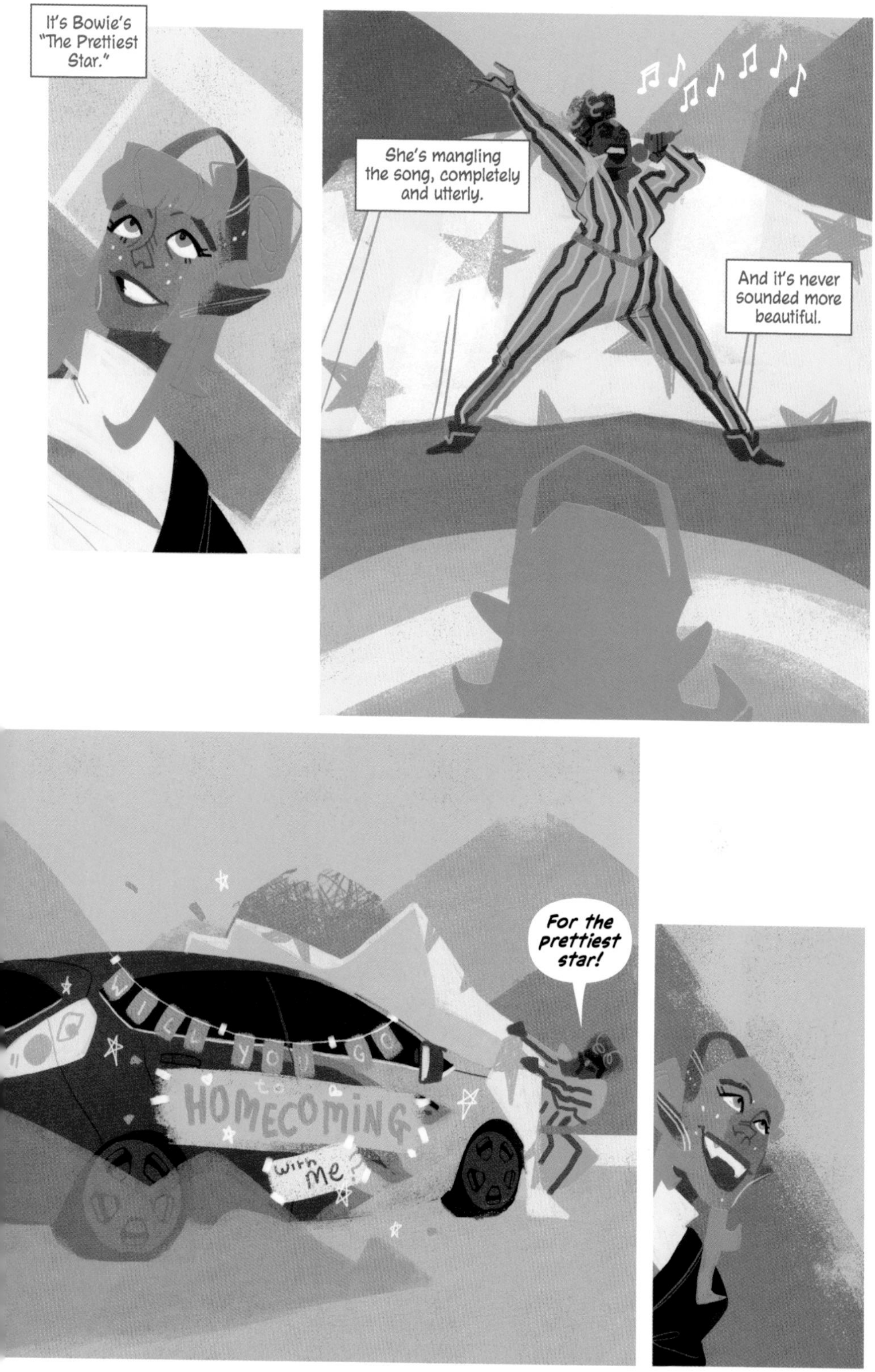
It's Bowie's "The Prettiest Star."
She's mangling the song, completely and utterly.
And it's never sounded more beautiful.
WILL YOU GO
to
HOMECOMING
with me
For the prettiest star!

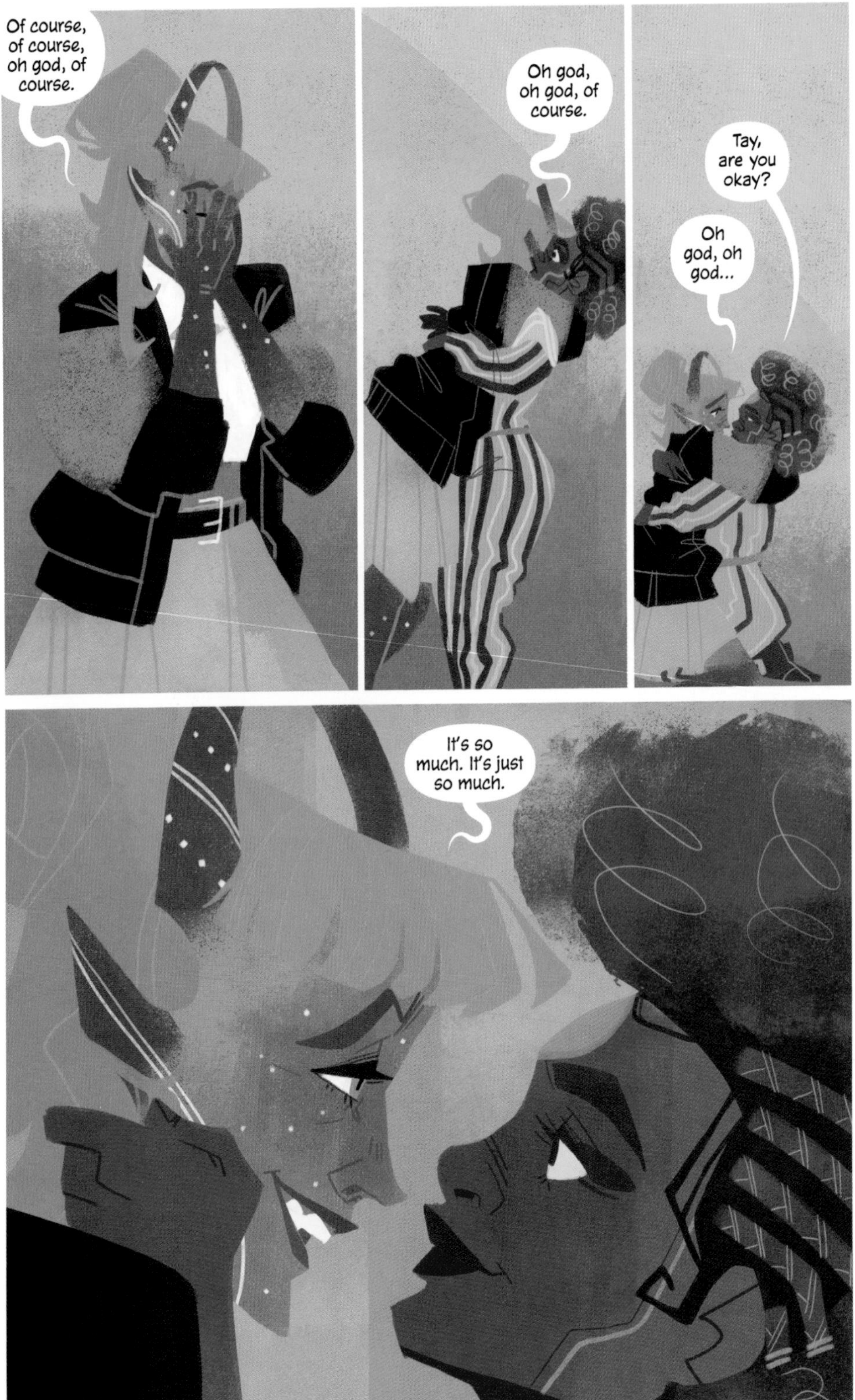
Of course, of course, oh god, of course.
Oh god, oh god, of course.
Tay, are you okay?
Oh god, oh god...
It's so much. It's just so much.

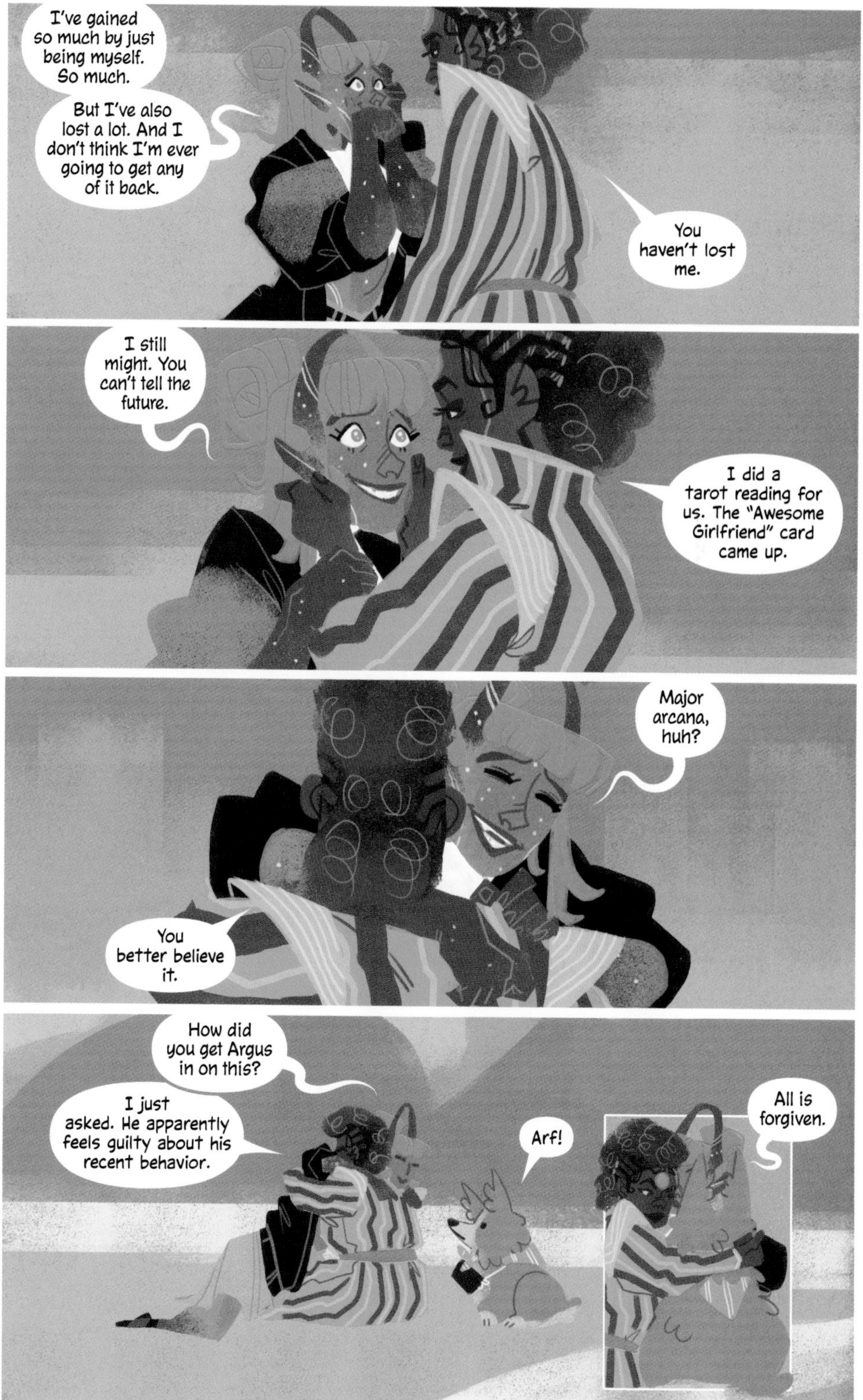
I've gained so much by just being myself. So much.
But I've also lost a lot. And I don't think I'm ever going to get any of it back.
You haven't lost me.
I still might. You can't tell the future.
I did a tarot reading for us. The "Awesome Girlfriend" card came up.
Major arcana, huh?
You better believe it.
How did you get Argus in on this?
I just asked. He apparently feels guilty about his recent behavior.
Arf!
All is forgiven.

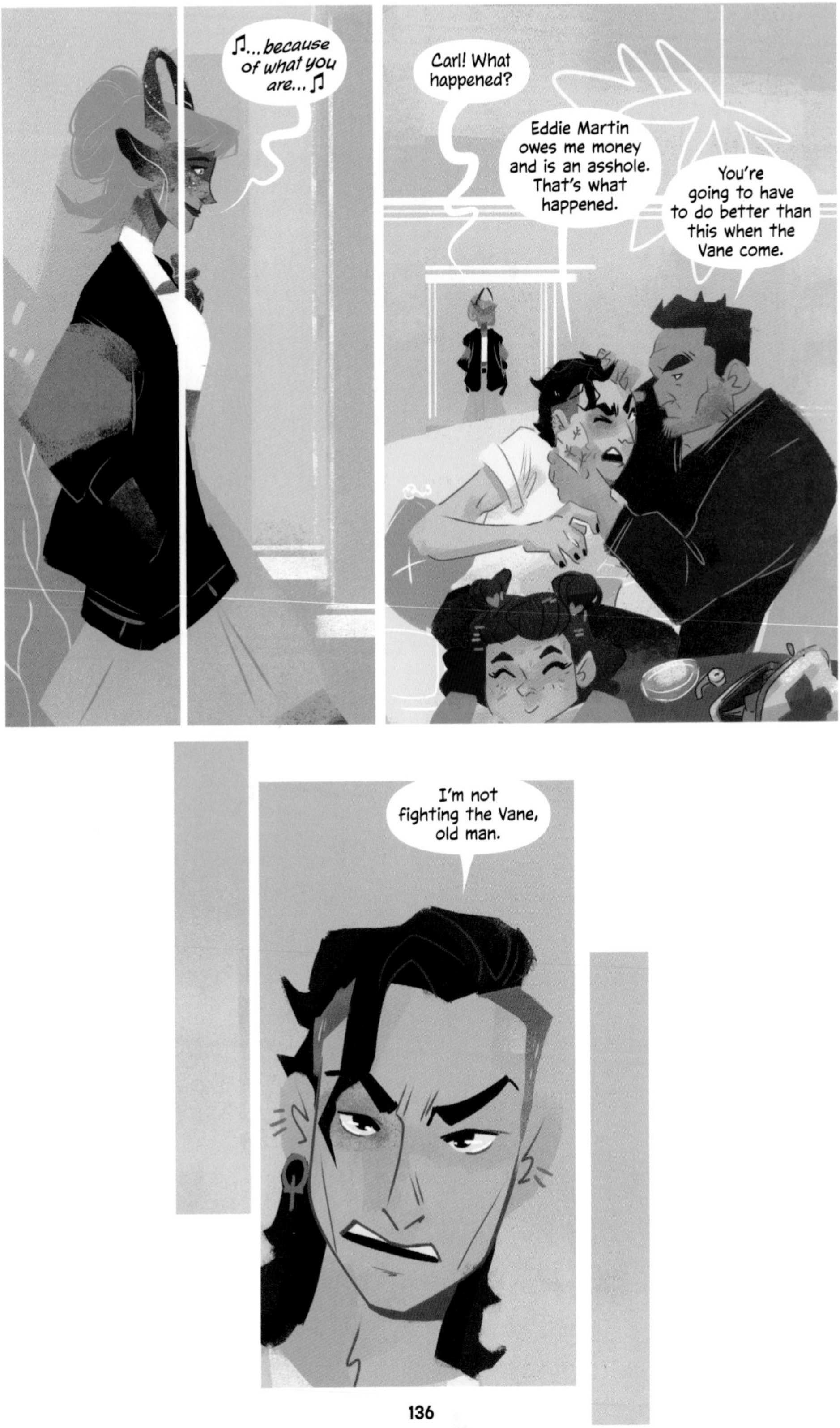
♫...because of what you are...♫
Carl! What happened?
Eddie Martin owes me money and is an asshole. That's what happened.
You're going to have to do better than this when the Vane come.
I'm not fighting the Vane, old man.

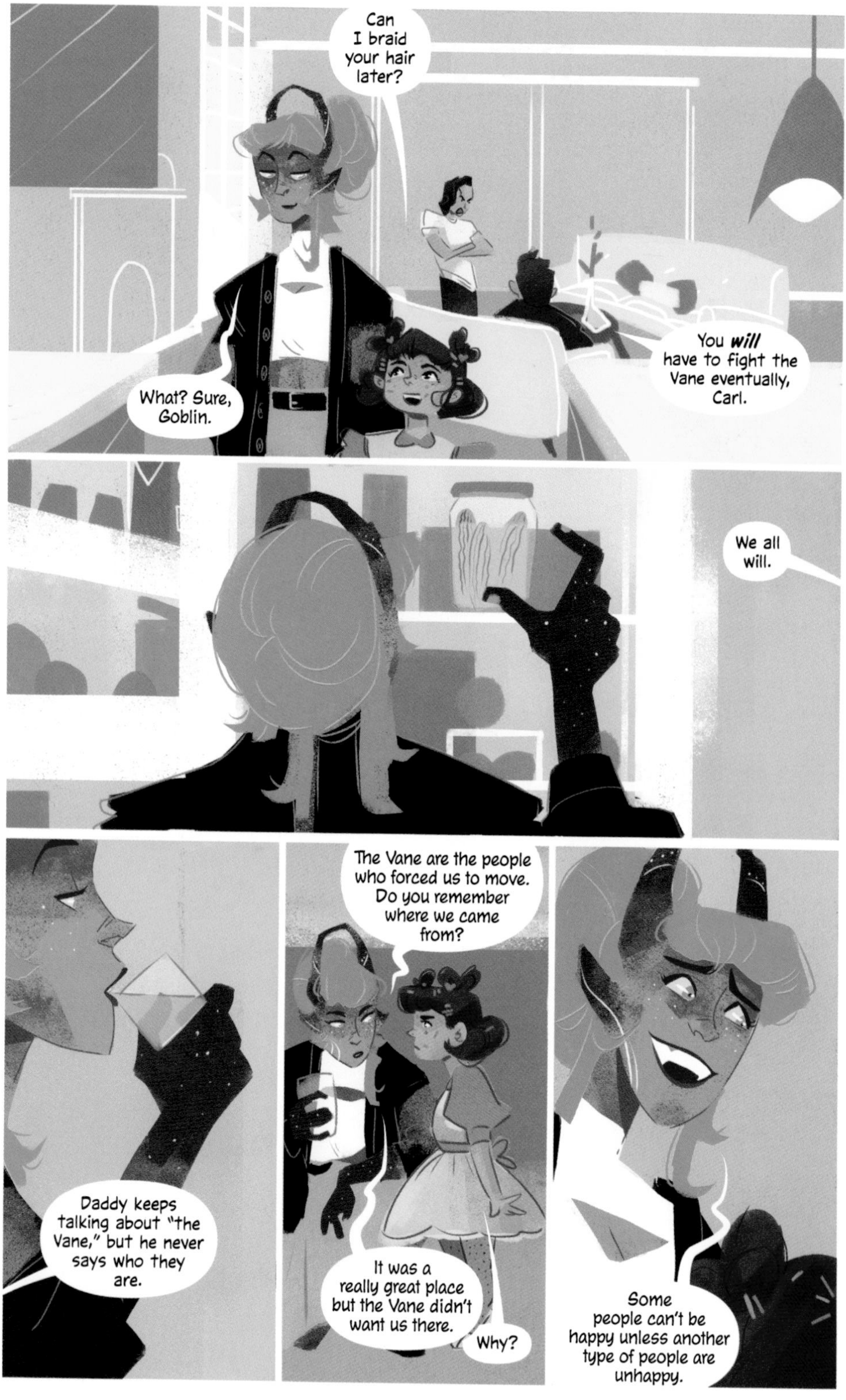
Can I braid your hair later?
What? Sure, Goblin.
You *will* have to fight the Vane eventually, Carl.
We all will.
Daddy keeps talking about "the Vane," but he never says who they are.
The Vane are the people who forced us to move. Do you remember where we came from?
It was a really great place but the Vane didn't want us there.
Why?
Some people can't be happy unless another type of people are unhappy.

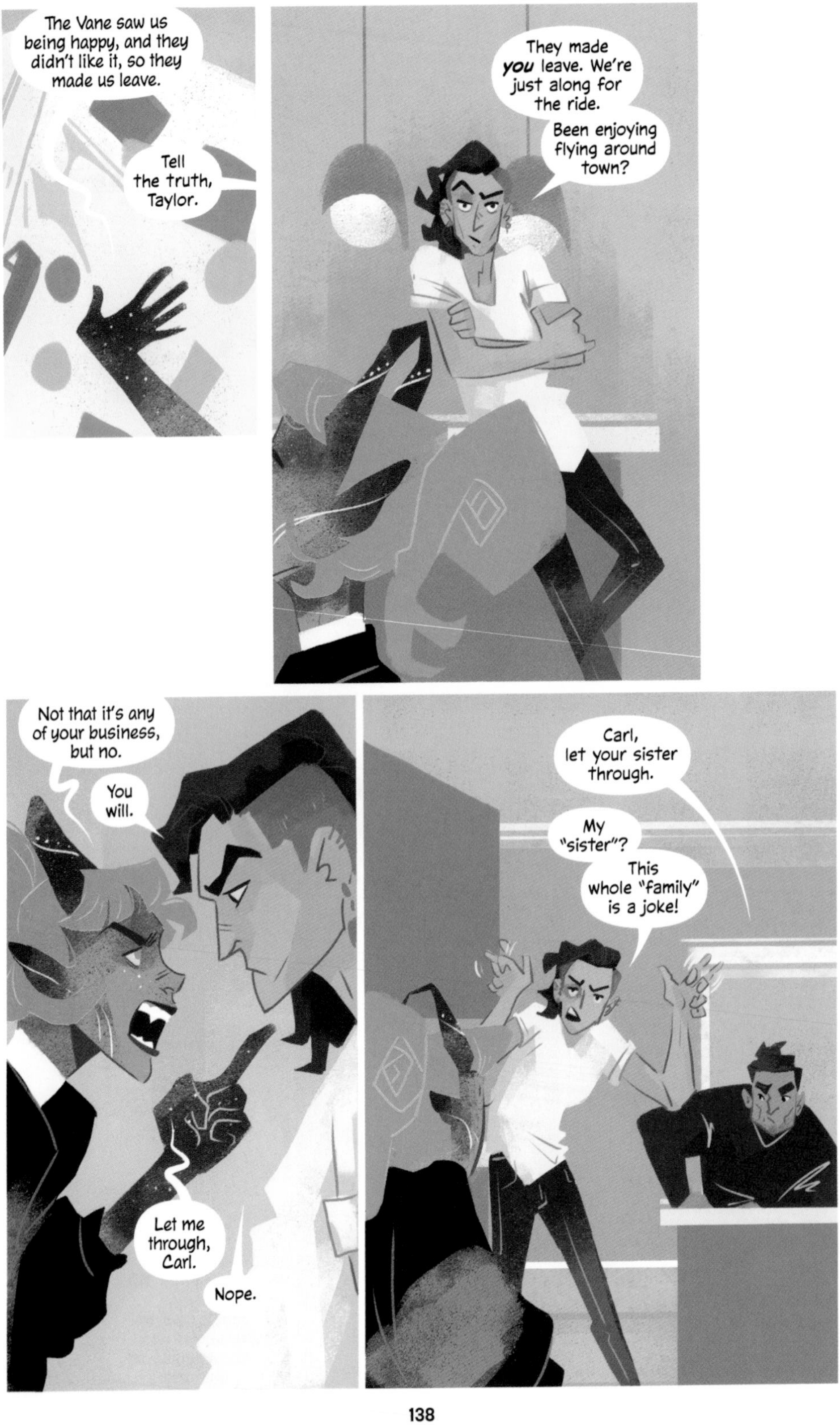
The Vane saw us being happy, and they didn't like it, so they made us leave.
Tell the truth, Taylor.
They made *you* leave. We're just along for the ride.
Been enjoying flying around town?
Not that it's any of your business, but no.
You will.
Let me through, Carl.
Nope.
Carl, let your sister through.
My "sister"?
This whole "family" is a joke!

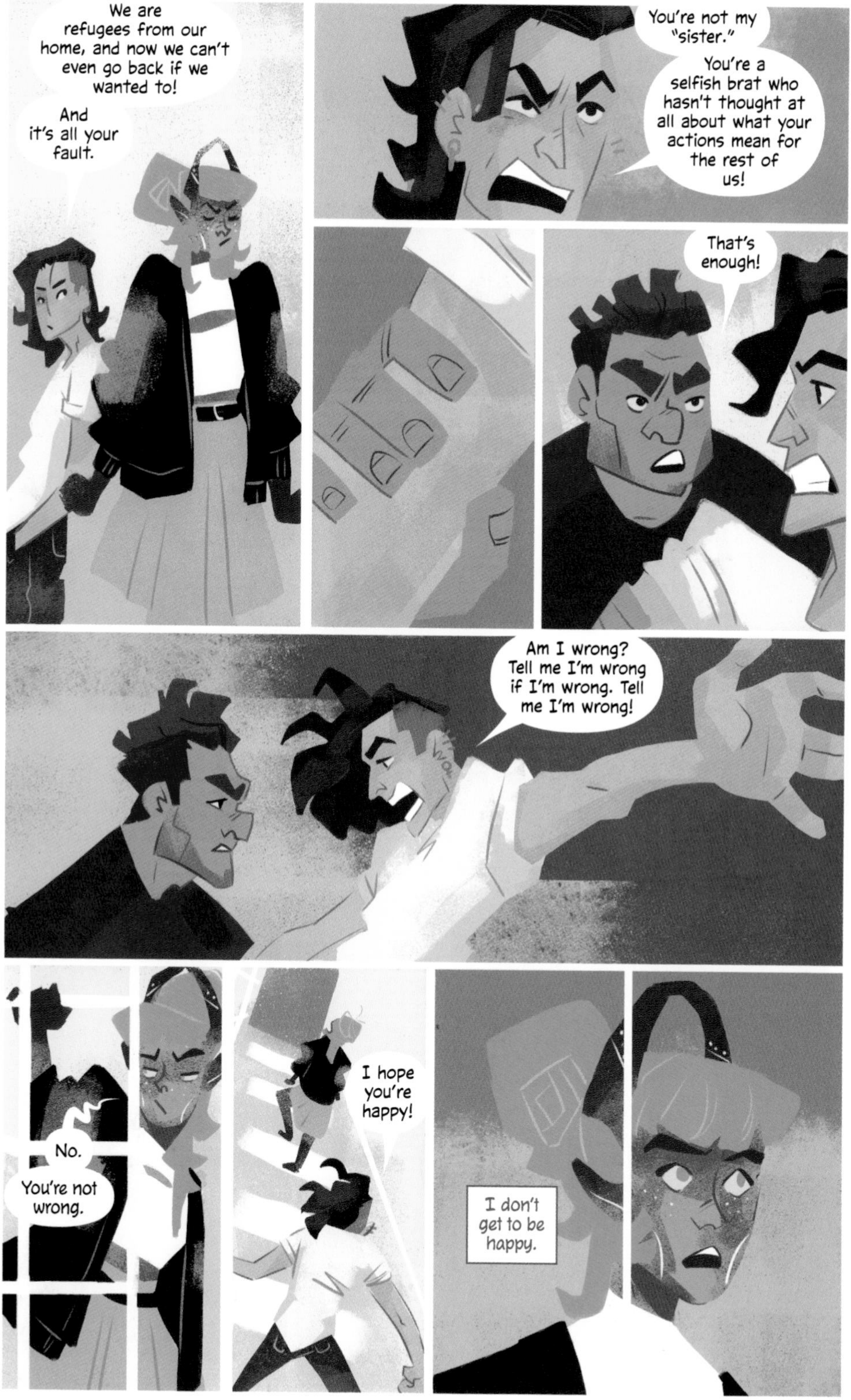
We are refugees from our home, and now we can't even go back if we wanted to!
And it's all your fault.
You're not my "sister."
You're a selfish brat who hasn't thought at all about what your actions mean for the rest of us!
That's enough!
Am I wrong? Tell me I'm wrong if I'm wrong. Tell me I'm wrong!
No.
You're not wrong.
I hope you're happy!
I don't get to be happy.

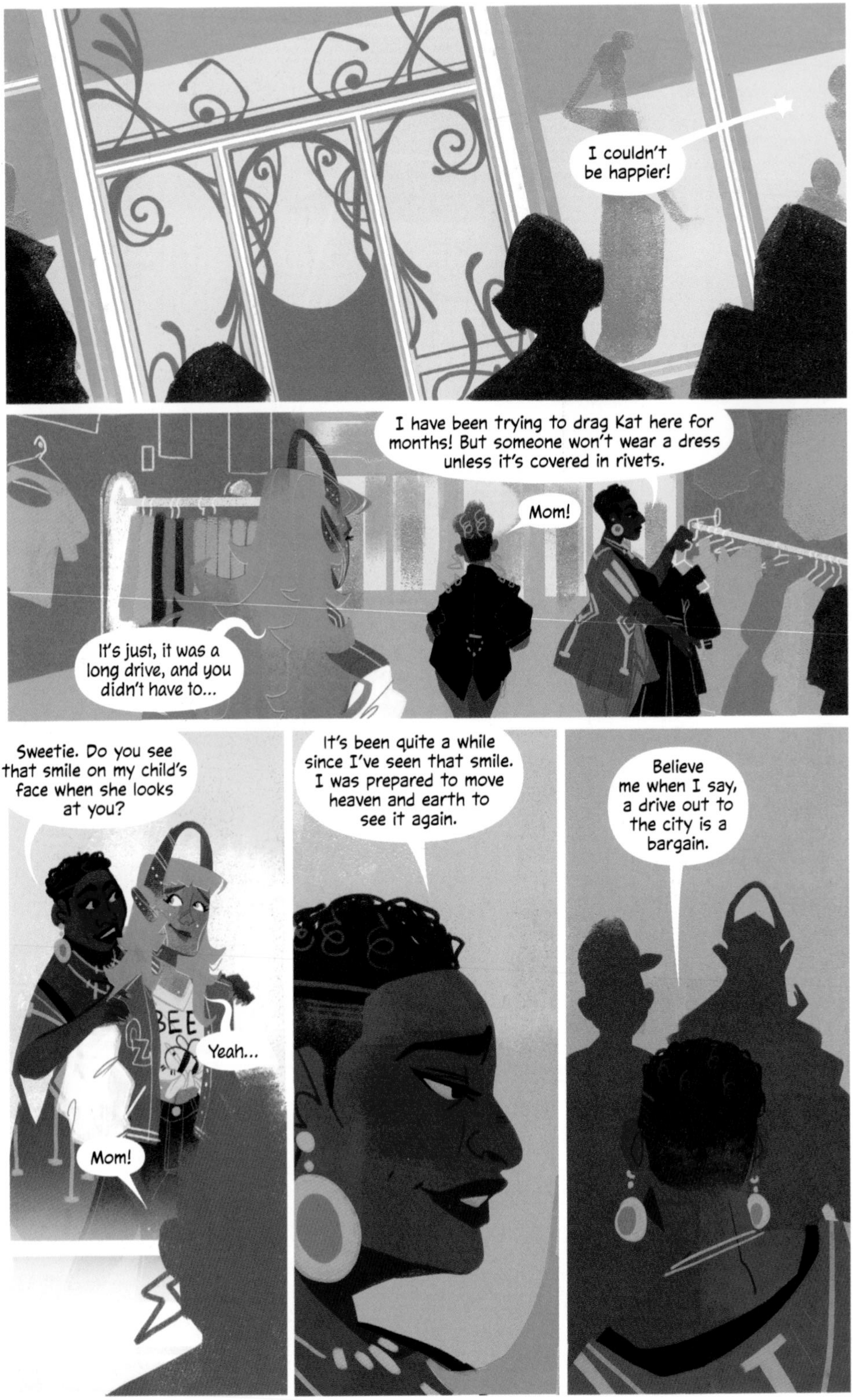
I couldn't be happier!
I have been trying to drag Kat here for months! But someone won't wear a dress unless it's covered in rivets.
Mom!
It's just, it was a long drive, and you didn't have to...
Sweetie. Do you see that smile on my child's face when she looks at you?
Yeah...
Mom!
It's been quite a while since I've seen that smile. I was prepared to move heaven and earth to see it again.
Believe me when I say, a drive out to the city is a bargain.

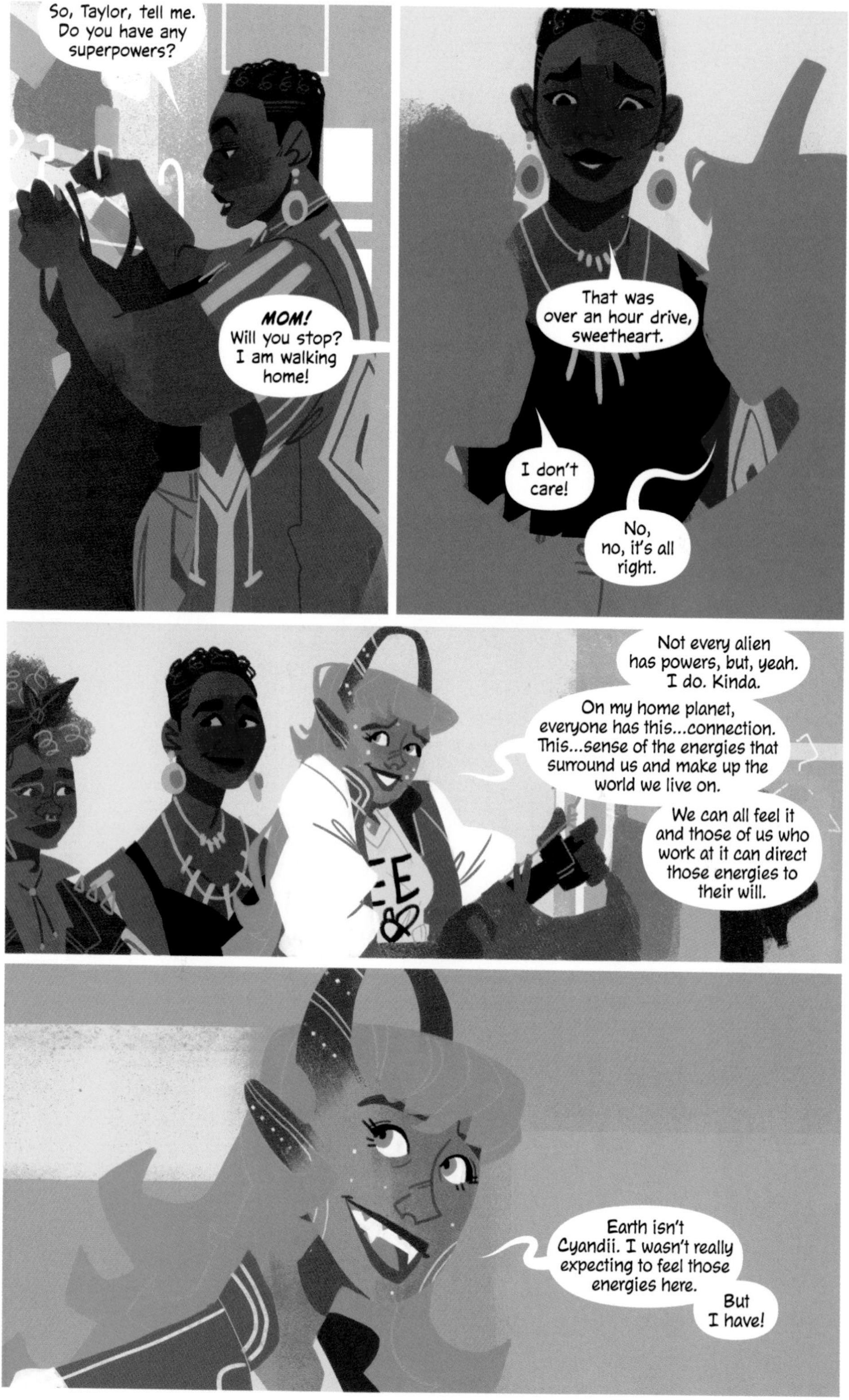

So, Taylor, tell me. Do you have any superpowers?
MOM! Will you stop? I am walking home!
That was over an hour drive, sweetheart.
I don't care!
No, no, it's all right.
Not every alien has powers, but, yeah. I do. Kinda.
On my home planet, everyone has this...connection. This...sense of the energies that surround us and make up the world we live on.
We can all feel it and those of us who work at it can direct those energies to their will.
Earth isn't Cyandii. I wasn't really expecting to feel those energies here.
But I have!

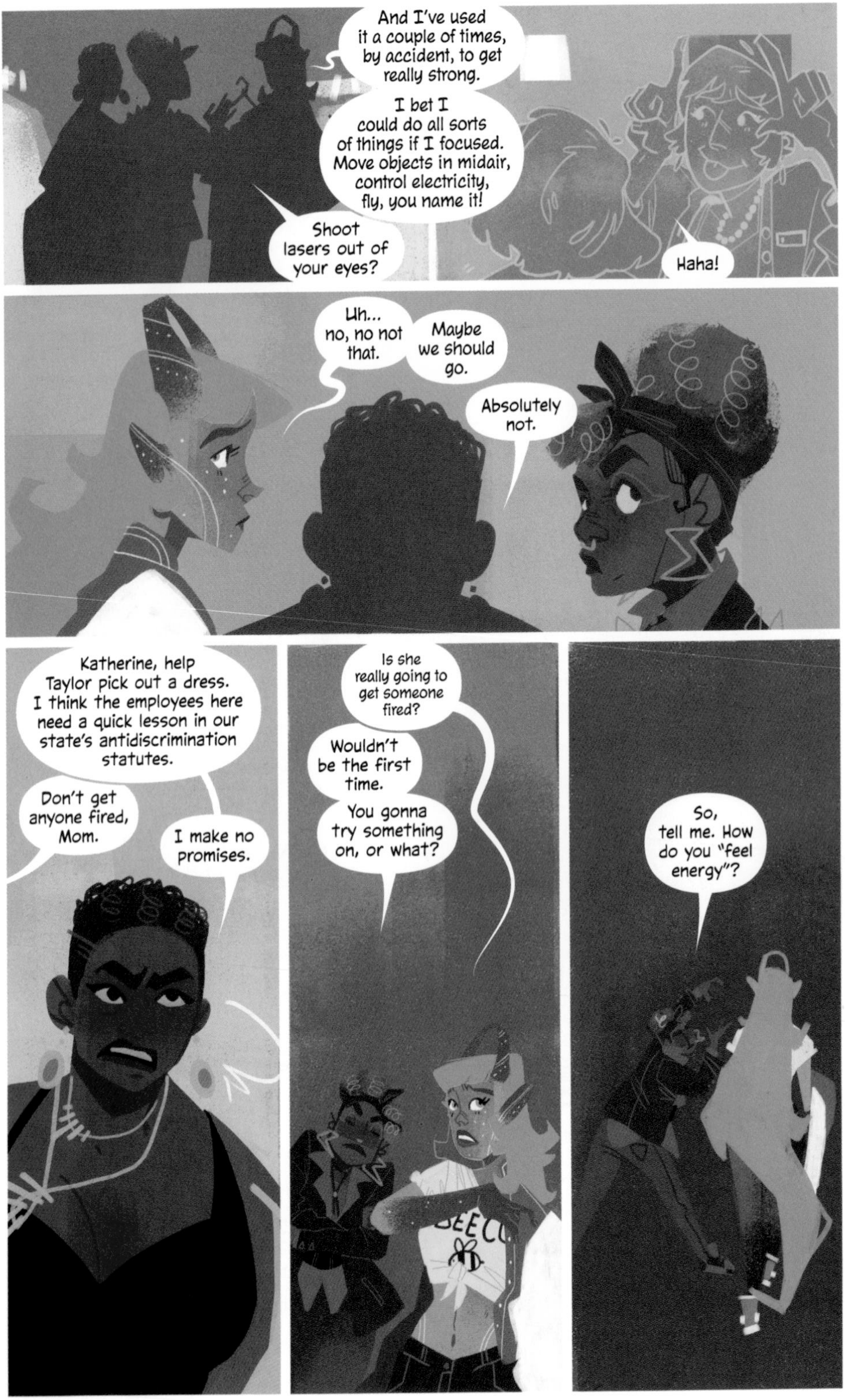
And I've used it a couple of times, by accident, to get really strong.
I bet I could do all sorts of things if I focused. Move objects in midair, control electricity, fly, you name it!
Shoot lasers out of your eyes?
Haha!
Uh... no, no not that.
Maybe we should go.
Absolutely not.
Katherine, help Taylor pick out a dress. I think the employees here need a quick lesson in our state's antidiscrimination statutes.
Don't get anyone fired, Mom.
I make no promises.
Is she really going to get someone fired?
Wouldn't be the first time.
You gonna try something on, or what?
So, tell me. How do you "feel energy"?

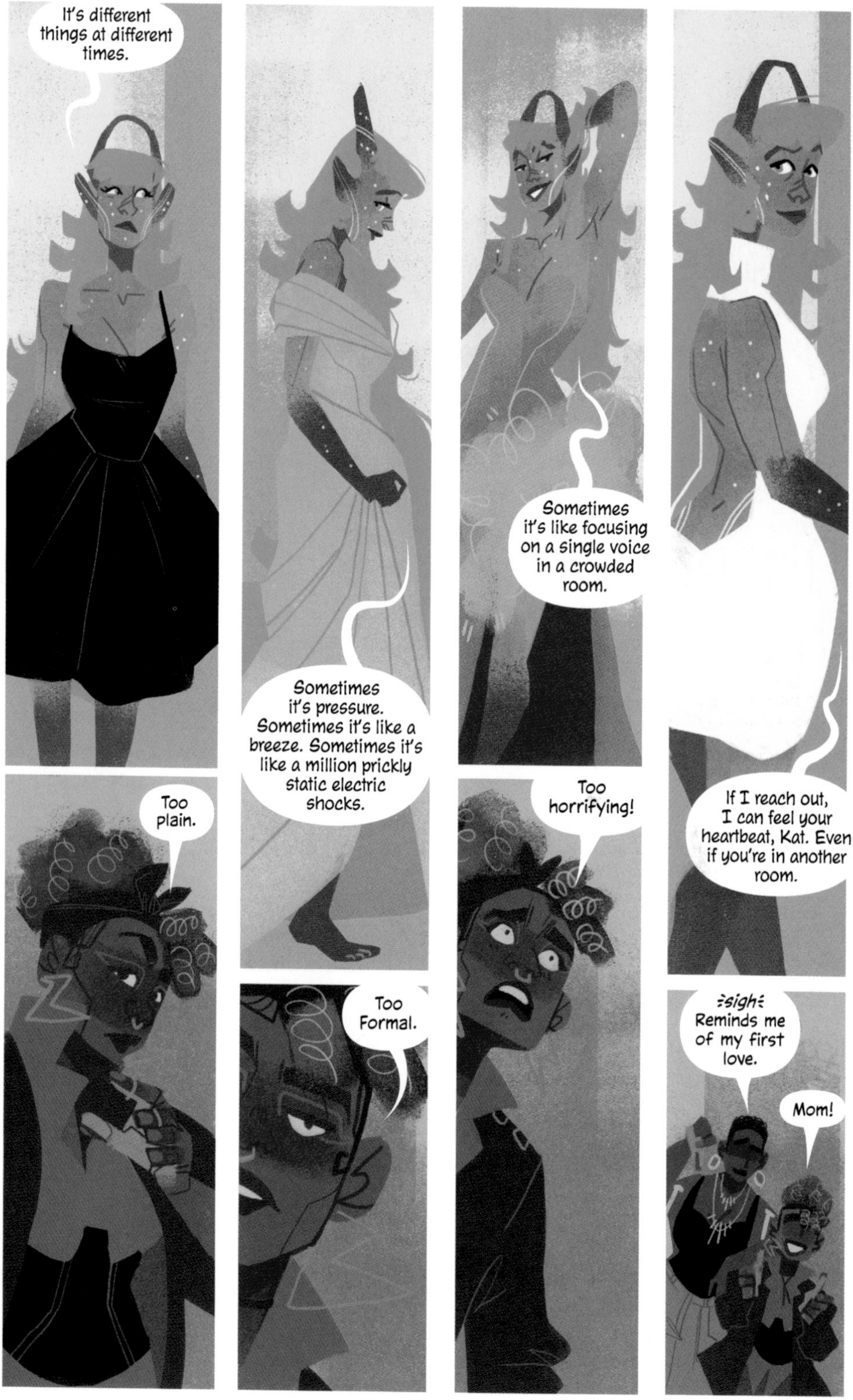
It's different things at different times.
Sometimes it's pressure. Sometimes it's like a breeze. Sometimes it's like a million prickly static electric shocks.
Sometimes it's like focusing on a single voice in a crowded room.
If I reach out, I can feel your heartbeat, Kat. Even if you're in another room.
Too plain.
Too Formal.
Too horrifying!
sigh
Reminds me of my first love.
Mom!

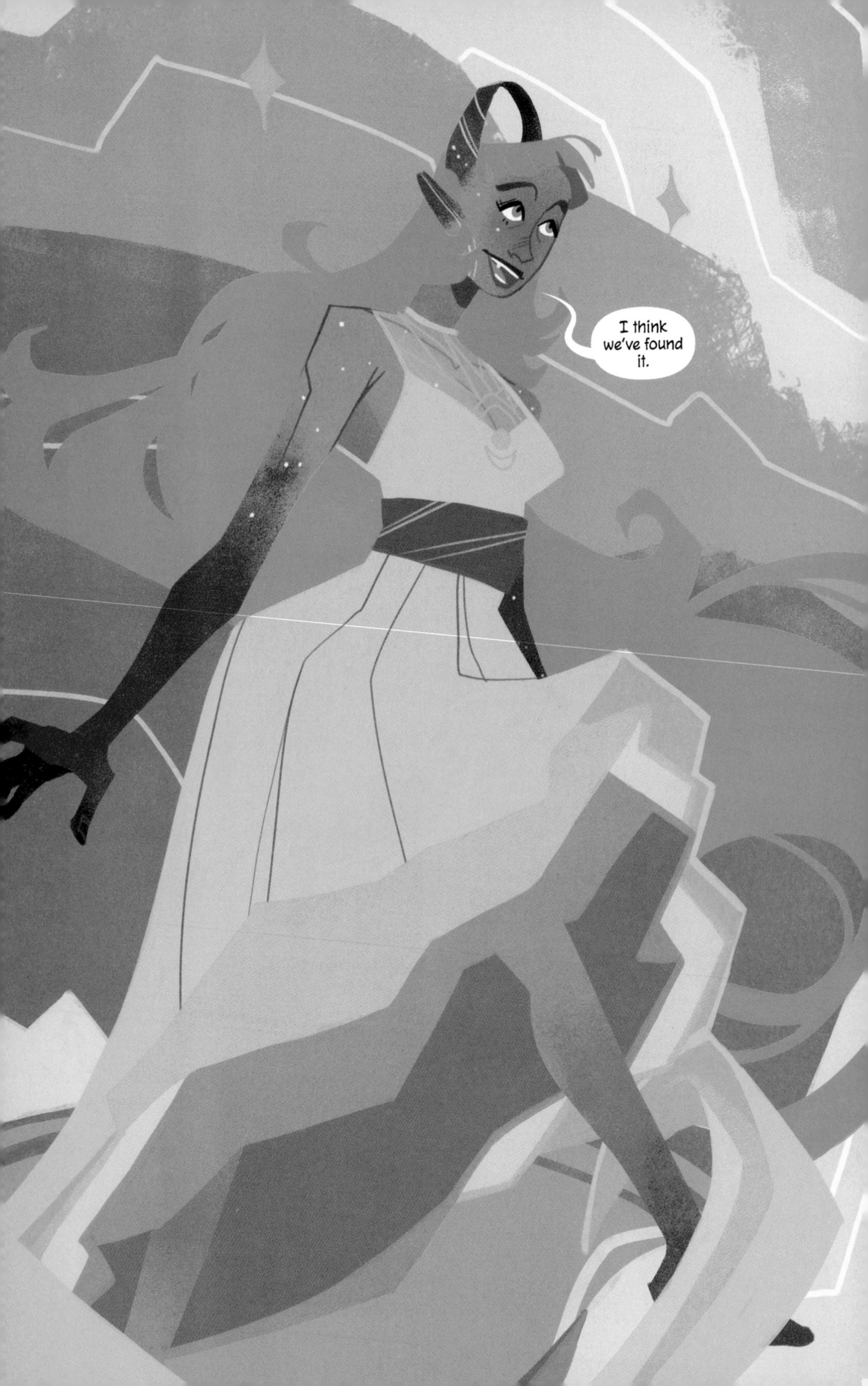
I think we've found it.

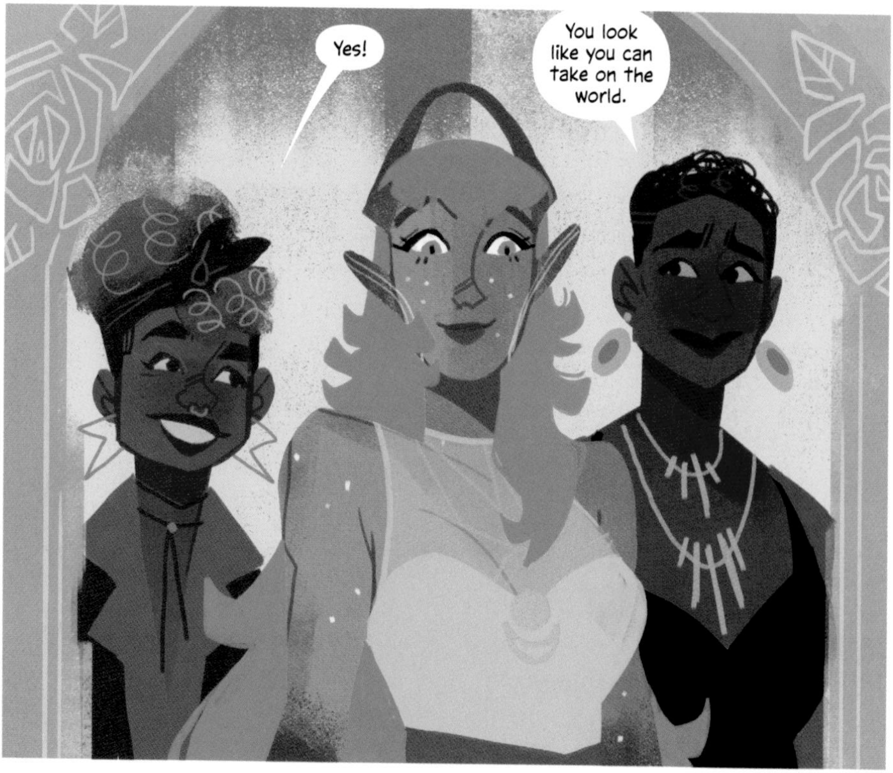
Yes!
You look like you can take on the world.

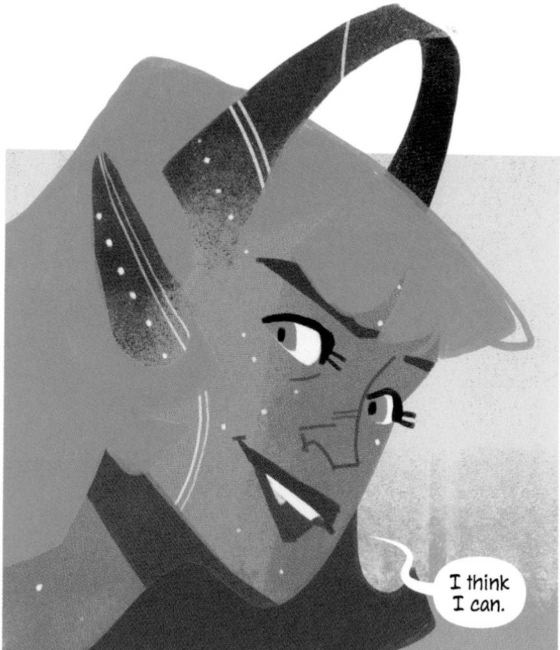
I think I can.

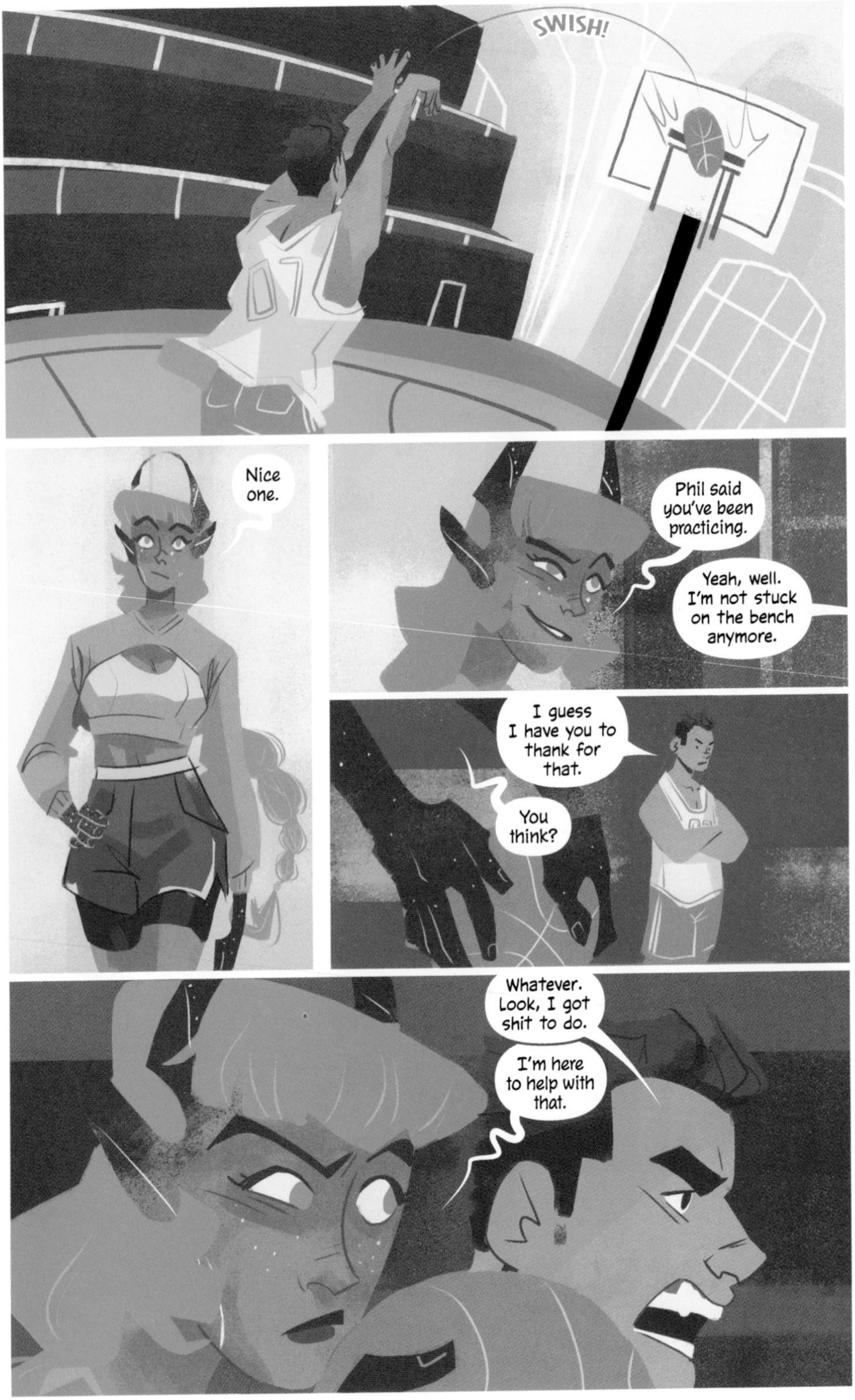
SWISH!
Nice one.
Phil said you've been practicing.
Yeah, well. I'm not stuck on the bench anymore.
I guess I have you to thank for that.
You think?
Whatever. Look, I got shit to do.
I'm here to help with that.

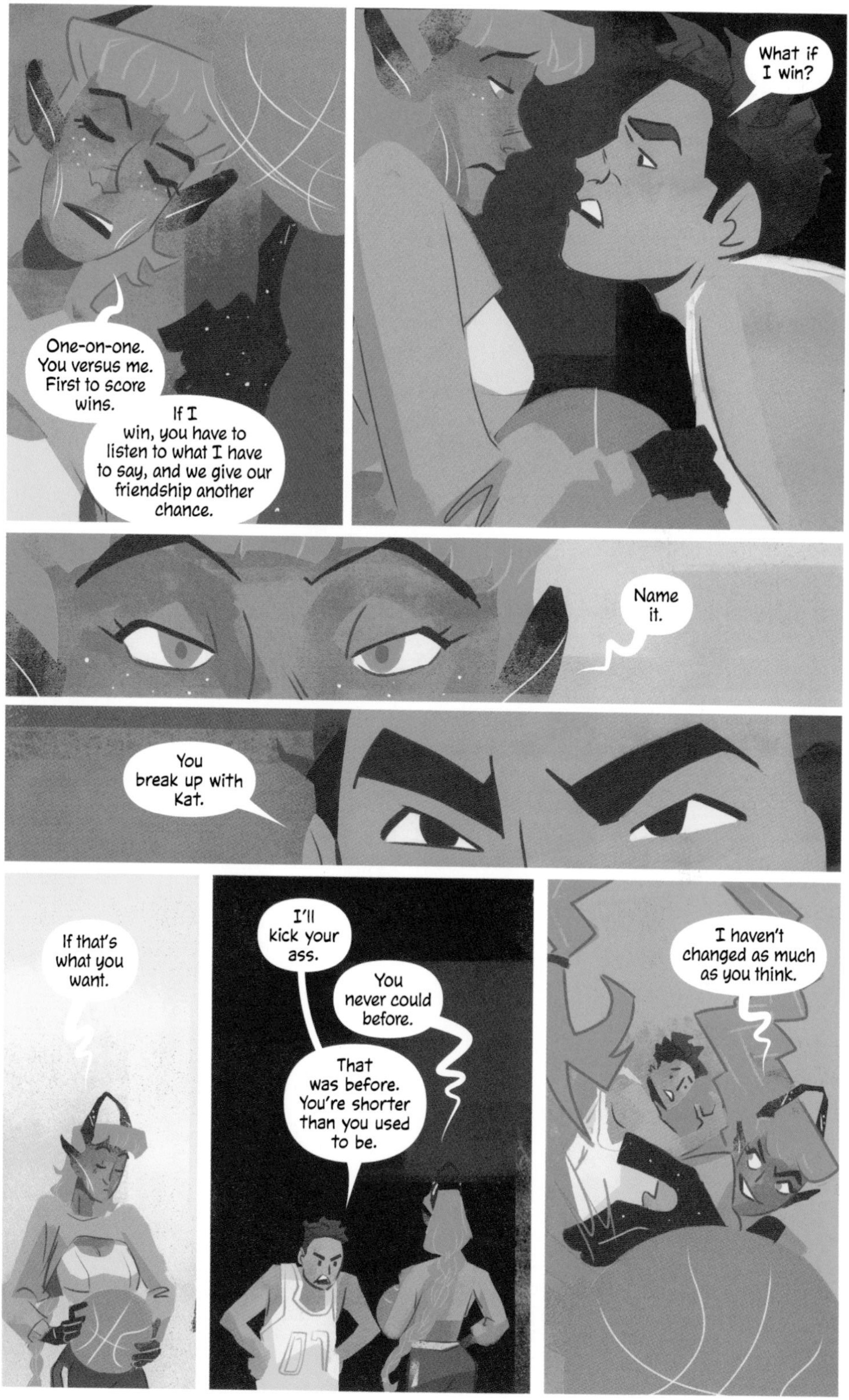
One-on-one. You versus me. First to score wins.
If I win, you have to listen to what I have to say, and we give our friendship another chance.
What if I win?
Name it.
You break up with Kat.
If that's what you want.
I'll kick your ass.
You never could before.
That was before. You're shorter than you used to be.
I haven't changed as much as you think.

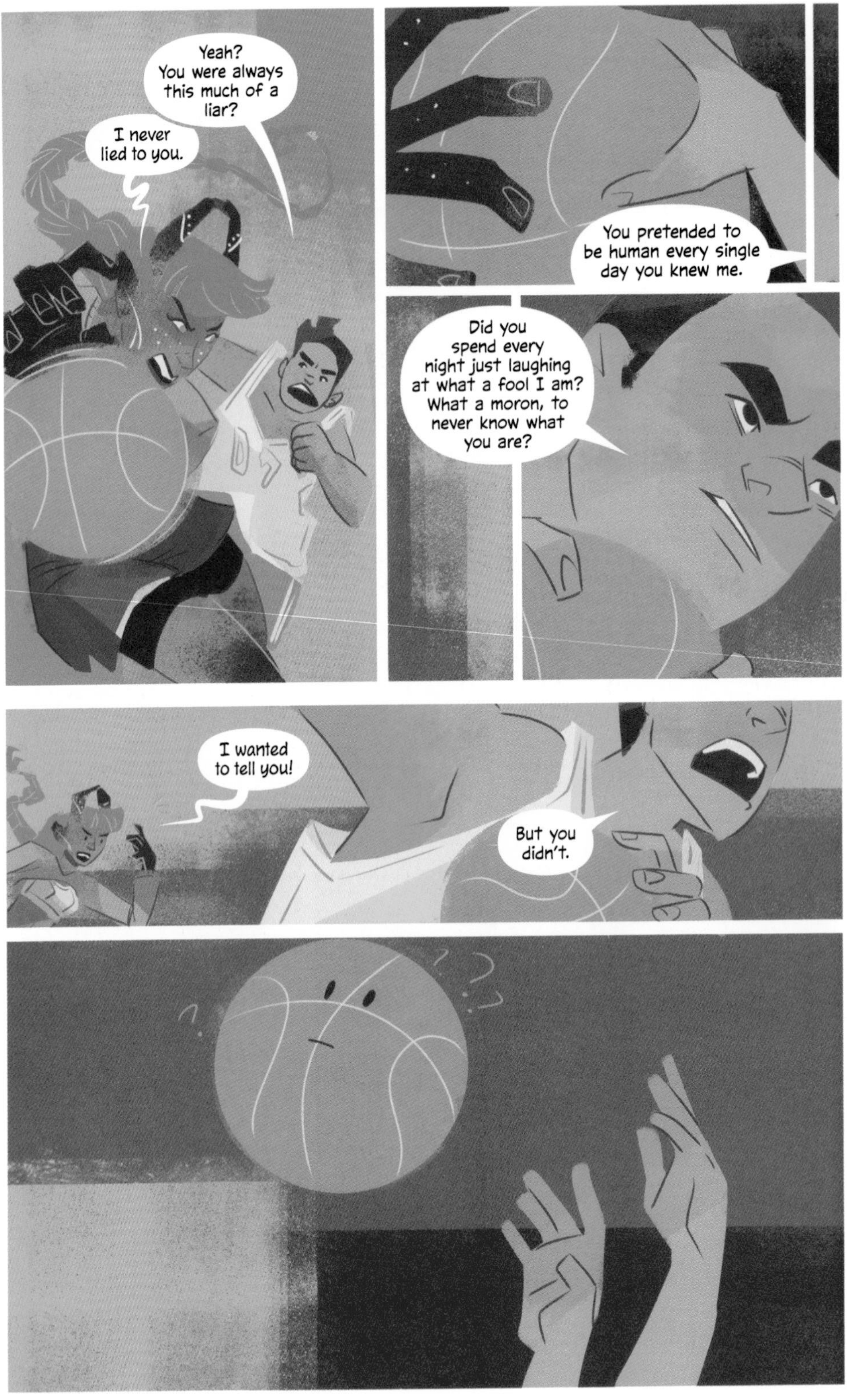

Yeah? You were always this much of a liar?
I never lied to you.
You pretended to be human every single day you knew me.
Did you spend every night just laughing at what a fool I am? What a moron, to never know what you are?
I wanted to tell you!
But you didn't.

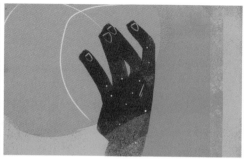

Sorry.

But that doesn't change the fact that I'm still the same person I was before.

Bullshit.

If anything, I'm more me than ever. I'm not wearing a mask.

That mask was my friend!

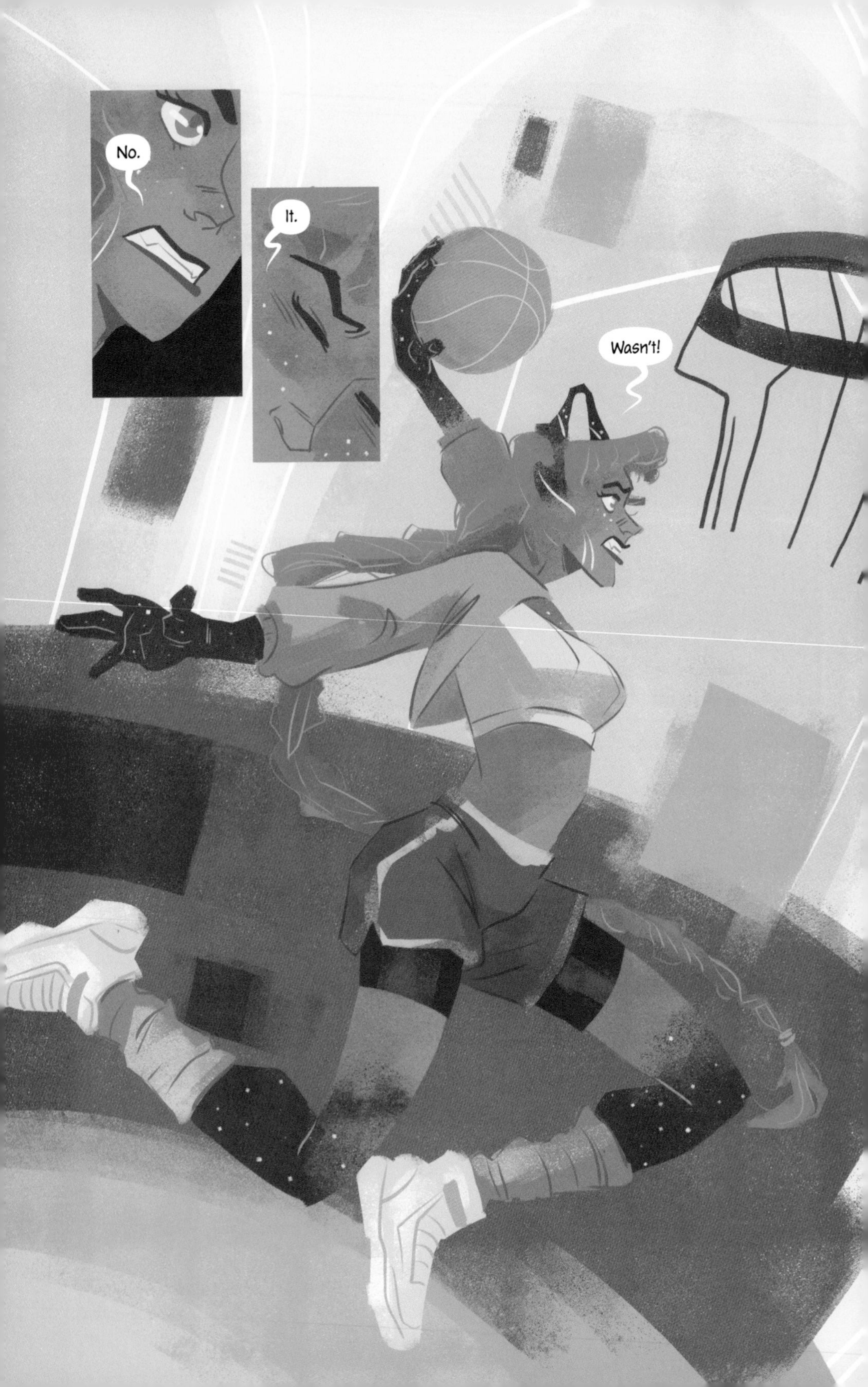
No.
It.
Wasn't!

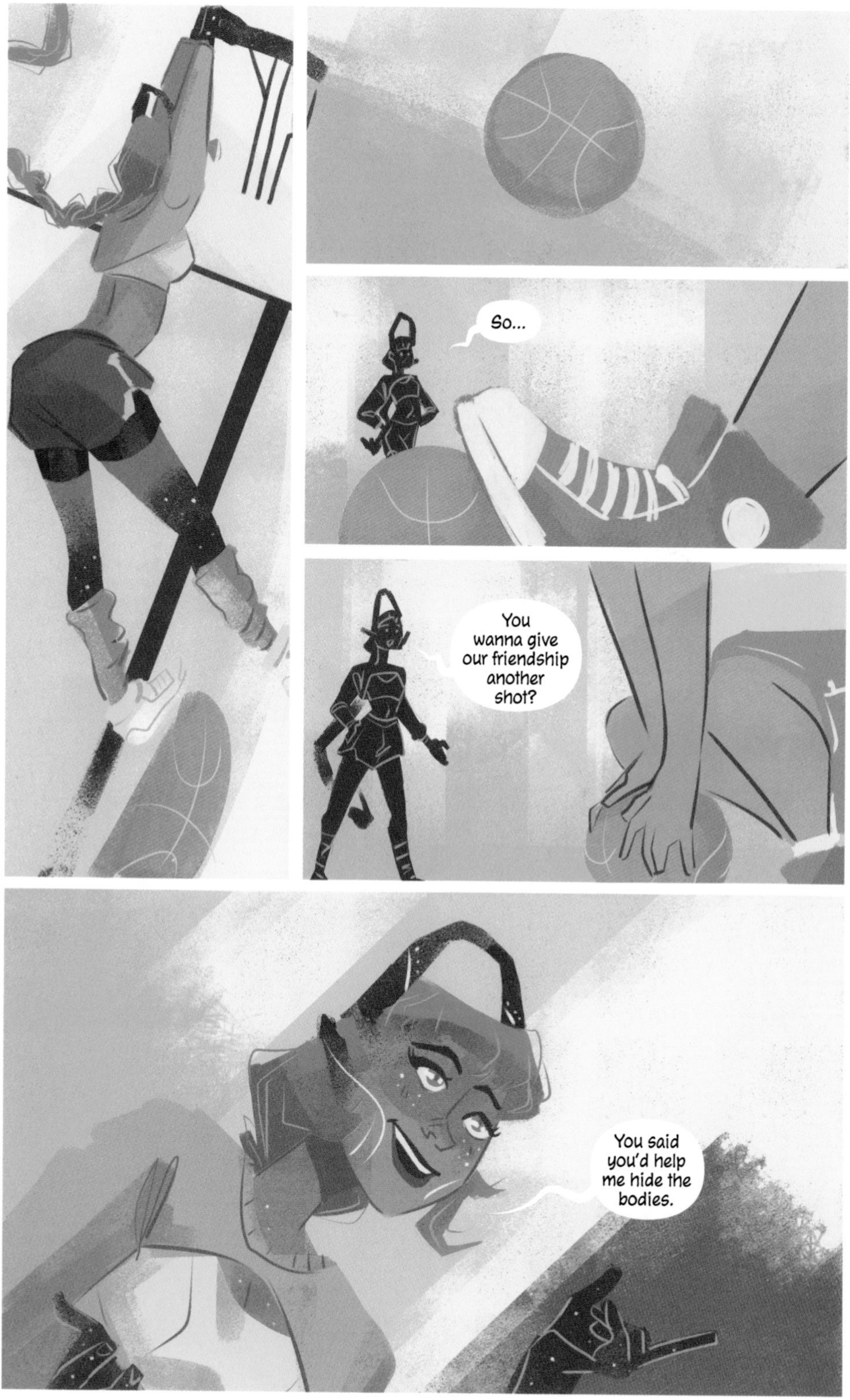
So...
You wanna give our friendship another shot?
You said you'd help me hide the bodies.

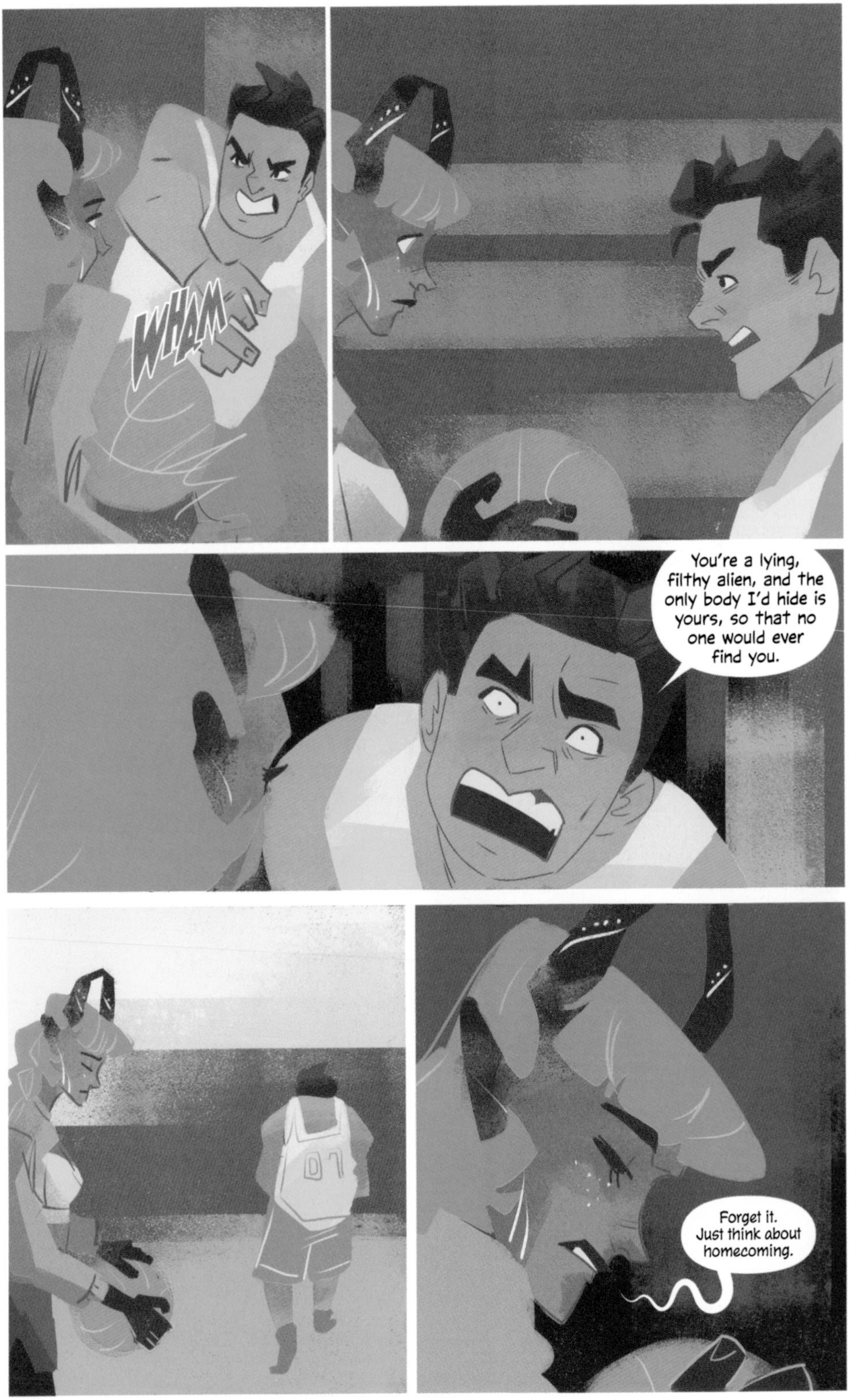
WHAM
You're a lying, filthy alien, and the only body I'd hide is yours, so that no one would ever find you.
07
Forget it. Just think about homecoming.

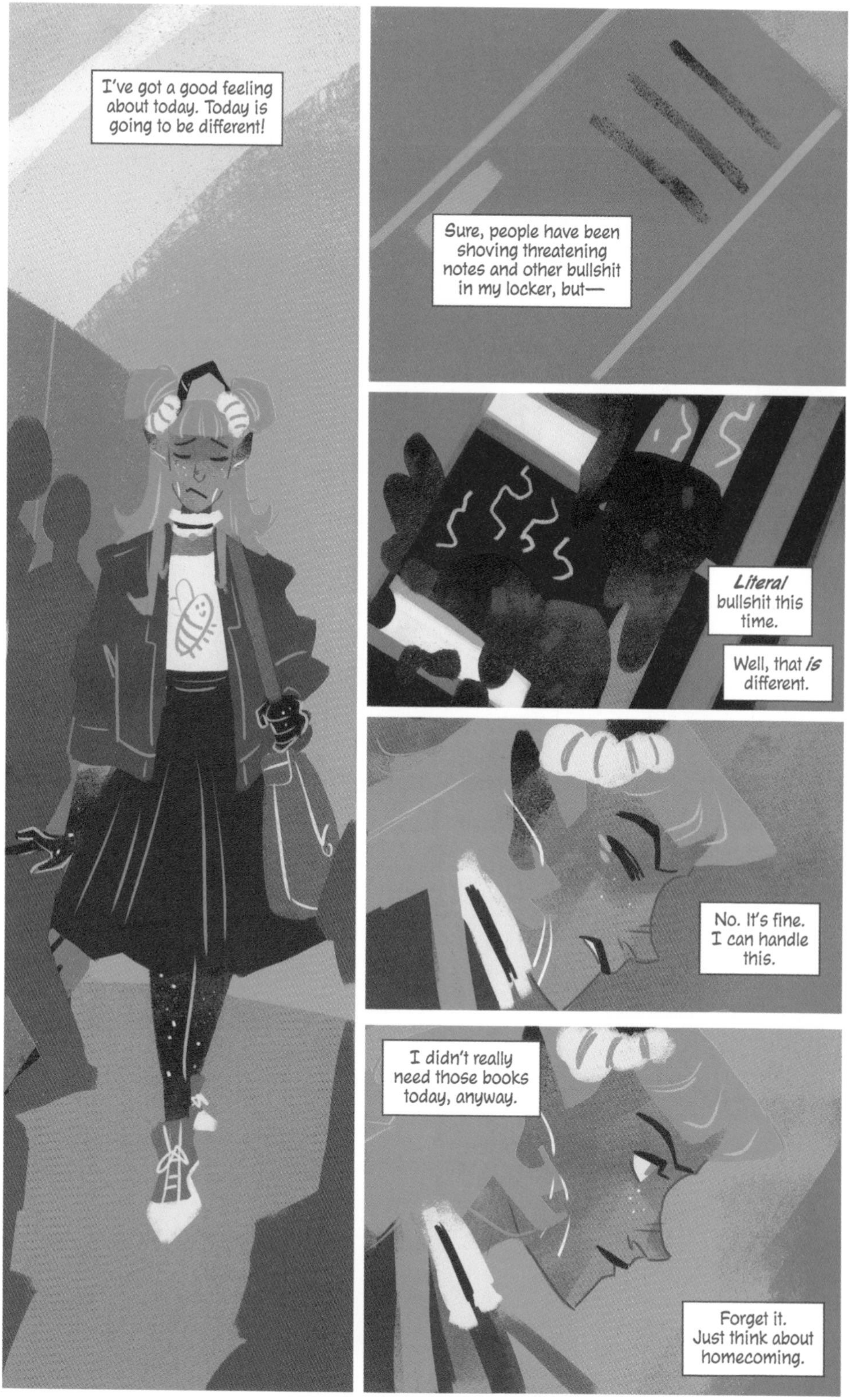
I've got a good feeling about today. Today is going to be different!
Sure, people have been shoving threatening notes and other bullshit in my locker, but—
Literal bullshit this time.
Well, that *is* different.
No. It's fine. I can handle this.
I didn't really need those books today, anyway.
Forget it. Just think about homecoming.

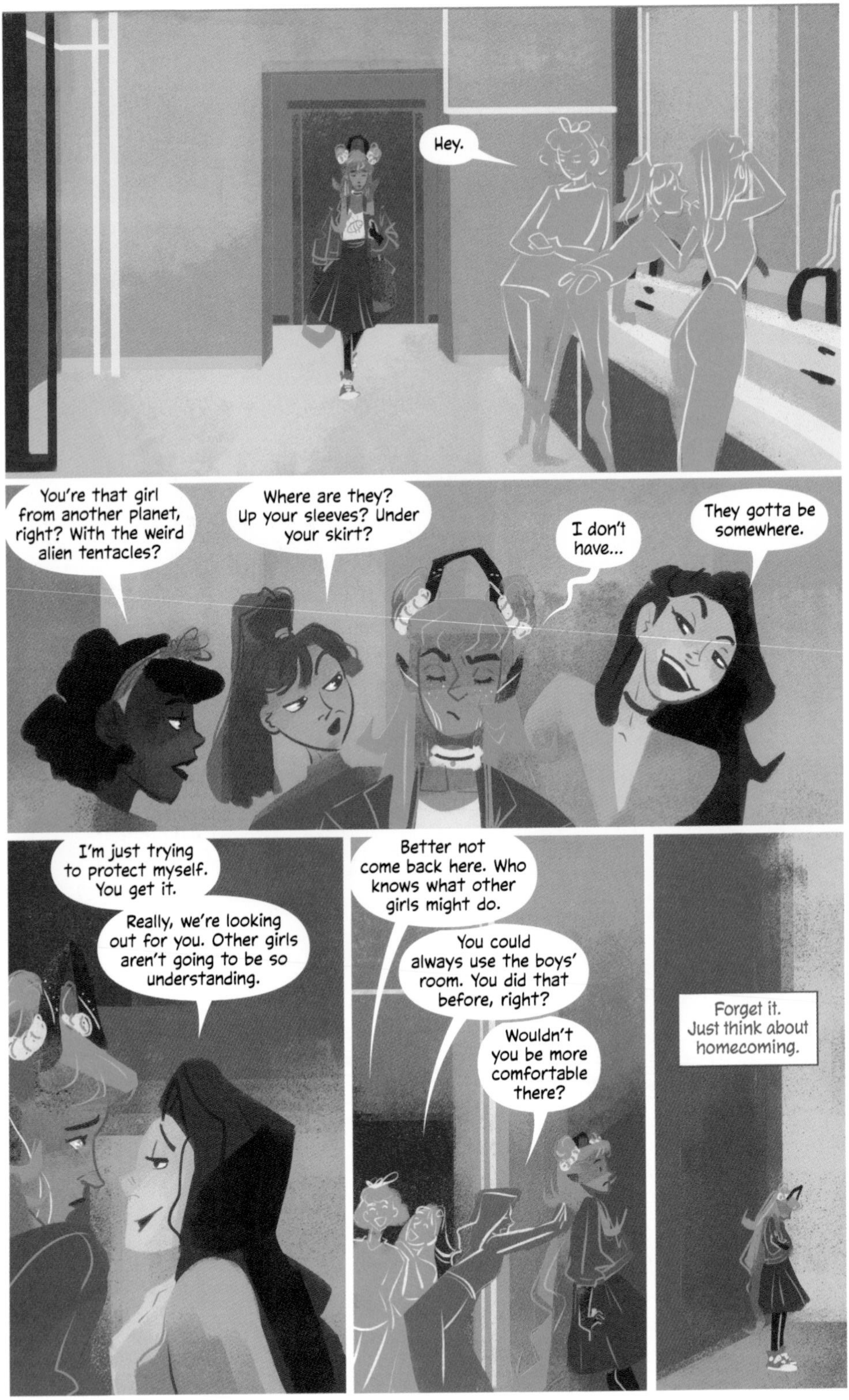

Hey.
You're that girl from another planet, right? With the weird alien tentacles?
Where are they? Up your sleeves? Under your skirt?
I don't have...
They gotta be somewhere.
I'm just trying to protect myself. You get it.
Really, we're looking out for you. Other girls aren't going to be so understanding.
Better not come back here. Who knows what other girls might do.
You could always use the boys' room. You did that before, right?
Wouldn't you be more comfortable there?
Forget it. Just think about homecoming.

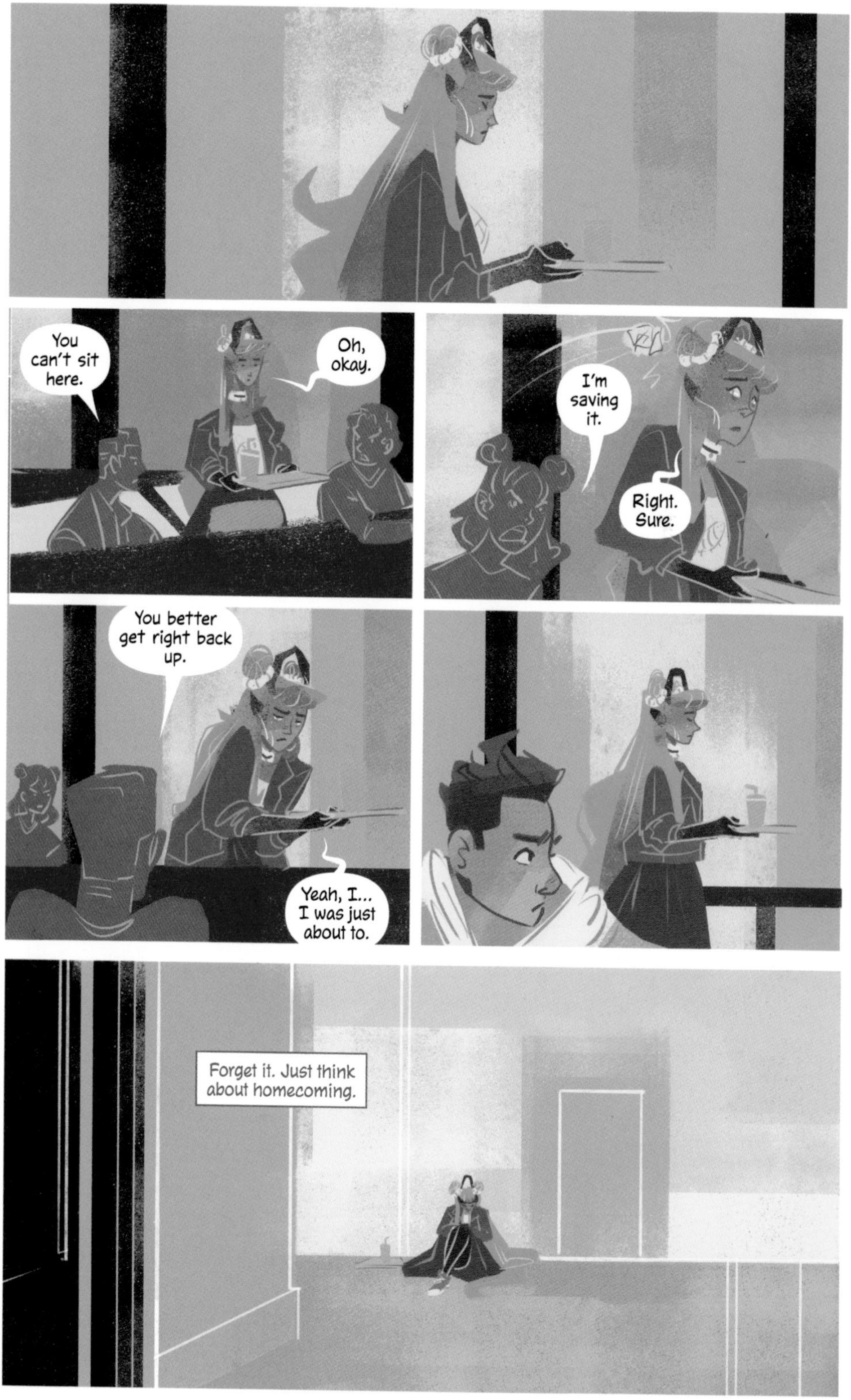
You can't sit here.
Oh, okay.
I'm saving it.
Right. Sure.
You better get right back up.
Yeah, I... I was just about to.
Forget it. Just think about homecoming.

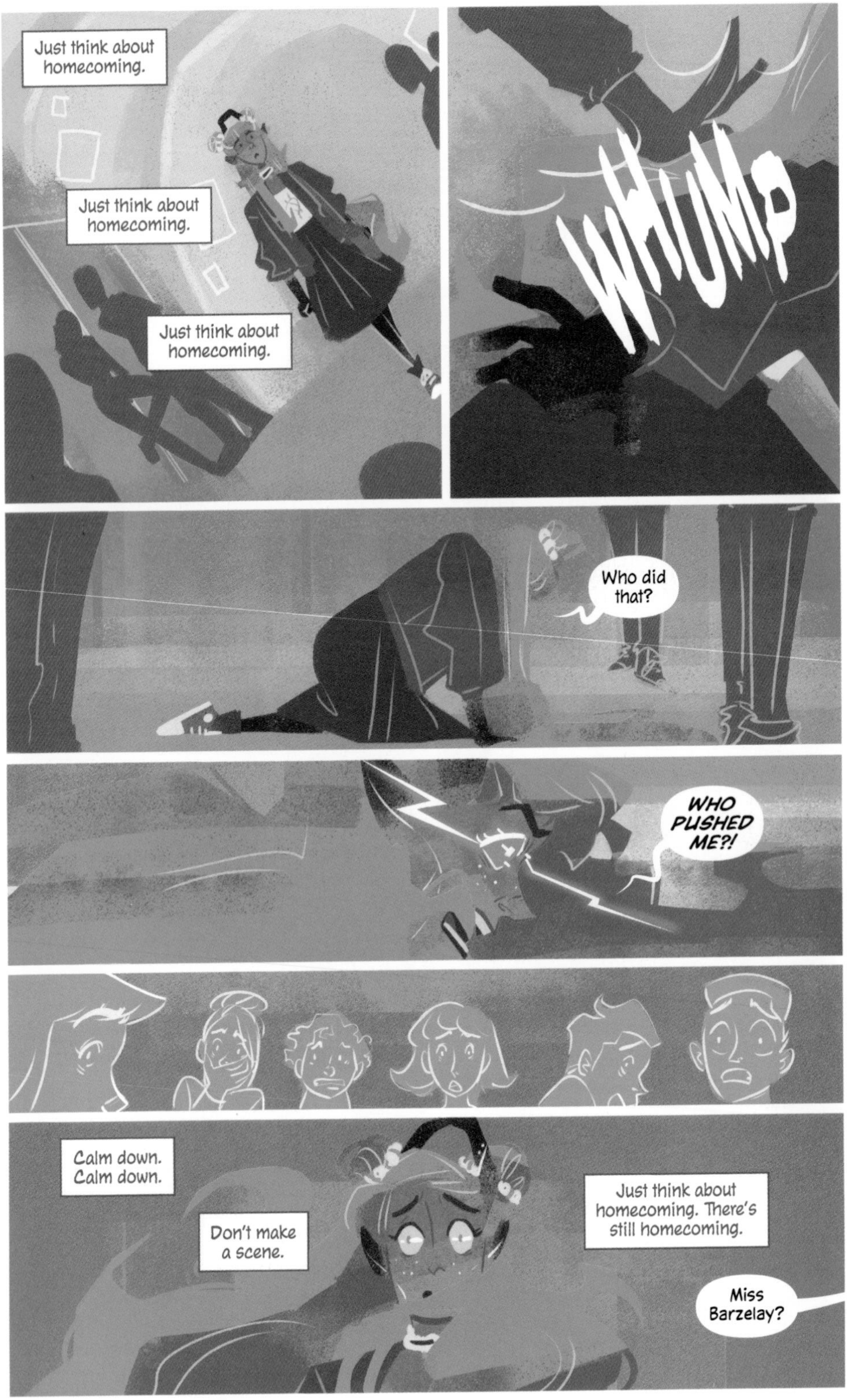
Just think about homecoming.
Just think about homecoming.
Just think about homecoming.
WHUMP
Who did that?
WHO PUSHED ME?!
Calm down. Calm down.
Don't make a scene.
Just think about homecoming. There's still homecoming.
Miss Barzelay?

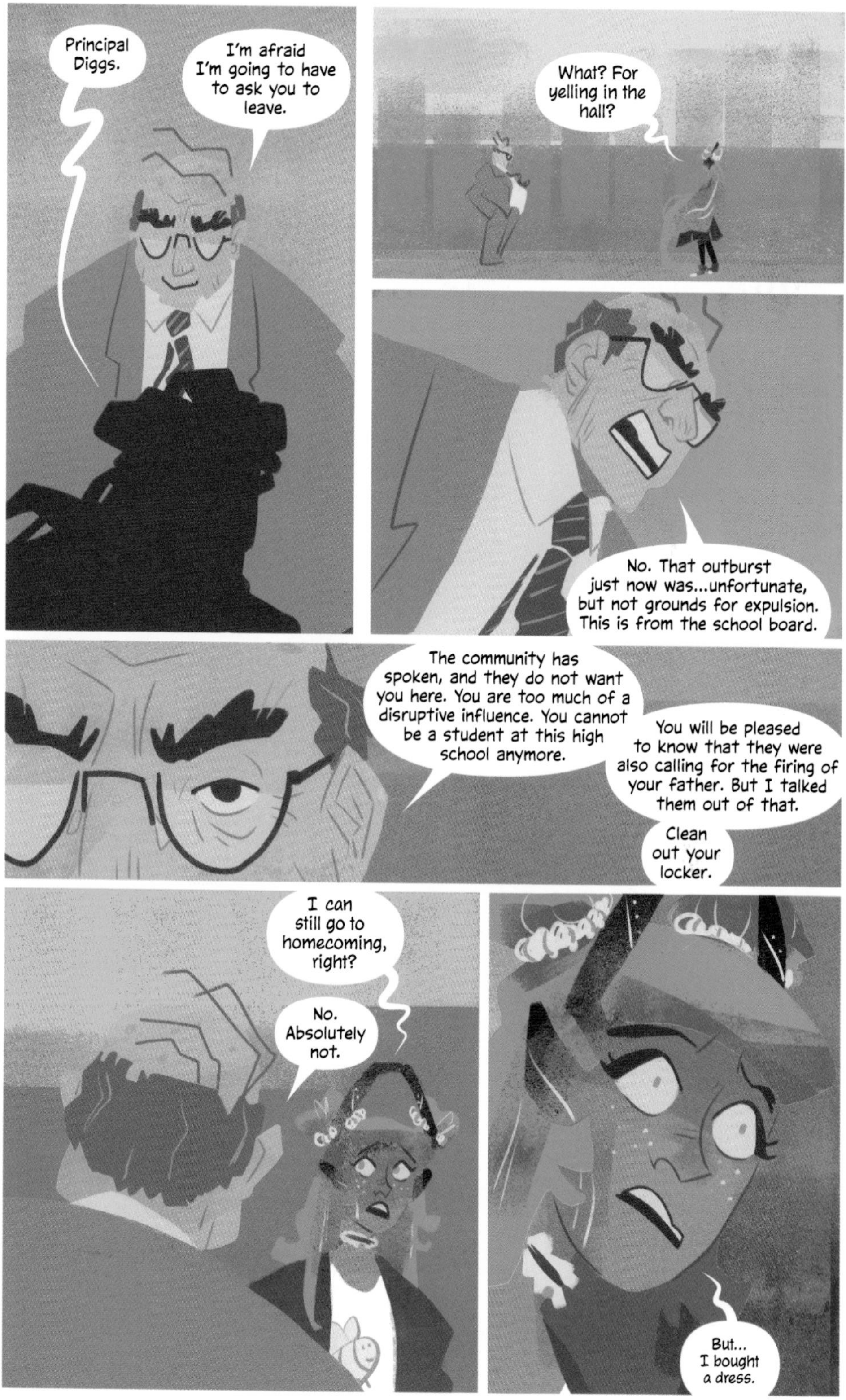
Principal Diggs.
I'm afraid I'm going to have to ask you to leave.
What? For yelling in the hall?
No. That outburst just now was...unfortunate, but not grounds for expulsion. This is from the school board.
The community has spoken, and they do not want you here. You are too much of a disruptive influence. You cannot be a student at this high school anymore.
You will be pleased to know that they were also calling for the firing of your father. But I talked them out of that.
Clean out your locker.
I can still go to homecoming, right?
No. Absolutely not.
But... I bought a dress.

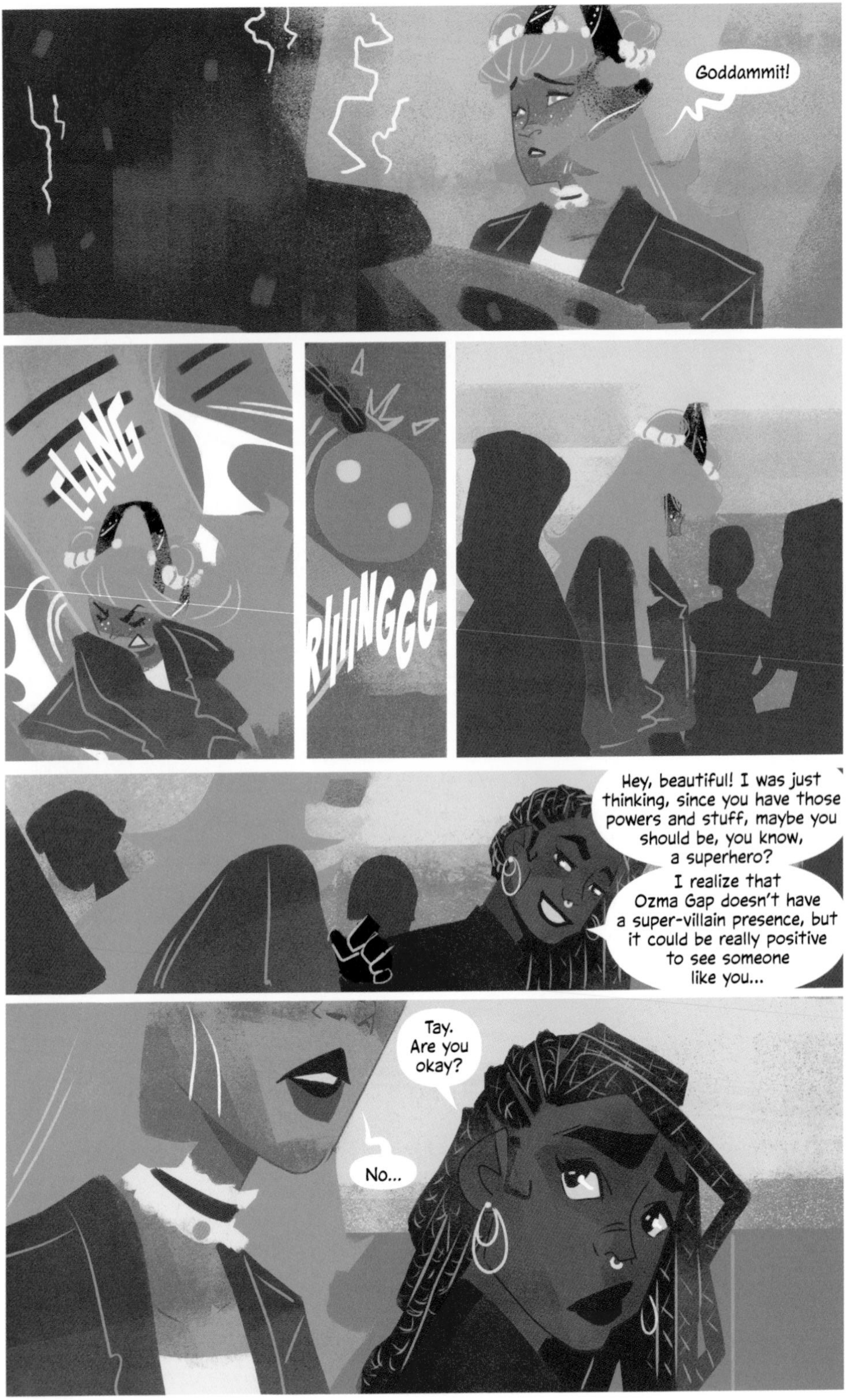
Goddammit!
CLANG
RIIIINGGG
Hey, beautiful! I was just thinking, since you have those powers and stuff, maybe you should be, you know, a superhero?
I realize that Ozma Gap doesn't have a super-villain presence, but it could be really positive to see someone like you...
Tay. Are you okay?
No...

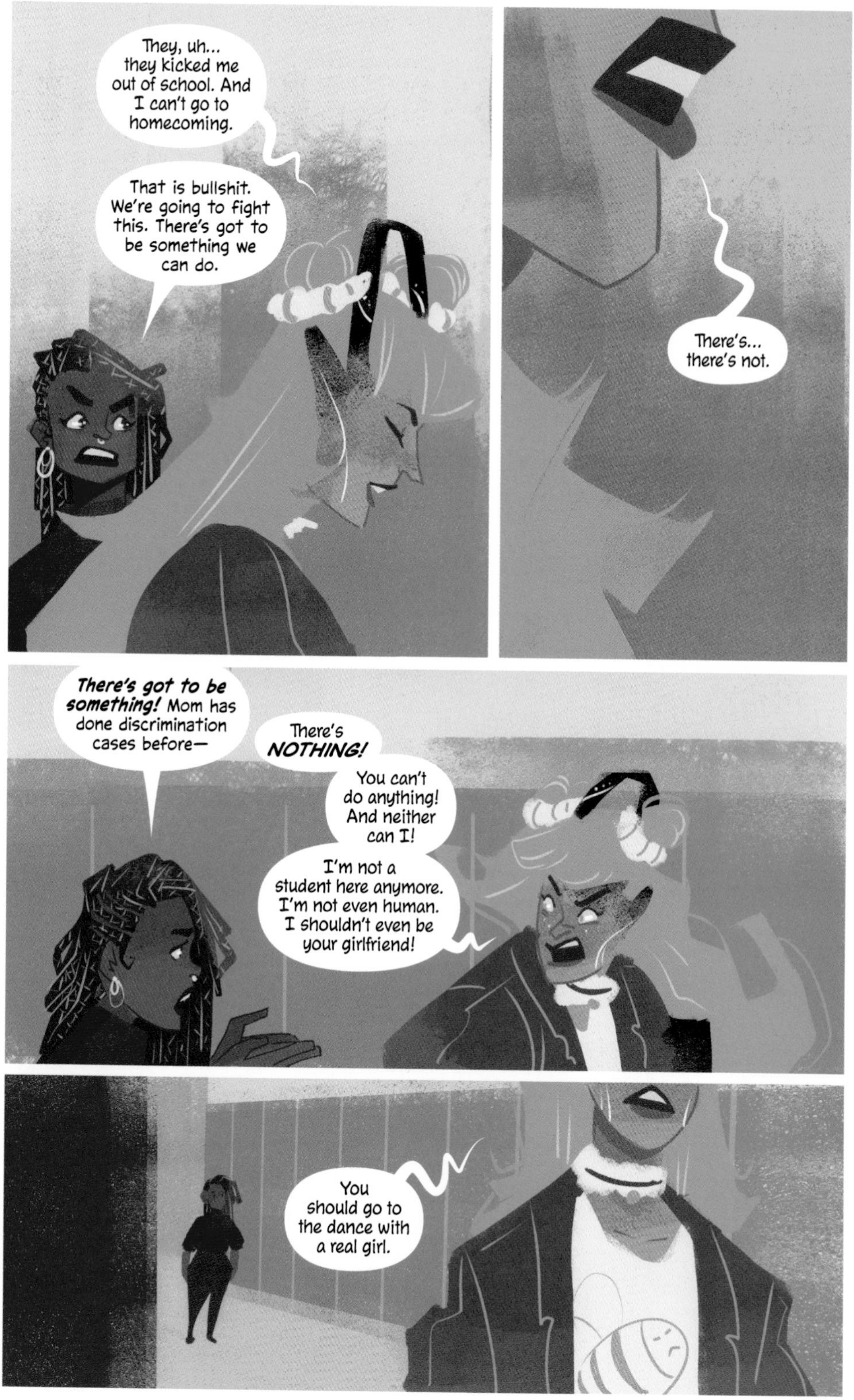
They, uh... they kicked me out of school. And I can't go to homecoming.
That is bullshit. We're going to fight this. There's got to be something we can do.
There's... there's not.
There's got to be something! Mom has done discrimination cases before—
There's ***NOTHING!***
You can't do anything! And neither can I!
I'm not a student here anymore. I'm not even human. I shouldn't even be your girlfriend!
You should go to the dance with a real girl.

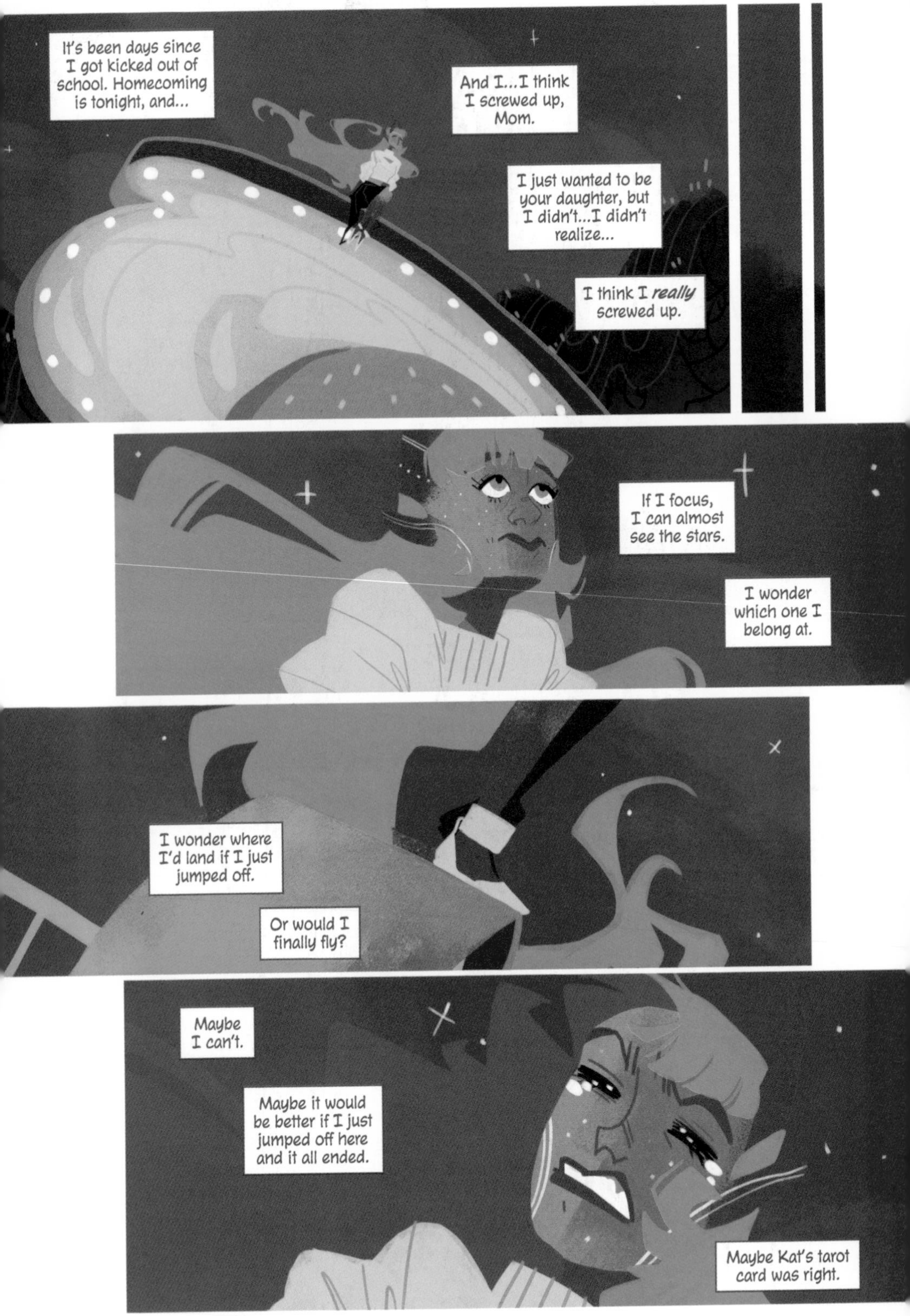
It's been days since I got kicked out of school. Homecoming is tonight, and...
And I...I think I screwed up, Mom.
I just wanted to be your daughter, but I didn't...I didn't realize...
I think I *really* screwed up.
If I focus, I can almost see the stars.
I wonder which one I belong at.
I wonder where I'd land if I just jumped off.
Or would I finally fly?
Maybe I can't.
Maybe it would be better if I just jumped off here and it all ended.
Maybe Kat's tarot card was right.

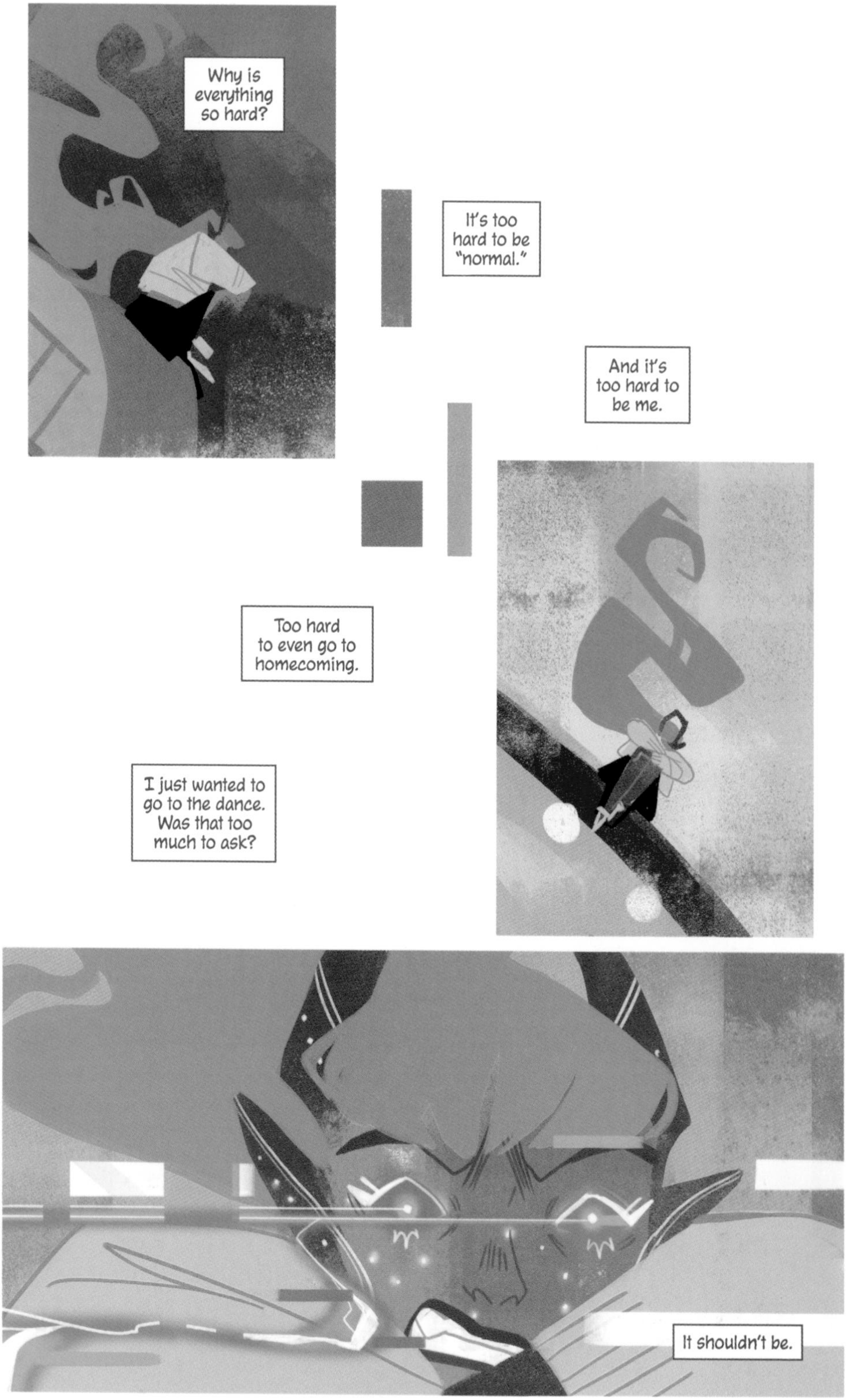
Why is everything so hard?
It's too hard to be "normal."
And it's too hard to be me.
Too hard to even go to homecoming.
I just wanted to go to the dance. Was that too much to ask?
It shouldn't be.

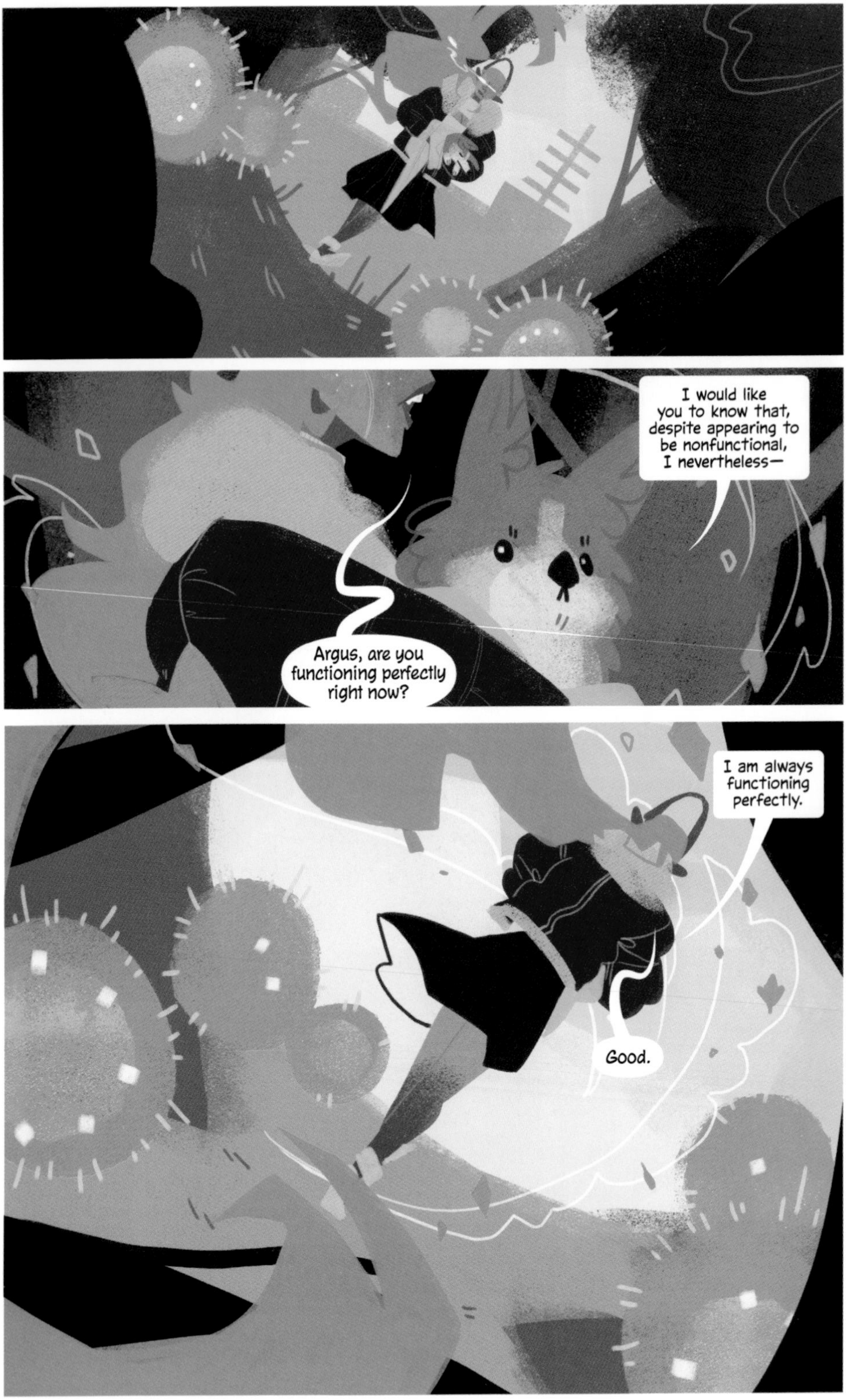
I would like you to know that, despite appearing to be nonfunctional, I nevertheless—
Argus, are you functioning perfectly right now?
I am always functioning perfectly.
Good.

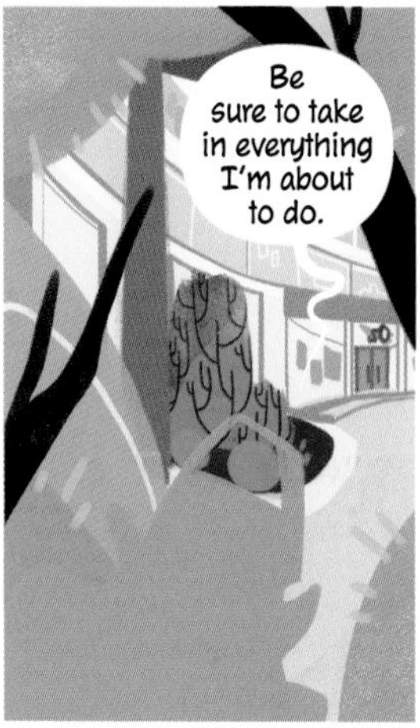
Be sure to take in everything I'm about to do.

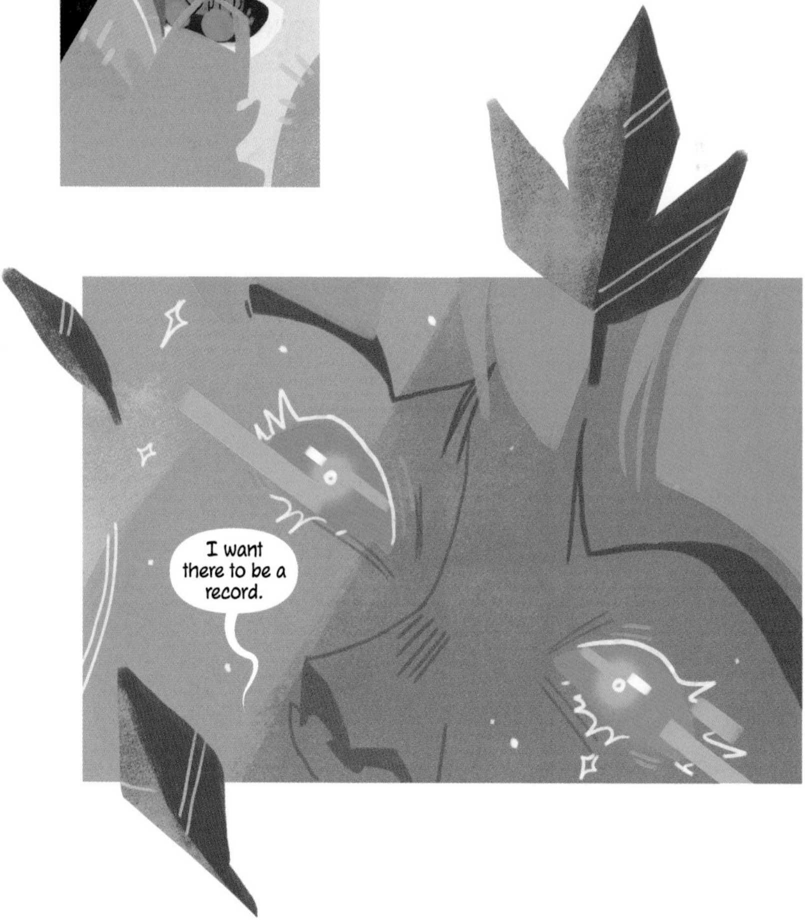
I want there to be a record.

chapter 5
Hang on to Yourself

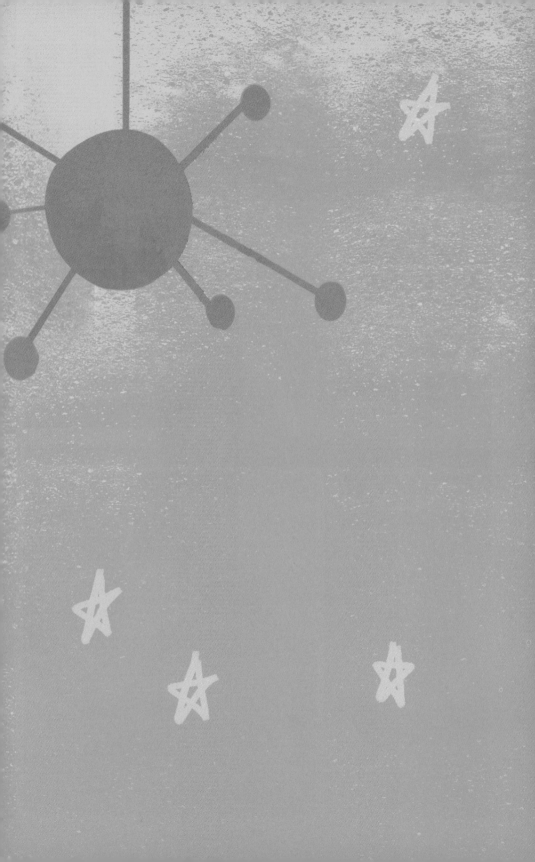

Good. That's the last of them.

The school's empty.

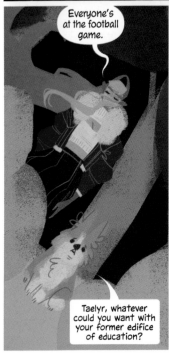

Everyone's at the football game.

Taelyr, whatever could you want with your former edifice of education?

I'm going to raze it to the ground.

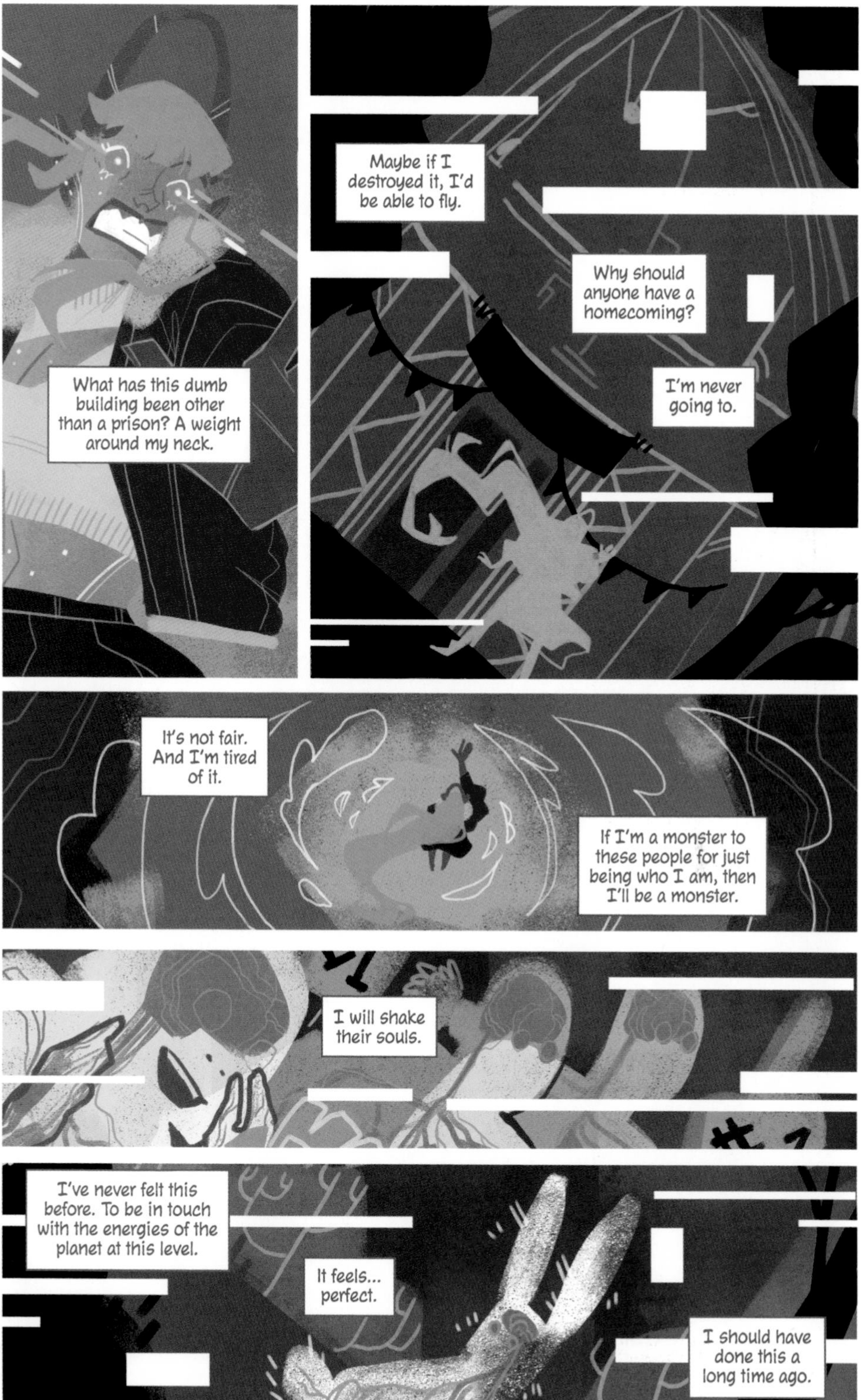
What has this dumb building been other than a prison? A weight around my neck.
Maybe if I destroyed it, I'd be able to fly.
Why should anyone have a homecoming?
I'm never going to.
It's not fair. And I'm tired of it.
If I'm a monster to these people for just being who I am, then I'll be a monster.
I will shake their souls.
I've never felt this before. To be in touch with the energies of the planet at this level.
It feels... perfect.
I should have done this a long time ago.

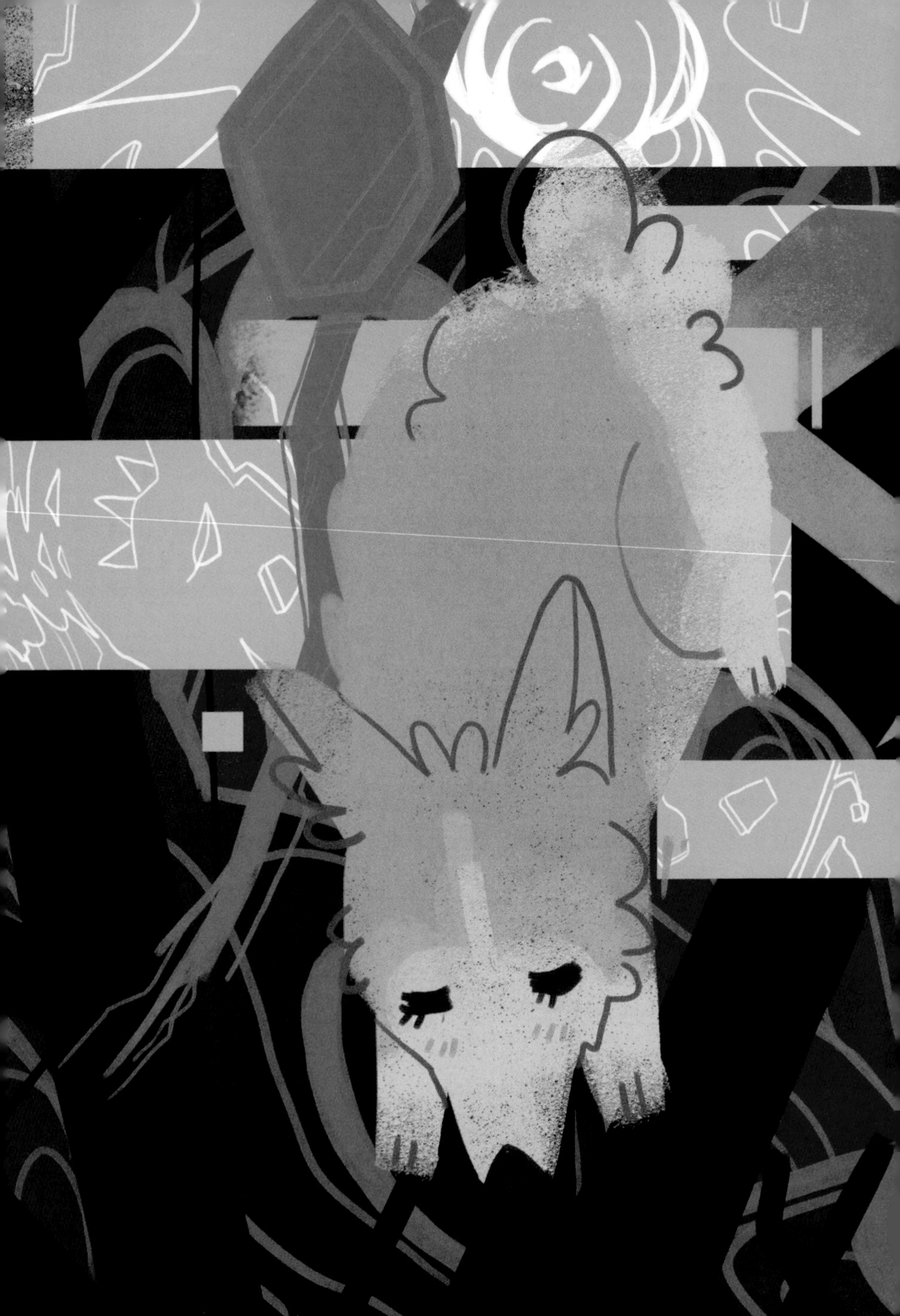

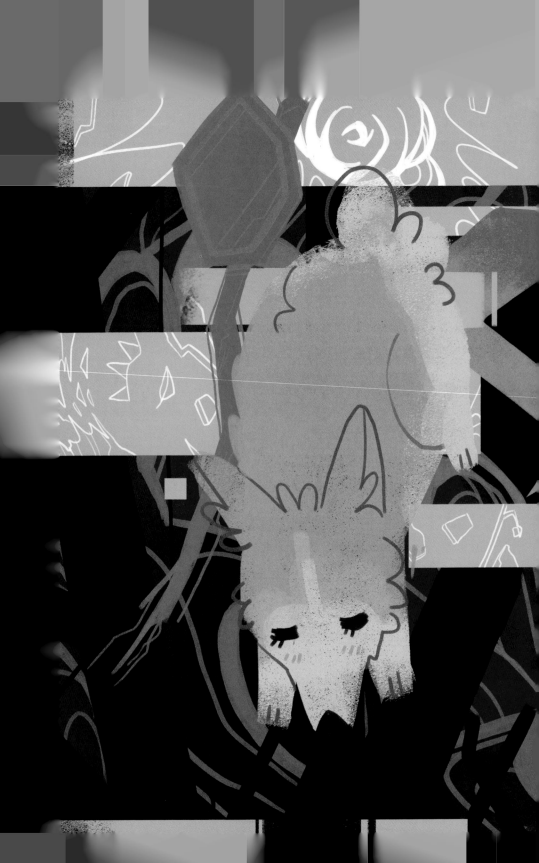

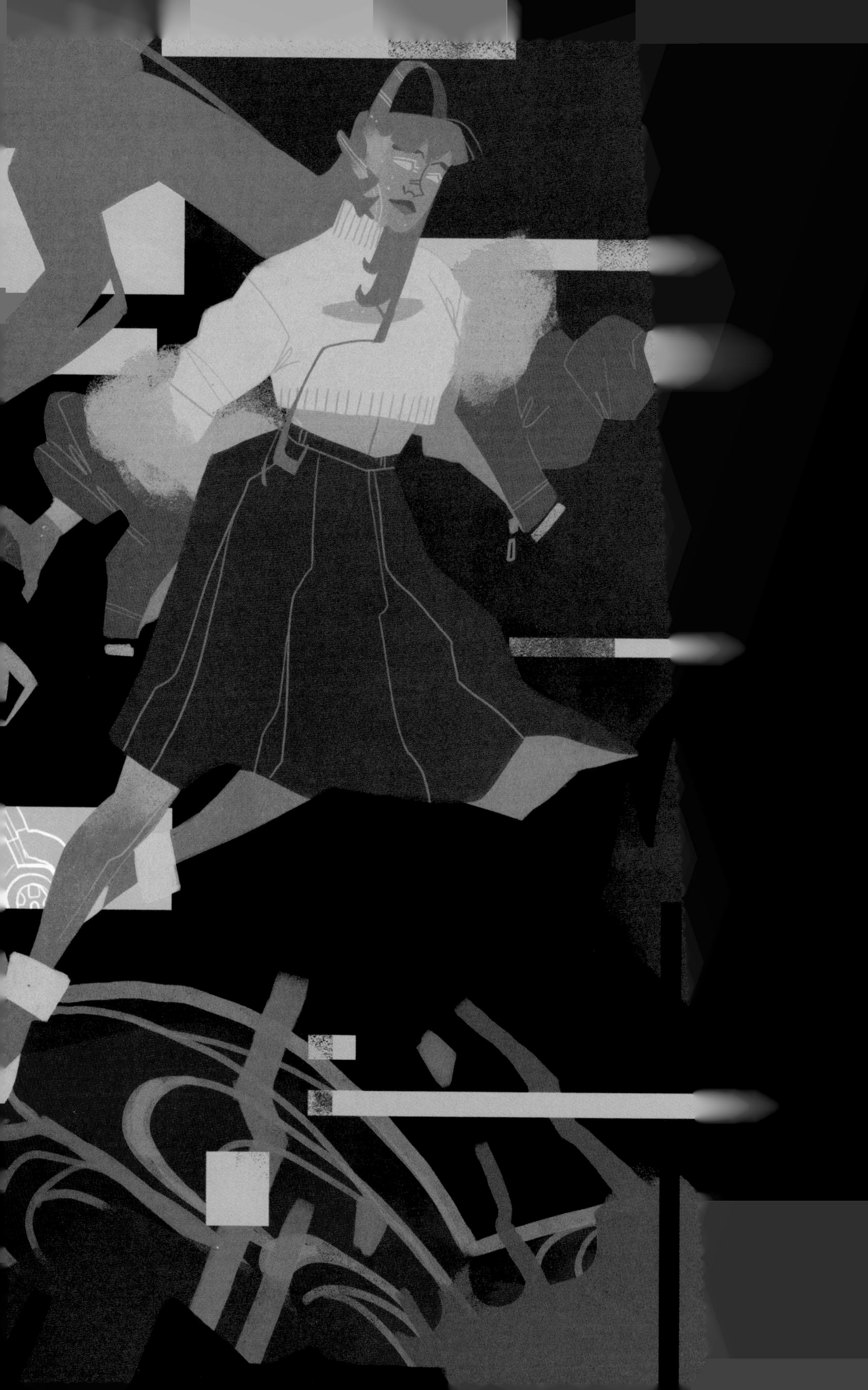

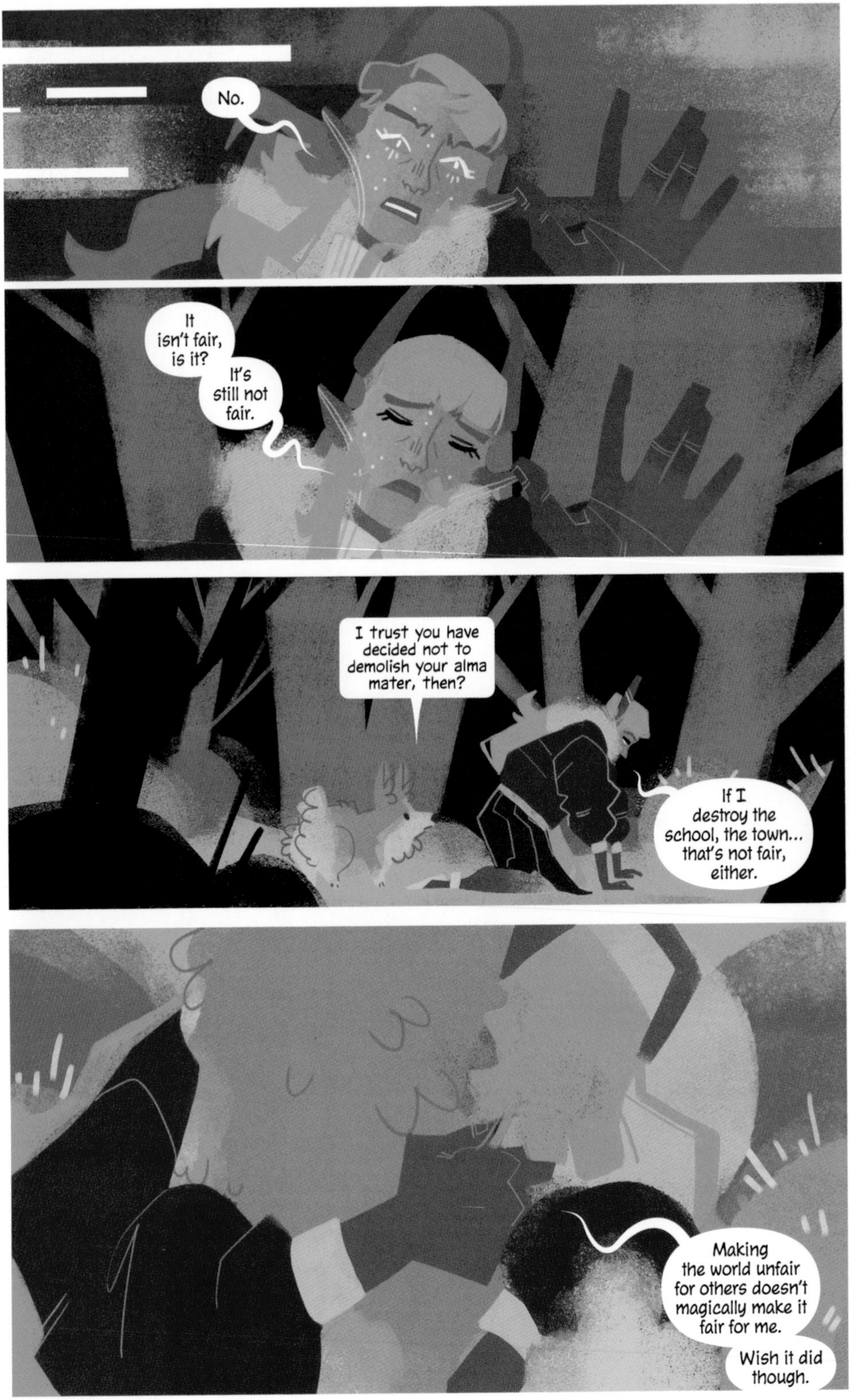
No.
It isn't fair, is it?
It's still not fair.
I trust you have decided not to demolish your alma mater, then?
If I destroy the school, the town... that's not fair, either.
Making the world unfair for others doesn't magically make it fair for me.
Wish it did though.

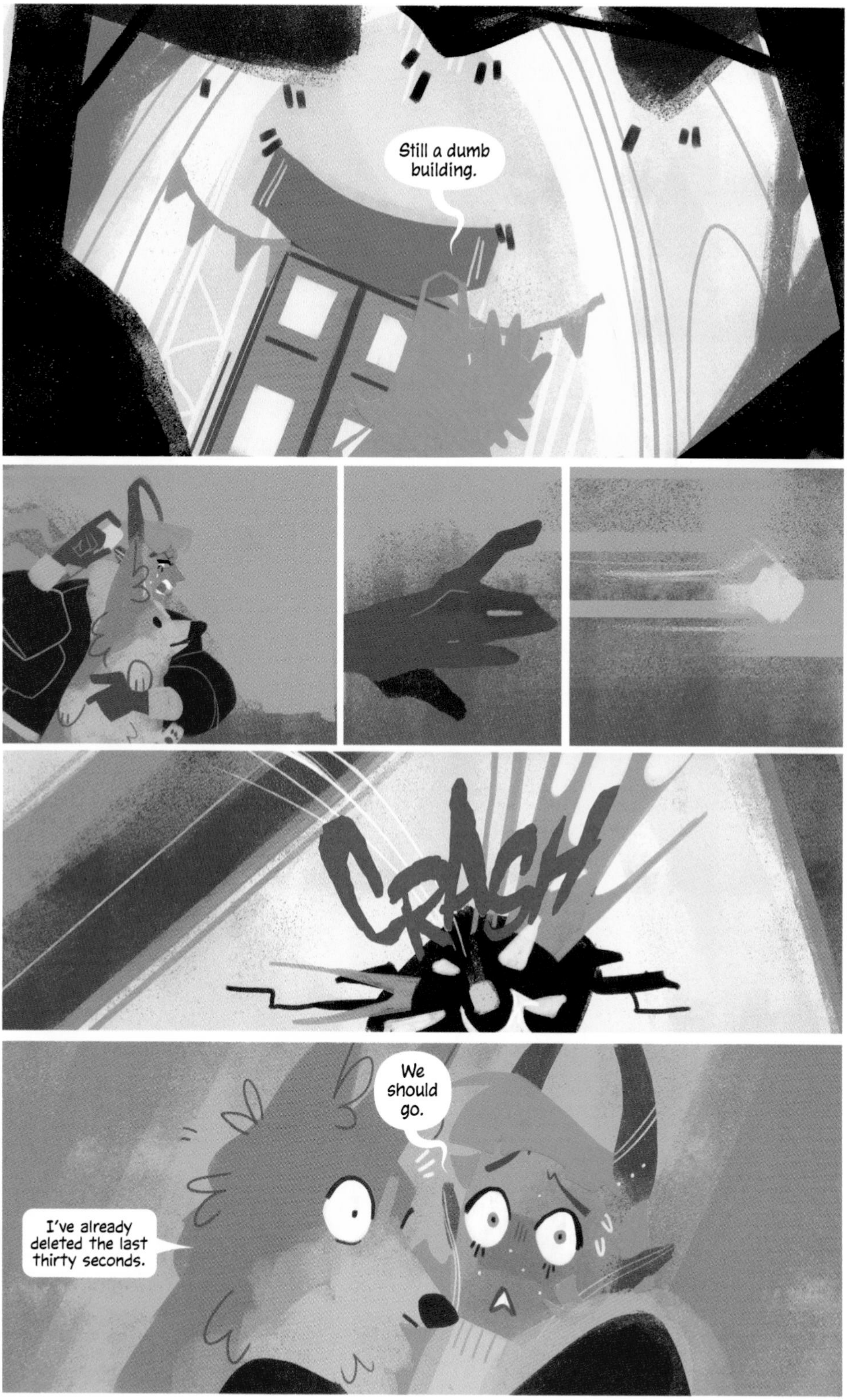
Still a dumb building.
CRASH
We should go.
I've already deleted the last thirty seconds.

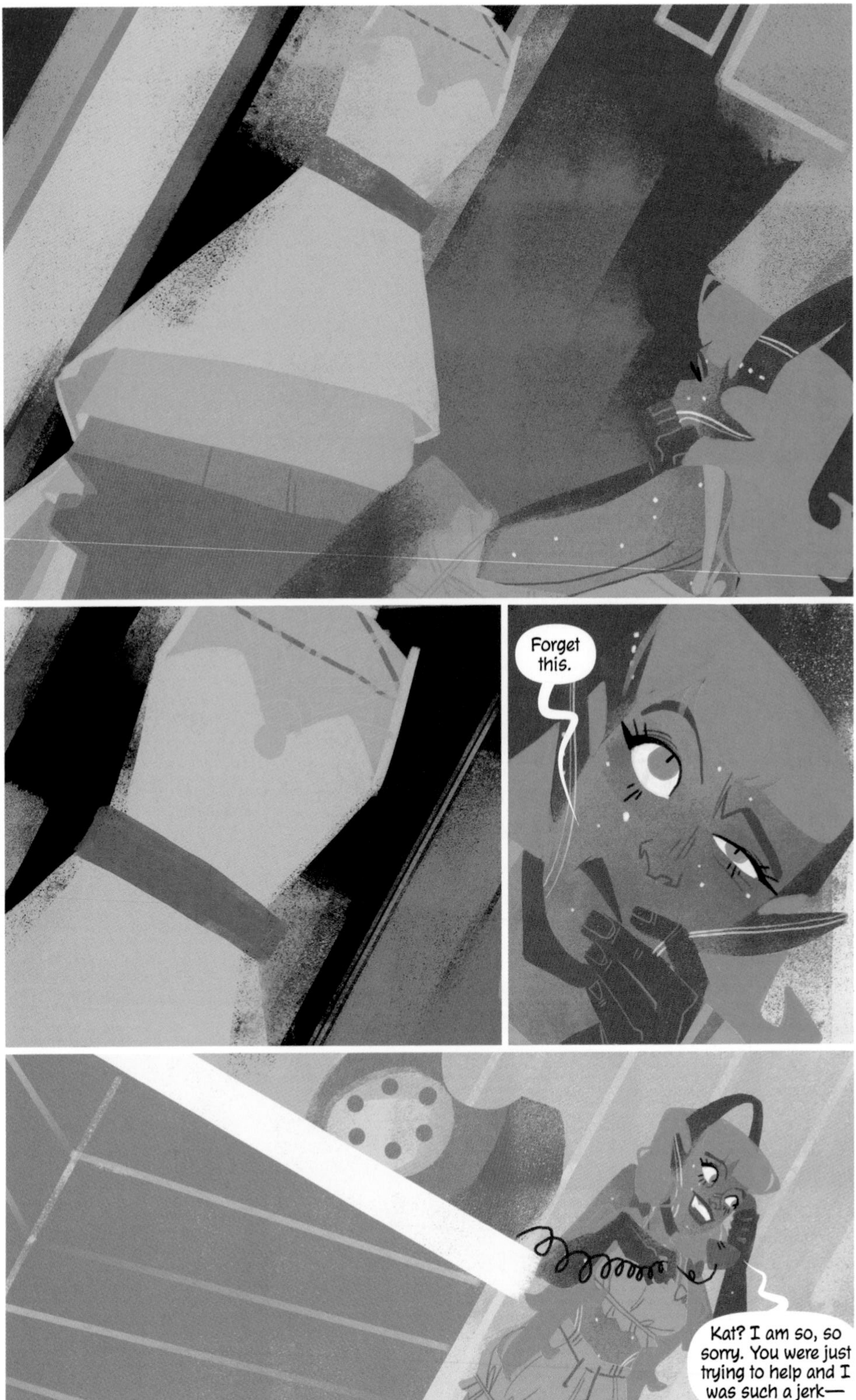
Forget this.
Kat? I am so, so sorry. You were just trying to help and I was such a jerk—

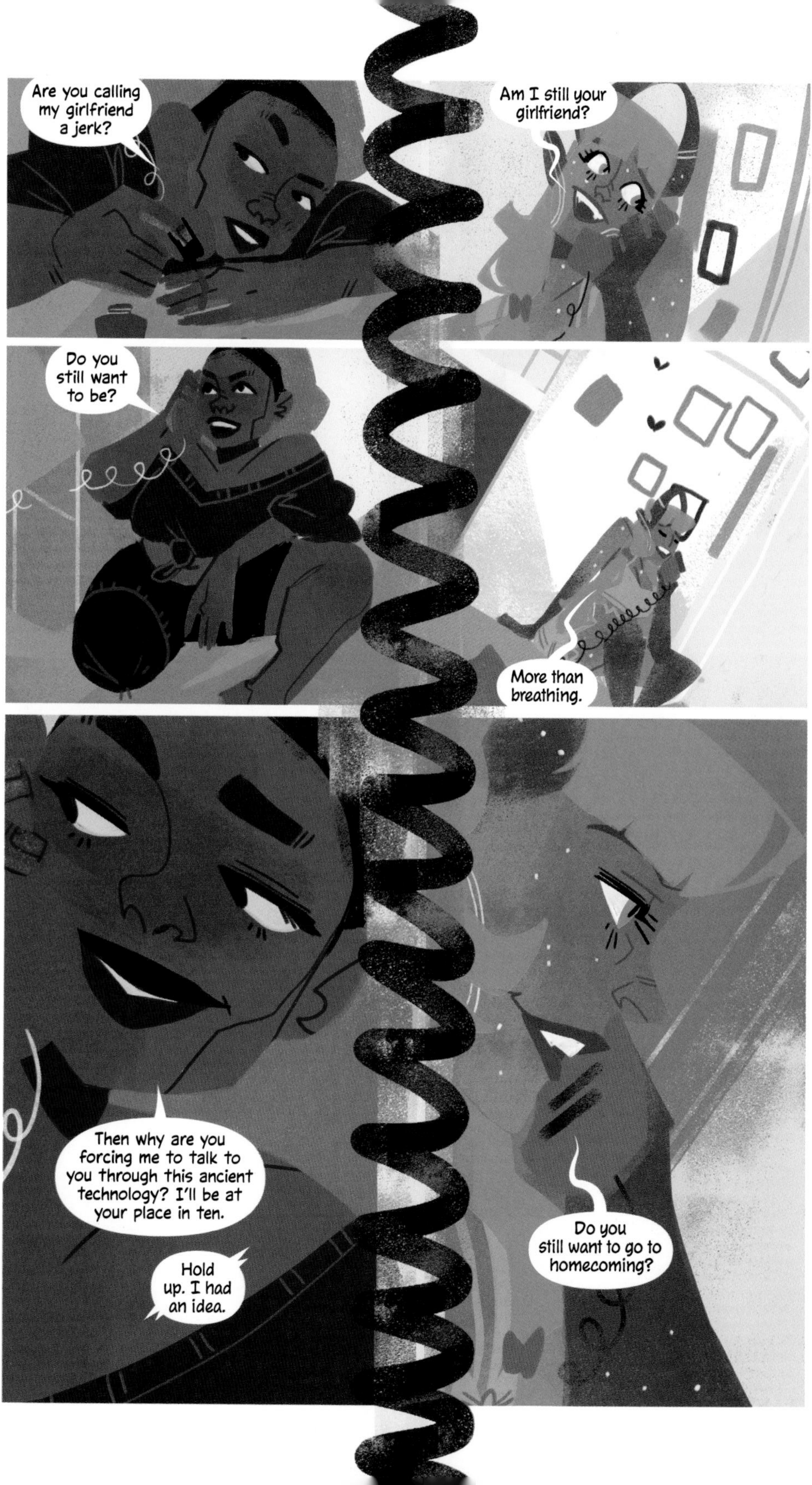
Are you calling my girlfriend a jerk?
Am I still your girlfriend?
Do you still want to be?
More than breathing.
Then why are you forcing me to talk to you through this ancient technology? I'll be at your place in ten.
Hold up. I had an idea.
Do you still want to go to homecoming?

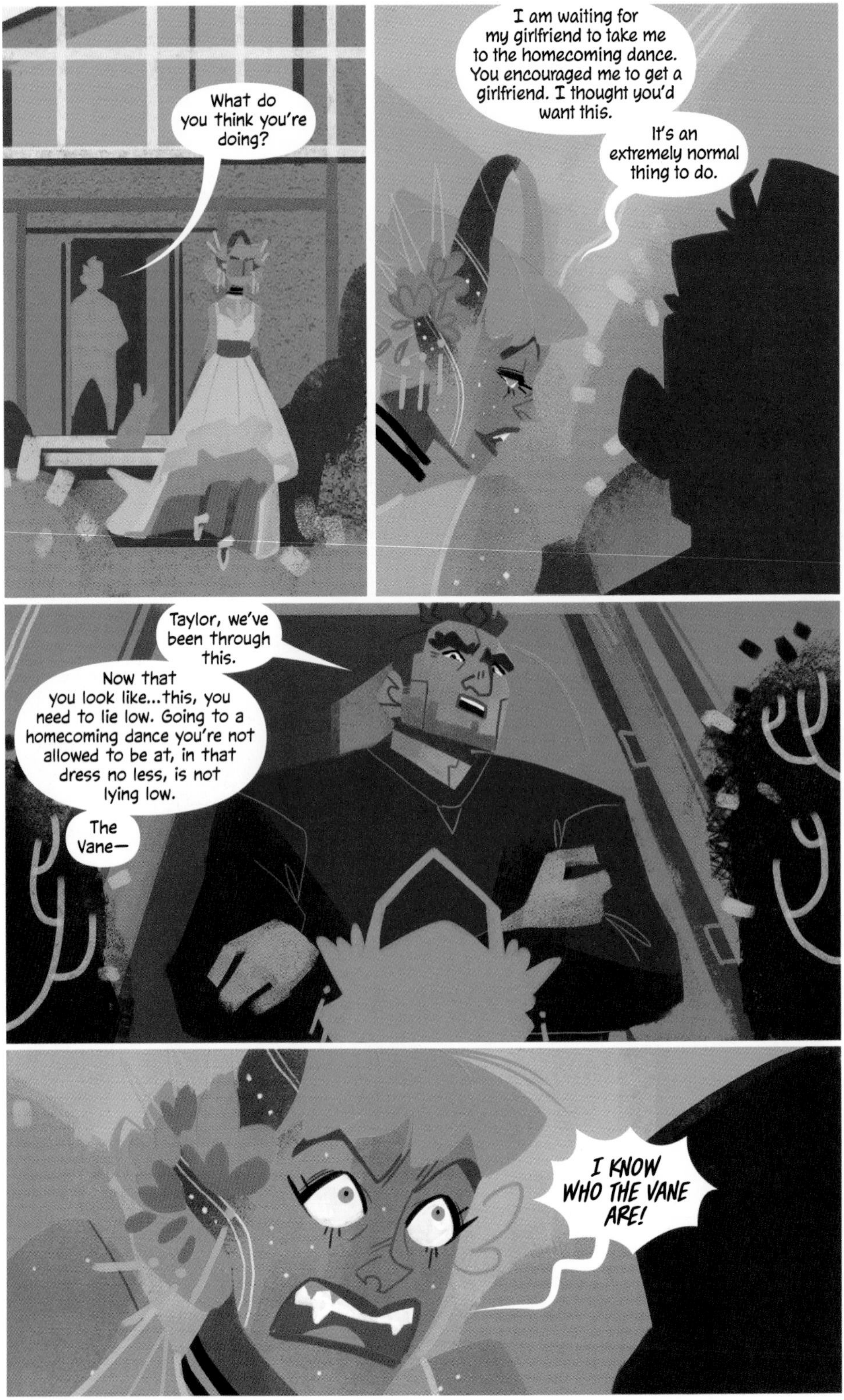
What do you think you're doing?
I am waiting for my girlfriend to take me to the homecoming dance. You encouraged me to get a girlfriend. I thought you'd want this.
It's an extremely normal thing to do.
Taylor, we've been through this.
Now that you look like...this, you need to lie low. Going to a homecoming dance you're not allowed to be at, in that dress no less, is not lying low.
The Vane—
I KNOW WHO THE VANE ARE!

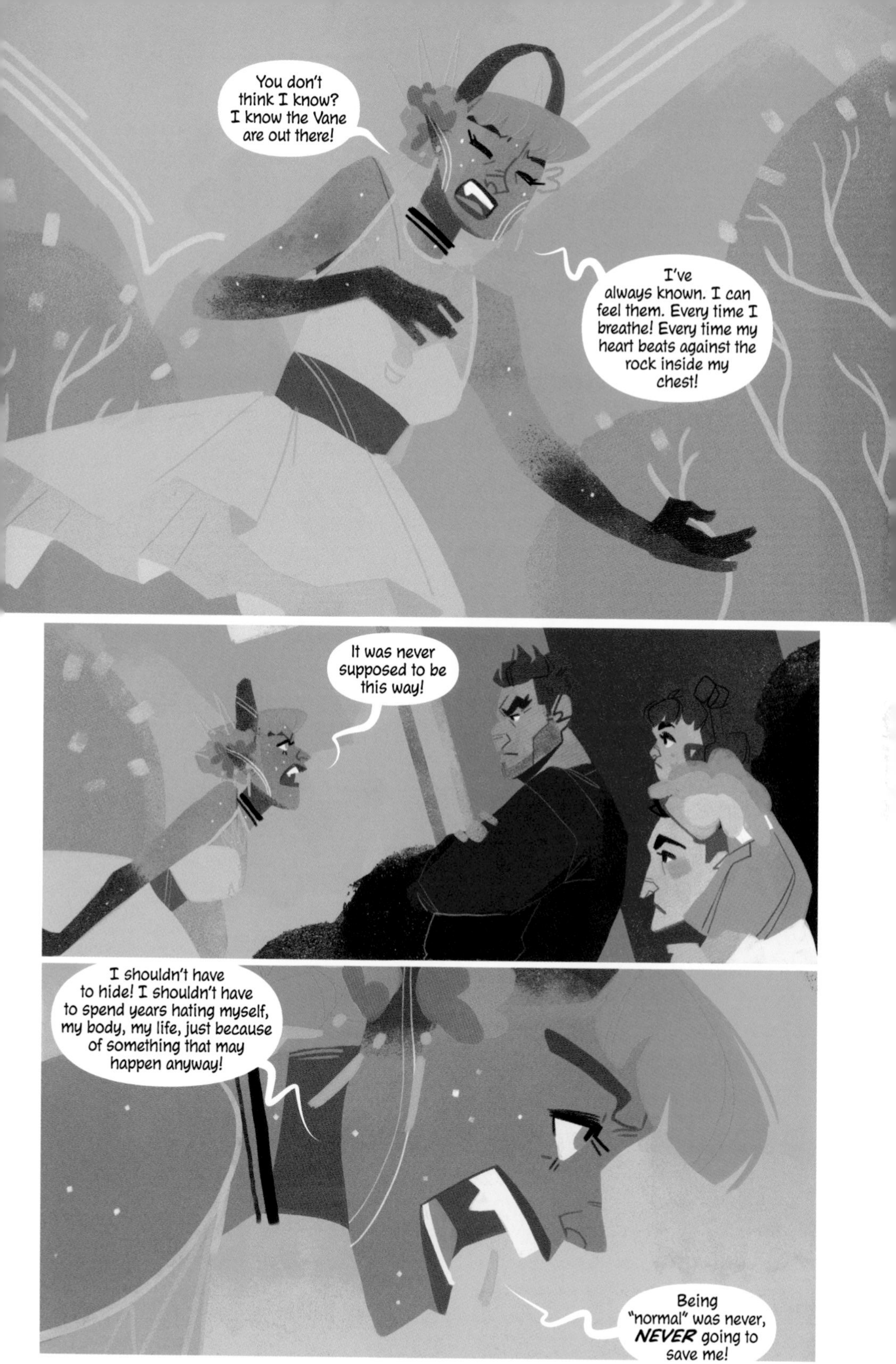
You don't think I know? I know the Vane are out there!
I've always known. I can feel them. Every time I breathe! Every time my heart beats against the rock inside my chest!
It was never supposed to be this way!
I shouldn't have to hide! I shouldn't have to spend years hating myself, my body, my life, just because of something that may happen anyway!
Being "normal" was never, ***NEVER*** going to save me!

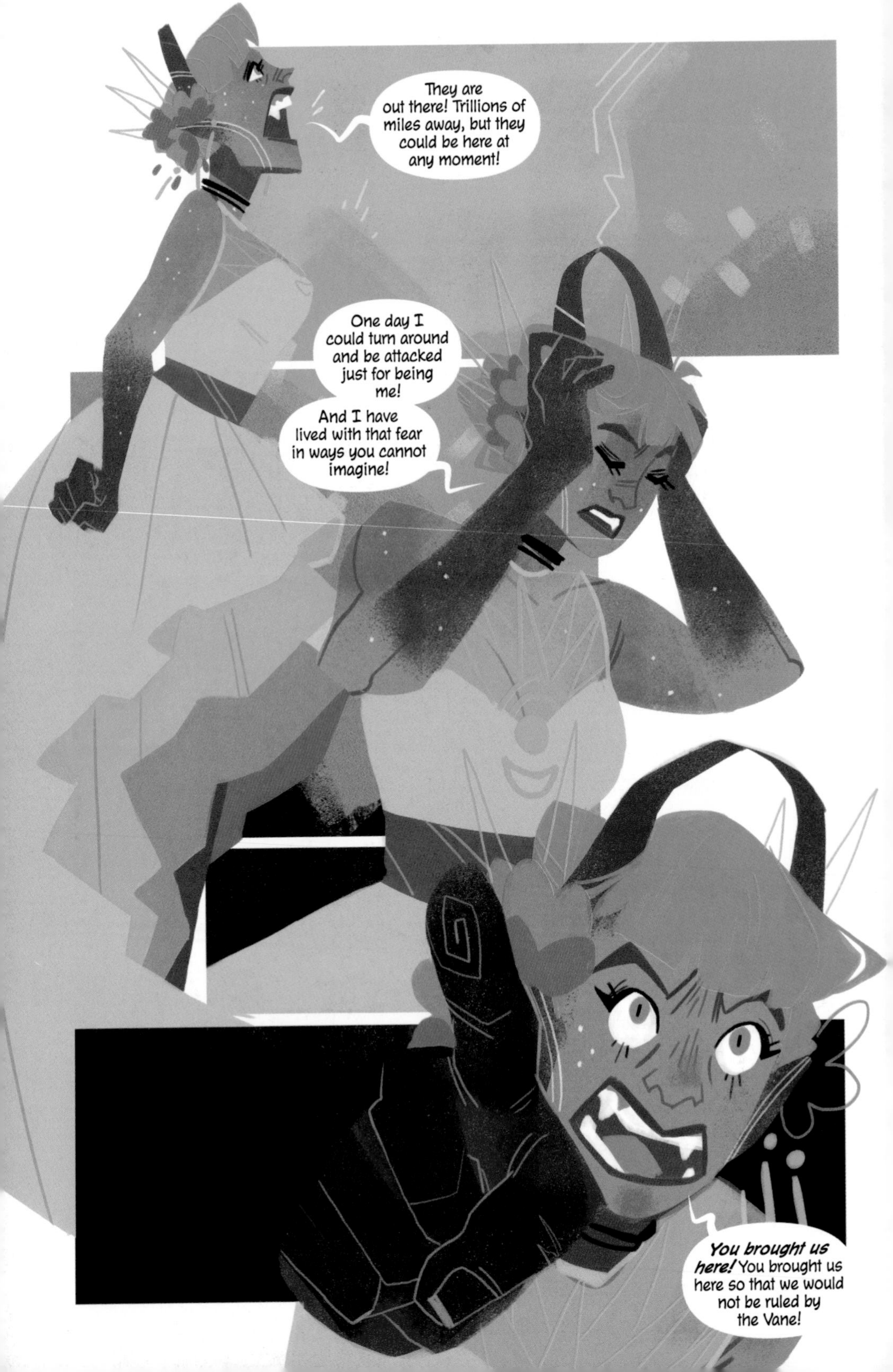
They are out there! Trillions of miles away, but they could be here at any moment!
One day I could turn around and be attacked just for being me!
And I have lived with that fear in ways you cannot imagine!
You brought us here! You brought us here so that we would not be ruled by the Vane!

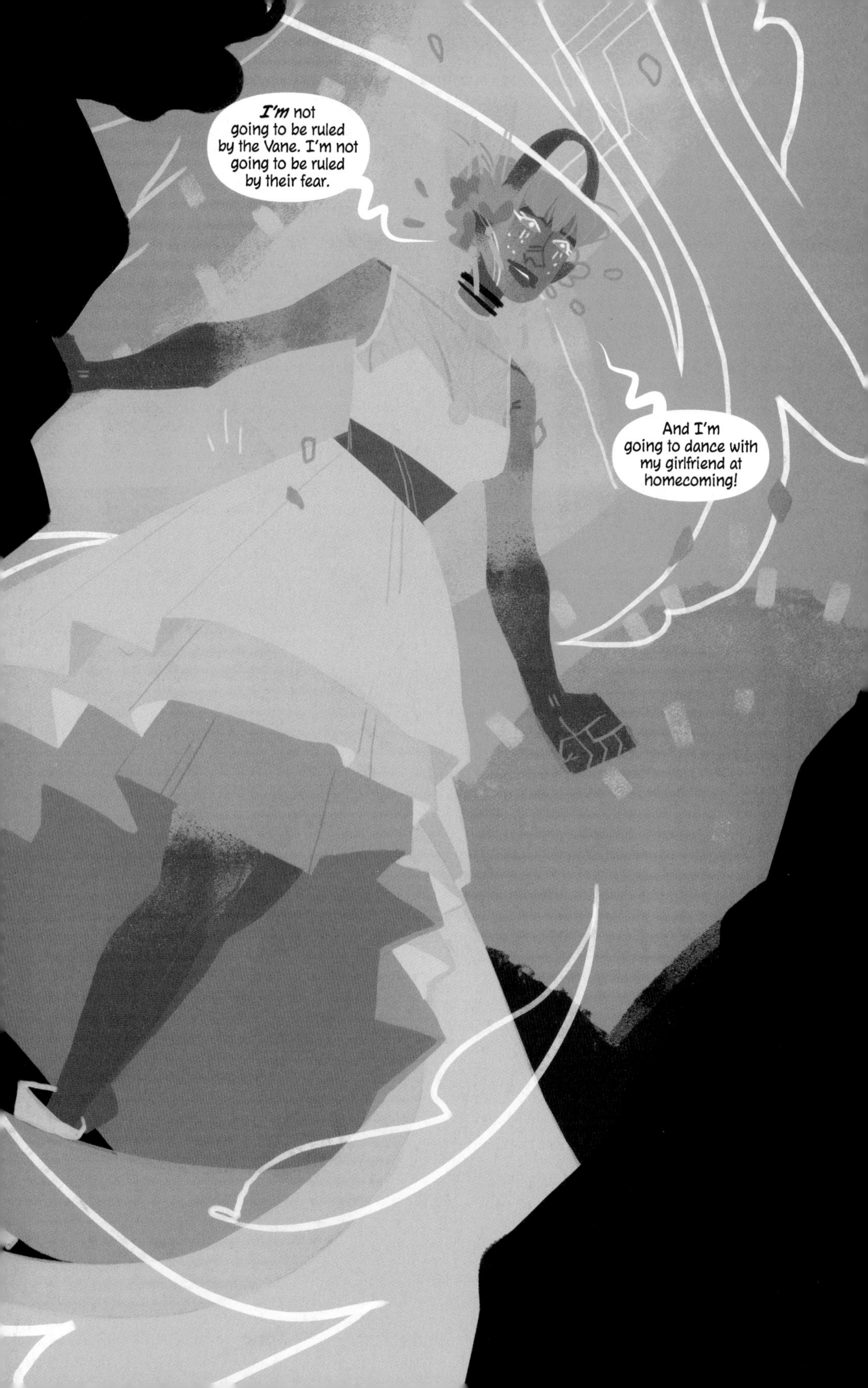
I'm not going to be ruled by the Vane. I'm not going to be ruled by their fear.
And I'm going to dance with my girlfriend at homecoming!

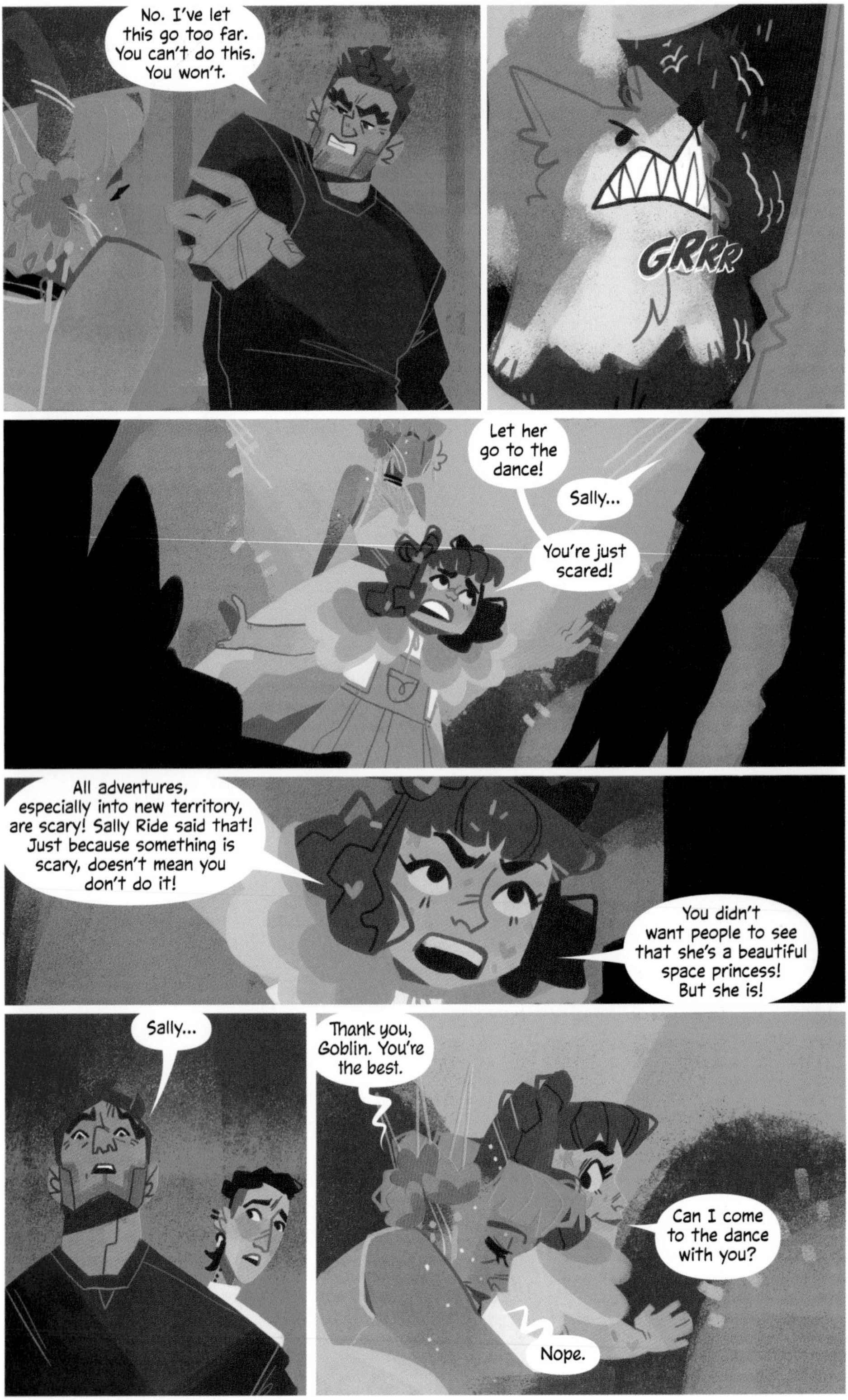
No. I've let this go too far. You can't do this. You won't.
GRRR
Let her go to the dance!
Sally...
You're just scared!
All adventures, especially into new territory, are scary! Sally Ride said that! Just because something is scary, doesn't mean you don't do it!
You didn't want people to see that she's a beautiful space princess! But she is!
Sally...
Thank you, Goblin. You're the best.
Can I come to the dance with you?
Nope.

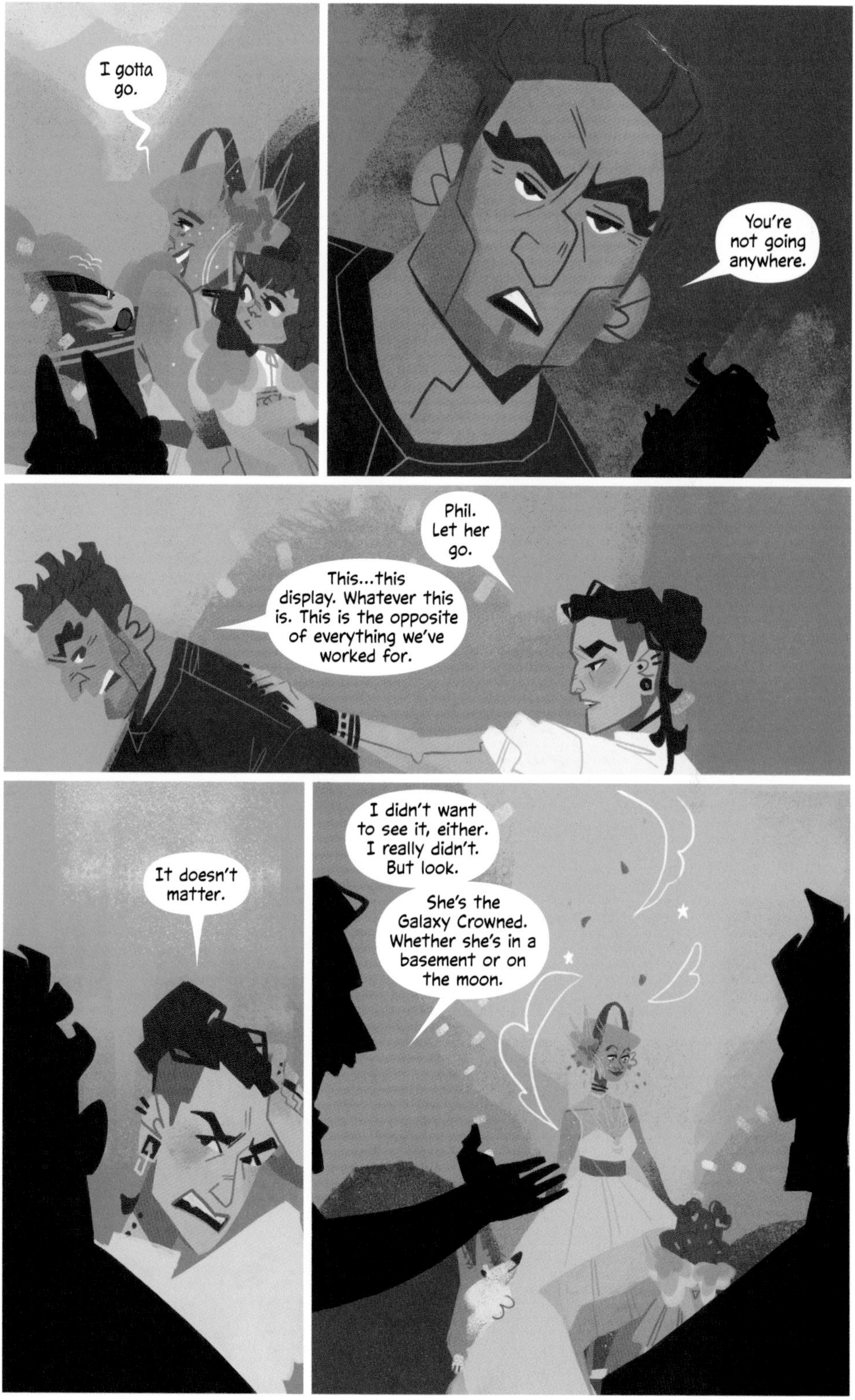
I gotta go.
You're not going anywhere.
Phil. Let her go.
This...this display. Whatever this is. This is the opposite of everything we've worked for.
It doesn't matter.
I didn't want to see it, either. I really didn't. But look.
She's the Galaxy Crowned. Whether she's in a basement or on the moon.

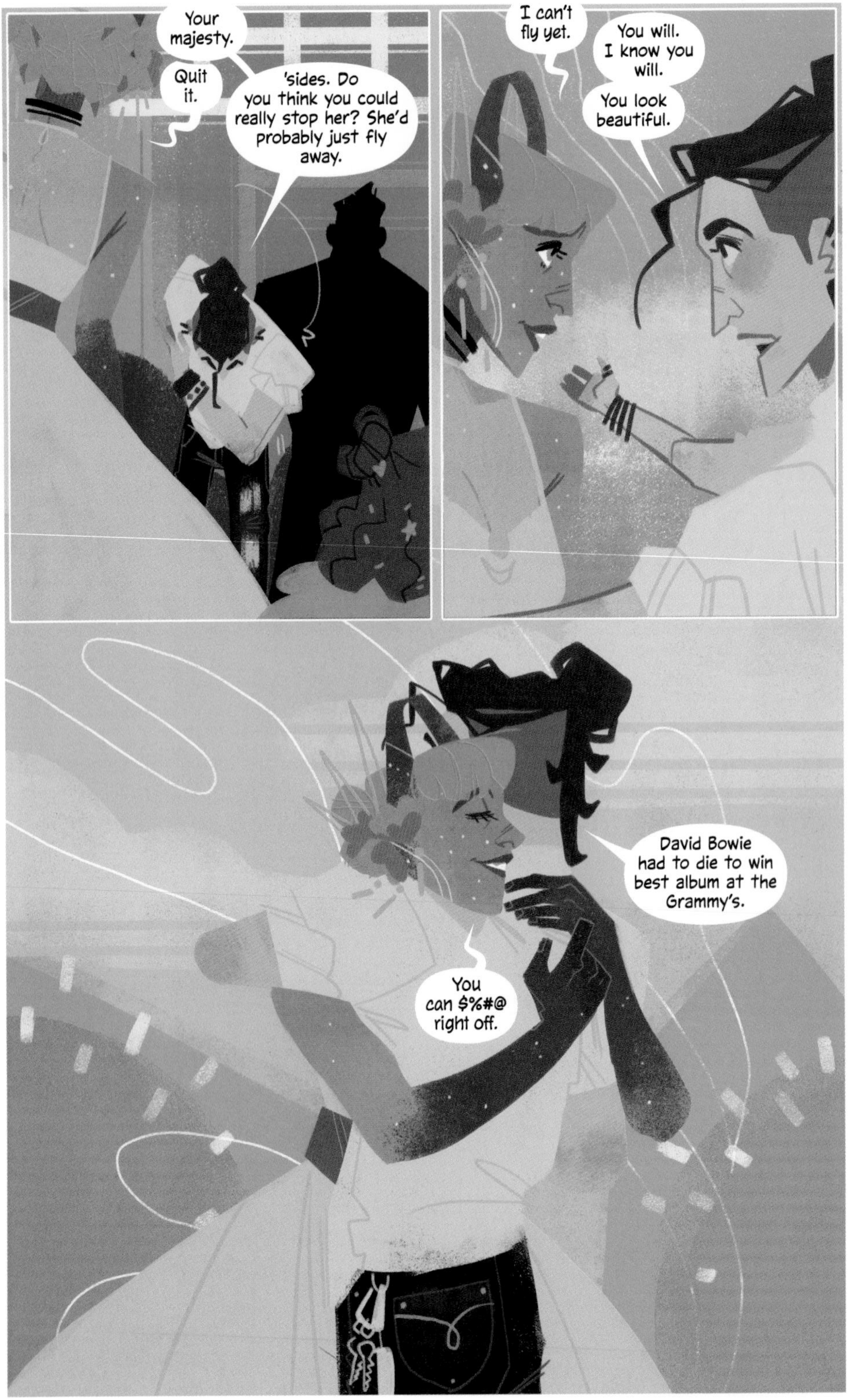
Your majesty.
Quit it.
'sides. Do you think you could really stop her? She'd probably just fly away.
I can't fly yet.
You will. I know you will.
You look beautiful.
David Bowie had to die to win best album at the Grammy's.
You can $%#@ right off.

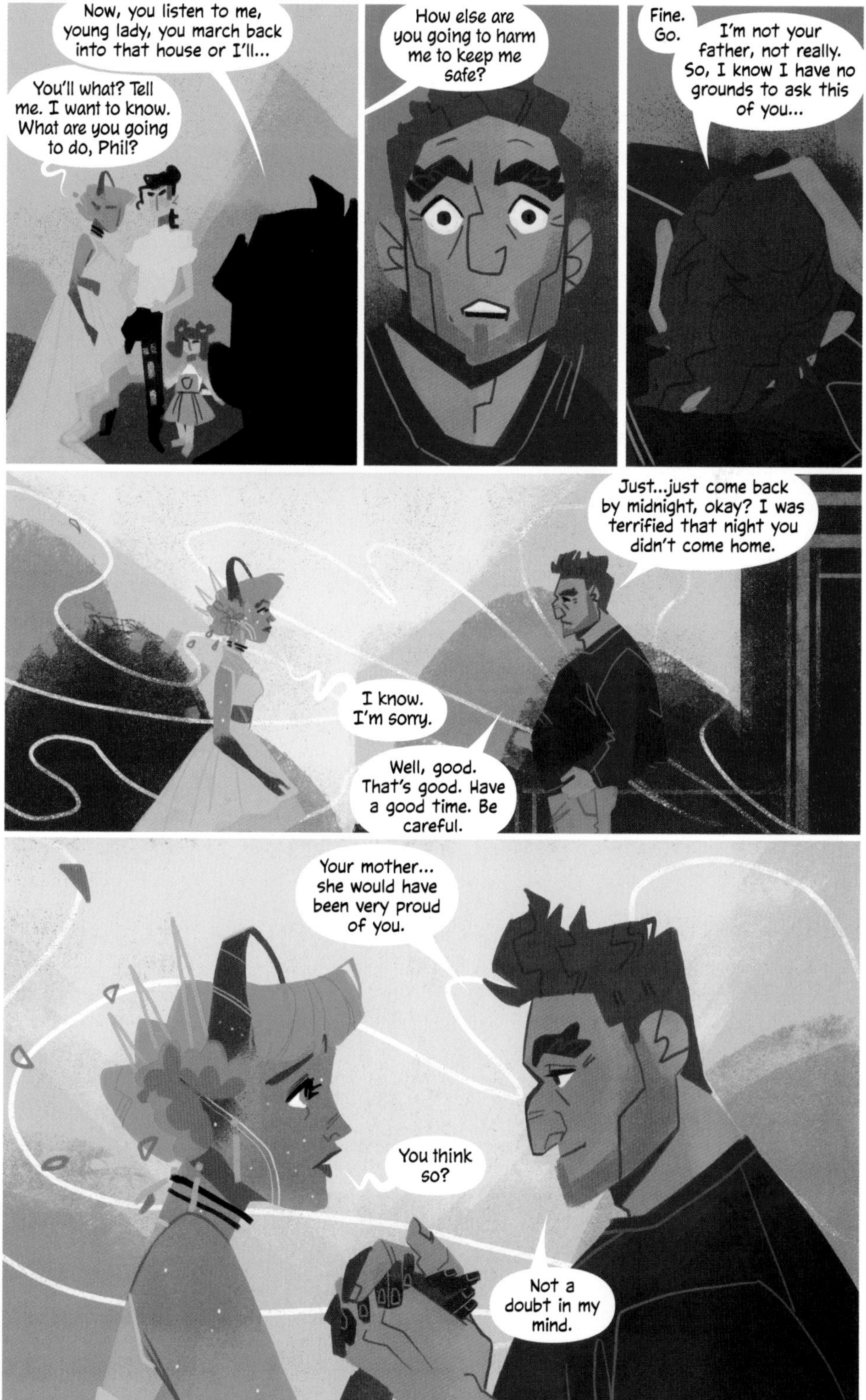
Now, you listen to me, young lady, you march back into that house or I'll...
You'll what? Tell me. I want to know. What are you going to do, Phil?
How else are you going to harm me to keep me safe?
Fine. Go.
I'm not your father, not really. So, I know I have no grounds to ask this of you...
Just...just come back by midnight, okay? I was terrified that night you didn't come home.
I know. I'm sorry.
Well, good. That's good. Have a good time. Be careful.
Your mother... she would have been very proud of you.
You think so?
Not a doubt in my mind.

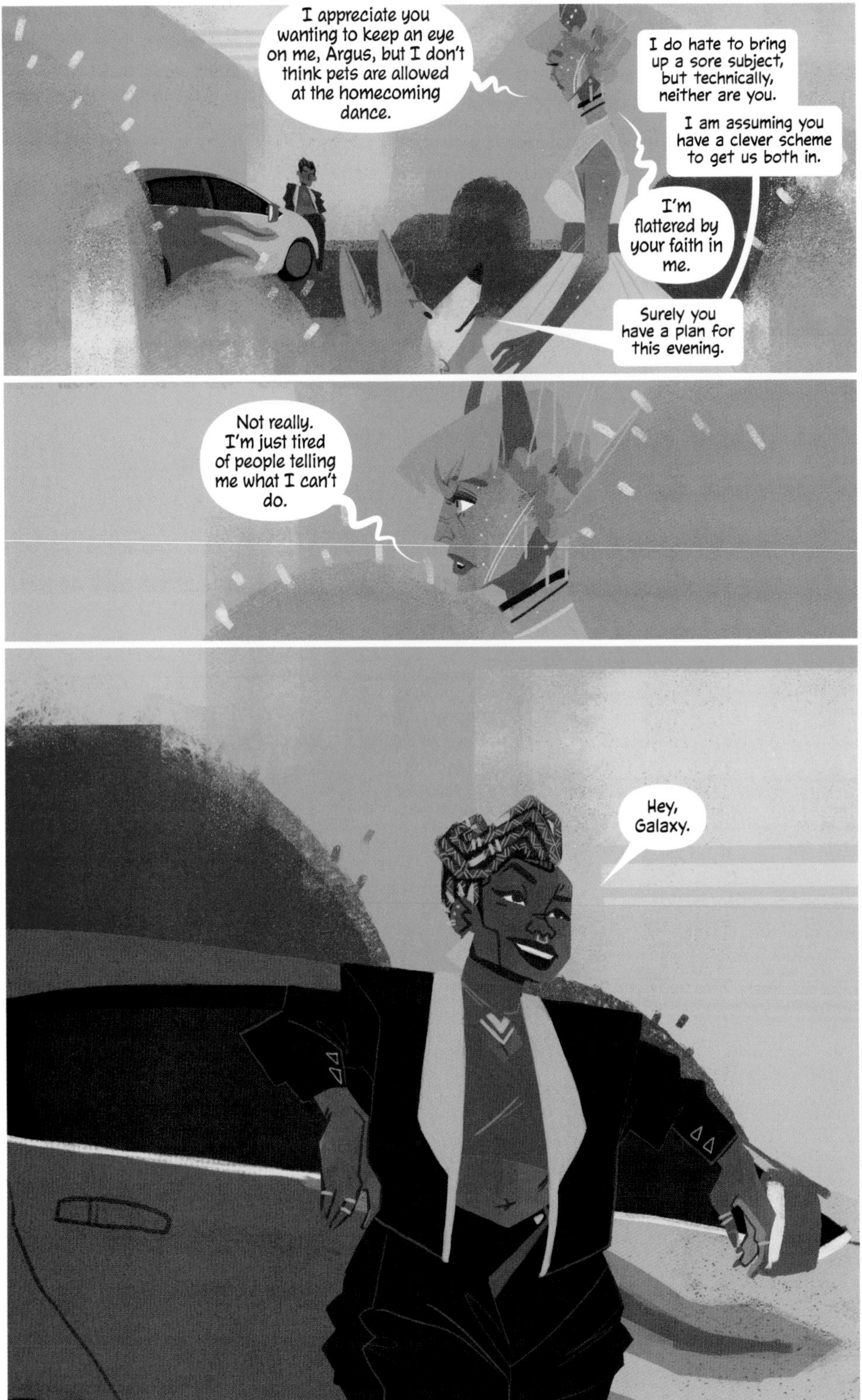
I appreciate you wanting to keep an eye on me, Argus, but I don't think pets are allowed at the homecoming dance.
I do hate to bring up a sore subject, but technically, neither are you.
I am assuming you have a clever scheme to get us both in.
I'm flattered by your faith in me.
Surely you have a plan for this evening.
Not really. I'm just tired of people telling me what I can't do.
Hey, Galaxy.

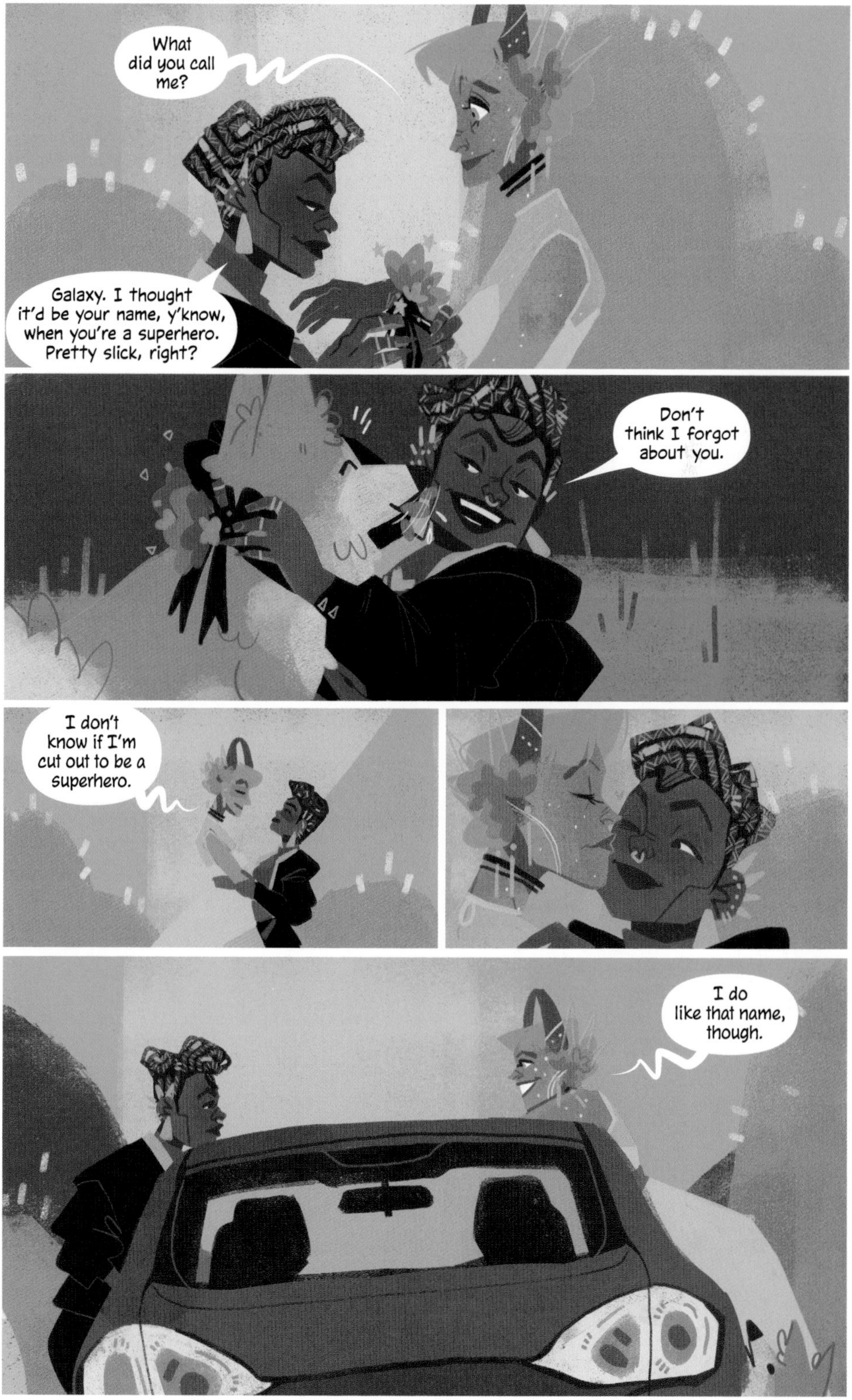
What did you call me?
Galaxy. I thought it'd be your name, y'know, when you're a superhero. Pretty slick, right?
Don't think I forgot about you.
I don't know if I'm cut out to be a superhero.
I do like that name, though.

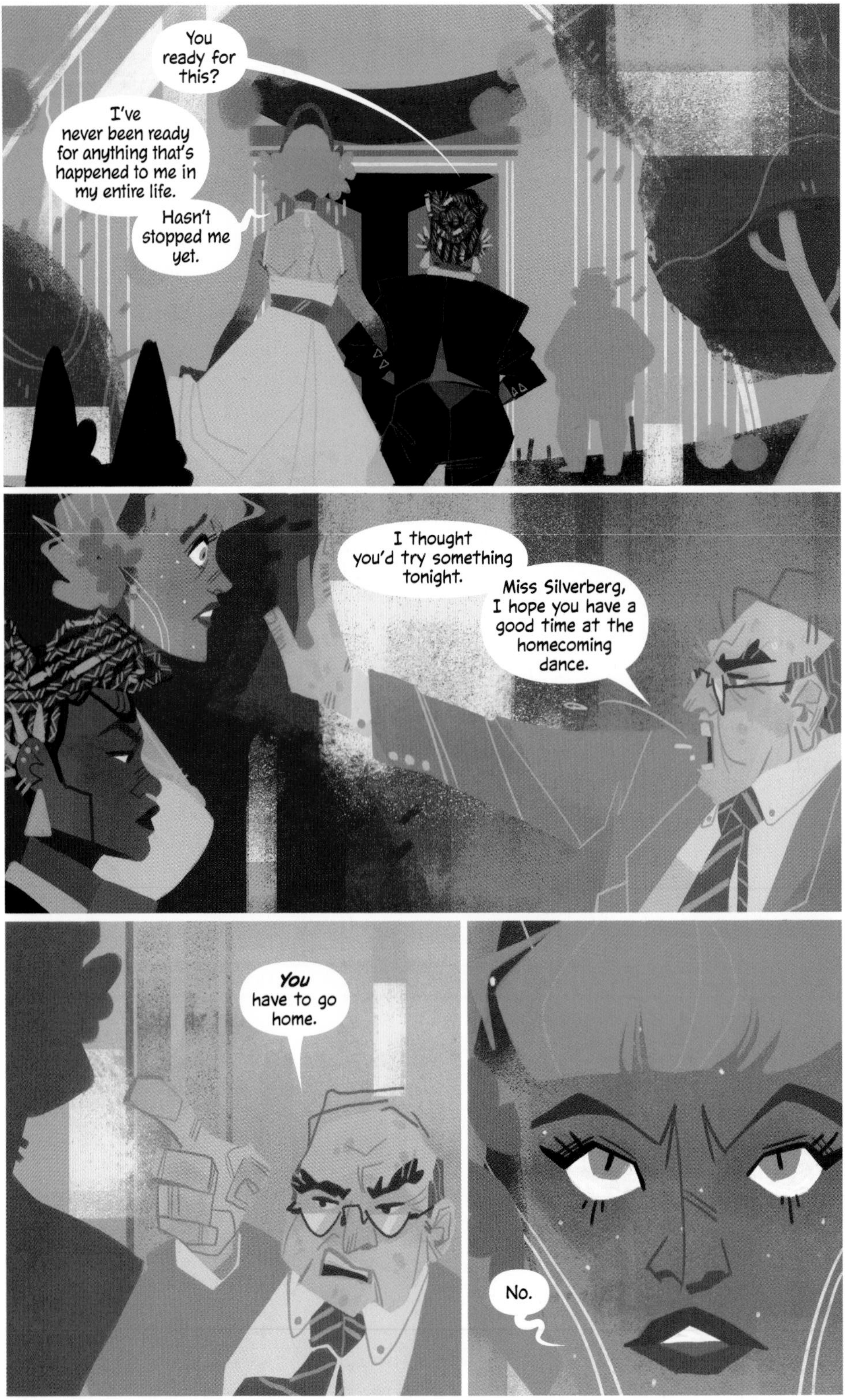

You ready for this?
I've never been ready for anything that's happened to me in my entire life.
Hasn't stopped me yet.
I thought you'd try something tonight.
Miss Silverberg, I hope you have a good time at the homecoming dance.
You have to go home.
No.

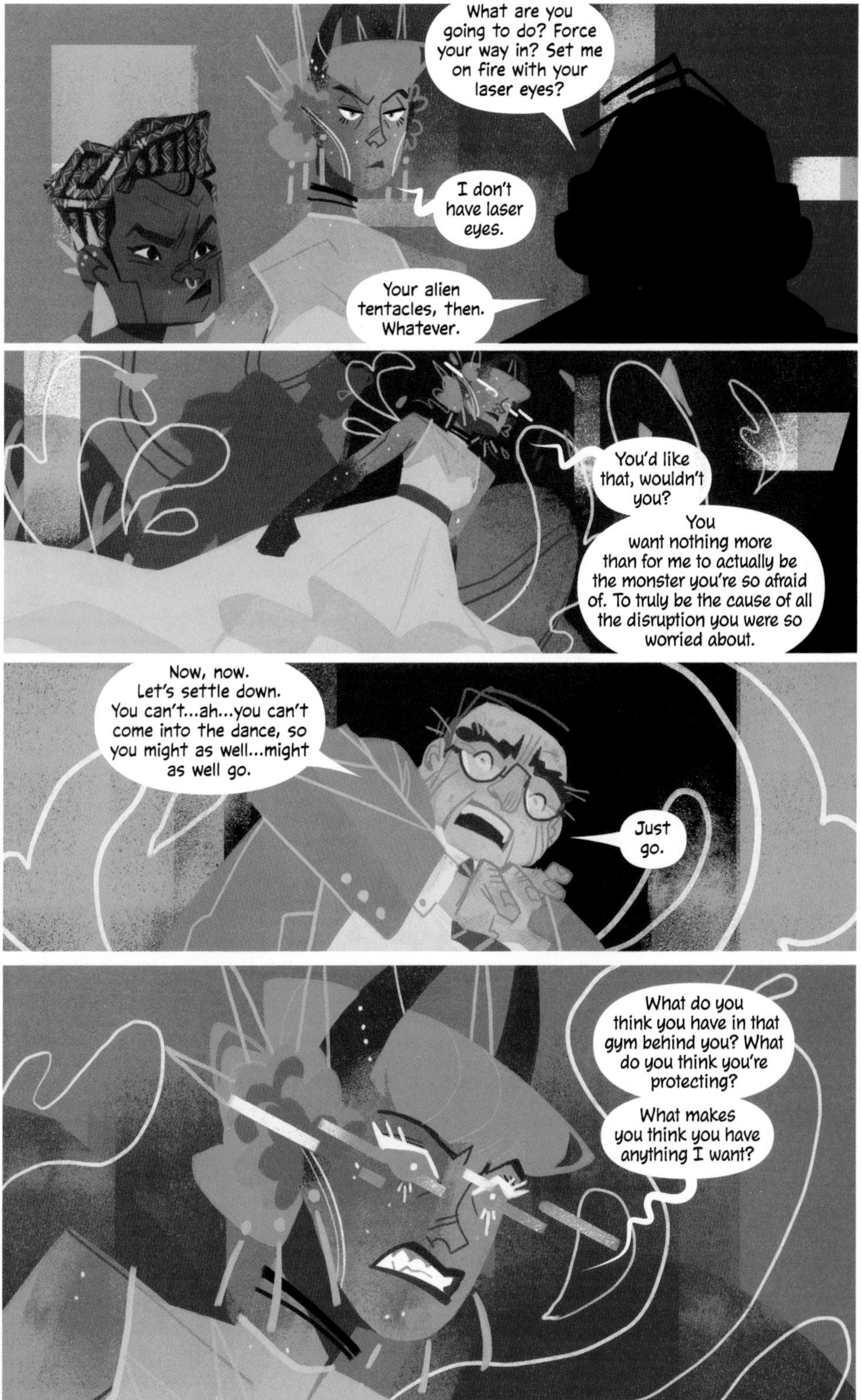
What are you going to do? Force your way in? Set me on fire with your laser eyes?
I don't have laser eyes.
Your alien tentacles, then. Whatever.
You'd like that, wouldn't you?
You want nothing more than for me to actually be the monster you're so afraid of. To truly be the cause of all the disruption you were so worried about.
Now, now. Let's settle down. You can't...ah...you can't come into the dance, so you might as well...might as well go.
Just go.
What do you think you have in that gym behind you? What do you think you're protecting?
What makes you think you have anything I want?

I know exactly what you are. I can see what you're made of, clear as day.

But you have no idea what I'm capable of.

You need to relax. Let me help out with that.

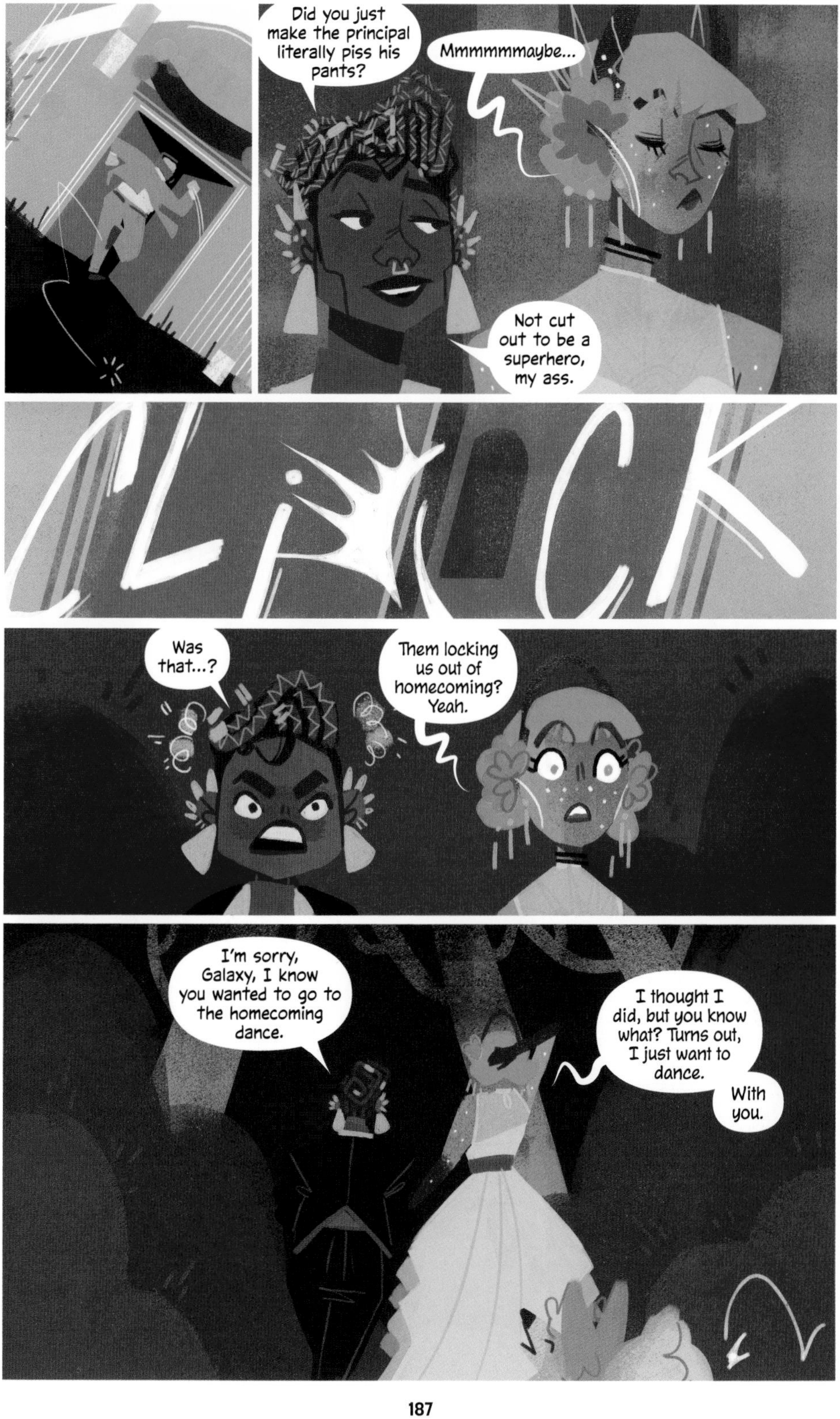
Did you just make the principal literally piss his pants?
Mmmmmmaybe...
Not cut out to be a superhero, my ass.
CLICK
Was that...?
Them locking us out of homecoming? Yeah.
I'm sorry, Galaxy, I know you wanted to go to the homecoming dance.
I thought I did, but you know what? Turns out, I just want to dance.
With you.

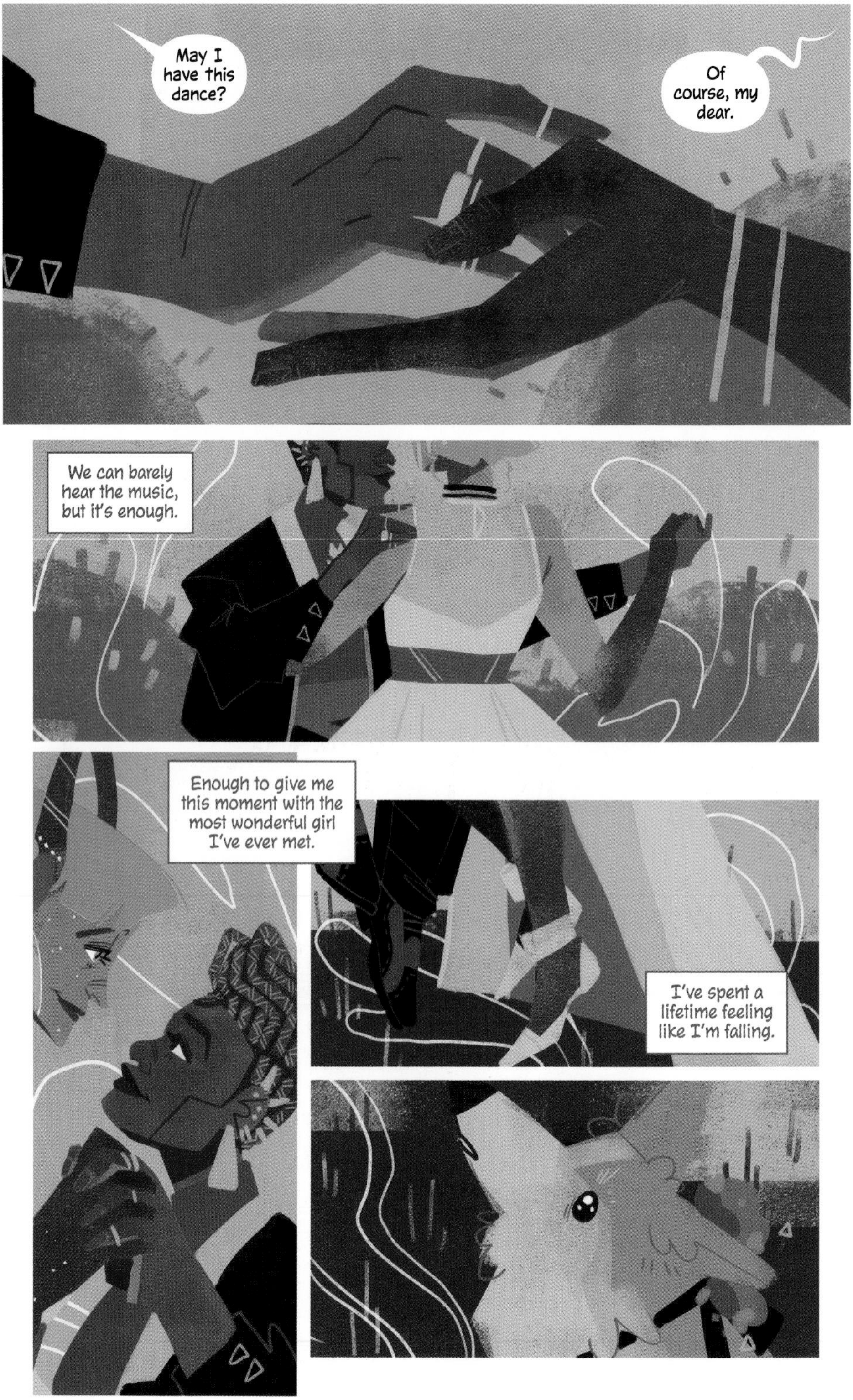
May I have this dance?
Of course, my dear.
We can barely hear the music, but it's enough.
Enough to give me this moment with the most wonderful girl I've ever met.
I've spent a lifetime feeling like I'm falling.

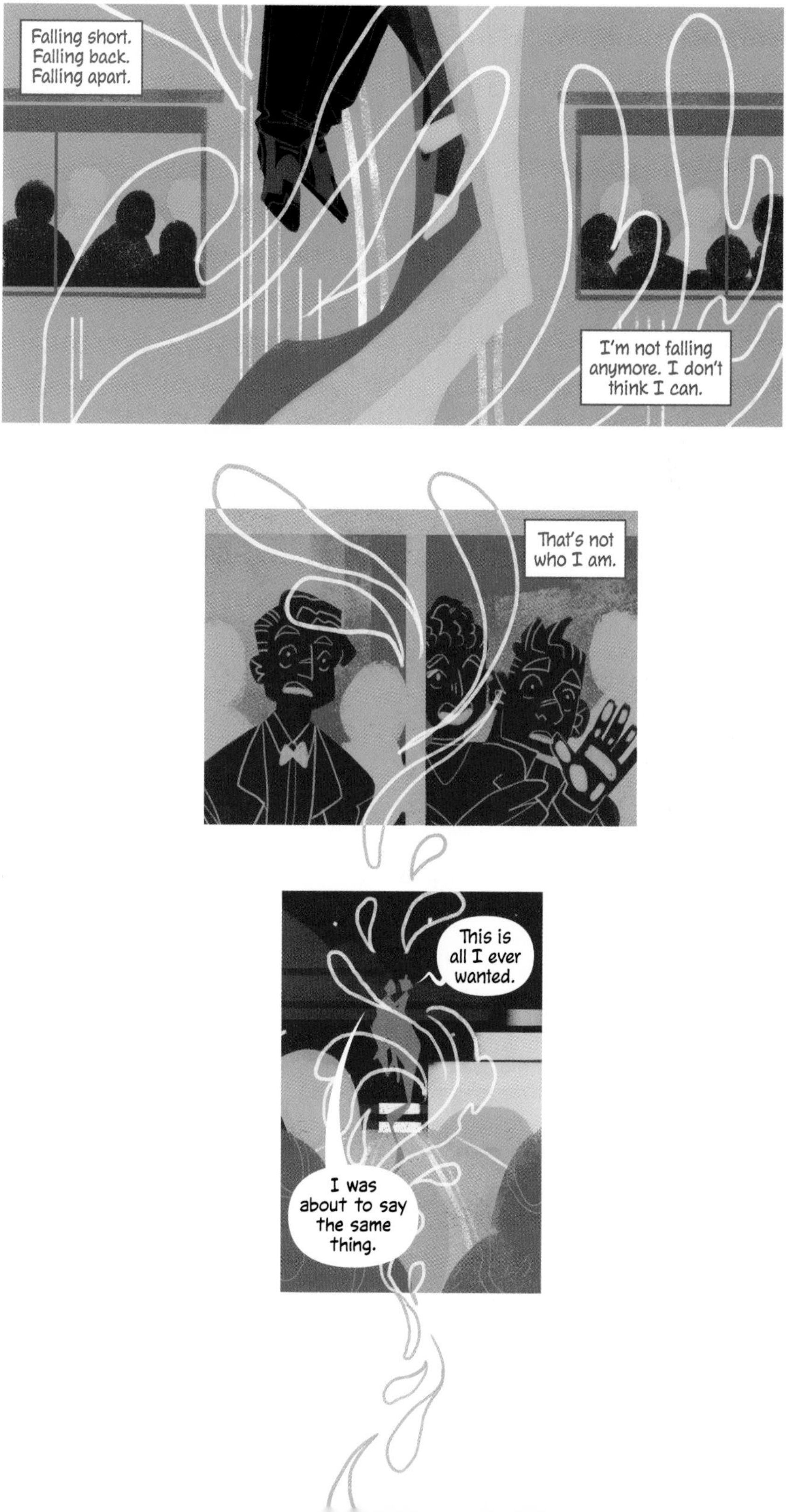
Falling short. Falling back. Falling apart.
I'm not falling anymore. I don't think I can.
That's not who I am.
This is all I ever wanted.
I was about to say the same thing.

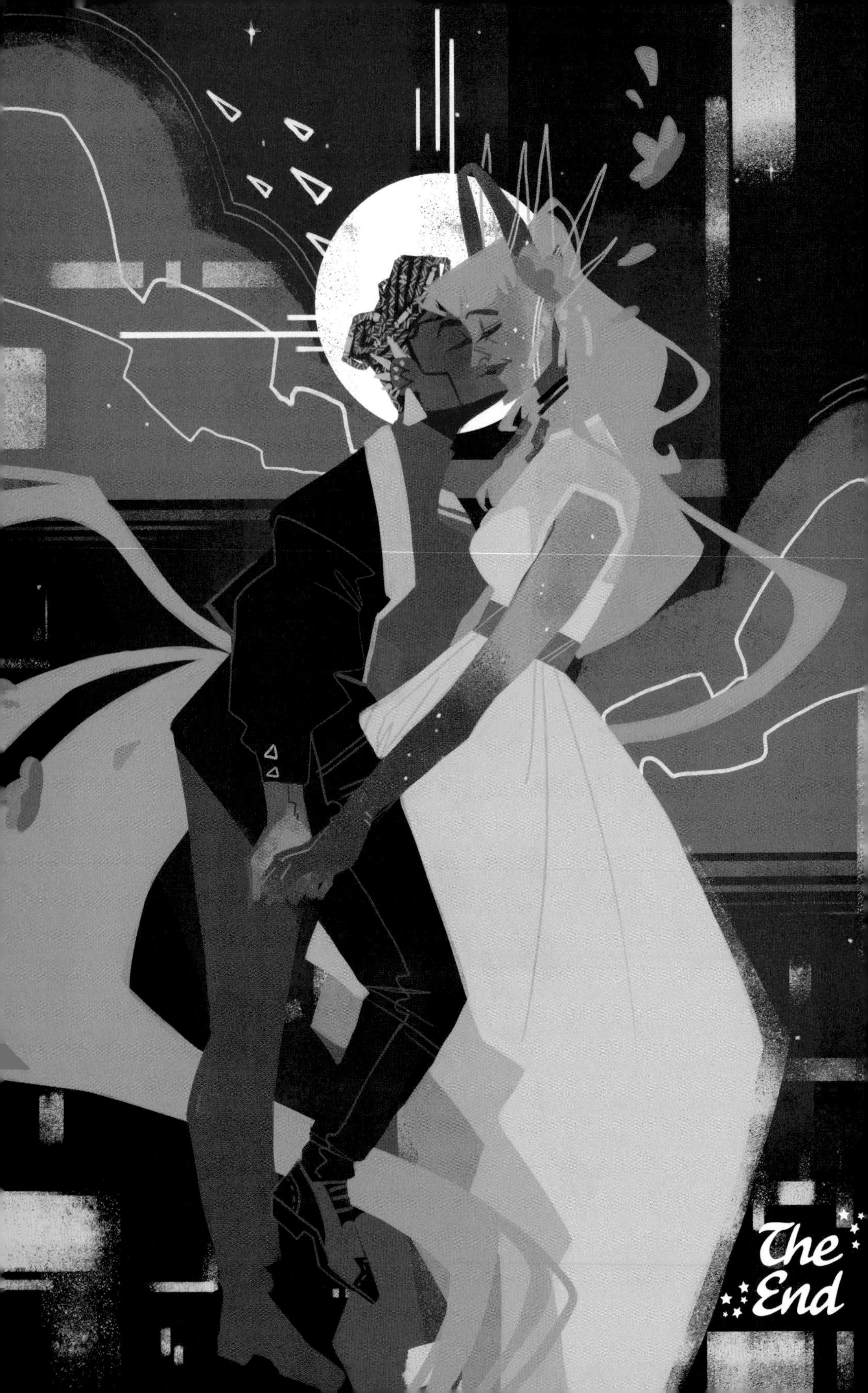
The End

Resources

If you, or a loved one, need help in any way, you do not need to act alone. Below is a list of resources that may be helpful to you. If you are in immediate danger, please call emergency services in your area (9-1-1 in the U.S.) or go to your nearest hospital emergency room.

The Trevor Project

The Trevor Project is the leading national organization providing crisis intervention and suicide prevention services to lesbian, gay, bisexual, transgender, queer, and questioning youth. Call their lifeline at 866-4-U-TREVOR (866-488-7386) or text START to 678-678. Visit them at https://www.thetrevorproject.org.

Trans Lifeline

Trans Lifeline provides trans peer support for the trans community and has been divested from police since day one. Run by and for trans people. Call 877-565-8860 or visit them at https://translifeline.org.

It Gets Better Project

The It Gets Better Project's mission is to uplift, empower, and connect lesbian, gay, bisexual, transgender, and queer (LGBTQ+) youth around the globe. Visit them at https://itgetsbetter.org.

RespectAbility

RespectAbility is a diverse, disability-led nonprofit that works to create systemic change in how society views and values people with disabilities, and that advances policies and practices that empower people with disabilities to have a better future. Visit them at https://www.respectability.org.

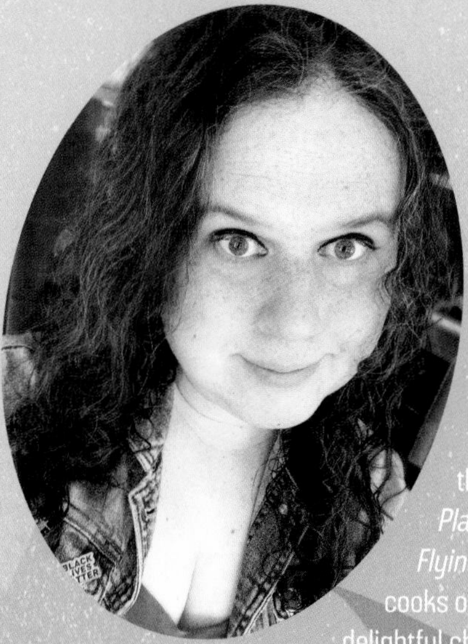

Jadzia Axelrod is an award-winning author, illustrator, activist, gadabout, style maven, and circus performer. She is a contributing author to *Wonderful Women of the World* and has written comics for Tor, Quirk Books, and Epic! Books. She is the writer and producer of the popular fiction podcasts *The Voice of Free Planet X*, *Aliens You Will Meet*, and *Fables of the Flying City*. She lives in Philadelphia, where she cooks overly elaborate meals for her wonderful wife and delightful child.

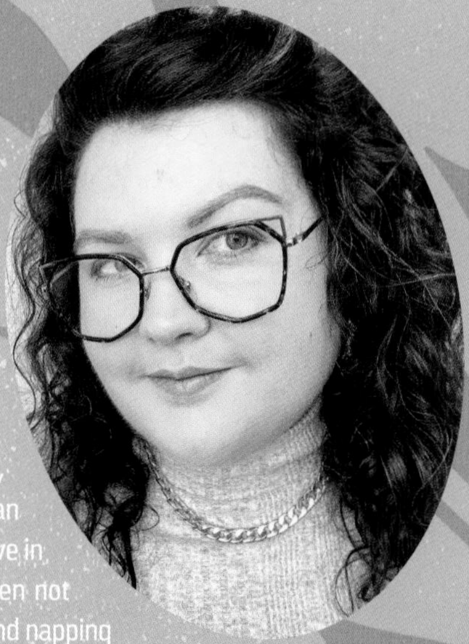

Jess Taylor is an almost-award-winning comics artist and illustrator with a penchant for cat photos. In between LGBTQIA+ activism and teaching they've contributed their work to titles such as *Adventure Time*, *Critical Role*, and *Stranger Things*. While having worked for Boom!, Legendary, Dark Horse, and Oni Press, Jess's indie work has seen them nominated for an Arts Foundation Futures Award. They currently live in Nottingham, skirting Sherwood Forest, and, when not advocating giving to the poor, they can be found napping in a spot of sunlight with their cat, Lottie.

When a mystic's quest for a powerful jewel puts Zatanna's whole life into question, she'll quickly discover that there's so much more to the mobsters, mystics, and mermaids at the last stop on the D/F/Q train: Coney Island.

From the bewitching mind behind *The Casquette Girls*, **Alys Arden**, and with enchanting artwork by popular Instagram artist **Jacquelin de Leon**, comes a fresh origin story for DC's fan-favorite magician.

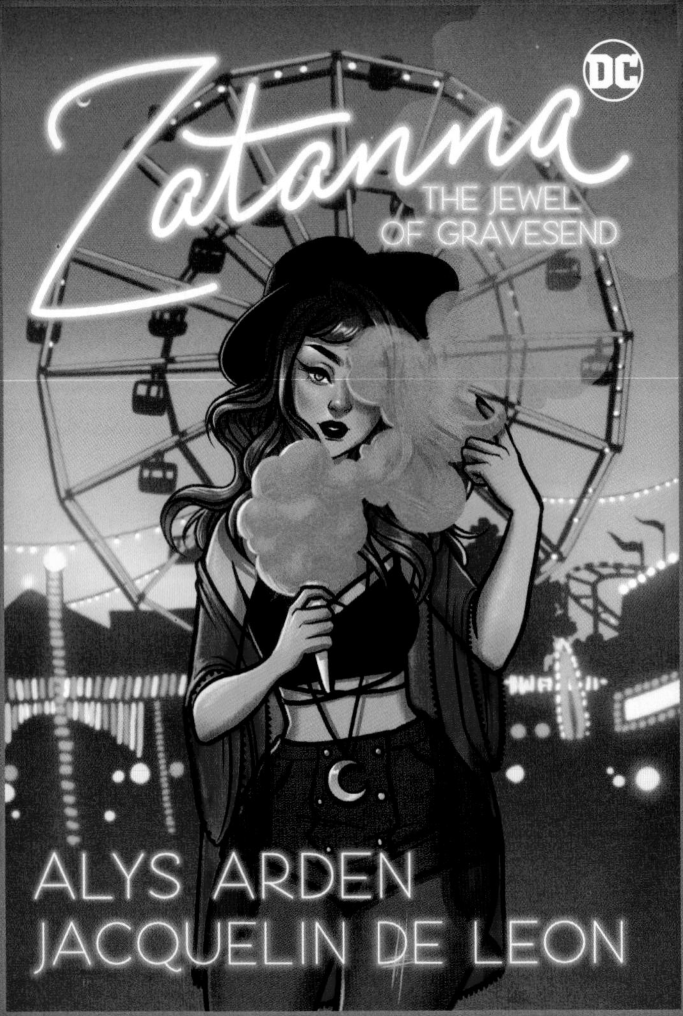
DC
Zatanna
THE JEWEL OF GRAVESEND
ALYS ARDEN
JACQUELIN DE LEON

IN STORES 7/26/2022

Keep reading for an exclusive sneak preview.

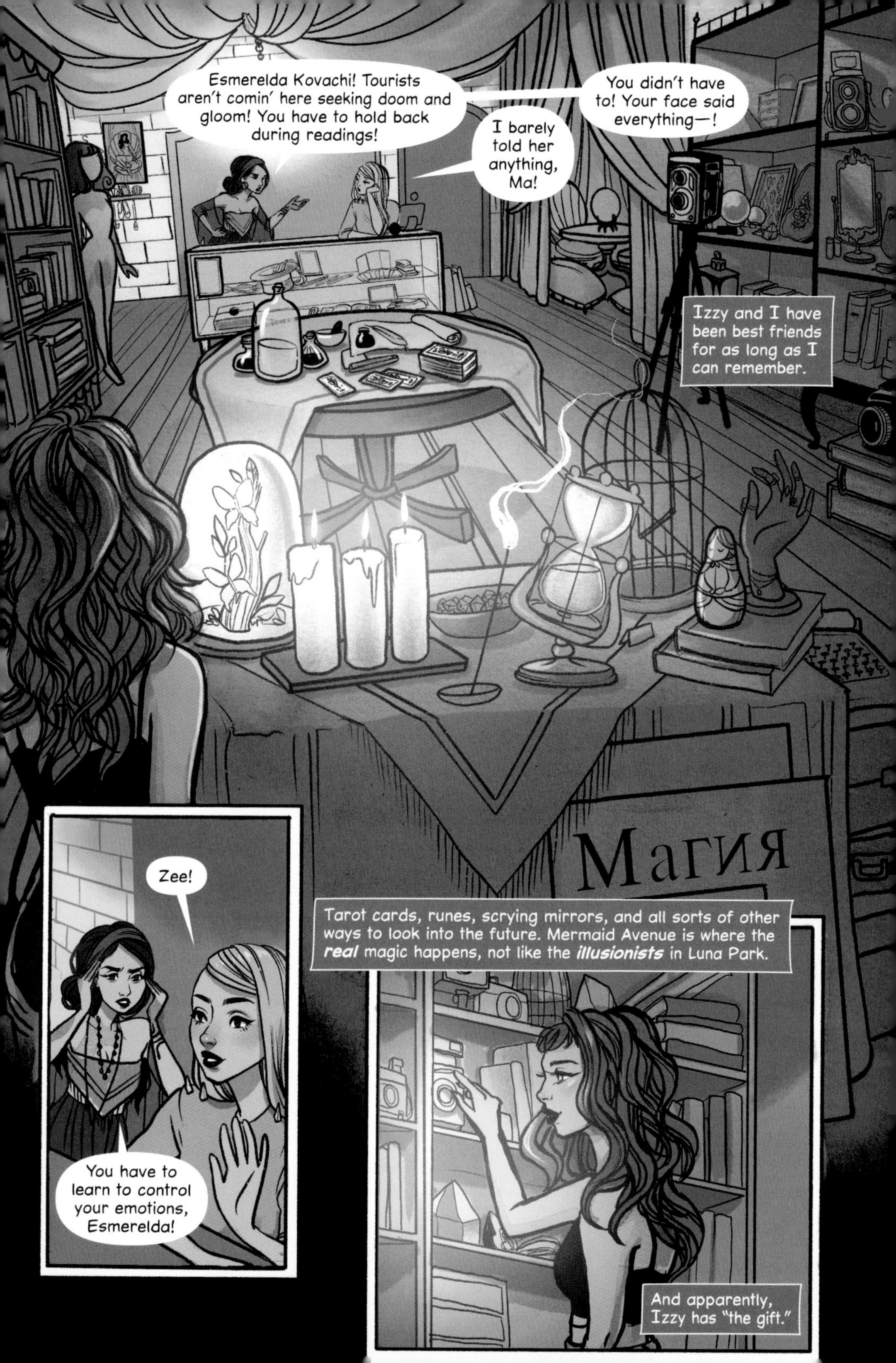
Esmerelda Kovachi! Tourists aren't comin' here seeking doom and gloom! You have to hold back during readings!
I barely told her anything, Ma!
You didn't have to! Your face said everything—!
Izzy and I have been best friends for as long as I can remember.
Магия
Zee!
You have to learn to control your emotions, Esmerelda!
Tarot cards, runes, scrying mirrors, and all sorts of other ways to look into the future. Mermaid Avenue is where the ***real*** magic happens, not like the ***illusionists*** in Luna Park.
And apparently, Izzy has "the gift."

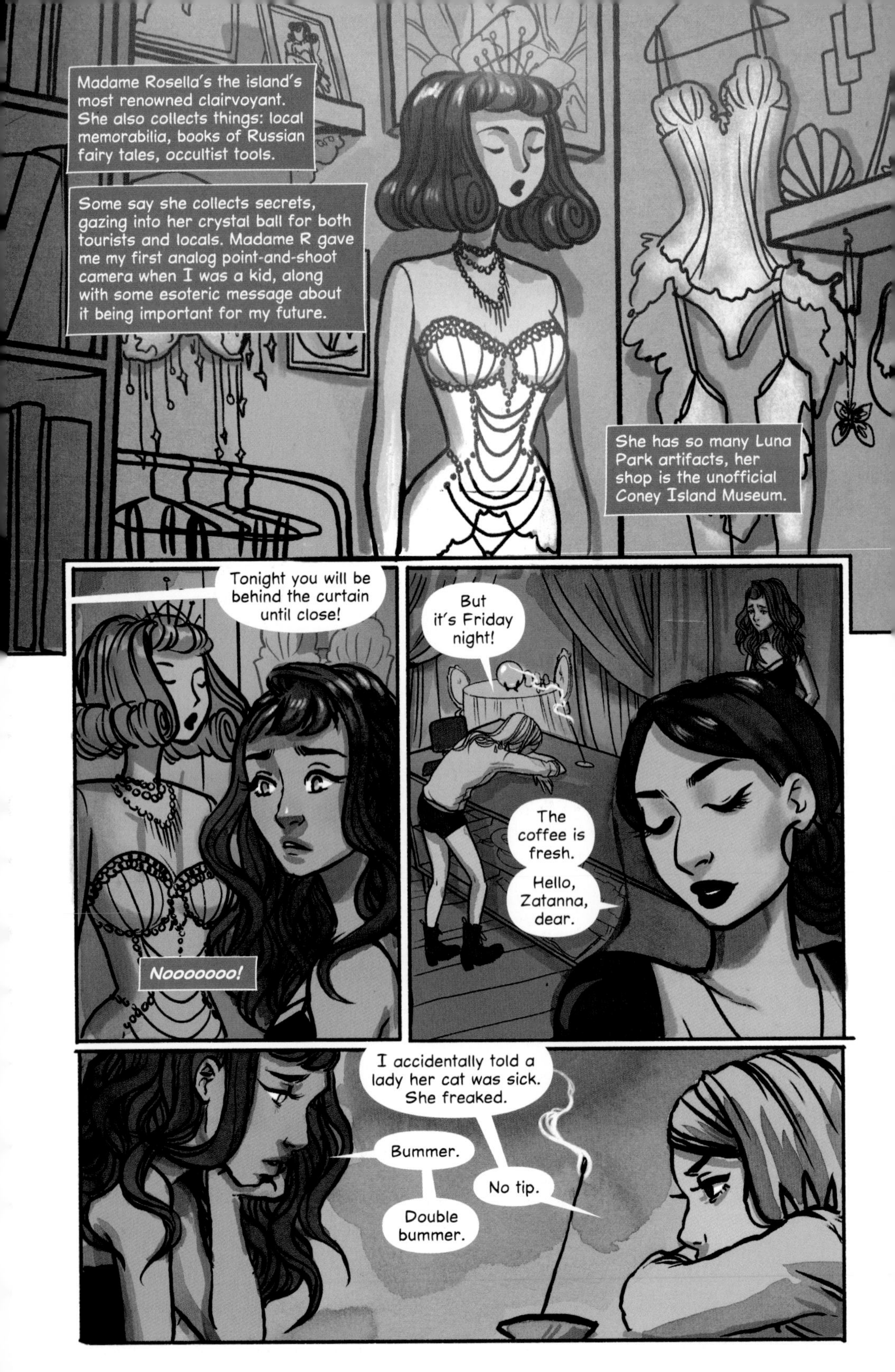
Madame Rosella's the island's most renowned clairvoyant. She also collects things: local memorabilia, books of Russian fairy tales, occultist tools.
Some say she collects secrets, gazing into her crystal ball for both tourists and locals. Madame R gave me my first analog point-and-shoot camera when I was a kid, along with some esoteric message about it being important for my future.
She has so many Luna Park artifacts, her shop is the unofficial Coney Island Museum.
Tonight you will be behind the curtain until close!
Nooooooo!
But it's Friday night!
The coffee is fresh.
Hello, Zatanna, dear.
I accidentally told a lady her cat was sick. She freaked.
Bummer.
No tip.
Double bummer.

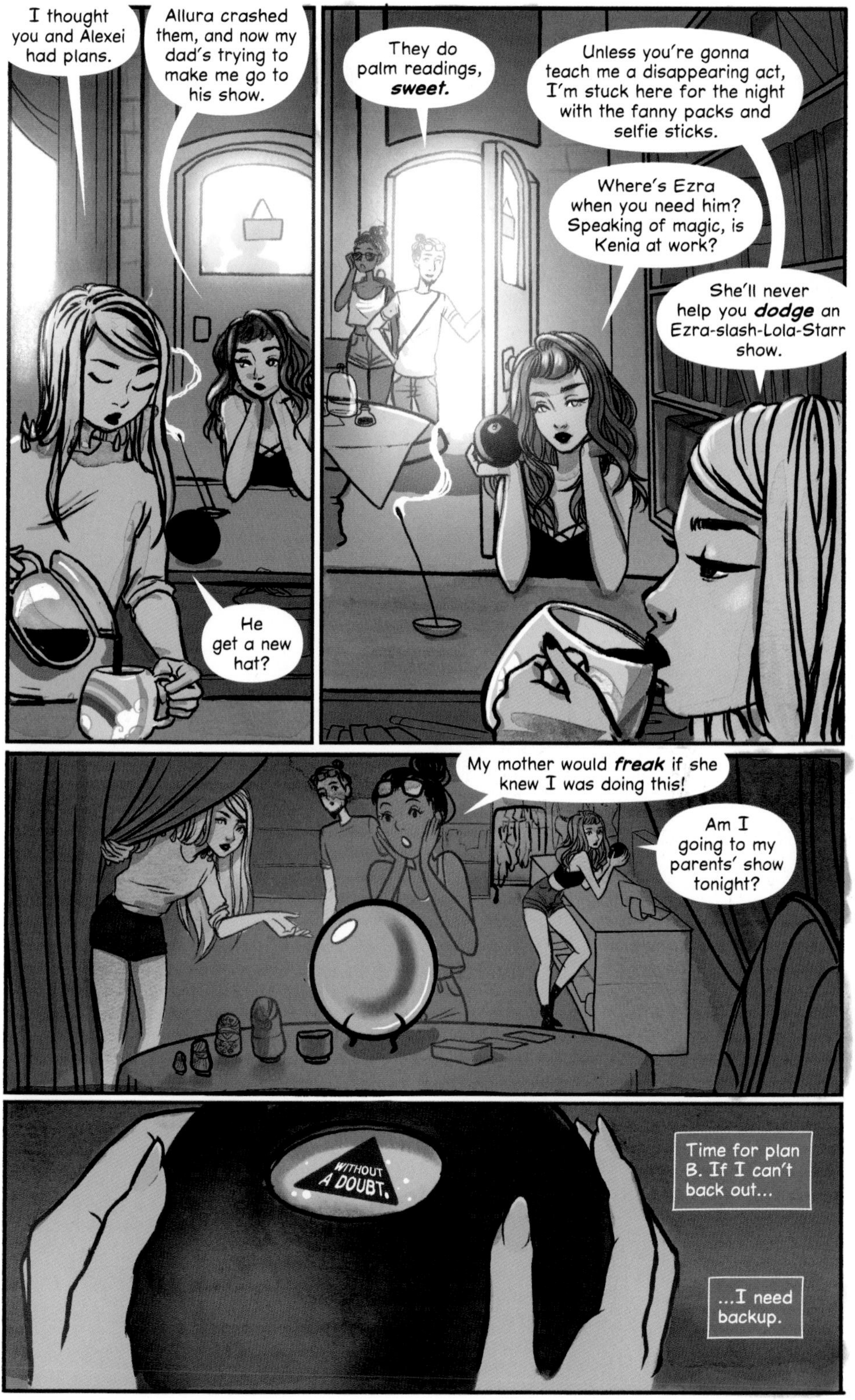
I thought you and Alexei had plans.
Allura crashed them, and now my dad's trying to make me go to his show.
He get a new hat?
They do palm readings, *sweet.*
Unless you're gonna teach me a disappearing act, I'm stuck here for the night with the fanny packs and selfie sticks.
Where's Ezra when you need him? Speaking of magic, is Kenia at work?
She'll never help you *dodge* an Ezra-slash-Lola-Starr show.
My mother would *freak* if she knew I was doing this!
Am I going to my parents' show tonight?
WITHOUT A DOUBT.
Time for plan B. If I can't back out...
...I need backup.

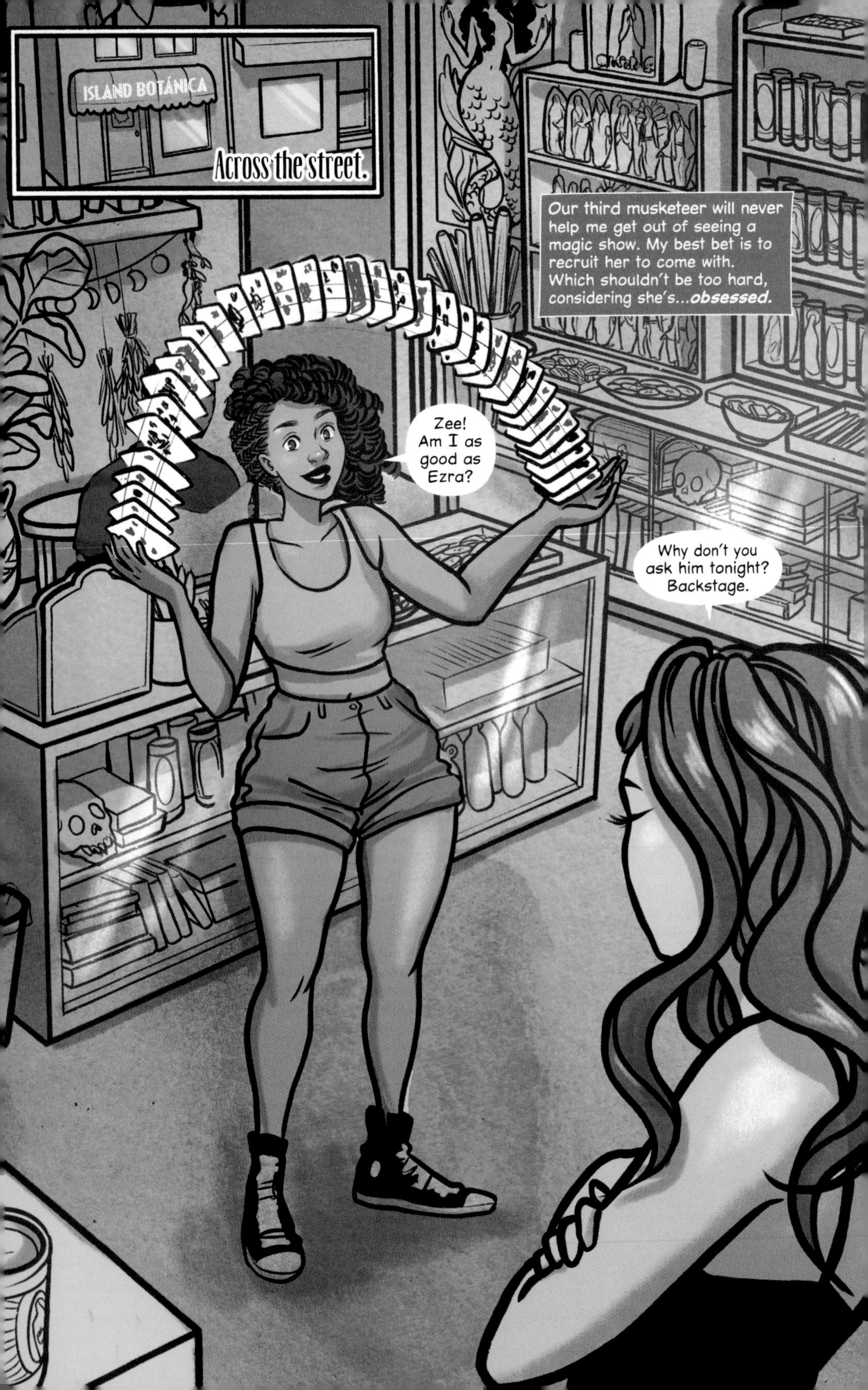
ISLAND BOTÁNICA
Across the street.
Our third musketeer will never help me get out of seeing a magic show. My best bet is to recruit her to come with. Which shouldn't be too hard, considering she's...*obsessed.*
Zee! Am I as good as Ezra?
Why don't you ask him tonight? Backstage.

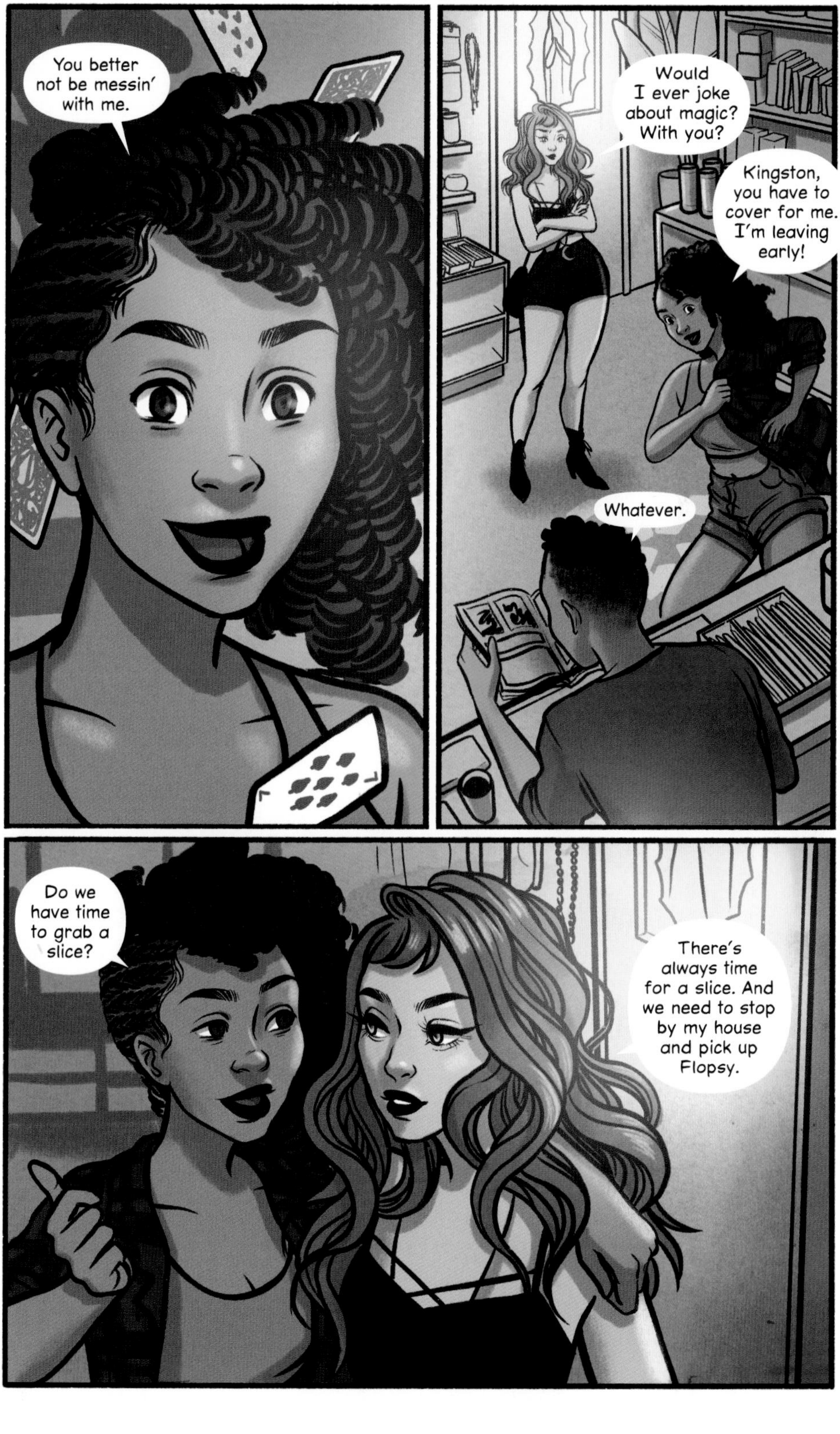
You better not be messin' with me.
Would I ever joke about magic? With you?
Kingston, you have to cover for me. I'm leaving early!
Whatever.
Do we have time to grab a slice?
There's always time for a slice. And we need to stop by my house and pick up Flopsy.

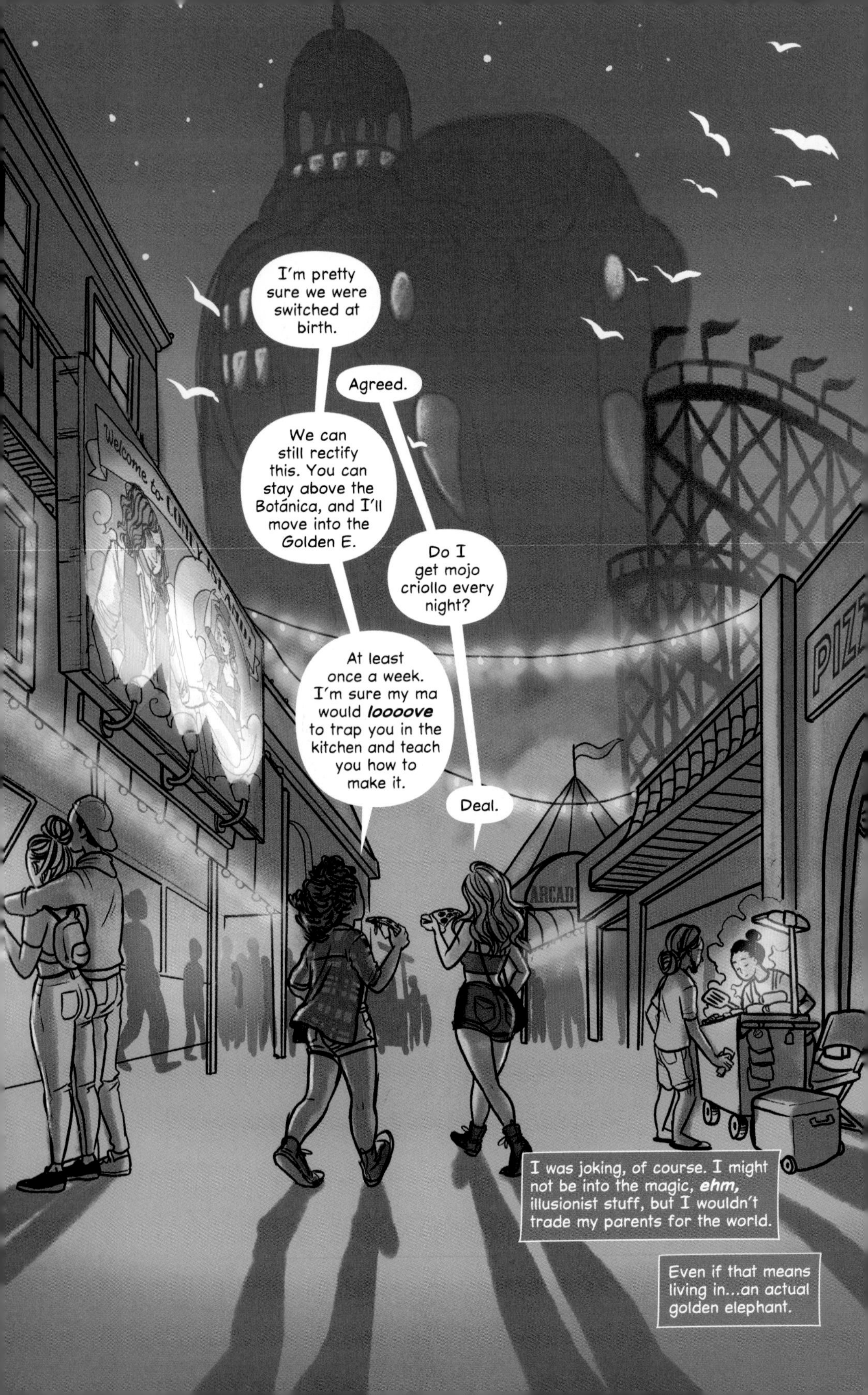
I'm pretty sure we were switched at birth.
Agreed.
We can still rectify this. You can stay above the Botánica, and I'll move into the Golden E.
Do I get mojo criollo every night?
At least once a week. I'm sure my ma would ***loooove*** to trap you in the kitchen and teach you how to make it.
Deal.
I was joking, of course. I might not be into the magic, ***ehm,*** illusionist stuff, but I wouldn't trade my parents for the world.
Even if that means living in...an actual golden elephant.
ARCADE

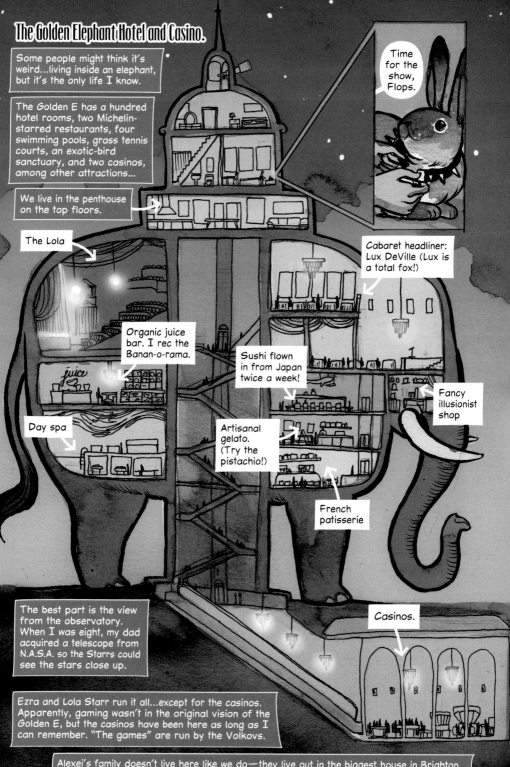

The Golden Elephant Hotel and Casino.

Some people might think it's weird...living inside an elephant, but it's the only life I know.

The Golden E has a hundred hotel rooms, two Michelin-starred restaurants, four swimming pools, grass tennis courts, an exotic-bird sanctuary, and two casinos, among other attractions...

We live in the penthouse on the top floors.

The Lola

Organic juice bar. I rec the Banan-o-rama.

Day spa

Time for the show, Flops.

Cabaret headliner: Lux DeVille (Lux is a total fox!)

Sushi flown in from Japan twice a week!

Fancy illusionist shop

Artisanal gelato. (Try the pistachio!)

French patisserie

Casinos.

The best part is the view from the observatory. When I was eight, my dad acquired a telescope from N.A.S.A. so the Starrs could see the stars close up.

Ezra and Lola Starr run it all...except for the casinos. Apparently, gaming wasn't in the original vision of the Golden E, but the casinos have been here as long as I can remember. "The games" are run by the Volkovs.

Alexei's family doesn't live here like we do—they live out in the biggest house in Brighton Beach. It's probably best for everyone. My dad doesn't really...get along with the Volkovs. I'm sure it has something to do with the rumors surrounding their "family business."

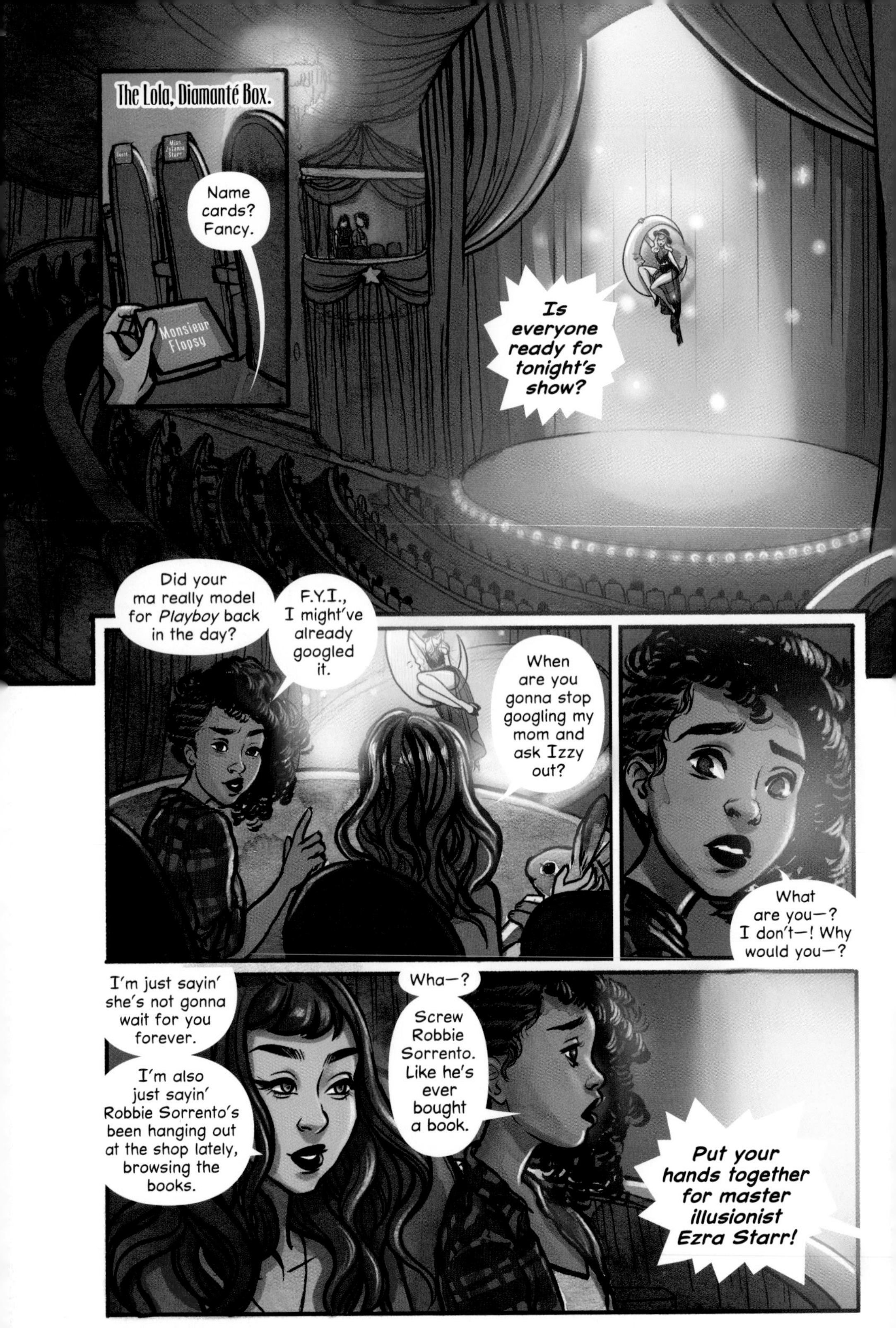
The Lola, Diamanté Box.
Name cards? Fancy.
Monsieur Flopsy
Is everyone ready for tonight's show?
Did your ma really model for *Playboy* back in the day?
F.Y.I., I might've already googled it.
When are you gonna stop googling my mom and ask Izzy out?
What are you—? I don't—! Why would you—?
I'm just sayin' she's not gonna wait for you forever.
I'm also just sayin' Robbie Sorrento's been hanging out at the shop lately, browsing the books.
Wha—?
Screw Robbie Sorrento. Like he's ever bought a book.
Put your hands together for master illusionist Ezra Starr!

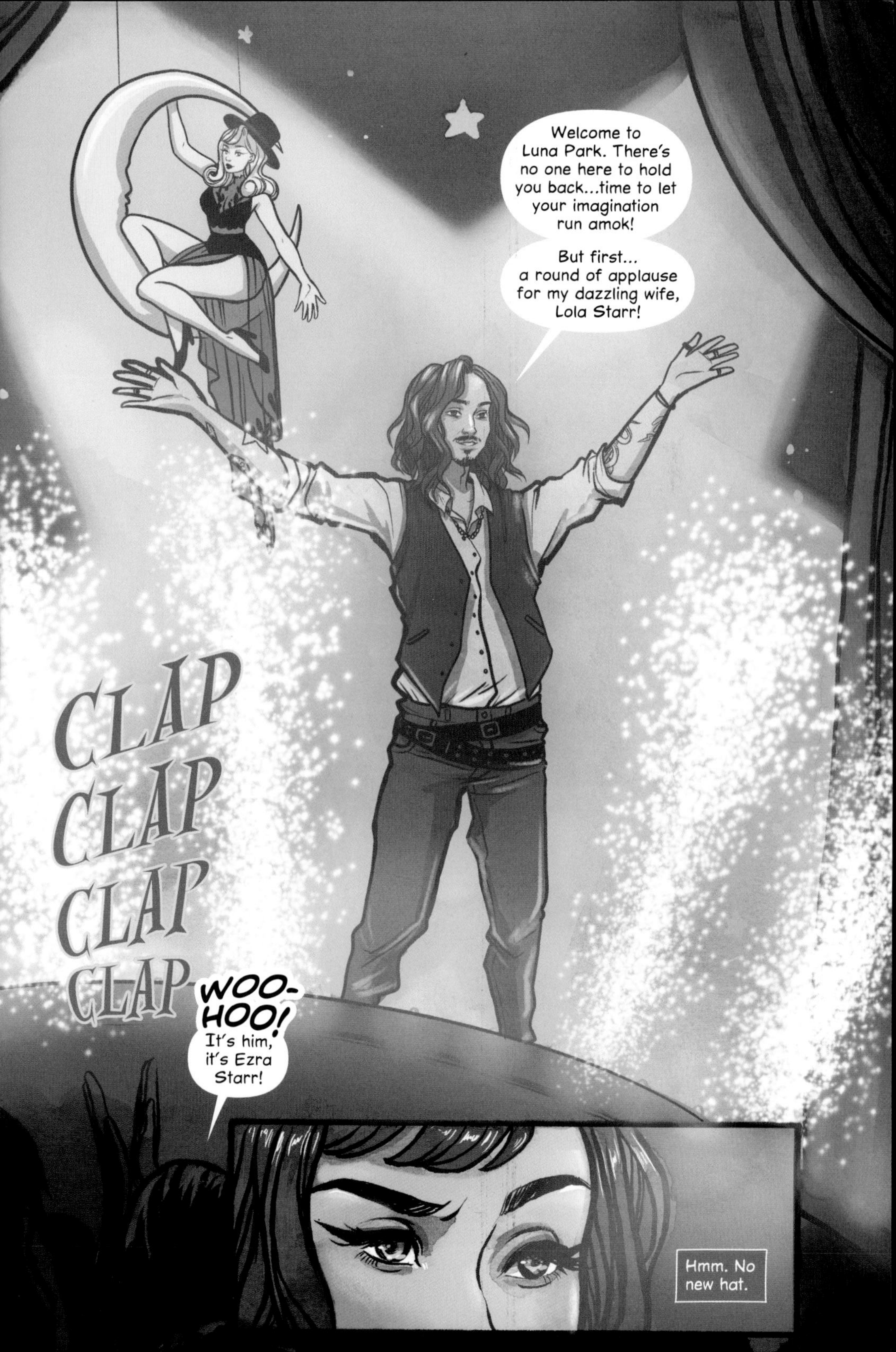
Welcome to Luna Park. There's no one here to hold you back...time to let your imagination run amok!
But first... a round of applause for my dazzling wife, Lola Starr!
CLAP CLAP CLAP CLAP
WOO-HOO! It's him, it's Ezra Starr!
Hmm. No new hat.

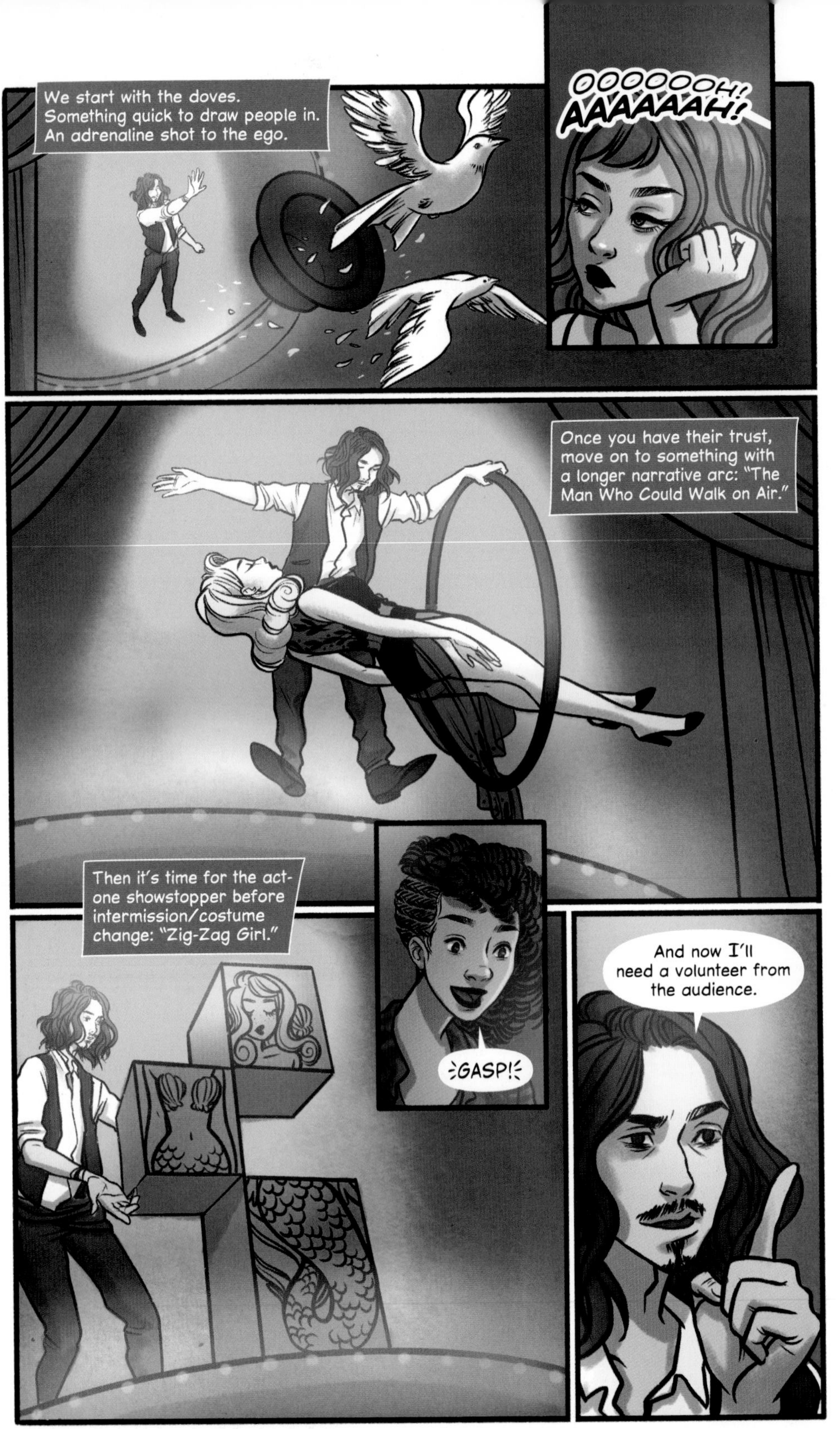
We start with the doves. Something quick to draw people in. An adrenaline shot to the ego.
OOOOOOH! AAAAAAH!
Once you have their trust, move on to something with a longer narrative arc: "The Man Who Could Walk on Air."
Then it's time for the act-one showstopper before intermission/costume change: "Zig-Zag Girl."
GASP!
And now I'll need a volunteer from the audience.

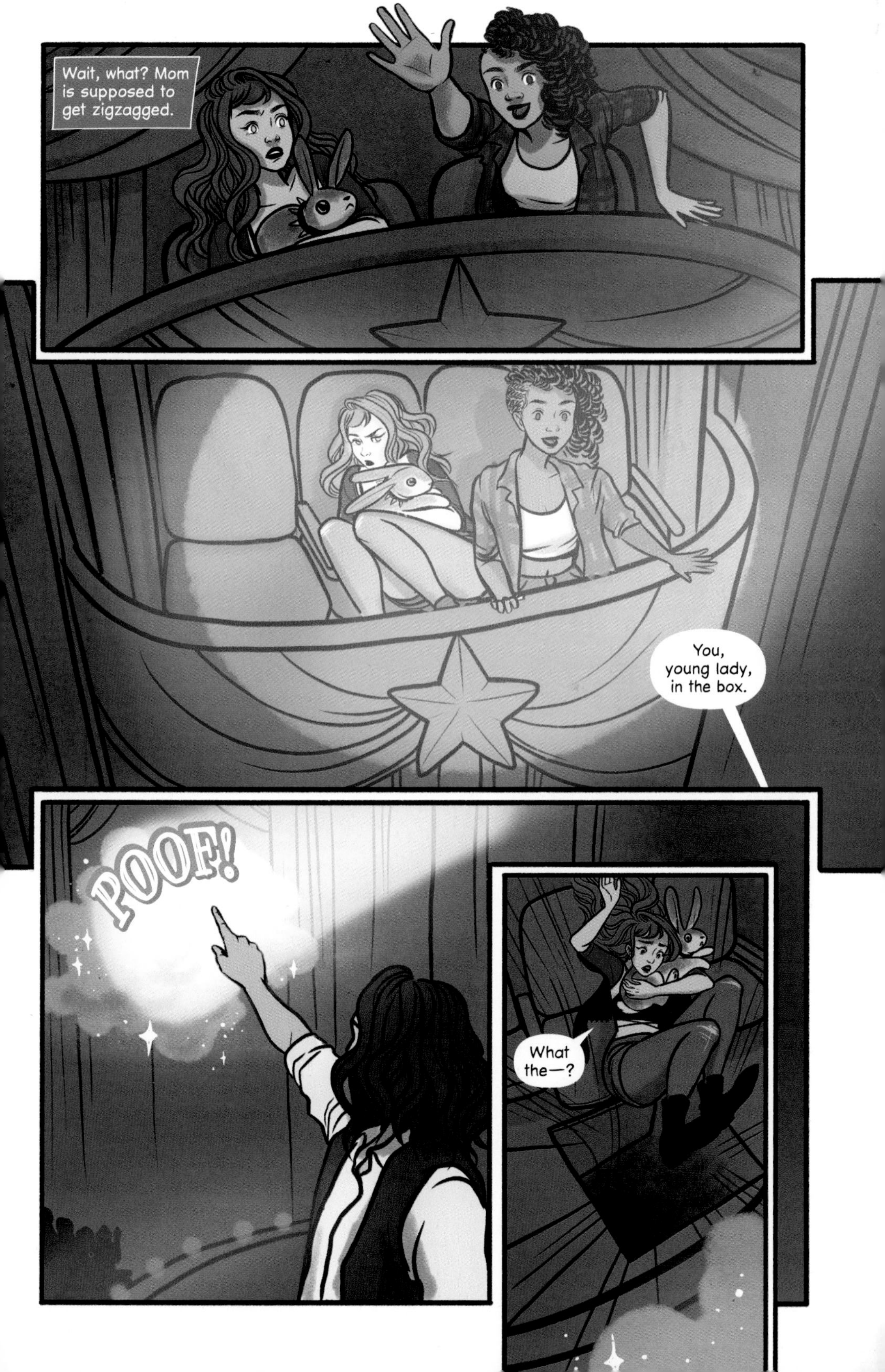
Wait, what? Mom is supposed to get zigzagged.
You, young lady, in the box.
POOF!
What the—?

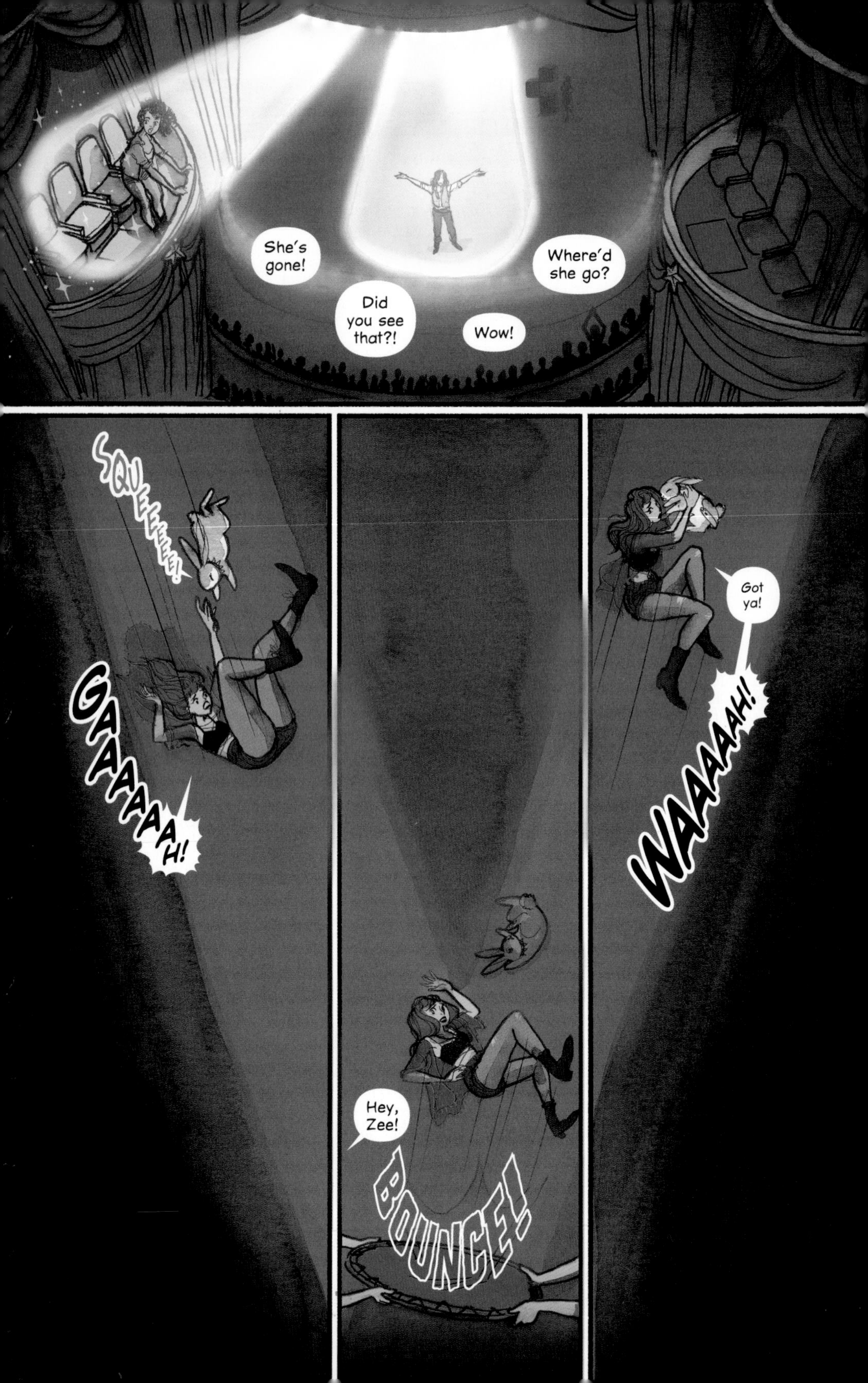
She's gone!
Did you see that?!
Wow!
Where'd she go?
SQUEEEEE!
GAAAAAAH!
Hey, Zee!
BOUNCE!
Got ya!
WAAAAAH!

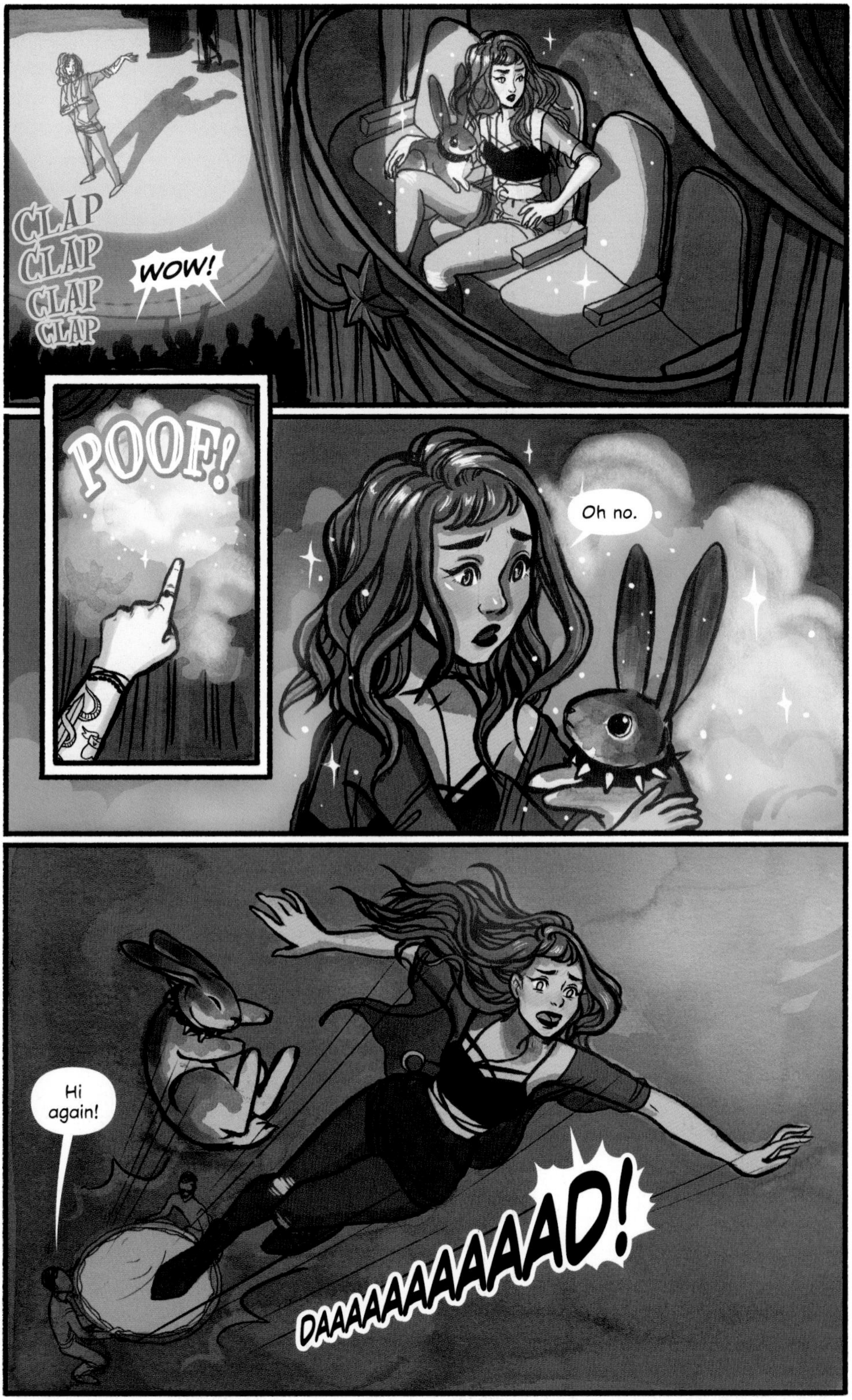
CLAP
CLAP
CLAP
CLAP
WOW!
POOF!
Oh no.
Hi again!
DAAAAAAAAAAD!

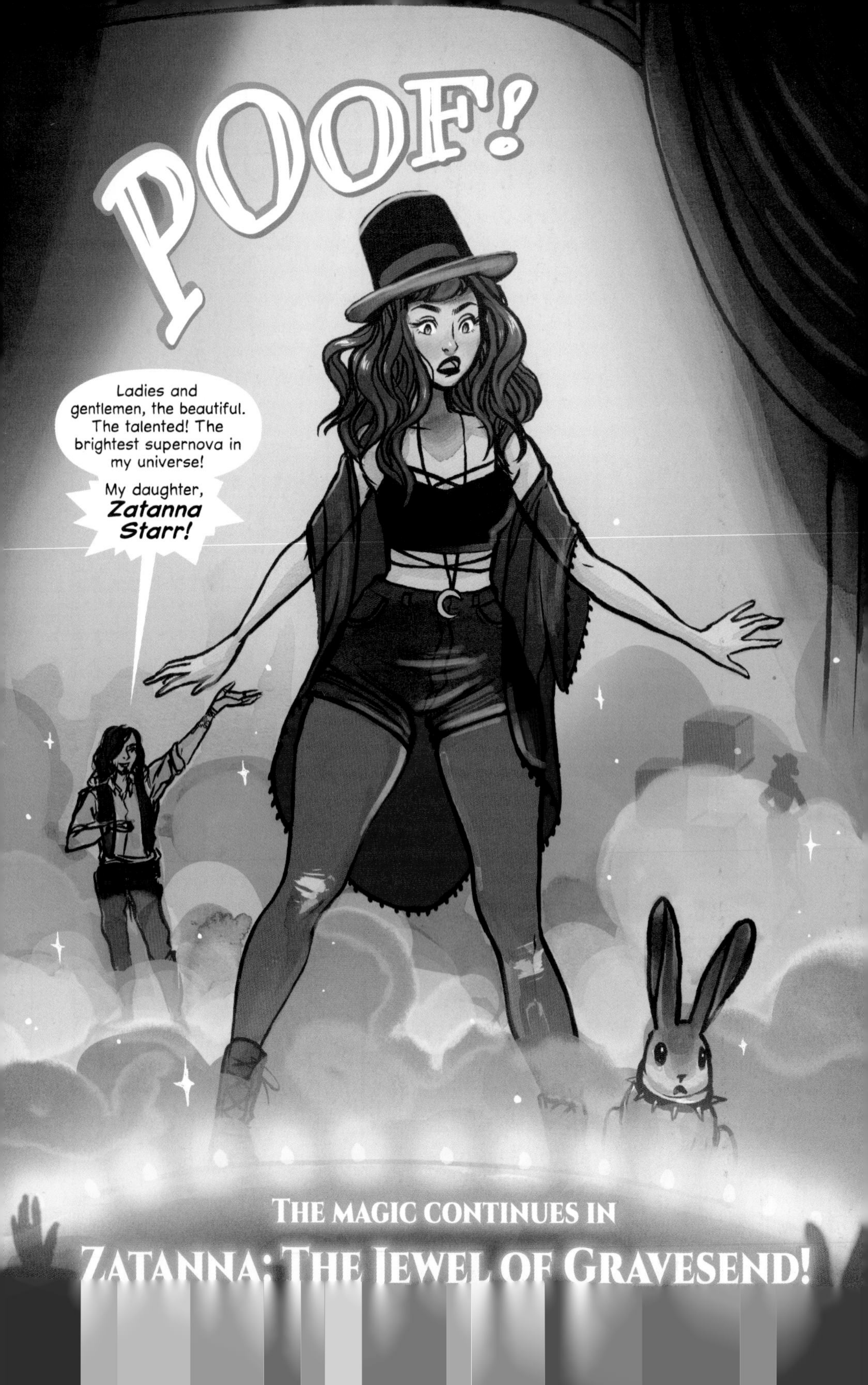
POOF!
Ladies and gentlemen, the beautiful. The talented! The brightest supernova in my universe!
My daughter, *Zatanna Starr!*
THE MAGIC CONTINUES IN
ZATANNA: THE JEWEL OF GRAVESEND!